No Inches Left to Give

No Inches Left to Give

DALLAS McCARTHY

RESOURCE *Publications* · Eugene, Oregon

NO INCHES LEFT TO GIVE

Resource Publications
An Imprint of Wipf and Stock Publishers
199 W. 8th Ave., Suite 3
Eugene, OR 97401

www.wipfandstock.com

PAPERBACK ISBN: 979-8-3852-3617-6
HARDCOVER ISBN: 979-8-3852-3618-3
EBOOK ISBN: 979-8-3852-3619-0
VERSION NUMBER 03/19/25

For my wife.
I would have never done this without you.

And for my children.
I hope this book brings more light to the world you inherit.

Take no part in the unfruitful works of darkness, but instead expose them.

EPHESIANS 5:11, ESV

Acknowledgments

THANKS TO MY FIRST readers for your patience and honesty: my wife Elsa, my mother, and my friend and mentor Randy Birkey.

Thanks to D. I. Riordan for talking through ideas and for countless creative contributions.

Thanks to Pastor Henry Knox for preaching about Jonah right when I needed to hear it.

Thanks to Don Pape for helping me when there was absolutely nothing in it for you.

And special thanks to my editor/coach/friend Jamie Chavez. Your feedback made this book so much better. And shorter.

Chapter 1

SHADRICK BENGOADE UNBUCKLED HIS seat belt after parking in his usual spot in the office parking lot. He gathered his insulated cup filled with his morning shake and his laptop backpack and opened his door, the fresh morning air of the parking lot greeting him. As he shut his door, another car drove up and parked in the spot next to his. It was Norma from Risk Management, whose office was down the hall from Shad's cubicle. Her small, two-door sedan was bright red and perfectly clean, save for the circular red sticker with the golden symbol of Baal in the center, a profile of the god himself with his uniquely elongated skull. The stickers were commonplace, a subtle way for Baalists to represent themselves as a member of one of the three culturally ascendent alternative religions. Shad could see that Norma's arms were bandaged in the familiar way of worshippers of Baal; clearly, she'd made an offering that morning before starting her day. "Hey Norma! Happy Monday," said Shad, waving at her as he walked past her car.

"Oh, hey Shad. Good morning!" she said, smiling back at him before turning to gather her things from her back seat.

Shad stopped for a moment and fumbled in his pockets for his keys, remembering to lock the doors on his six-and-a-half-year-old small sport utility vehicle. Truthfully, there wasn't much sport in it, but it was reliable and practical—new top priorities for a young father. Making his way through the parking lot, Shad spotted cars with stickers signifying followers of Moloch and Asherah, the former a silver square with a black bull's visage in the center, and the latter a multicolored outline of a voluptuous woman in a pose that looked like a sensuous dance.

A brisk breeze put an extra spring in his step as he looked up at the place where he spent at least forty hours of his week. Located in a heavily treed area on the north side of Mapleton, the midsize city where Shad was born and raised, the rectangular office building was as nondescript as could be. Constructed of beige brick, it had dark-tinted windows lining its four-story façade, a look emblematic of office architecture in the late eighties and early nineties. The exterior included some old oak trees that were prolific acorn factories, resulting in a robust squirrel population that terrorized the building's maintenance staff. The perimeter of the building was edged with Japanese boxwood shrubs, all trimmed in meticulous cubes. Aesthetically, it was exactly the kind of building that one would expect to house a company like E-Tech Data Systems, where Shad had been a data analyst for the last five years.

After swiping his ID card to open the door, he made his way through the lobby, nodding at the guard at the security desk. Skylights four stories above bathed the open lobby with morning sunlight. "TGIF, right?" said the security guard, smiling beneath his push-broom mustache.

"You know it, Frank! Long weekend too!" Shad said, forcing a friendly chuckle as he walked.

"What? Long weekend?" Frank asked. "Shoot, you're right! I had forgotten about the Blood Moon Equinox! Well, that's a pleasant surprise."

"Glad to be the bearer of good news! This week sure has made us earn it. Have a good one!" Shad said as he passed the desk, automatically spitting out small talk without a second thought.

"You too!" Frank replied.

Shad continued through the lobby and passed the communal idols that were now common in many public spaces. Alternative religious freedom had been occupying much of the political discourse in recent years, with the three major cults garnering increasing support and prominence. As a result, accommodations were being made in nearly every facet of public life to afford practitioners of these faiths the opportunity to worship openly and easily.

He first passed a large, golden statue of Baal, standing with his right hand pointing at the sky and his left extended forward with the palm up. This morning there were a few Baalists kneeling at the base of the idol, using the ceremonial knives to make their morning offerings, but Shad made it a point not to look too closely. If he were honest with himself, it was more out of aversion than respect for their privacy, but if anyone asked, he'd probably swear otherwise.

A little further through the lobby was the elaborately embroidered banner for the goddess Asherah, with dozens of silk ribbons hanging from the ceiling that Asherians would use to dance in celebration of their seductive deity. This morning there was only a single man wrapped in one of the silk banners, spinning slowly around and muttering something to himself. There were no prostitutes there now—they only visited this office building on Tuesdays from noon to 1:00 p.m. Every week during that hour-long window, Asherians who worked in the building would line up in hopes they could spend their lunch break copulating in the lobby, shedding their worldly worries and ascending to Asherah's advanced consciousness. Afterward, the lobby sandwich stand would stay open an extra hour to satisfy their other appetites.

And finally, he passed the altar to Moloch, where the followers of the bull god at E-Tech Data Systems would leave daily sacrifices to their bovine deity in exchange for promises of true, individual freedom. Thankfully, the altar also had two incense burners that were kept active at all times to help mask the smell.

Shad passed each idol quickly, not looking up at any of them. He'd seen all three many times over the years, but they still gave him the creeps. Something about them was off-putting, leaving him with an uneasiness that always took a while to shake off. He always had the feeling that they pulled at him a little as he passed, like there was some kind of gravity drawing him in, asking him to concede, to stop resisting—not to give up *everything*, only just to kneel. *Bow to me and let the anxiety flow from your arms, Shad,* whispered Baal. *Embrace your body's desires and there will be no more pressure,* promised Asherah. *Offer me your sacrifice and I will give you true freedom in darkness,* guaranteed Moloch.

Focusing on the floor as he walked briskly to the elevator bank, Shad promptly punched the upward arrow as soon as it was within reach. While he waited, a few other employees arrived to wait for the next elevator. Shad nodded at each of them: Todd from IT, Mike—no, Mark—from Sales, and Norma, whom he'd seen in the parking lot. He knew who they were and assumed they knew who he was, but wasn't more than professionally cordial with them. He didn't really have anyone at work he would call a friend, no one he kept up with outside of work hours. In some ways that made him sad; he didn't have much fun with his coworkers and mostly had to force his way through personal interactions. On the other hand, it made it easy for him to compartmentalize work and keep it separate from his private life. No one here really knew much about him, and he was OK with that.

The four of them stood quietly, awkwardly looking anywhere but at each other as the soft, forgettable music played in the lobby's ceiling speakers. The elevator door opened, and they all filed in and pushed their respective buttons. Shad hit three, where the data analysts were housed along with Norma's department. He stood back in the corner of the elevator, looking down at his shoes. The others each stood quietly in variations of Shad's pose, like automatons awaiting their next command. The light for the second floor lit up, and the doors slowly opened. Todd began to walk forward, but his shoe scuffed on the elevator's tile floor, squeaking loudly and causing him to stumble clumsily. He had been sipping at his coffee as he exited, so his stagger caused him to spill the hot brew down his tie and shirt.

"Oh, dang it. Just perfect!" Todd said. The other three elevator riders tried to avoid acknowledging the misstep and quietly urged the elevator doors to close with all of their mental energy. Todd walked away, wiping at his chest and conspicuously never looking back as the elevator doors mercifully shut. Shad waited for the elevator to rise one more level to his floor. The door let out a pleasant *ding* and Shad exited behind Norma, who walked quietly ahead through the elevator bank, making a right where Shad made a left toward their offices. He wondered for a moment if she was in pain or feeling lightheaded from her morning offering to Baal. Shaking his head, he banished the thought and kept walking to his desk.

He arrived at his workstation, a basic six-foot-by-six-foot square with half walls that allowed Shad to see into his neighbors' cubicles. The half walls were covered in a soft, light-brown fabric that acted as a bulletin board where employees would tack photos and other personal decorations to give the space a modicum of personality. In some work environments, this kind of layout would facilitate discussion; however, in a room populated by data analysts there was never much discussion taking place. At most, there were periodic whispers as analysts talked about whatever batch of information they were parsing, deliberating about the best methods of organization and which formula would be most effective for analysis. Beyond that, the room was filled with the sound of clicks on computer mice and the pitter-patter of keyboards. As Shad unpacked his bag and set his things out for the day, those subtle sounds were already permeating the room. He was comforted by the familiar noises, ready to dive into the numbers and zone out. Just after he sat down, he heard a skittering in the next desk over.

"Hey, Nate," Shad said.

"Hey, man. How'd you know I was here? You didn't even look over the side."

"The rats, dude."

"Oh, yeah, my offering! Sorry, are they being loud? They'll be gone after lunch," Nate said.

"No, it's not bad. It's just how I know when you're there in the morning, doesn't bother me. No worries," Shad said. A dedicated follower of Moloch, Nate often brought field mice or rats to work in a small cage that he would use as an offering during his lunch hour. "Got plans for the long weekend?"

"Definitely! Heading downtown for the Blood Moon Equinox. It's going to be huge, all of Mapleton Square Park in front of city hall is going to be roped off. Supposed to be thousands of people coming. Can't wait! You going?"

"I don't think so, dude, probably too many people for Isla. She gets weird with crowds, you know?" Shad said.

"There's going to be tons of kids there, man. It's family friendly," Nate said.

"Oh yeah, I'm sure. It's more about her, she's just kind of introverted. Gets that from me, I guess!"

"A data analyst, introverted? Who would have thought!" Nate laughed.

"I know, man, I'm a walking stereotype," Shad said as he booted up his work computer and typed in his log in information.

"Yeah, I hear you. Aren't we all?"

A skinny, middle-aged man with a perfectly groomed goatee half stood in his workstation, three cubicles to the left. "Could you guys take it to a break room? Some of us are already working."

"Sorry, Ben," Shad said. "We'll stop, just catching up a little bit." Shad smirked to himself and heard Nate snicker quietly in his cubicle. A direct message from Nate popped up on Shad's screen as he began to read through his inbox.

Dude needs to relax, lol!

No joke, it's 8:15 a.m., maybe take it easy on the coffee? Shad replied.

Look, I'm a loyal servant of Moloch, but that guy should look into Asherah, know what I'm saying? Would loosen him up! Nate replied.

Haha for real. All right, back to the grind, bro! Got a beast of a file to append today. Have to get it done before the weekend! Shad typed.

Cool, talk to you later.

Shad sent a thumbs-up emoji, then pulled out his phone and opened up Spinstagram to see if his wife Alina had posted anything that day. He refreshed the app a few times, but she hadn't posted anything new. Must be a slow day at home—she almost always posted updates about Isla in the mornings. Looking back at his email program, he continued scanning through unread messages and replied to a few. One was a reminder for that day's Blood Moon Bash, a small party the company sponsored for employees who celebrated the alternative religious holiday. He minimized that window, opened up his spreadsheet program and began clicking and typing away, focusing on the data append he wanted to complete that day. He wasn't exactly living the dream working as a data analyst—especially as each day got him that much closer to turning thirty—but it paid the bills, allowed him to take care of his family, and also happened to favor his introverted disposition.

A few hours quickly elapsed as Shad squinted at his screen, doing his best to keep his attention on the numbers he'd been wrestling with for most of that day. As simple as the process was, it required his full concentration to complete correctly. Distractions meant potential errors, which would doom him to spending even more time with the grids, numbers, and formulas than he'd already forfeited—something he *really* wanted to avoid.

"Slim Shadddddyyyyy!"

He winced as he heard the shrill crowing of his exuberant coworker.

"Where's the *real* Slim Shaddy? Found him!" cackled Mayra, a portly woman in her mid-thirties. She walked gracelessly on wedge heels, her well-insulated body squeezed into a jean skirt and cheetah-print blouse. "Aren't you coming to the party, Shad? You're going to miss out!"

"Oh, uh, sorry—I am just really trying to get this file done. I don't think I'm going to be able to make it."

Nate stood up from his workstation. "Dang, I'm late! I'm coming, Mayra. Ben, you coming? There's free food!"

"I'm sick. I don't want to spread it around," Ben said without looking up from his computer screen.

"Gross, you're sick? Then why'd you come to work? You should have stayed home!" Mayra recoiled.

Ben coughed lightly. "I know, I'm sorry. I have this project I need to finish; I'm trying to keep to myself so I don't get anyone else sick."

"OK, then. Shad, you sure you're out, man?" Nate said, looking his way.

Before Shad could respond, Mayra turned her sights back on him. "Shad, come on! The data will wait. You can't miss this! The Blood Moon Equinox only happens once a year," she said, her hands on her hips as she cocked her head to the side scoldingly. "You know how important this is to us," she added, eyebrows raised as she looked over her tortoiseshell eyeglasses.

"Yeah, I'm sorry guys. I'm super focused, I don't want to lose my stride, you know? These numbers, they're unforgiving" he said with an apologetic smirk, hoping to be excused the way that Ben had been.

"This is when we celebrate Baal's return from the underworld when his first blood sacrifice brought rain and fruitfulness to the earth. It's really important to Molochians too—right, Nate?" she said.

"Yeah, absolutely. This is when we make our most significant sacrifices of the year. These sacrifices are more important than any other we make until the next Blood Moon Equinox, they kind of set the tone for each worshipper and establish our status with Moloch," Nate said.

"Ehh, I uhh . . ." Shad muttered, trying to find any exit from this highway leading somewhere he didn't want to go.

"*Everybody* is there already. Come on, it'll be fun," Mayra said, making her best attempt at a pouty face as she took another swig from a can of beer. Shad just now noticed that the can was red and had an image of the moon on it, some kind of special edition can made for the Blood Moon Equinox. Human Resources allowed some alcohol consumption in the office on special days. Apparently, the Blood Moon Equinox was one such occasion.

"It's just not my thing, I'm sorry. I'm not a part of any of those groups, I wouldn't feel comfortable there."

"Not *comfortable*? That's really surprising, Shadrick. And disappointing. I'm disappointed in you." Shad could smell the beer on her breath as she spoke, her tattooed eyeliner compressed into a scowl. "I would have never expected you to be anti-alt. I thought you were better than that, but I guess I was wrong!" Her words dripped with performative woundedness. With that, she abruptly turned and left Shad's cubicle before he could respond, her wedge heels thumping loudly on the thin office carpet.

Shad watched Mayra storm off and then looked at Nate and shrugged. "You know I'm not anti-alt, dude. It's just not for me, you know?"

"I get it. I'll bring you back some blood cake. It doesn't have actual, like, blood. I mean, sometimes they do, but this one doesn't. It's cherry flavored," said Nate. "Anyway, I'll grab you some. Want an HR-approved beer?"

"Sure, thanks. Tell everyone I said hi, and uh, Happy Blood Moon Equinox."

Nate chuckled. "No one says that. We say 'Hail the Blood Moon,' but yeah, I got your back. Later buddy."

Taking a deep breath, Shad shook off the weird interaction and turned his strained eyes back to the familiar lines of the spreadsheet. Two eternal hours later, Shad clicked the anachronistic disk icon to save his work. He clicked over to his email program and opened a new email draft to his supervisor. He attached the completed spreadsheet with a short note: "Just finished, finally. Will head over soon with notes."

He clicked Send and leaned back in his well-worn mesh office chair, drawing a familiar creak from its unoiled joints. He ran his hands over his forehead and into his hair, exhaling the weariness he felt after completing such a tedious task. Shaking his head a little to rouse himself, he got up and began to make his way to his supervisor's office. He walked through the fluorescent-lit corridors with walls lined with completely forgettable art, passing dozens of cubicles just like his own. As he went, he thought through what he was going to say to his boss Eddie, the data processing supervisor at E-Tech Data Systems.

A loud cheer jarred him out of his thoughts and drew his eyes to the breakroom he was just passing to his right. The room was packed with employees, many carrying red, blood-moon-adorned cans like the one Mayra had sipped greedily. As he passed, he saw Mayra earning the applause of her coworkers by bowing to a golden statue the size of an office chair. It was a smaller version of the statue of Baal in the lobby and featured a small, round bowl-like base. Rising from the ground where she had bowed, Mayra stood up and pulled the golden blade from the statue's right hand. Raising the blade skyward, she said something that sounded like an ancient language, and brought the knife down across her forearm, blood quickly spouting from her separated skin onto the extended hand of the statue. Shad turned and continued toward Eddie's office as Mayra completed her ritual offering, reciting something else in the ancient language he didn't understand.

He arrived at Eddie's office and knocked on the doorframe. "Hey Eddie, is now a good time to go through that append I just sent over?"

Eddie spun around in his leather chair, throne-like in comparison to Shad's creaky excuse for a butt holster. "Shad! Glad you're here. Yes, now's a great time. Come on in."

Shad walked in and began to sit down, but Eddie stopped him. "Ah, ah—go ahead and get the door."

"The door?"

"Yep. Close it, would you?" Eddie said through the kind of artificial smile only a middle-manager can muster. Shad awkwardly rose and walked to the door, closing it. At first, he didn't use enough force, so the door didn't fully close. He was halfway turned around before he realized his error, so he had to turn back around and retrace his steps to fully close the door before he made his retreat back to the chair in front of Eddie's desk. Sitting down felt like a refuge after the awkward dance he had just performed.

"Uh, sorry about that. Anyway, I sent you this week's append. I brought my notes so we could go through it before the day is over," Shad said, pulling out his spiral notebook. He liked to take notes with paper and pen. In a world of digital *everything*, it was nice to have a few things that were made of more than just electrons.

"I saw that, thank you! There's something else we need to talk about first," Eddie said, folding his hands over each other on his desk and looking at Shad seriously.

"Oh, OK. Sure, what's up?" Shad said, reflexively adopting a tone that was far too jovial.

"We need to talk about today's Blood Moon Bash."

"The what?"

"The party. In the breakroom?" Eddie said, motioning with his head in the direction of the breakroom where Shad had passed Mayra in the middle of making her offering to Baal.

"The cult thing?"

"No, it's not a *cult thing*. We don't use language like that here, Shadrick. They're alternative religions. I have you marked down as having completed the Alternative Religions in the Workplace webinar two weeks ago. You did attend that, correct? Faking attendance to a training is an immediate write-up."

"Yes, I did attend it. I did, I'm sorry. I meant to say *alt*, not *cult*."

Eddie nodded, clearly skeptical of Shad's sincerity. "Then you should know that the Blood Moon Bash is a celebration for all of the diverse religious backgrounds represented at E-Tech Data Systems. It's an important part of the company's cultural inclusivity initiative. Why didn't you attend?"

"I was just too busy with this data file. I really wanted to get it done, you know. So that we could talk through it today, before the weekend. And not on Monday, next week." Blindsided by this line of questioning, Shad was flailing.

"That's not what I was told, Shadrick. I received a call earlier and I was told something very different," Eddie said, his face a stone façade of corporate condemnation. "I was told you were disrespectful to your coworkers, even *hateful*. That you're anti-alt. It sounds very realistic given the language you just used. Care to explain yourself?"

"What, I—hateful? No, of course not. I'm not anti-alt. Is this about— is this about when Mayra came to my desk?"

"Whoa, whoa, we're not talking about anyone else here, Shadrick. We're talking about *you* and *your attitude* toward your coworkers who practice alternative religions." Eddie raised his hands above his desk in a stopping motion. "Bringing up someone else as a deflection isn't a helpful way to address these important issues. Let's not try to avoid what you did."

"I—I'm not trying to avoid what I did. I mean—I didn't do anything. I didn't *mean* to do anything, at least. I'm not anti-alternative religious, or alternative religions, whatever. I'm not anti-alt," he continued, words dribbling weakly out of his mouth like a baby's spit-up. He stopped him-self for a moment and took a breath, gathering his thoughts. He knew he hadn't done anything wrong, he just needed to say it in the way that Eddie needed to hear it. He had to find the right piece of corporate jargon to fit into this particular Human Resources puzzle. "Let me explain what happened. A coworker came to my desk to invite me to the party—the Blood Moon Bash. And you're right, it doesn't matter who it was, exactly. The coworker came to my desk when I was really deep into this data ap-pend. I was on a roll and I was focused on my work, so I might have come off as more abrupt than I intended. I see now that I should have been more intentional about adapting my message and tone to her personality type, just like we talked about in that training a few months back, right? I should have spoken in a way that she could hear it. But I was so focused, I just wasn't intentional in the way that I should have been. So I apologize for that. I'll do better. I really didn't mean any offense."

Eddie sat, nodding as he listened to Shad's explanation. "Mmmm, I appreciate that, Shad. I'm glad to hear you really thinking through this.

If we really want to embody the company's values—empathy, morality, passion, and thoughtfulness—"

"Empty."

"*Excuse* me?"

"Empty. The acronym spells *empty*, just without the Y," Shad said.

"Um, that's *not* how it's presented, no. I'm not sure where you heard that and I certainly hope you're not repeating it with your coworkers, because that's not correct. It's EMPaTh, OK? E for empathy, M for morality, Pa for passion, and Th for thoughtfulness," he said, clearly enunciating each letter and word as he ticked them off on his fingers. He put extra emphasis on the *a* and *h*, just to be sure to communicate his point. "We're each supposed to be empaths, exemplifying those words as we live out those values."

"Oh, right. Of course. That makes more sense. Sorry."

"*As I was saying*, if you really want to embody the company's values, you need to think through how what you say will be received. You have to change what you say so that it's most acceptable to the person who hears you. Otherwise, you may offend someone. I think that's part of what happened here, so I'm glad to hear you're owning it." Eddie's tone reminded Shad of his daughter's elementary school vice principle.

"Yeah, again, I'm sorry about that. I'll be more intentional," Shad said, thinking he had found his way out of the maze.

"That's not everything though, Shadrick." Eddie crushed Shad's sense of relief. "Your tone and delivery were definitely a problem, but only *part* of the problem. The other part was what you actually said. I was told you said that you weren't comfortable being around employees who practice alternative religions. That celebrating with your coworkers wasn't *your thing*. That's just not an EMPaTh attitude. That kind of anti-alt behavior doesn't belong here." He paused, attempting to give more gravity to his words. "As you know, at E-Tech Data Systems, we celebrate each other's differences. Those differences are what makes this a great place to work. It's what makes us so strong and successful—the third largest database and analysis firm in this entire region! Without those differences, where would we be? Without Baalists, Molochians, and Asherians, we'd be weaker, Shadrick. We'd be nowhere. We need a variety of perspectives, a variety of backgrounds in order for us to find unique ways to tackle modern data challenges. Today was an opportunity to celebrate all of the ways that these diverse groups contribute to our success—to *your* success. And it's an opportunity you wasted."

Shad paused, trying to figure out how to respond in a way that would end this conversation quickly and with the least bad outcome possible. "I guess I just thought that since it was a religious thing, it wasn't mandatory."

"Uh, what? *Of course* it isn't mandatory."

"Oh, well, then . . . if it isn't mandatory, then it's OK that I didn't go, right? I didn't do anything wrong, I just chose not to attend."

Eddie shook his head slowly, looking down at his desk. "You really don't get it, Shadrick. That's just so far off of the mark."

"But—"

"No, no," Eddie held up his hand, cutting Shad's protest off at the knees. "No, I think I understand. I've heard enough. We'll have to continue this conversation on Tuesday next week, after the long weekend. And that conversation will *include HR*. Unfortunately, this *is* going to need to go into your permanent file. You understand?"

"No, I don't understand."

"Yes, you've made that clear enough. We'll have to work through that with HR and see what trainings are available to educate you on why you need to celebrate all of the backgrounds here at E-Tech Data Systems. Baalists, Molochians, Asherians—they all contribute unique, valuable viewpoints that should be treated with respect and dignity." Eddie stood up, signaling that the meeting was over. "I'll go through the append on my own. You can leave your notes with me or email them. I know you like your notebooks."

"Oh, uh, yeah. I'll email them to you." Shad stood and gripped his notebook closely.

"I know this was an uncomfortable conversation, Shad. But it's a step in the right direction. You'll see that soon." Shad turned and began to walk to the door to leave. "Got big plans for the weekend?" Eddie said, his face transforming from stern authoritarian to jovial buddy-guy in an instant.

"Oh, you know, um, I'm not sure. I need to check with Alina." Shad was desperate for the excruciating interaction to be over.

Eddie pushed out a phony laugh. "I hear that! Gotta get permission from the old ball and chain, right?" he said, his chummy grin freshly remanufactured.

Shad forced out a chuckle in return. "Oh yeah, you know how it is." He clenched his teeth as he realized he wasn't sure if Eddie was married.

Panicking, he threw out a question as a diversion from his potentially devastating blunder. "What about you, any plans?"

"I'll be heading down to the Blood Moon Equinox festival at the park downtown."

"Really? I didn't think you were a member of one of the, uh, alternative religions." Shad just barely caught himself before referring to them as cults again.

"Oh, I'm not. I'm just going with some friends to show my support for their beliefs and rich culture. I want to make sure that they know I am not just their friend, but also their advocate. We can practice the EMPaTh values in *and* out of the office." Eddie winked gracelessly. "All righty, well, have a good weekend. Hope the old lady has something fun planned!" he said with another counterfeit chortle, finally concluding the visit.

"Thanks. You too, boss," replied Shad, incredibly grateful for the reprieve. As he walked away, he cringed as Eddie continued speaking.

"Not here to be a boss, Shad!" Eddie tapped the sign he always kept on his desk that said *Life Sherpa*.

Shad turned back uncomfortably to face his boss, fearing he was trapped in some corporate version of Sisyphus's curse. "Yup, right. Thanks for the guidance, um, sherpa Eddie," he said, nodding goodbye. He quickly turned and walked away as fast as he could without breaking out into a full-on sprint.

When he got back to his desk, he logged back into his workstation, typed up his notes, and emailed them to Eddie. After clicking Send, he sat in his desk and stared past his computer monitor. It was close to 5:00 p.m. and he was more than ready to call it a day. He felt guilty, even if he didn't regret his choices. He knew he didn't do anything wrong when he spoke with Mayra, but the entire situation left him discomfited. Maybe it was getting reprimanded by his boss that troubled him, or maybe it was an overall sense of injustice. He wasn't sure what was making him feel so uneasy, but he was sure of one thing—he was going to stand his ground, regardless of the cost.

Chapter 2

SHAD TURNED OFF HIS workstation, packed up his things, and left the office to begin his weekend with his wife and daughter and flee the vexing experience he'd just had. He speed-walked through the lobby, past the idols that stared at him ominously as he went. Years of practice had taught him the optimal speed to walk when he hit the doors that would get him out fast without slamming the door and sending it swinging wildly. After a perfectly executed exit, he quickly made his way across the parking lot to his reliable, boring vehicle. He turned the car on, popped on the seat-heaters even though it wasn't cold outside, and plugged his phone into the audio system. Eager to zone out, he queued up his latest sci-fi audiobook and began his journey home.

By most city standards, his commute wasn't terrible. With forty-five minutes one way, he had plenty of time to escape to new worlds through mediocre narratives. Shad enjoyed the classics and some nonfiction, but he mostly enjoyed listening to what most would consider airport reads—entertaining but totally forgettable stories. Years of listening to those kinds of books had convinced him that writing books required a little bit of talent, but mostly just discipline. Putting the car in gear, he began his mental escape and made his way to the freeway, where he'd crawl through stop-and-go traffic toward the house he and his wife rented in suburbia. He went back and forth, from paying attention to the narrator to reading the billboards and bumper stickers he passed as he drove. "Moloch me like a hurricane" read one neon-colored sticker on a small sports car ahead and a couple lanes over. After a few ambulance-chaser law-firm billboards, he spotted one with a photo of beautiful, dark eyes staring down at each driver. Outlined in heavy dark makeup, the eyes beckoned viewers to Asherah's temple, just two exits down.

While altars and idols for the three alternative religions had been installed all over the place—in parks, office buildings, department stores, and even some fast-food restaurants—the actual central cult temples were another thing entirely. Large, imposing structures, each cult had its own exclusive architecture that was tailored specifically to its deity and unique worship rituals. The temple for Asherah that this billboard advertised was a beautiful wooden building. Welcoming and cozy, the interior was replete with soft, red-velvet cushions in numerous, dimly lit alcoves situated around a central hall. Unlike Shad's office building that used elaborately embroidered banners (since space was limited), the temple's main room included the full idol of Asherah, her busty, attractive visage cast in hand-polished bronze, surrounded by multicolored sheer ribbons hung from the ceiling for dancing rituals. Throughout the area around the idol were more sporadically placed plush couches. These cushioned areas were where Asherah's temple prostitutes would lie in wait for loyal followers who hoped to spend some time and energy "ascending." They might ascend right there in the main hall with the help of these "spiritual guides," or make their journey skyward in one of the more secluded alcoves around the perimeter of the building. Since Asherians believed their bodies were themselves offerings to the goddess, they made sure to stay well-groomed and in peak physical shape. Temple servants who hoped to achieve the rank of temple prostitute would serve the faithful in a number of ways, from providing refreshments to the parched believers who had exerted themselves in worship, to beating hypnotic rhythms on large drums that were situated around the perimeter of the main room. Priests and priestesses of Asherah dressed in sheer, loose-fitting, multicolored linen lined with gold stitching that didn't leave much to the imagination. Once prostitutes themselves, they would walk quietly around the temple, supervising the "acts of worship" and sometimes partaking, depending on the social status of the participants. Wealthy or powerful worshippers tended to receive more intimate attention from the priests and priestesses, or even the High Priestess herself. Participants of lower social position would be lucky to receive the attention of one of the temple prostitutes. Some people would attend the temple frequently for months or even years before being able to make their first copulate offering.

Asherian temple prostitution had been legalized a decade or so ago after years of heavy lobbying and an all-encompassing cultural blitz using the slogan *Free Worship*. Polls showed that most people approved of legal temple prostitution as long as it was between consenting adults. Many still had the weathered stickers on their cars that signaled their support for legalization: a dark silhouette of Asherah within the word *free* in a blocky, all-caps font.

A few exits after the temple to Asherah, Shad passed a billboard advertising the Temple of Moloch's homeless outreach program. It had been heavily promoted recently with ads on TV, radio, and even postcards in the mail. According to the ads, the homeless population of Mapleton was invited to come to the temple any time, day or night, and they would be provided with a place to stay, food, and any resources they might need. It was an impressively generous initiative and had garnered a lot of support in the community. Molochians in Shad's office had sold chocolate bars for a couple of weeks to raise funds for the program. After they explained what it was all about, Shad was happy to buy a few and even donated the change. After all, it was hard to argue with feeding and housing the needy. The chocolate bars sucked, though.

Just a half mile after the billboard, Shad drove past the monolithic stone temple for Moloch. All blocks and pillars, it looked like something out of a history book. A square building with an exposed central courtyard, the whole structure was open to the air. Driving by, Shad could see the torches lit inside the temple and the fire around the base of the huge statue in the center where sacrifices were made throughout the day and night. The statue was all black—cast completely in iron and polished to a mirror's clarity. Either made of metal or stone, Moloch was always portrayed in the deepest of blacks. Shad had once been to a wedding at a temple to Moloch in another city, which was built almost exactly like this one. He managed to make it through the entire ceremony despite the disturbing cries of animals sacrificed at the altar, screaming as their throats were slit by black-clad Molochian priests and priestesses with exotic-looking bronze blades, their blood spraying over the bride and groom to sanctify their vows before the bull god. After that experience, Shad always found a way to be busy when he was invited to other Molochian nuptials. He didn't have anything against his Molochian friends—he wasn't a vegan or anything like that—he just didn't want to actively *participate* in it again. He also didn't like that the temple priests and priestesses wore a dark hood that completely obscured their faces. He assumed they could see out of it, but he hated that he felt like they were always watching him.

The Temple of Moloch marked the halfway point for Shad's commute to his little slice of suburbia, leaving just about twenty minutes in his drive. Traffic slowed, and he instinctively switched to the lane furthest to the right. His phone's map program just showed red ahead, indicating a serious traffic slowdown but providing no other helpful information. Obviously, there was an issue, but was this a "suck it up and get past it" issue, or was it an "exit and risk it on the side roads" issue? He paused his audio book, and flipped over to the radio to get traffic updates. Of course, the first thing Shad heard were commercials. A jingle for a local car dealership chain, an announcement for a local concert, some weird pharmaceutical ad that seemed like it had more disclosures than actual advertising. Finally, the traffic updates began. As he crawled slowly toward whatever was causing the slowdown, Shad listened to updates about pretty much every highway in the Mapleton metro area except the one on which he drove. *Must have just happened, the radio helicopter hasn't gotten here yet,* Shad thought.

After five years of driving the same route to get home five days a week, he could guess what was probably the cause of the slowdown, but he kept listening to hedge against the unexpected. Almost without fail when traffic ground to a halt during his drive home, it was due to a wreck that had happened between the fast lane and the high occupancy vehicle, or HOV, lane—the two lanes on the left side of the highway. Today was no different—sure enough, as he neared the clot in the traffic artery, he observed what looked like a pretty minor fender bender between two large trucks, one in the HOV lane with its front fender jammed into the rear quarter panel of the other, which sat halfway between the HOV lane and the fast lane.

As Shad passed the crash and sped up, a new commercial came on for the Blood Moon Equinox festival: "All weekend long! Come to Mapleton Square Park downtown and celebrate the Blood Moon Equinox with the followers of Baal. Come and make your offering to receive the blessings of our beautiful golden man, our god and our savior, Baal!" He switched from the radio back to his audio book as he returned to his normal commuting speed.

The temple to Baal wasn't along Shad's drive, but he was still familiar with it. Shad had attended the University of Mapleton, which was located mostly downtown, and the temple was near his campus. A huge, imposing pyramid in the middle of an open park, it was built entirely of stainless steel and thick glass. With floors of white marble, the interior was extremely bright on a sunny day. In the exact center of the pyramid stood a huge, golden statue of Baal in the same pose as the idols at E-Tech Data Systems, with one hand pointing skyward and one extended. Baal was oriented to face the front entrance of the temple, greeting the faithful as they came to make their offerings. The statue sat on a huge, white marble base in the shape of an upside-down star, with Baal being the center of the star and the "top" point of the star pointing out from the front of the idol. Each point of the star was connected by a stainless-steel trough, making a circle around the entire idol. The circular trough fed to radial troughs that ran through the middle of each point of the star and then fed into a central pool that surrounded the golden god at the focal point. At equidistant points around the circumference, large golden knives sat in golden sheaths, their handles pointing skyward. Worshippers would kneel at the trough and use one of these knives to draw their sacrifice forth from some part of their body and let it run into the trough, where gravity would take it through the aqueduct-like system to the central pool. Unlike the idol that Shad passed in the lobby of work every day, this one didn't have tables with bandages for the faithful—those were distributed by Baalist priests and priestesses who served in the temple day and night. Dressed in red robes, the priests and priestesses all had clean-shaven heads and wore copious amounts of white makeup on their faces, making themselves appear androgynous. They would make their way around the room, giving out bandages and even administering stitches where necessary.

Shad had visited the temple of Baal out of curiosity during his junior year, drawn to the stunning architecture of the huge structure. It was known for being kept immaculately clean and as quiet as a library, so Shad thought he'd visit and maybe do some reading for class inside the large building. As soon as he arrived, he realized he'd miscalculated. Not only were there no places for him to sit and read, but the room wasn't as silent as he thought it would be. As he walked around the interior, the sound of Baalists making their offerings filled the room. It wasn't loud, exactly, but the cacophony of hushed sounds was impossible to ignore. The sound of knives being unsheathed and sheathed, the slick sound of metal against skin, the occasional sound of liquid drip-dropping into the steel trough, and—most distracting of all—the sharp inhalations of worshippers, teeth gritted as they withdrew and deposited their offerings. Shad abandoned his plan and opted to do his studying in the actual library for the rest of his collegiate career.

Reminiscing about his college-year adventures had helped Shad pass the time for the rest of his commute; before he knew it, he was in his subdivision. He parked in the garage, turned off the engine, unplugged his phone, and got out of the car. As he entered his home, he was greeted by the familiar smell of pizza and cheese bread.

"I'm home!"

"Daddy!" screamed his six-year-old daughter, Isla, as she ran to him from the living room.

"Hello, princess. Did you start pizza night without me?"

"Of course not!" she said, embracing her father with the uniquely effervescent adoration a daughter can only produce for her father. "We would never do that, Daddy! Pizza night, pizza night, pizza night!" she chanted musically.

Shad pumped his hand in the air with every exclamation of *pizza night* as he laughed at his daughter's excitement. "All right princess, let me put my stuff away, OK?"

"OK, Daddy, I'll be waiting for you."

"Where's your momma?"

"I think she's in your room."

"Thanks, Pickle," he said as he walked through the living room toward the hallway, using the nickname she had earned as a child. When she first started eating solids as a baby, she was incredibly picky. There were very few foods she would eat without a fuss, and one of them was pickle slices. This trend continued until she was a talkative toddler. She'd also eat anything they put pickle juice on, so they began telling her if she kept it up, she'd turn into a pickle. Isla loved that idea, so she started introducing herself as "Pickle" to anyone they met. "I ate too many, so now I'm a pickle, that's what Daddy said," she would say. And from then on, the new moniker was hers.

The master bedroom door sat slightly ajar. The light was on inside, and as Shad entered, he saw his wife sitting on the king-size platform bed, her laptop open and resting in the location for which it was designed. "Well, hello, beautiful."

His wife Alina looked up at him and smiled. "Hey, babe. How was work?" she asked, closing her laptop and setting it on the bed.

"Eh, it wasn't great. We can talk about it later. I'm ready for some cheap pizza and cheese bread."

"Isn't pizza just cheese bread, really?"

"Don't overthink it, my love. Just enjoy the cheesy goodness." He placed his bag and phone on a small desk against the wall in front of their bed. "You ready?"

"Oh, yeah!" They made their way to the kitchen and began their Friday night tradition. They each ate to their heart's content as they watched an animated movie on the couch. Isla sat between her parents, loving every moment of the evening. It was a fun, goofy movie for kids, one of the latest that they rented on one of their many streaming services. As usual, Isla was drowsy about three-quarters through the movie and was fully asleep on Shad's lap by the time the credits started to roll. He picked her up as Alina turned the TV off and began cleaning up the plates and pizza boxes. Shad carried his little girl to her room and laid her gingerly on her bed, pulling her covers up to her chin. She cooed a bit, bringing to mind sweet memories of snuggling with her as a baby. He flipped on her night-light and closed the door after taking one last glance, filling his heart to the brim. Smiling warmly to himself, he turned and walked to the kitchen where Alina was pouring a glass of wine for them both.

"Some vino, huh? Make mine a double. Is that a thing with wine? Pour me lots of wine, is what I mean," Shad said.

"That bad?"

"Yeah, pretty bad," he said, taking the glass she handed to him gently, trying to avoid spilling the precious contents.

"All right, spill it! Not the wine. The details."

"Don't get smart with me, little lady," Shad said. "Well, I guess I got in trouble. I went to Eddie's office to go over the final append for the week, and instead of talking data I got chewed out. Felt like I was a little kid in the principal's office, like I was going to get detention or get suspended or something. Which would be getting fired in adult terms, right? Or written up? I think I'm going to get written up next week. I had that anxious twist in my stomach, that feeling where the bottom of your guts just drops out. Felt like a dog that was getting scolded for pooping on the floor."

"So where did you poop?"

"Very funny, I set you up for that."

"You did."

"I don't know, *I* don't think I 'pooped' anywhere." Shad made quotes with his fingers. "They had this thing at work and I didn't want to go to it, and apparently it wasn't optional like I thought it was? Except Eddie insisted it *was* optional. According to him, I offended a coworker."

"Well, at least you have a boss to get mad at you and coworkers to offend. Isla is my boss and my coworkers are her teachers," she said. "I really miss working, I miss my career. Designing new things every day, the pressure, the deadlines. I miss making art! Remember that, when I was more than just a nanny?"

"Babe, come on. You're way more than a nanny, you're a *mom*. Most important job in the world. Besides, you wanted to stay home with Isla after she got sick, you didn't even hesitate. No doubt in my mind that she got better so quick because you were so dedicated to her. That was a huge sacrifice, Alina, don't forget that. Once she got better, we could have put her in day care, but you wanted to be with her, you didn't want to be apart from her."

When Isla was just a year old, she had come down with a serious case of pneumonia. She was hospitalized for over a week, and even after being sent home she required daily treatments to recover. Alina had cared for her tirelessly, quitting her job and staying home full time.

"Yeah, I know. I'm glad I was able to be there when she needed me. And after she got better, I *wanted* to stay home at first. I did. It was sweet at the beginning. We had such a bond after what we'd gone through, you know? Now that she's older, it's just so much of the same thing *every single day*. And I miss the excitement of my job. Getting promoted, making my own money, talking to executives and big shots. Taking their vision and bringing it into reality. I loved being a designer. I meant something there, remember? They were so upset when I left," Alina said.

"Come on, you mean something here. You mean *everything* here. And you know, she's in school now. Why not draw and paint here at home?"

"Ugh, I just don't have the energy. With all of the school stuff, all of the Moming I have to do every day, when I have some time to myself, I never feel like creating something. I just want to tune it all out. I really miss being creative, but I just don't feel like I have the space for myself anymore."

"Well, maybe you should look into going back to work? That might help restart your creative juices," Shad said. "I definitely don't have a problem with it. You used to make more money than me!"

"And start at the bottom again? No way. Only way I'd go back is if I would be able to go right back to where I was when I left, and that's just never going to happen. I've been gone too long."

"Think about it. We can always try something different if you change your mind. I'm sorry you miss your career. I know that was a huge sacrifice, but I'm grateful you did that and I don't think you should regret it. You're the reason she pulled through, I really believe that."

"I just wonder what could have been sometimes, that's all." Alina stared past Shad into her memories. She was quiet for a moment, lost in her thoughts. "Sorry, I made this about me."

"You totally did."

"Where were we? What was this thing you got in trouble for not going to? Training or something? How did you offend someone? I have so many questions" Alina said.

"It was for the Blood Moon Equinox. Just a party or something, a celebration for the culties at work."

"Culties? Come on Shad, that's rude."

"It's not rude, that's what they are. They're a part of cults, why avoid saying it? It's not like they're ashamed."

"It's derogatory, Shad. You're not saying it with acceptance. We're not raising Isla to be like that. If you're going to call them anything, call them *alts*. That's what they prefer."

"Fine, alts, whatever. The point is, they had an event for the Blood Moon Equinox and I didn't want to go. I just don't want to be around it; it weirds me out. The blood and the sacrifices and the dancing, whichever cult it is, it's not my thing. I have my religion, and I mean I'm not super into it, but we go on holidays and that's enough for me. I'm not having Easter parties and forcing everyone to watch me take communion, you know? I really don't understand why I need to participate in their thing." Shad exhaled in relief as he finished venting thoughts that had been building up since he left work. "And of course, Eddie wouldn't tell me who complained about me. He made me feel like I was trying to reveal someone in the witness protection program when I brought it up, like it was so out of bounds to even ask. Now I have to talk to Eddie and HR again next week, and I'm sure that means I'm going to have to do some kind of training about tolerance for the alternative religious. And I'll probably get written up. This is going to screw my performance review all to hell. It's just all so overblown."

"I get being uncomfortable, it's not something you're used to being around. I would think people would understand that," Alina said. She looked down, processing everything Shad had said.

"I know, I didn't expect this. You know me, babe. I don't discriminate against anyone. I honestly don't have the energy to discriminate against anyone. I don't care what they do or believe. That's the truth, I really don't care. They're adults, they can do what they want. Free country, and all that. Just leave me out of it. Why is that so much to ask? I don't want to have to see people cut themselves or cut an animal's throat or screw a priestess. Why is that a problem?" The wine was acting as a wrecking ball, tearing down the walls that held back Shad's exasperation.

"I hear you. I understand why that was frustrating."

"Thanks, babe, thanks for letting me vent. I don't have anyone else I can talk with about this."

"Of course. That's what I'm here for. I know you, you're a good person. You didn't mean to offend anyone. Eddie will understand that; I'm sure you'll be fine."

"I hope so, I don't want to have to update my résumé, I don't even know where I saved it. I really don't want to go through the job-hunting process again, it's worse than dating. But maybe it's time for a change, maybe I'm stagnant. Maybe our family could use a change?" Shad replied, partly to Alina and partly to himself.

"Let's not get ahead of ourselves. Getting written up sucks, but it's not the end of the world. We don't have to upend everything over this. You'll be all right. Who knows, the conversation with Eddie and HR could help. Maybe there is something there that you need to work through. Have you considered why your coworkers wanted to you to go to the party?"

"What? My coworkers?"

"Yeah, the ones who invited you and then complained about you. Have you thought about why they did that?"

"Uh, no, I guess I hadn't. I think it seemed like Nate just wanted me to hang out. Mayra was super pushy, though," Shad said.

"OK, so maybe they were just trying to include you?"

"Yes, OK. I guess so. I'm pretty sure Nate was just being friendly because we're usually cool at work, joking around and everything. But I'm honestly not sure what Mayra's deal is, I think she might be trying to convert me. Why does that matter anyway?"

"Well, you rejected them, Shad. They were accepting you into their celebration, it seems like they just wanted you to accept them too."

"Accept them? I do accept them. I walk with them, I work with them, I'm nice to them. And I accept that they're in a cult. I just don't accept an invitation to participate."

"Shad. Come on, stop with the cult stuff."

"It's true. I walked by and saw the 'party' as I was going to Eddie's office. The knives, the idols. I saw Mayra cut her arm open, babe. It was deep, it bled *a lot*. I hate blood, it grosses me out. Seeing her skin split open like that . . . ugh!" He visibly shivered the thought away. "It's so disgusting, it's not for me. It's great that the culties—sorry, the alts—accept me and I'm sorry if I offended anyone. I told Eddie that, I *told* him I was sorry! But I don't regret what I did. I don't think it's fair that I'm forced to attend something that I don't feel comfortable attending. They wouldn't punish anyone for not attending some other religious party, and I wouldn't want them to, either. They don't even allow *other* religious celebrations in the office anyway! It's a double standard, and it's not fair."

"I just think you should reconsider your attitude toward the alts, Shad. It sounds like they just want you to accept them as they are. Golden rule, right? Treat others as you want to be treated?"

"Yeah, I agree! I'm not trying to force them into my religion, I don't want them to force me into theirs. That's my golden rule right there."

"OK, OK. Let's just talk about something else."

Shad sighed, frustrated. He was clearly wound up and took a moment to calm his righteous anger and comply with his bride's request. "All right, fine. What do you want to talk about? How's Isla doing at school?"

"Good! She's doing really good. They had a party at the school today too. It sounds like she had a lot of fun."

"A party? That's cool. What was it for? Do we have any pics?" One of the benefits of the age of smartphones was that teachers now often took pictures during the school day to share with parents. This was especially true of younger kids like Isla, particularly when they had special days like parties, birthdays, or field trips.

"Yes! Ms. Meyerson-Smith sent me some really good ones. Let me stream them to the TV." Alina made her way to the couch in the living room. Shad slurped the last portion of his wine out of his stemless glass and walked over to the counter where he grabbed the bottle and poured a generous refill. Taking a sip, he turned and followed his wife back to the living room. She sat down in her spot on the sectional, turned the TV on, and scrolled to the photo-sharing app. Shad settled in to his spot and got comfortable, genuinely excited to see joyous images of his sweet daughter enjoying a school party with her friends. "Found it! Here's the first one." She tapped a few more times and the first image filled their large flatscreen television.

Shad's anticipatory smile melted away. He leaned forward toward the screen, staring in disbelief.

"What the hell is this, Alina? Is this some kind of joke?"

"What? What are you talking about? This is from the party today, Isla had a great time."

"After the conversation we just had, you show me this? You let Isla participate in this? Are you serious?"

"Don't talk to me like that, Shad. It's just a party, the kids had fun. They had snacks and party favors. Look at her, she's loving it," Alina said, gesturing angrily at Isla's smiling face on the screen. She knelt at a kid-sized statue of Baal, laughing as she drew a red line across her arm with what looked like a paint pen. The statue was more of a highlighter yellow than gold, with playful, exaggerated features including a silly-looking smiley face instead of the stoic visage of Baal. Clearly this was an attempt to make the idol more cartoonish and kid-friendly. Shad recognized the robes of a Baalist priest in the background. Other kids were in the photo, also looking happy as they pretended to make their offerings to Baal.

"Is that what I think it is? Is she pretending to cut her arm?"

"Yeah, they're learning about alternative religions since it's the Blood Moon Equinox."

"And why in the world do six-year-olds need to learn about cutting themselves to give blood offerings to a golden idol for a godforsaken *cult*?" Shad raised his voice more than he intended. The wine that had helped him open up earlier was also causing him to lose his grip on his anger.

"You do *not* need to be rude to me. Calm down. These religions are a huge part of our society and our kids need to learn about them so they're prepared for the real world. They'll have friends that are alts. We can't shelter them, Shad."

"She's six, Alina. We can absolutely shelter her. We *should* shelter her! She's a kid, for God's sake!"

"Stop yelling at me!"

"Stop yelling? That's what you're upset about?" Shad began again, but stopped himself. "All right, you're right, I'm sorry. I shouldn't raise my voice. But honestly, Alina, she's a child, she shouldn't be pretending to cut herself! That's insane! And what was a Baalist priest doing there in the first place? You're really OK with this?"

"Yes, I'm more than OK with it. I support it. I think it's good to explore those cultures."

"OK, so are we going to be allowed to have our pastor do a demonstration about the birth of Jesus on Christmas?"

"You know that's not the same. Our religion is the majority, alts don't have the same position in society. They're marginalized. It's good for the kids to engage with people who are different from them and not just the mainstream. It's how we teach our kids to have an open, tolerant worldview. And this party was a fun way for them to learn about what alts believe."

"Wait, this wasn't just a Baalist thing? They had stuff like this for the other ones?"

"Yes, of course they learned about the other alternative religions, Shad. The Blood Moon Equinox is important to all three of the alternative religions, you know that."

"Show me the rest of the pictures."

"No, you're just going to get mad and it's not productive."

"Show them to me, Alina."

"No, I'm not going to—" She was interrupted by Shad grabbing her phone out of her hand. "What the hell, Shad? Give me my phone!"

"I want to see what our child learned today at school, Alina. I'm her parent, I have a right to see it too," he said as he unlocked her screen and tapped to the next photo. He gritted his teeth as he swiped along the screen, scrolling through a few more photos of Isla pretending to make offerings to the silly lemon-colored idol as the bald Baalist priest oversaw the children gleefully. The Asherian photos were next. The photos showed the kids dancing in a group together in front of a miniature figure of Asherah. It almost looked like a doll, with pretty features painted on its face and body. The children held colored, silky ribbons as they were taught to dance by a young, enticingly-dressed woman Shad assumed was an Asherian temple prostitute. "At least they're only *dancing*," Shad said.

"Come on, Shad. They're kids. They're not going to do anything inappropriate."

"I'm not even going to respond to that." He shook his head as he scrolled through the remaining photos. The final pictures were of the children with a black-clad priest of Moloch. They stood in front of a black, bull/man statue. Unlike the previous two idols, this one looked like a regular idol to Moloch. It wasn't changed for a child audience. "They didn't give this one the cartoon treatment?"

"No, you can't alter the visage of the bull god, it's against the core tenets of Moloch. At least, you know, that's what I read."

"What are you talking about? How would you even know that?"

"I looked into some of this stuff after Isla got home and told me about the party, I wanted to know what she had learned," she said, speaking quickly and shrugging off his baffled tone.

Shad continued to scroll until he got the point where the kids were participating in the mock sacrificial ceremony. Each child beat on a drum in the large school gym while the Molochian priest set a stuffed dog in front of the small black statue of the shirtless man with the bull's head. The next pictures showed the priest take a knife to the stuffed dog's abdomen, plunging the blade inside and pulling it down from the top of the chest down to the toy's legs. Polyester fibers burst out of the laceration and spilled out onto the small altar as the priest raised his hands up toward the sky, and then knelt. The photos showed some of the children smiling as they were beating on the drums, but some, including Isla, looked sad.

"Does this look like Isla is having fun?"

"She just didn't understand the ritual and the meaning of sacrifice. I explained it to her and she felt better about it."

"You explained it to her? Since when are you a Molochian scholar?"

"I told you, I read about it when I found out about the party they were having."

"Wait, I thought you read about it today, after she got home and told you about the party. You knew this was happening before today? Like in advance?"

"Yes, it was on the school calendar. It's up on the refrigerator," she said, pointing toward their kitchen.

"Why didn't you tell me about it? We could have pulled her out of school today."

"I didn't think you would care. And why would we have pulled her out of school? She had fun and she learned a lot about what alts believe and practice."

"She had fun pretending to cut her skin open? She had fun dancing with a prostitute? She had fun watching someone cut open a stuffed puppy? Alina, this is crazy! She's six years old, she's a *child*. We can't let her get exposed to stuff like this! She's probably going to have nightmares tonight. I can't believe you didn't talk to me about this when you found out it was happening." Shad stood up and began to pace.

"It's school, Shad. She's learning, that's what they do in school."

"This is religion, Alina. We should be making decisions about whether or not she learns about religion, not the school. That's a decision for the parents," he said, stabbing his finger toward the ground.

"You need to calm down, Shad."

"I'm not going to calm down, I'm pissed off!" Shad threw his hands in the air in frustration. "They shouldn't have brought this stuff into a school, much less an elementary school! They're first graders!"

"I'm glad they did it! Isla has friends who are alts, she has teachers who are alts. That's the real world, she needs to know what's out there!"

"Know what's out there? Have you thought this through? We don't even show her some PG movies because you worry they'll scare her and she'll have trouble sleeping. But you're not worried she'll have nightmares about *cutting herself*? Or how about sexualizing a six-year-old girl with that disgusting temple prostitute, huh? No problems there? And you really saved the best for last, Alina—you're not worried that beating a drum while she watches some freak in all black gut a toy dog is going to give her bad dreams? You really think that's just *normal kid stuff*? Have you completely lost your mind?"

"Freak? Really, Shad? That's what you think of alts? Freaks? And you're calling me crazy? That's hurtful, and it's not productive. Is this really how you want to raise Isla? To think that alts are freaks?"

"Yeah, Alina. Yeah, I do. I want her to think the people who cut themselves and gut animals and have orgies are *freaks*. Because that's what they are! And if you think any of that crap is normal, then you *are* crazy."

Alina gasped. She stood up and walked a few steps away, then turned back and faced him. "I know you had a bad day at work, Shad, so I'm going to let that go. That's a terrible and mean thing to say. I know you don't mean it."

"I absolutely mean it, Alina. I fully and completely mean it. There's something off about these people, and I don't want Isla anywhere near it."

"Then I don't want to be anywhere near *you*, Shadrick. We're going to stay with my mom. I can't be around you right now." She spun on her heels and walked toward their bedroom. Shad followed her.

"You're just going to leave? Just like that? You don't want to defend the culties?" Shad said as he followed her into their room. Alina didn't stop or even acknowledge him; she just shook her head as she walked. "Turn around and talk to me, Alina."

Ignoring his entreaties, she took a duffle bag out of their closet, placed it on their bed, and began to pack it with clothes. She had just called his bluff, and Shad folded. "Alina, no. Come on. We can talk this out. I'm sorry, I'm just drunk. Don't leave."

"You're definitely drunk, but there's truth in wine, right? This is deeper than you having too much to drink. I need to think, you said some really serious things that I need to process. And I need to be away from you and your anger."

"OK, take some time and some space, but you can do that here. I'll sleep on the couch. I'll leave you alone, I promise. Just don't go, don't take Isla." He was still angry, he still felt righteous, but he didn't want to watch his wife and daughter walk out of his house to win an argument.

"Shad, I'm not just going to get over this overnight. Your anger, the yelling, those hurtful things you said . . . I'm overwhelmed, this was too much. I just—I just didn't expect this from you. There's clearly some serious distance between us and I need to figure out how we move forward from this. We both do." Alina looked at him with the feigned mercy of someone who knows they have the upper hand.

"Can you at least commit to come back tomorrow? Or Sunday?"

"I don't know. I really don't know." She looked away and walked past Shad to their laundry room where she began to gather some clothing for Isla.

"Babe, please. Is this really what's best for Isla?"

"That's exactly what I'm thinking about, Shad. What's best for her." Alina placed more clothes and other personal items in the bag and zipped it up.

"Don't you think this is a little extreme? I had a bad day at work, I had some wine, I vented, give me a break."

"What about everything you said about her party at school? All of that stuff about alts? You didn't mean any of that?"

Shad hesitated before responding.

"That's what I thought."

"Alina, these are parenting decisions we should be making together. I was just upset that I got left out of the decision process. I mean, we go to church, Alina. I thought we were on the same page with religion. I felt blindsided. We can talk this out and decide how to move forward together, you don't have to leave for that."

"*Do* we go to church, Shad? Do holidays count? And how *do* we move forward together? I want Isla to learn about alts. I want her to accept them, to understand them. I want her to be able to decide for herself what she thinks of alternative religions. Maybe she'll even be an alt herself! You think they're *freaks*. What are you going to do if she wants to be an alt?"

Shad started to speak and then stopped himself. He didn't know how to deescalate a fight that had already gone way beyond his control without surrendering his principles. So he stayed silent.

"If you can't even answer that, how exactly can we compromise?"

"We can find a way; we can figure something out. We always have, Alina."

"I hope so," she said, picking up the bag and walking past him. She walked to their garage, opened the passenger door of their minivan and placed the bag inside. Shad followed her quietly, trying to think of what he could say that might make a difference.

"Please, Alina. Please don't go, don't take Isla. I love you, don't leave!" Shad slit the throat of his pride like a Molochian sacrifice. Alina kept walking through their house. When she reached Isla's door, she slowly and quietly opened it and walked in. She uncovered their daughter, whose peaceful sleep was the perfect dictionary definition of serenity. Gently picking Isla up in her arms, she turned to leave. Shad hesitated, blocking the doorway. Alina made eye contact with him, the moment pregnant with tension as their daughter became some kind of hostage. He relented, stepped aside, beaten. She walked to the garage, opened the sliding door of the van and set Isla gently in her booster seat. Alina adjusted the back of the seat so that Isla was slightly reclined, helping her stay asleep. She closed the door and turned to Shad.

"It's only my mom's house, Shad. You know where we'll be. I just need to think. I'll call you." Shad leaned in for a kiss, but she dodged him and walked around the front of the van to the driver's side.

"I love you." Shad's voice quivered, his pride having completely bled out on the altar of desperation.

"Me too." The door of the van closed with a *thunk* of finality. She pressed the button on the visor to raise the garage door, turned the van on, and began to reverse out onto the street. Shad stood in front of the van in shock, bathed in the bright headlights. He didn't run after her, he didn't wave goodbye; he just watched, frozen and helpless, as his whole heart drove away, leaving him alone in their now-hollow home.

Chapter 3

ALINA LEANED AGAINST THE cafeteria wall as she watched the children dance whimsically to the Asherian music. She caught Isla's eye as she twisted around with a multicolored ribbon and gave her a warm smile, which Isla returned with an ear-to-ear grin. She was having so much fun; Alina was delighted to see Isla engaging freely with something that was totally foreign to her. She had worried that Isla would be scared or apprehensive, but all of the kids had been surprisingly open to learn about the alternative religions and dived in to the activities with giddy enthusiasm.

Why was it so hard for adults to open up like this? Alina wondered as she pulled out her phone and opened up Spinstagram to post about the event. Isla was having such a blast and looked completely adorable; she knew she'd get tons of hearts on her post. If she used the right hashtag, it might even get picked up by a Spinfluencer and go viral. As she lifted her phone to record the video, she stopped herself. Shad followed her on Spinstagram. He would definitely see her post, and Alina hadn't told him anything about this event. Frowning to herself, she locked her phone screen and put it back in her pocket. She didn't want to explain it to him, not yet. She wasn't ready for him to know about this part of her life before she had fully worked out her feelings.

"Hail the Blood Moon," came a voice from out of her periphery.

Alina started, the voice jarring her from her thoughts. "What? Oh, yes. Hail the Blood Moon!"

"Thanks again for volunteering, Mrs. Bengoade," Isla's teacher said.

"Oh, please Ms. Meyerson-Smith, call me Alina. I'm glad I could be here. What a fun day for the kids!"

"Well, if I'm going to call you Alina, you'd better call me Bella!" said Ms. Meyerson-Smith, Isla's first grade teacher.

"That's fair. Thanks for inviting me to help, Bella."

"I'm thrilled that you decided to come. You've been a lot more engaged than most parents, and this is such an important subject, especially now. There's so much hate, so many people whose minds are closed. I see so many parents like that, so it's really refreshing to have a parent who's, like, totally opposite! Ever since you started following my Spinstagram, I feel like we've had some great, raw conversations. You've been so perceptive and unbiased; it's been really encouraging. I wanted to make sure to thank you in person."

"Oh, that's so nice of you to say!" Alina blushed, putting her hand over her heart. "I was afraid I was being intrusive by asking so many questions!"

"Not at all! I've really enjoyed the discussion. It's a joy for me to share about Moloch and how the bull god has changed my life. Dominick!" she yelled, turning toward the kids. "Stop stepping on Amber's shoe laces! I see you; I know you're doing it on purpose. Amber, tie your shoes! Step out of the dance first, silly!" She turned back to Alina. "Sorry about that! Anyway, ask as many questions as you want! I really love talking about it."

"I've been so inspired by your story. Hitting rock bottom and finding your way back through Moloch . . . It just really touched my heart."

"I wasn't even sure anyone was watching those clips! I hope you don't mind me asking, but why does my story resonate with you? You have such a beautiful family, is everything OK at home?" Bella asked with the counterfeit concern found uniquely in the heart of gossips.

Alina sighed, looking back at the children as a new song started and they began to run around with silk ribbons above their heads. "Yes, everything is fine. I don't know, maybe that's the problem? I feel like I'm in a rut. Shad goes to work, I take care of Isla, on the weekends we watch a movie or go to the park or to the store. Rinse and repeat. Same thing all the time, I just feel like I'm missing something important. And I know that's not the same as what you went through, but the way you described how you felt back then, isolated, disconnected, you put words to a lot of my feelings."

Bella put her hand on Alina's forearm. "Alina, if it can work for me, it can work for anyone. I mean that. You know what? You should talk to the high priest today. He's here for the Molochian demonstration, you should connect with him after our class completes the ritual lesson."

"No, no, that's OK. I don't want to bother him, I'm sure he has much more important things to do than talk to some suburban mom."

"Of course not! I'll introduce you. I promise, it'll be great. I'll find you, don't leave before we talk, all right?"

"Sure, yes, that sounds good. Thank you, Ms. Meyer- uh, sorry. Thank you, Bella."

"Don't mention it, I'll see you soon. Now I have to get back to wrangling these crazies!" Bella said as she smiled and turned back to the crowd of dancing children. Alina continued to help the teachers as kids were ushered around the school to the different alternative religion exhibitions. Isla's class had started the day with the Asherian demonstration in the cafeteria. The kids loved that lesson, as it gave them an excuse to run, dance, and generally go wild. Their next lesson about Baal took place in the library. The children weren't as excited about the Baalist experience, despite how much the priestess tried to make it fun and engaging. A few children got scared of the knives and the blood and refused to participate, and two of them cried.

The class headed to the gym to complete their Blood Moon Equinox experience with the Molochians. This was the demonstration that Alina had been looking forward to; she'd been learning about Moloch from Bella for weeks online. She'd asked tons of questions and done some separate research on her own, but she'd never actually visited the temple of Moloch or even one of the smaller idols throughout the city. Reading Bella's descriptions of her experiences with Moloch struck a chord in Alina that she hadn't even been aware of before. Just the simple act of messaging through social media with Bella made Alina feel more a part of something than she had in years; maybe even since before Isla was born. Something was missing and she couldn't help but jump at the opportunity to share her feelings to an empathetic ear. She hadn't even told her husband how she'd really felt about her life, about their lives. Now that she'd told someone, now that she'd said out loud what had been brewing in her heart for so long, she couldn't ignore it anymore.

And she didn't *want* to ignore it anymore. Alina could hardly stop thinking about Moloch lately. She even imagined—fantasized—about what her first sacrifice would be and exactly how she would offer it to the bull god. It had to be a very expensive cut of meat. However, she also knew it couldn't be so pricey that it would set off any red flags if Shad reviewed their credit card statements. She wasn't ready for him to know that she was considering becoming an alt. Considering? She was past that. She had decided. Alina imagined herself placing the offering gently on the altar as the priest and the other worshippers looked on, beating their drums rhythmically. Gripping a ritual blade, she would slowly slice it, taking care to ensure that the blood dripped down the front of the obsidian stone *just right* so that no single drop was wasted. She'd look up at Moloch as she made her offering, releasing herself to him and accepting his gift, that same freedom that Bella described for which Alina yearned so deeply.

And now at her daughter's school, she was going to be closer to an idol to Moloch than she'd ever been before. She was so tingly with excitement and anticipation that she felt a little embarrassed, like a teenage girl at her favorite boy-band concert. Sure, it was just a kid's version of the idol and it wasn't the *real* ritual, but it was like an appetizer before the main course. After all, the Blood Moon Equinox festival was that weekend; what better time was there to make her first real offering to Moloch? And with Bella helping her talk to the priest, she was so much closer to bringing her fantasy into reality.

Isla's class entered the double doors of the elementary school gym and Alina held her breath, trying to conceal her eagerness. The wooden bleachers were collapsed into the walls, opening the gym up to the maximum size to accommodate multiple classes at once. The idol was positioned in the center of the large space, with an assortment of drums placed all around the room. Each one had drum sticks placed on top, waiting for one of the children to beat the rhythm of worship during the sacred ritual. Since it was a demonstration for children, the drums were multicolored, some with smiley faces on the drum head. Molochians believed it would be blasphemy to present Moloch in any other form than the black bull-man portrayed in their traditional idols, so the figure at the center of the room wasn't altered to be kid-friendly the way the other demonstrations had been.

After a short introduction by the Molochian high priest and lower priests and priestesses, the children began their pretend rite. They beat the drums as the high priest offered the mock-sacrifice, a stuffed animal which was split open and laid on the altar. The drum beats were inconsistent and scattered, as the children hit the drums wildly. Many of the kids were just enjoying the drums and ignoring the mock-sacrifice entirely. Isla beat her drum, looking on dejectedly as the priest split the animal open. Alina, on the other hand, was close to euphoric. Even with the drum beats being completely arhythmic and the sacrifice consisting of a polyester puppy, being present in a facsimile of the real ritual was enough to give her goosebumps. She continued to look on, savoring the experience as the high priest explained as much as he could about the process in a way a first grader would understand, jittery with anticipation of her conversation. Finally, the lesson concluded and children began to line up with their teachers and other parent volunteers before they would file out of the gym, back to their home room classes. Bella gathered her students in one area and had them continue to play on the drums and then made her way over to Alina.

"Hey! What'd you think of that?"

"It was amazing. Really great. I'm so glad I was able to be here to share that experience with Isla. I know it wasn't the real thing, but it was still so powerful!"

"I know. I felt it, too. Come on, let's go talk to high priest Lord Malochus." Moving through the gym, she ushered Alina toward the high priest, who was dressed in the traditional black robes with a black hood. Through the hood, Alina could just make out a face, but not with any detail. The only thing that differentiated the high priest from the other black-clad Molochian clergy was that Lord Malochus wore a golden crown over his black hood. A simple piece, it was a smooth gold band that went around the circumference of his head, with only a pointed piece that went down over his nose.

"Hail the Blood Moon, Lord Malochus. Please guide us to the freedom of our liberator, Moloch the great and wonderful," Bella said, bowing. Alina also bowed, awkwardly. "This is Alina, she's the friend we've talked about. Her daughter is Isla, the one I pointed out earlier," she said, gesturing toward Isla.

"Hail the Blood Moon, initiate," he said to Bella. He then turned to address Alina. "Alina, may the grace of Moloch free you from tyranny," he said with a thick Middle Eastern–sounding accent, returning their bows.

"Thank you for taking the time to speak with me," Alina said, her endless fidgeting betraying her nervousness.

Malochus nodded in acknowledgment. "Bella has told me much about you, Alina. I welcome you here, to the presence of our liberator. I understand you are seeking liberation for yourself and for your daughter?"

Alina jerked involuntarily, jolted from her stunned self-consciousness. "For myself, yes. I hadn't thought about including Isla," she said, looking at Bella, who was staring at her intently.

"You only want freedom for yourself?"

"What? No, I mean, I want her to be free too. I just, I hadn't thought . . ." She paused.

"You thought only of your own liberation?"

"Of course, I want liberation for her. It's just that when I have been thinking about Moloch, about making offerings, it's always been for me. Now that you bring it up, I feel so selfish."

"There is no need to feel embarrassment, bonded-one. Only our liberator, the great bull god Moloch can unbind you. We all seek to be unbound selfishly. This selfishness is normal. There is no shame in it. It is not for you to unbind yourself; it is for our liberator to do this. I am the liberator's high priest; it is for me to guide the bonded like yourself. It is for me to show you that your progeny is also bound and in need of the liberator."

"I'm sorry, I'm not sure I understand. Why do you call me bonded? What do you mean?" Alina said.

Malochus looked at Bella. "I was told that she had received guidance?"

"Forgive me, my lord. I didn't use the sacred terms when we spoke about the liberator."

He continued to face Bella for a moment. Even with his appearance entirely shrouded by his dark hood, it was clear he was looking at her with stern disapproval. "My apologies, bonded-one. This initiate has been liberated; she should have given you better guidance. I will explain. You are bound to this world. Your progeny is, too, bound. You are bound to everything around you, every person around you. Your family, friends, colleagues. You are never free; you are always bound by demands. To the obligations that these things impose upon you," he said, his accent producing "obligations" as *oh-blee-gah-shins.* "You cannot live freely; you cannot live for *yourself.* You are restricted to serve others first. You must follow the rules set upon you. Even your morality, this is a boundary set for you by the light of the world. These are bonds for you, they tie you down. They keep you from serving yourself. This is why I call you bonded-one. All of those who live under the tyranny of the light are bonded-ones. Only the darkness of the great liberator, our bull god Moloch, *only he* can break the bonds of the light and grant you the true freedom to embrace yourself and shed all else. No bonds. No needs. No obligations. True fulfillment. Your desires, granted in his darkness. Bonded-one, you must understand one thing. In one word, this singular term, in this is the essence of the dark one, the void heart of Moloch," he paused, looking at her through his dark veil. "*Freedom.* Moloch is freedom from the light of this world. Liberty in darkness." Malochus stood silently, still facing Alina as she stood quietly and digested his words, overwhelmed.

"How . . . how can I be freed?" Alina asked. "What do I have to do, what do I need to offer?"

"You ask the right questions. You are on the path to darkness," he said, nodding approvingly. "The initiate will guide you now." Malochus turned to Bella. "I trust the guidance she provides now will be complete. This is correct, Bella?"

"Yes, Lord Malochus. I will provide true guidance," Bella said, bowing her head.

"Good. You know what will please the liberator during this Blood Moon Equinox. Do not fail him, or initiate you will forever be," Malochus ordered. He turned to Alina. "I look forward to your liberation, bonded-one," he bowed to her. "Now I must return to the temple to prepare for the sacred rituals. Please, excuse me."

"Yes, of course," Alina said, also bowing. "Thank you so much for taking the time to speak with me. I will follow Bella's guidance. I promise." Malochus nodded to her and walked away toward the hooded priests and priestesses who were gathered quietly near the idol. Alina looked to Bella. "Wow. That was . . . intense."

"Yes, as our high priest Lord Malochus carries so much responsibility on his shoulders. He's so connected to the liberator, even interacting with bonded-ones is a challenge for him. But he does it anyway, that's how much he cares."

"Malochus? Is that his real name? I don't think I've ever heard that before."

"When one ascends to the level of the priesthood of Moloch, you are unbound from your previous life entirely. That includes your birth name. You take a new name which is given to you by your high priest. Malochus received his name years ago in Lebanon, the old world."

"I thought his accent sounded Middle Eastern," Alina said, looking at Malochus, who was directing the other priests and priestesses as they gathered and prepared to transport the idol of Moloch. Two large wooden beams were attached to the base of the idol on the right and left side. Each beam had an indentation padded with dark leather toward the end. As she watched, the priests and priestesses knelt down and lifted the beams up onto their shoulders. They all stood and hoisted the idol up as Malochus turned to lead them out of the gym. Alina turned back to look at Bella. "I'm sorry if I got you in trouble by asking those questions, I didn't know that would happen."

"It's fine. Don't worry about it," Bella said.

"Why does he call you initiate?"

"It's my status in the temple. I am attempting to join the permanent service of the liberator, but it's a very long process that involves a number of tests."

"Oh, I feel terrible! I'm so sorry, I had no idea I was screwing things up for you, Bella!"

"It was my fault, but I'll provide you with better guidance about what's next. That will return me to the good graces of Malochus and, more importantly, our liberator. But you need to follow my instructions. Will you do that?"

"Yes, yes, I will."

"Promise me, Alina. This is important."

"I promise, I'll do what you tell me to do. I want to do this right, I want to be liberated by Moloch."

"OK, good. You know the Blood Moon Equinox festival in the park downtown this weekend?"

"Yes, of course. It's supposed to be huge, all three alternative religions will be there celebrating, right?"

"That's right. I need you to come on Sunday night. Can you do that?"

"Sunday night? What time? I guess it's a three-day weekend, I should be able to come once we get Isla down for bed. I don't know what I'll tell Shad . . ."

"No, Alina. You have to bring Isla with you. That's extremely important."

"What? I can't bring her if it's at night, Bella. We're pretty strict about her schedule. Shad will never let me do that. I can't just—"

"You can. And you will. It's just one night, Isla will be fine. Shad doesn't need to know, does he?"

"You're saying I should sneak her out without Shad knowing? I don't know, if he finds out he's going to be furious. And we never keep her up past her bedtime, and definitely not outside of the house. I don't understand why I need to bring her, are you sure I can't come alone? I'm sure I could sneak away by myself."

"Yes, I'm sure. You can only be liberated if you are liberated together *with* Isla. If Isla isn't with you, you can't be liberated." Alina looked down, clearly very uncomfortable. Bella decided to change tactics, gently placing her hand on Alina's shoulder. "This guidance comes straight from Lord Malochus. And if it comes from him, it has the blessing of the true liberator, Alina."

"You mean, from Moloch?"

"Yes, I mean Moloch, the breaker of bonds."

"He knows about me? About Isla?"

"You're special, Alina. This is important to all of us." Bella gave Alina the same look she would give a first grader who was struggling with self-confidence. "It'll be fine, I promise. I know it's out of your comfort zone, but that's what this is all about, right? Getting free of your burdens, letting go of the things that are holding you back. The same is true for Isla. This is going to be life-changing for both of you. We'll make it like an adventure for her. She'll love it, it'll be fun and exciting. Trust me!"

"That's true, I could treat it like a special occasion. Like we're going camping or something."

"Yes, exactly!"

"I could tell Shad I'm giving him a break, that I'm taking Isla to my mother's house so he can have a guy's night, or even the weekend." Alina's apprehensions began to vaporize.

"That's a great idea. He'll never even know."

"What about offerings? Am I going to need to bring something for both of us? I hadn't planned on that but I can just buy more so we have enough for me and Isla."

"You don't need to worry about that, we'll have plenty there to offer for both of you."

"Really? I thought I needed to bring something for myself. Everything I've read has said that it's important that your first offering be something special, so your introduction to the bull god is positive, so it impresses him with your loyalty and dedication. It should be personally significant, or expensive. At least that's what I read, I don't really know."

"You have been reading a lot, haven't you? You're right, that is normally how the initial liberation should go. The bonded-one usually brings an important sacrifice. But this is a special situation, Alina. It's the Blood Moon Equinox and you'll both be liberated at once, which is extremely unique. In situations like this, especially with the high priest involved, the offerings are provided for you."

"Oh wow," began Alina before taking a breath. "That sounds like a big deal."

"Like I said, there's something special about you. Lord Malochus knew it as soon as I told him about you."

"What could be special about me?"

"You may not see it in yourself, but Lord Malochus sees it. He chose you. It's deep down in your heart, in your blood. And most importantly, Moloch sees it too."

"This is kind of overwhelming. But also really exciting!"

"I know it is! This is going to be great, Alina. I'll be there with you every step of the way!"

Alina turned and hugged Bella enthusiastically, surprising her. "Thank you for helping me through this! I know it's taken a ton of your time. It means the world to me that you're investing so much in me, and in Isla. Thank you, thank you!"

"It's my pleasure, Alina. I'm happy to serve the liberator by leading bonded-ones to freedom from the tyranny of the light of this world. I was a bonded-one before too." Bella looked down at her watch. "Oh, shoot. We're late for the final ceremony in the auditorium! Let's round up the kids!" They both rushed toward the class and began to herd the children to the doors. Alina's mind was racing, overwhelmed with excitement. *Is this really true? Of all people, I'm special enough that the high priest knows who I am? That Moloch himself knows me, has chosen me? What's so unique about me?* She thought to herself, heart aflutter. She could hardly believe it. She was just a boring house wife, just a regular suburban mom. Her thoughts were swirling as they walked to the final ceremony of the day. Isla turned around and caught her eye, beaming with blissful happiness. Alina returned the giddy smile. She wasn't sure what it meant that they were special enough to be known by Moloch, but they were going to find out together.

Chapter 4

SHAD WOKE SLOWLY TO the annoying whine of a leaf blower being operated in his neighbor's yard. He began to get up, struggling to open his eyes, disoriented by his pounding hangover. Before he realized where he was, he fell off the couch. Groaning, he got up and sat back down, rubbing his forehead in a pointless attempt to make the headache go away. After Alina left with Isla to go to her mother's house, Shad was aimless. He had stood quietly in the kitchen for what seemed like hours, leaning against the counter, stunned that everything had gone so wrong so quickly. He checked his phone over and over again, hoping to see a message from his wife. He had tried texting her, asking if she made it safely. It was marked to show she had read the text, but she never responded. Conceding, he had left his phone on his charger in his bedroom and decided he didn't want to think anymore. Then he'd opened another bottle of wine and committed to the most deliberate pursuit of drunkenness he'd ever made in his life. His hazy memory after the first couple of glasses of wine from that second bottle indicated his pursuit had been wildly successful. Apparently, the night ended when he had passed out on the couch.

Sitting there, massaging his temples, he ran through the events of the previous night in his mind as a form of self-flagellation, reliving the train wreck of a conversation that led to the love of his life taking his precious daughter away to his mother-in-law. He thought through each exchange with Alina, hearing the words again in his mind, his anger rising back up in his chest as he recalled her responses. *What was she thinking? There's no defense for exposing Isla to this, not this young. It's one thing to be tolerant, it's one thing to be accepting, but to force it on kids? The violence, the sexuality—how could she think this was good for our little girl? She's so sweet, so impressionable. She just wants to make people happy; she'll go along with anything. Completely innocent. And what about Alina? Where did this come from? Maybe I was too intense last night. Maybe I was too hard on her. I know she's been in a rough patch with being a stay-at-home mom, but that's temporary. Surely, she knows that? She knows we can get through this like we have with everything else. The woman I was arguing with last night is not the same woman I married. But when did she change? How could I have missed this? And what the hell am I going to do about this now? I have to convince her that this stuff is harmful to Isla. That we need to protect her innocence. I have to show her that I'm not against her—that I love her and Isla more than anything. And I have to show her that these alts, these cults are not more important than our family.*

Shad got up from the couch, feeling reinvigorated by his plan. He'd find a way to convince his wife of the danger that the alternative religions posed to their young daughter, to their family, to their future. But first, he had to deal with the ogre of a hangover that was plunging a battle-axe into his skull. After a quick shower to rinse off the wino stink, he threw on fresh clothes and headed out to the store. Like every good suburbanite, Shad lived only about ten minutes from the nearest Bullseye department store. The location nearest him was an Ultra Bullseye, meaning it was larger and had a full-fledged grocery section. They shopped at the store often, procuring everything from frozen pizzas to underwear, from shoes to external hard drives. Walking the aisles was a favorite pastime, providing Shad and Alina with ample opportunities to judge and criticize merchandise—and very often other shoppers—while Isla got to run around the store. As he walked through the doors, the memories both warmed his heart and dug a pit in his gut. He shook it off, and focused on his shopping list.

He entered the store near the clothing department, grabbing a shopping cart more out of habit than necessity. Making his way through the store almost on autopilot, he grabbed the club crackers and Pedialyte, his time-tested hangover cure. He cut over to the toy section and selected a cute plush elephant for Isla that was so soft even Shad wanted to cuddle it, and then went to the front of the store to the floral section. A dozen red roses seemed to fit; he considered two dozen but felt that might seem too extreme, and any other flower just didn't seem to have the same gravity as a red rose. His objectives complete, he made his way to the checkout lines.

As he exited the grocery section of the store, he was greeted by a huge Blood Moon Equinox display, filled with special merchandise that celebrated the alternative religions and the holiday. The display was filled with items of all kinds for all three groups—a Baalist stainless steel knife set featuring an upturned five-pointed star, surrounded by an ornate circle on the handles of each blade; tantalizing, skimpy silken Asherian clothing; Moloch-themed coloring books with depictions of the bull god, the temple, and Molochian sacrifice rituals. There were stickers, posters, toys, backpacks, temporary tattoos, hats and anything else someone could want to proudly declare their—or their child's—adherence with and allegiance to one of the alternative religions. Shad even saw children's "Blood Moon Equinox Beginner's Kits" for each of the alternative religions, which included items similar to what he had seen in the images of Isla at school. Small, kid-friendly versions of each idol—with the exception of Moloch, whose miniature idol still looked like the real thing—fake knives that would squirt red paint when you pushed a button for the Baalist ritual, a small drum and stuffed animal "offering" for Moloch, and some silk ribbons for dancing in worship of Asherah. He stood there, leaning on his shopping cart, his jaw clenched as he took it all in. So much of the merchandise being targeted at children gave Shad the feeling that the odds were stacking up against him. If even regular people disagreed with him, people who shopped at the same Bullseye where he had shopped with his family for years, people with day jobs like his, people with young families and little daughters just like his . . . if they all thought this was normal, then maybe Shad was on the wrong side of this fight?

"Freaking unbelievable, right?"

Shad jumped, startled by the voice bursting his mental bubble. A man stood a few feet from him, staring at the Blood Moon Equinox display. He wore a suit, but looked as haggard as Shad felt. "Huh, what?"

"This crap they're selling. This is supposed to be a normal store, you know? This is where I shop with my kids. Where I used to shop with them, I mean, before she took them from me." Shad got a whiff of what smelled like whiskey coming off the man's breath.

"They even have toys. Pretend sacrifices. How did it come to this?" Shad said to the man, and also to himself.

"Culties just can't leave it alone! We gave them the prostitution thing, you know? We gave that to them. They can bang all their prostitutes in their temples and it's legal. They can cut themselves and kill animals too. They said they just wanted to be free to live their religion. They just wanted to practice the way it was meant to be practiced. That's what they told us. Big freaking lie, man! Total trojan horse!" the man said, his voice loud enough that he began to draw attention from other shop-pers. "I've had enough. Not anymore, not my kids!" he said, gesturing at the display. Shad began to look around, noticing that others in the store were beginning to notice them. The last thing he needed was to end up in some viral online video with a guy raging about the cults for Alina to see, that would just guarantee she'd leave him for good.

"I get it man, but let's calm down, all right? How about we take a walk?" Shad said as a portly man with glasses approached them looking perturbed. He had an unshaven face and the waddle of someone who spends too much time on the couch.

"Hey! Hey, you! You got a problem with alts? You one of those anti-alt bigots?" the neck-beard said.

Shad's suit-wearing acquaintance quickly turned in the graceless manner that comes with a high blood-alcohol level. "Yeah, yeah, I do have a problem with culties! They're going after kids!"

"Listen here, you intolerant douchebag, we like to be called alts. Watch your mouth!"

"Oh boy, you're one of them, are you? You look like you would be, you fat idio—" He was cut off by Shad grabbing his arm to pull him away from the confrontation.

"Sorry! My friend got carried away, we were just leaving," Shad said as he led the man along.

"What, no, I was just getting started!" the suited man said as Shad dragged him toward the exit.

"Dude, shut your mouth and come with me. I agree with you, but we're drawing a crowd, and I guarantee security is on the way. There's about ten cell phones pointing at us right now, and I can't afford to get into trouble over this," Shad yell-whispered at the man. "My name is Shad, what's your name?"

"I, uh, I'm Thomas. Tom."

"Tom, you got something to lose? Because I've got a lot to lose. If you insist on doing this right now, I'm going to turn around and leave you here. What do you want to do?" Tom began to look around, the reality of the situation slowly dawning on him. "Yeah, yeah, OK. Let's go. Where are we going?"

"Out of here. But first I have to pay." Shad continued leading him to the checkout lines. The bespectacled neck-beard continued to follow and yell at them.

"Yeah, you go and run away, you stupid bigot! Get out of here!"

"Yeah, we're out of here. Sorry!" Shad said over his shoulder. People began to put their cell phones away, realizing the ripening confrontation had died on the vine before it could come to fruition. Luckily, there was a lane open in the self-checkout, so Shad was able to pay for his purchases and quickly exit the store with Tom.

"Listen, uh, thanks for that. You saved my bacon."

"I saved us both, hopefully. I think we got out of there before anyone recorded anything that was worth uploading for likes on PostSpace or VidHole. If we're lucky," Shad said as he closed the back door of his SUV.

"Yeah, I just kind of lost control there. I've had a little bit to drink."

"I can tell, hard to miss."

"Been a tough week. Look, I hate to ask for another favor, but think you could give me a ride? I'm definitely not good to drive. I shouldn't have driven here in the first place, but I'm sober enough now to know I'm not sober enough to get home. I can call a rideshare, but I'm not sure if I want to be waiting around here for someone else to call me out."

Shad sighed. "Sure man, where to?"

"Brookhollow. It's about ten minutes east of here."

"Yeah, I can do that. That's in the direction I was heading anyway." They got into the car and Tom told Shad his address. They drove quietly at first, but Shad began to feel uncomfortable and thought Tom might want to sound off more now that they were safe to speak freely. "Think you could reach back there and grab the Pedialyte and crackers?"

Tom was looking out the window contemplatively. He looked back at Shad and then to the back seat. "Oh, yeah. Definitely." He reached to the back and grabbed the Bullseye shopping bag. Shad grabbed the Pedialyte out of the bag and opened it, using his knee to keep the steering wheel steady as he twisted the cap off. He chugged half of the bottle before coming up for air.

"Want some? I got two bottles."

"Are you sick? Why are you drinking Pedialyte?"

"I smelled like you this morning. Got obliterated last night, this is my personal hangover cure."

"Worth a shot at sobering up, I guess," Tom said, pulling out the other bottle.

"Mind handing me the crackers?"

Tom complied, and Shad opened them one-handed as he continued their drive. "Thanks. So what's got you day drinking on a Saturday?"

"My ex. She married this guy, he's really into one of the cults. The one with the hookers."

"The cult of Asherah."

"Yeah, Asherians. With the dancing and the orgies. Just my luck, she leaves me for cheating only to remarry a guy who turns cheating into a religion. It's all right, you can laugh," Tom said after he noticed Shad was suppressing a smile. "I got over that, she's a grown woman and if that's what she wants to do with her life, that's fine. But now she's got my son going too. Not for the sex, at least as far as I know, but the dancing and the rituals. She's getting him into it. We never even went to church, you know? Not even on the holidays. My parents were strict, really tough on me. I stopped going to church as soon as I could. My ex always wanted to go, but I was against it. Now I wish I had listened to her, maybe things would have been different."

"Hindsight sucks, right? Looking back, trying to find where you missed it, where you lost the chance to save it all. I get it."

"You too?"

"Not the same thing, not as bad, but yeah, me too. My wife seems like she's getting sucked in to all this alt stuff and I'm afraid she's trying to drag my six-year-old daughter along with her. And for the life of me I can't figure out where it all went wrong. But I guess that doesn't matter, right? All that matters is what we do *now*," he said, punctuating the last word by jabbing his index finger into the steering wheel.

"I don't know what to do now," Tom said.

"Yeah, me neither. But I can tell you that getting piss drunk and picking fights at Bullseye isn't the solution."

Tom laughed. "You've got that right." Shad slowed the car as they arrived at Tom's house, a massive McMansion on a large lot at the back of a cul-de-sac. "Thanks again for getting me out of there. Saved me a headache. Now I only have the hangover to deal with."

"I hear you. You're welcome, Tom. Pay it forward, or whatever." Shad was never much with goodbyes.

"Here's my card. If you ever figure out what to do about your situation and you have a tip for me, give me a ring," Tom said as he pulled a business card out of his cellphone's case wallet. He opened the door and got out of the car. "Good luck, Shad." Tom closed the door and Shad examined his business card. It was thick, with deeply embossed lettering, clearly not a cheap card. It read "Tom Rodriguez, Managing Partner, Rodriguez, Hamilton, and Singh, Attorneys at Law." Shad looked up from the card to see Tom enter the front door of the massive house and close it behind him. *Lawyer, mansion. Makes sense.* He put the car back into gear and began to drive toward his mother-in-law's house. *Maybe she's cooled off and we can defuse this today, maybe she just needs this gesture of peace to let her guard down,* he thought to himself, taking a generous shot of hope-ium. Shad was trying to stay positive; he knew he had to do anything and everything he could to try to fix this situation and avoid his personal life turning into a wasteland, but the dread growing in his gut was like a sinkhole, swallowing anything in its vicinity.

It was midafternoon when he parked the car in the street in front of Alina's childhood home. The day was warm and sunny; the contrast between the bright sunlight and Shad's inner turmoil somehow made him feel worse, like the weather was also against him. He pulled his phone out and sent Alina another text, hoping that giving her advanced warning would avoid any unwanted surprises and emphasize to her that he was just trying to make peace. He waited a few beats to see if she would respond. She didn't.

He got out of the car, opened the back door, and grabbed the flowers and the stuffed elephant. As he walked up the sidewalk to the front door, he saw the curtains move, indicating someone was peeking out. His heart skipped a beat as he imagined it was Isla. An involuntary frown captured his face when his mother-in-law opened the front door before Shad even reached the threshold.

"What are you doing here, Shadrick? She doesn't want to see you," Eliana said.

"I just wanted to drop off gifts for her and Isla. It's OK if she doesn't want to talk," Shad said, holding up the flowers and the stuffed elephant. Eliana made a grimace and stepped out of the door toward him. He handed her the flowers and the toy. "I'd like to see Isla."

"I don't think that's a good idea," Eliana said, stepping back into the doorway.

"The disagreement is between me and Alina. Isla isn't involved in this, she's just a kid. Please let me see my daughter." Shad worked hard to keep his anger in check.

Eliana hesitated. "I'll go talk to Alina." She went inside and closed the door behind her. Shad stood there on the front porch, doing his best to act nonchalant as the minutes passed. The door opened and his heart jumped into his throat as he saw Isla burst out at a full run toward him.

"Pickle!"

"Daddy! I'm so glad you're here! Mommy said you couldn't come on our trip to see Nana because you were busy with work. Are you done with work now? Can you come and play with us?" she said, all in one breath.

"I'm sorry, sweetheart, but Daddy still has some work to do. But I'll come to play with you very soon, as soon as I can. I promise." He hugged her tightly and gave her a kiss on the forehead.

"You shouldn't work, Daddy. You should play with me instead." Isla said with the matter-of-fact decisiveness that comes so naturally to kids.

Shad laughed. "I wish I didn't have to, my love, but Daddy has to work so we can pay our bills. But don't worry, I'll be here with you soon. Do you like the elephant I brought you?"

Isla had brought the elephant out with her and lifted it up toward her father. "I love it! Can I name him?"

"Of course, you can. What should he be called?"

"Earl. Earl the elephant!"

"That's a fantastic name. How about you and Earl get back inside and play?" Eliana was watching through a crack in the open door. The last thing Shad wanted to do was end this moment with Isla, but he didn't want to push his luck and make the situation worse. "I'll see you again soon, OK? Give Mommy a big hug for me."

"Will you be here for bedtime?"

Shad's voice caught in his throat. He took a breath. "I'm sorry baby, not tonight. I wish I could. Mommy will be there. Can I have the biggest hug ever? It has to be a really big hug to last me until I see you tomorrow." She tried to maintain her frown, looking away from him. "Come on, I know you can give me a really huge hug. Can you show Earl how big a hug you can give? I told him on the way that you give the biggest hugs. Want to show him?"

Isla began to grin. Shad smiled at her and opened his arms to her. Isla put Earl down on the ground behind her and turned to her father, spreading her arms as wide as she could manage. She ran to him, her smile wide with a daughter's pure joy. "I love you so much, Isla. I will always love you."

"I love you too, Daddy!" she screamed in his ear. Eliana stood in the doorway, having opened it more now that she heard their time concluding. Shad locked eyes with her, pleading. She looked away from him.

"Come on, sugar. It's snack time," Eliana said to Isla. She hesitated, looking up at her father.

"It's OK, Pickle. Go get some delicious snacks with Nana. See you soon."

"Bye, daddy!" She planted a kiss on his cheek and ran past Eliana into the house.

"Thank you, Eliana. I'll be back again tomorrow."

"You're welcome," she said, beginning to close the door.

"Eliana, wait." She held the door slightly ajar, looking up at him. "You're really OK with this? This cult stuff? You support that?"

"I support my daughter," Eliana said, shutting the door with finality. Shad stood for a moment, looking at the closed door. He took a deep breath, doing his best to remember his daughter's hug, and retreated to his car where he sat staring blankly at the steering wheel. A fissure began to form in his soul; he just wanted to be with his family. And he couldn't. He began to feel the aches of desperation crack his resolve. He imagined banging on the door, begging to be forgiven and allowed back into Alina's good graces. He imagined scooping Isla up in his arms, kissing her sweet cheeks and hugging her like he had just done. In this vision, he knelt before Alina, surrendering. He heard his voice tell her she was right, agreeing that Isla should learn about the alternative religions, even agreeing to participate himself. He saw himself next to Alina, holding her hand as she held Isla's next to her, the three of them standing before the huge obsidian bovine deity. Looking toward her, he saw Alina look into his eyes, raise a black blade up and plunge it into his chest.

He screamed inside the car, which had never felt so small. Banging his fists against the steering wheel, he vented his heartache through fury. He had no idea what to do next. All he wanted was his family, but he knew he couldn't give in. There was no compromise to be had. He had to convince Alina that she was wrong, he had to change her mind. He had no choice, because if he failed, he'd lose everything he loved. Breathing deeply and rubbing his knuckles, he tried to regain some of his composure. He happened to look down the driveway just in time to see Eliana walk out and drop the flowers into the trash can. She didn't notice him. *Perfect. Just perfect.* Shad thought to himself. He pulled out his phone and texted one of his longtime best friends, Deckard Culpepper.

Deck. You free tonight? Shad saw the "read" confirmation show up. He then saw the dots appear as Deckard typed his reply.

Sure, brother. What did you have in mind?

Want to get blasted?

With you? Definitely. Alina is cool with that?

No idea.
Oh, I see. All right. When do you want to hang?
How about now? I'll bring the booze.
I'll get the grill ready.

Chapter 5

It took Shad about twenty minutes to drive to Deckard's bungalow. He lived on the other side of Mapleton from Alina's mother. Luckily, or unluckily depending on how you viewed the circumstances, there was a cavernous liquor store on the same exit as Deckard's neighborhood. Shad stopped in and picked up a handle of his favorite bourbon and a pack of the cigarettes he used to smoke at parties in college. *If I'm going to go off of the deep end, I might as well dive in headfirst.*

Deckard lived in an old neighborhood. It was filled with small, but very posh houses from the fifties. All of them had been completely redone, and most were populated with people just like Deckard—single yuppies or childless artsy couples with enough money to invest in transforming an old house into a status symbol. Deckard was a one-man advertising agency. His creative talent got him noticed in his early twenties, and he'd been a hired gun for agencies all over the state ever since. He never even went to college to study his craft—he was just *good.* He was Shad's oldest friend, but they didn't get to spend much time together since Shad had become a family man. As Shad drove up, he saw a beautiful young woman walking down the sidewalk away from Deckard's front door. Deckard stood on the front stoop, his button-down shirt open in the front and billowing listlessly in the light breeze. He was gesturing his arms in a conciliatory fashion that was crystal clear to Shad—*come on baby, don't be mad.* The young woman walked to her car defiantly, clad in shorts that barely qualified for the classification, heels that were high enough to need special training, and a silken blouse that left very little to the imagination. She didn't turn around as she left, but gave Deckard a single-fingered salute as a goodbye. Shad pulled up behind her little hybrid as she got to the driver's door. She turned to him, made eye contact, and gave Shad the same salutation. He smiled awkwardly and waved as she slammed her door and drove away.

Deckard made his way down the sidewalk toward Shad's car as he was getting out and retrieving the liquor store bag from the back seat. "Sorry about that, Tracy's usually really nice."

"She certainly looks nice."

"She does, doesn't she?"

"Think she'll still want you to take her to prom after today?"

"Screw off, she's twenty-three."

"Right, still following Theo's Law?" Shad asked, referring to Theobardo Decrapio's reported penchant for only dating women twenty-five years old and younger. Deckard shrugged in the affirmative. "Figured that. Sorry to spoil your plans."

"Ah, she'll get over it. In fact, she'll probably be even crazier about me after this. Want what you can't have, absence makes the heart grow fonder, you know, all that. She'll hate you, though."

"I really thought we'd be besties. I'm crushed."

"Let's get to the back porch. I have some steaks marinating and the grill is warming up. Seems like the weather is going to cooperate too."

They made their way inside. Deckard's bachelor pad was as perfectly decorated and laid out as you would imagine an ad man's home would be. Beautiful, expensive furniture in all of the right places; rooms felt full but not cluttered. Walls were amply adorned without being crowded. Art pieces expertly curated for every room, each piece aesthetically pleasing enough for the layman to appreciate while also maintaining enough chic exclusivity to impress even the snobbiest of connoisseurs. Even the lighting was immaculate, casting shadows perfectly to frame the room; not too bright, not too dim, like the baby bear's porridge, it was just right. He followed Deckard into the living room toward the bar, walking past a high-end sound system where a vinyl record spun out some kind of rock music that sounded like it predated Shad's birth by a decade or two. Deckard took the bag from Shad and lifted out the handle of bourbon. He examined the bottle. "You're nothing if not consistent, my friend."

"I like what I like."

Deckard nodded respectfully at him. He did a double take and looked back in the bag. "What do we have here?" he said, pulling out the cigarettes. "Wow man, we're going hard tonight, huh? Props to you for going old school and not buying one of those battery powered fruity things. People just don't enjoy good things anymore."

"Well, I'm not saying I won't enjoy it, but enjoyment isn't exactly my goal," Shad said as Deckard poured the brown liquid into two ornately etched old-fashioned glasses.

"Still like it neat?"

"Definitely.

"So, if enjoyment isn't the goal, what is? What's going on? We haven't hung out in a while, brother. I'm not saying I'm not happy you're here—it's great to see you—but your texts were pretty cryptic."

"Let's head outside, this is a long story." Shad grabbed the cigarettes and the handle of whiskey and walked toward the back porch. He opened the pack of cigarettes and took out the matches that he got for free from the liquor store, struck a match and effortlessly lit a cigarette that sat limply in his mouth, the muscle memory from his intemperate youth still fully intact.

"Let me just start out by saying that I'm not a bigot, OK?"

Deckard burst out in laughter. "Bro, that's kind of the exact thing a bigot would say! Hand me one of those," he said, gesturing toward the cigarettes.

"I know, I know how it sounds. Just listen, all right?" Shad took another drag on the cigarette, sat forward in his chair, and began to recount the entire series of events of the past twenty-four hours, starting with the Blood Moon Equinox celebration at work, through the fight with Alina, the debacle with Tom at the Bullseye, his heartbreak at leaving Isla, and ending with Shad texting Deckard that afternoon. He spared no detail, and didn't pull any punches about how angry he was—at his coworkers, at his wife, and at himself. "Man, I just want to keep to myself, you know? I really don't give a crap about the culties and their weird cult stuff. Do your thing, just stay away from me. And my family. But now it's messing with my job, and they've got their hooks into Alina—it's even getting to Isla. I'm just so pissed off about it. I'm pissed at myself, too, for losing control. For pushing Alina out the door. Even if I still think she's wrong, I shouldn't have lost my cool like that. I don't know what to do, Deckard. I don't know how to fix this. So I came over here to get drunk, because that's the only thing I could think of that might make me feel better. Or forget that I feel bad."

"Well, I'm glad you came, Shad. I'm glad to see you and I'm even more glad to be here to help one of my oldest friends through a tough time." Deckard clinked his glass against Shad's. "Now, where to start?" Deckard said, looking down at his glass and taking another pull off of his cigarette. He finished it, and motioned to Shad for another. "I'll start where you did—you're not a bigot. None of what you did was driven by hate. I've known you almost two decades, I know how you operate, and hating people for their religion or whatever, it's just not you. Not that you don't hate people, I'm sure you're capable, but hating people for that kind of thing just takes too much effort. You don't care enough to hate people like that."

Shad laughed. "You're making me sound like such a sweetheart!"

"Yeah, that didn't come out exactly how I meant it. Look, I mean you do your thing and you let other people do theirs. You've never been judgmental. You may crack a few jokes here and there, but who doesn't? Hating someone is a whole different level of energy and effort, and you're just not going to do that unless you're invested in someone. Like this situation you have with Alina. You're bent out of shape over it because *you love her.* You always have. You can't help yourself; you're worked up because you're invested. But your coworkers? Maybe they're your friends, maybe you care about them, but nobody is that invested in their coworkers unless they're boinking on their lunch break. You don't care enough about these people to truly hate them. When you really, really *hate* someone, that's an investment. You're tied to that person, you're spending energy, active negative energy directed at them. Maybe they hurt you, or someone like them hurt you, or hurt someone you love. The point is, you just don't understand them, their way of life. You don't get it. And you know what? *You don't have to.* They are trying to *force you* to get it, but it's not your responsibility to approve of their beliefs or their lifestyle. You're not disapproving, either, but they're interpreting your lack of positive affirmation as hatred. They want you to hate them because that would mean you *care.* The reality for them is much worse. You don't actually care at all."

"I hadn't thought of it that way, but now that you're putting it into words, that's exactly right," Shad said as he refilled his glass with Kentucky's finest export.

"I know it is, bro, because *I feel the same way.* You have no idea how much this cult stuff comes up in my job. It's every single day, someone is talking about Baal this or that, putting a little Moloch on their desk, getting some kind of Asherian tattoo. I work with a bunch of artists, man. They're all into it. They just want attention. '*Look at me, I cut myself for Baal, I'm interesting!*'" Deckard mocked as Shad laughed. "Maybe they really do believe it, I don't know. I just know they can't stop talking about it. It's on their shirts, it's on their bumper stickers, it's on their freaking lunch boxes. I gotta hand it to the big businesses, they've really figured out how to capitalize on this thing, like what you saw at Bullseye with that guy."

"Yeah, it's unavoidable, it's everywhere. And you know what, I never really cared. I just ignored it, blew it off. It wasn't in my world, right? Didn't affect me. But now it's coming after my family, my *daughter*. Now I'm paying attention. Now I'm starting to care. Now I really am starting to hate them, but not for what they believe. I hate them for what they're doing, for how they're pushing it on me. I know the difference."

"They want to be the victims, the minority, the oppressed. It gets them the attention they want, which is what they really worship. I'm not religious, you know that." He raised the glass of whiskey and gestured toward his house. "This is my religion. I make money, I spend it, I enjoy my life. That's my religion. But those serious religious types who just live it and don't shove it in your face all the time? I respect those people. When you talk to them about it, you know it's real for them. You can just tell, and they're not pushing it on you, but just the gravity it has when they speak, that alone has a draw to it. But these stupid culties? It's like teenage girls talking about a trendy boy band, like the latest fad diet," he paused to take a drag off of his cigarette. "Like vegans, but on cocaine. The same mindset, but exponentially more intense." They both laughed at the comparison and sat back in their chairs, looking out at Deckard's well-manicured backyard.

"So what do I do now? How do I fix this with Alina?"

"Shad, look at me. My current love interest graduated from college four months ago. You're asking me how to fix your marriage?"

"It's better than what I've got now, which is nothing."

"All right, I'll do my best," Deckard said, standing up and walking to the edge of his porch. He turned his back to Shad, unzipped his pants, and began to urinate into his yard. He kept talking over his shoulder. "I think your best bet is to be honest with her, but without the anger. Alina is too soft, man; she can't handle your intensity. Not when it's directed at her that way," he bounced up and down on the balls of his feet a couple of times and then zipped up his pants. "It's obvious to anyone that you care about her and Isla. She knows that, she's just on the defensive, probably feels guilty. You can get through to her, you just have to put your guns down, you know what I mean?"

"I really messed it up, didn't I?"

"No, Shad, no, that's not what I'm trying to say. I don't think this is all on you. Alina has clearly been keeping some big secrets from you.

She's got a lot to answer for. But what *I am* saying is that fixing it is going to be all on you, I don't think Alina is going to bring you an olive branch. My guess is that she's feeling a mix of guilt for keeping things from you and hurt for how mad you got, that's a tough combination. And as far as the cult stuff at school, it sounds like she's definitely had a sip of the Kool-Aid, so she thinks she has the moral high ground here. She's convinced herself that she's the one who's tolerant, she's moved beyond your level of enlightenment. Which is what all of the culties do, right? That's why they call us all hateful and bigots, all that crap. They have to keep the moral high ground, because otherwise they lose the argument. By making you into the villain and themselves into the victim, you're engaged on their level. You feel like it's your responsibility to show that you're not the bad guy, so how do you do that? You have to care—or pretend to care—about them, their beliefs, the cult, the rituals, all of the insanity just to prove that you don't hate them. But that's the only weapon they have, because they can't beat the truth—and the truth is that you just don't care. No one really does."

"They found a way to make me care, they're bringing this stuff to my kid, to her school. They're pushing every boundary."

"I know. Nothing is off-limits. It's even in video games. Remember *Pinnacle Champions*? All of the new champions are culties now. All of them. They all have these cultie backstories, all these cutscenes about how they serve Baal, or how they came to know Asherah's freedom, or whatever the crap. I just want to play a battle royale game, I just want to shoot people in a computer game with my friends. I didn't sign up to get preached at about 'alts' and 'alternative religious freedom,'" Deckard said, making air quotes with his hands. "And it's not just gaming, either. Movies, TV, everyone's an alt now. They're even changing old movies to make characters into culties. And comedians are into it, too, so much so that they're not even funny. In a sane world, they'd be making hay out of this cult stuff. A sex cult? People who willingly cut themselves like the emo girls when we were in high school? Offering filet mignon to a statue? There's so much material there, but no one will touch it. Late night TV should be all over it, but those shows haven't been funny in a long time. Their monologues are basically sermons now. They're not comedians anymore, they're just alt-scolds."

"It's even in kid shows. You ever hear of Gluey? It's a show about a blue horse. Recently they had an episode where he visits a temple of

Moloch. It's like they don't even recognize the irony, a horse attending a temple where animals are frequently gutted," Shad said.

"You let Isla watch that?"

"Nah, she doesn't like that show. There's another one called Boca Pelon that she watches that had an episode about an Asherian wedding. I put a stop to that and blocked it from our account. Those weddings are basically orgies, completely insane that they'd put that into a kids show. Now that I think about it, Alina did get mad that I blocked that episode. I didn't think much of it at the time," Shad said.

"You couldn't have known it would end up like this, man. Don't overthink it."

"Yeah, I guess."

"You know it's in the military now, too? I saw someone share a post from the army on PostSpace showing a bunch of recruits running and carrying flags for each of the three cults to honor the Blood Moon Equinox. The hell does that have to do with being in the military? They don't do that for anything else, why are they doing it for the alts?"

"You're still on PostSpace? I deleted that a long time ago, it's a cesspool. Everyone's angry all the time. You gotta delete it, bro, it'll improve your life."

"I know, I know. I don't use it much anymore except for work; someone texted the post to me. Wasn't that billionaire Peelong Dusk going to buy it? Maybe he'll turn it around. Anyway, like we were saying, this stuff is in schools now, it's in the government, it's in business, universities. It's everywhere. You know it's all going down the tubes when the military cares more about making sure everyone knows they're cool with culties than they do about, you know, war stuff. People need a reality check, but everyone is afraid to speak out about it because they don't want to get canceled." They both sat quietly for a moment, mentally drained from their mutual rage session. "You hungry? The grill has been on this whole time."

"Starving. What's on the menu?"

"Come on man, where do you think you are? Rib eyes!" Deckard got up and walked inside. He quickly returned with a dish covered in foil, and Shad followed him to the grill. Deckard grilled the steaks to just barely medium-rare as they returned to recollecting good gaming memories, joking and laughing. They ate outside with paper plates and what appeared to Shad to be pearl-handled flatware. As expected, Deckard owned equally spectacular dishware, but he didn't want to have to do the dishes, so they used the disposable option. The steak sobered them a little bit, but they continued to drink as they ate. "So what's the deal with the Blood Moon Equinox, anyway?"

"No idea," Shad responded in between chews of the delicious beef. "Some kind of important holiday for the culties, all three of them. I don't really understand it, but obviously it has something to do with the moon's cycle, astronomy, stuff like that? I just know it's significant for all of the cults."

"You mean astrology?"

"Yeah, that, whatever."

Deckard laughed. "Idiot. All right, so what about the festival down-town? Just a party or what?" he said as he cut another large bite.

"They're doing special rituals, I think. It's a big deal in Mapleton Square Park. They've cordoned off the whole area. You can't drive any-where near it, lots of streets blocked off. Parking is a mess. I'm sure the rideshare drivers are making a killing. Supposed to be a huge production."

"Want to see what it's all about?" Deckard asked.

"What do you mean?"

"Let's go down there, man. Let's see for ourselves what all of the fuss is about. Maybe we'll convert?"

"Screw off, Deckard, we can't just go down there."

"Why not? Is it closed?"

"No, I think it goes on twenty-four hours, every day this weekend. But we just, we can't go down there. We're not culties, we're not into that crap."

"So what? Is it only for the faithful? What about the cult-curious?" Deckard said, his impish grin only growing.

"Are you serious? We can't do that."

"I'm completely serious. Yes, we can, and we will," Deckard said, pulling out his phone.

"What are you doing?"

"Getting us a rideshare. Finish your steak, Lexi is only seven min-utes away."

"Lexi? You call a rideshare and our driver is a chick?"

"What can I say, I'm magnetic."

"Oh man, this is a bad idea."

"This is a *great* idea. I'm going to go get ready," Deckard grabbed his plate, tossed it in the trash, and jogged indoors. Shad finished his steak and took another shot of whiskey. Anxious energy was quickly obliterating his buzz. Deckard came outside and stood facing Shad, his hands extended out as he presented himself with sarcastic pride.

"Dude, is that a fanny pack?"

"Shad. Come on, it's tactical. Look at it, it's got carabiners!"

"All right, why not? If anyone can pull it off, it's you."

"Ready? Lexi is almost here," Deckard said as he turned, walking inside. He stopped and turned to Shad with a serious look on his face. "And I'm calling it right now, so there's no confusion—I'm riding shotgun."

Chapter 6

A BRIGHT RED, FOUR-DOOR Mini Cooper pulled up to the curb next to a park entrance in the core of downtown Mapleton. Shad got out of the back passenger-side door, which faced the sidewalk. True to his word, Deckard got out of the front passenger door. Some modern rap spilled out with them, featuring a female rapper who apparently enjoyed discussing her own body parts in graphic detail to the tune of a standard 4/4 beat and some synthesizer noises.

"Thanks for a great ride, Lexi!" Deckard said, leaning his head back into the car.

"My pleasure, Deckard. You know how to find me when you need me," said the buxom brunette with a wink.

"I do, and I will. Drive safe!" Deckard said as he closed the door.

"Did our driver really just give you her phone number? What is your life?" Shad asked.

"I'm a decent-looking bachelor with money, approaching middle age. Laboratory scientists couldn't invent a better magnet for chicks with daddy issues."

"Good point. Gonna call her?"

"Eventually, of course. Gotta let it marinate for a bit. I'll probably text her a little, ghost her for a week or two, and then call her after that. She'd leave her mother's funeral to get to me at that point."

"What about Tracy?"

"Who?"

"Shameful. But I'd be lying if I said I wasn't impressed. Speaking of shameful, what the hell was that garbage that we were listening to?" asked Shad.

"That was Jizzo, this really fat chick. Very popular right now, for some reason."

"I'm getting old, man. New trendy music just sounds bad to me, I don't get the appeal at all."

"Nah, man, you're not that old. Jizzo is actually terrible. There's other new music you'd probably like. But she's legitimately not good, so don't get down on yourself about it." Deckard started to walk down the sidewalk. "Get your game face on. Time to pretend we're culties!" he said, making a serious face at Shad. They both broke out laughing, still drunk enough to offend a Breathalyzer.

"All right, for real, where do we go from here? Ah, over there. See the fire? That's got to be an entrance." They could see large groups of people in the distance lit by flickering firelight. The two inebriated friends made their way in that direction. As they walked, the reality of the setting and the situation began to have a sobering effect on them both. Grins and snickers were gradually replaced with truly serious expressions by the time they approached the entrance they had spotted. Two large copper braziers stood on either side of the entrance gate, flames dancing from their basins and filling the area with shimmering light. The gate was manned by priests and priestesses of the three cults, each one running their own respective turnstile. The faithful would go to the priest or priestess that corresponded with their alternative religion of choice and receive a bracelet that they'd wear in the park. While admission was free, it seemed like these bracelets were required as a part of the entry process. Two uniformed police officers stood near the gate, chatting and keeping an eye on people as they entered the festival area.

"You want the orgies, the bleeders, or the stabbers?" Deckard whispered.

"Let's go with Moloch, that's the one I need to learn about." They both queued up behind other festivalgoers who were patiently waiting to receive their bracelets from the hooded Molochian at the gate. Shad was in front of Deckard and reached the entry first.

"Hail the Blood Moon, worshipper. Are you bonded, or are you liberated?" the feminine voice said, indicating to Shad that he was facing a priestess of Moloch.

"Uh, what?"

"Bonded-one, give me your right arm, please," she said, extending her hand. He complied, and she placed a white bracelet over his hand, removed the paper covering the adhesive, and stuck the two ends together so that the circle it formed around his wrist was now complete. As she did that, he saw that she wore a black bracelet.

"Why do you have a black bracelet? Is that for priests and priestesses?" he asked.

"It is because you ask that you must wear white, bonded-one." She gestured for him to move forward. He nodded, more in acknowledgement than understanding, and walked forward so Deckard could get his bracelet. Having eavesdropped on Shad's interactions with the priestess, Deckard said that he was liberated and received a black bracelet. He bowed to the priestess solemnly and walked over to where Shad was waiting for him. Looking around at the other entrances, Shad noticed that while all three cults gave out white bracelets, they each had a unique color for those which Shad assumed were "liberated." The Baalists used their signature red and the Asherians a multicolored swirl.

"Got the cool black one! No idea what 'liberated' means to them, but I'd say I'm kind of a libertine, so that's gotta be close enough, right? What'd she call you? Bondage one?"

"*Bonded* one. Bond-ed."

"Are you sure? That's not what I heard."

"Screw off," Shad said, flipping his friend the middle finger.

"What does 'bonded-one' mean?"

"No idea, but obviously there's a significant difference between being a bonded-one and being liberated. Doesn't get much clearer than black and white."

"Yeah, true. So she had the black bracelet, right? I guess the ones who are liberated are the insiders and the white bracelets are for the noobs."

"Sounds plausible to me, let's go with that. Where to now?"

Deckard looked around. The crowd wasn't dense, but there were enough people that they could blend in with the other worshippers. "Beware, the direction of the herd," he said, following the movement of the throng and nodding in the direction that people were walking. Shad and Deckard folded themselves into the flow of people moving toward the park's central field. The trail was lined with more copper braziers, bright with energetic flames that echoed the excitement of those whose paths they lit. Observing the others as they walked, Shad spoke to Deckard under his breath.

"Looks like a bunch of college kids. Some odd ones too," he said, gesturing toward a single, middle-aged woman who appeared to be walking alone.

"Yeah, this is a weird mix. Definitely a lot of young people, but not everyone. Plenty of people who don't really fit a mold. They all have one thing in common, though." Shad looked at him inquiringly in response. "Their eyes. They all have the same look. It's . . . desperate."

Shad casually glanced around, his inebriation inhibiting his ability to appear inconspicuous. He quickly saw what Deckard meant—each person around them, regardless of age, race, or class, had the same look in their eyes. The eager, trusting anticipation of partisans heading to the breadline for their portion. Some were clearly more confident than others; the true believers moved with an assurance that set them apart. The seekers moved forward with an inherent hesitance, unsure of themselves but just as yearning as the rest of the group. Shad imagined Alina in this multitude. Would she be moving boldly forward, or shuffling along reluctantly? Ahead of them, another pair of police officers were walking more slowly and aimlessly than the festivalgoers. They ambled along casually, eyeing people as they walked along toward the gathering ahead. Deckard elbowed Shad and nodded in their direction. "You see that? Even the cops here are culties," he said. Both officers had black bracelets on their right wrists, indicating that they were liberated worshippers of Moloch.

The path curved around and opened up to the main festival grounds, set up in a gigantic circle. Huge bonfires greeted them and kept everything brightly lit, built in various places throughout the area, seemingly without design. Worshippers danced and performed other "religious acts" around the fires as drums were beat by mesmerized celebrants. One huge pyre burned magnificently in the center of the round park, with three distinct sections of the circle set apart for each alternative religion. The closest as they entered was the golden idol for Baal. Next in the counterclockwise direction was the deep black of Moloch, almost invisible against the night sky, if not for the brilliant firelight. And on the other side of the fire from where the path had introduced them was the beautiful idol to Asherah. Deckard and Shad continued with the crowd for a dozen or so yards as people began to target their respective idols of choice, but then they peeled off to the edges where they could observe without being observed. They spotted a table along the perimeter where offerings for followers of Moloch were being provided in exchange for donations. They slowly made their way closer to investigate.

The offering table was staffed with priests or priestesses of Moloch; their dark robes and hoods were very effective at obscuring the person inside, so one could never be sure who was staring back from behind that black cloth. Many offerings were featured, presumably for varying levels of religious dedication. The introductory offerings included stacks of plastic-wrapped cuts of meat of various sizes and quality. For the truly dedicated offeror, there were small cages available. Skittering and chittering inside were an assortment of small rodents and even some small birds. The language was explicit that donations were not required, but it was also obvious from everyone's behavior that they were strongly encouraged. A skinny older man who looked in his fifties or sixties feebly shuffled up to the table to acquire an offering for himself. He chose a modest cut of meat, nodded in reverence, and turned to leave.

One of the priests or priestesses reached out and grabbed his arm. "Donations are welcomed, bonded-one," the priest said. Shad was close enough to hear the statement and its clear implication. He rolled his eyes.

"I, I'm so sorry, I don't have any money. My treatments, they've taken it all. That's why I'm here, this is my last hope. This is all I have left," the man said. Shad, still eavesdropping, grimaced.

"You still have a watch, do you not?" The priest motioned to the man's wrist which bore a bulky gold watch, evidently old and valuable.

The old man hesitated. "Yes, yes, I do, this was my father's, I, I don't know . . ." he trailed off, looking at his watch.

"True liberation requires sincere sacrifice, bonded-one. Do you desire to be liberated from the bonds of the light of the world?" Shad gritted his teeth and turned to walk toward the table. Deckard, also eavesdropping, grabbed his arm to stop him.

"Not our problem, brother. Not why we're here," he said under his breath, shaking his head. Shad took in a deep, frustrated breath and stood back in his place.

"Yes, yes, of course I do. I truly want to be free from this disease," The old man's frail hands struggled with the watch clasp. After some excruciatingly long moments, he managed to release it and hand it to the priest.

"The liberator rewards those who genuinely sacrifice, bonded-one. Your affliction is a serious one?"

The old man looked dejectedly down at the table. "Yes, they . . . they tell me it's terminal."

"And you desire true freedom?"

"Yes, yes, I do! I want Moloch to free me!"

The priest nodded. "Tonight, you will be free and bask in Moloch's deepest darkness," the priest said, stepping around the table. He walked to the old man and grabbed his arm gently. "Come with me, bonded-one. I will guide you." The pair began to walk away from the table, the old man's face bright with astonished joy at the special treatment he was receiving.

"Well, that ended differently than I expected," Deckard whispered. Shad grunted in response, turning back to the crowd. He watched a few more people receiving offerings in exchange for "donations," all of them receiving an approving nod from the Molochian clergy in addition to sacrifices. A young woman with a black bracelet bowed and handed over some money in exchange for a cage containing a rodent, Shad couldn't tell if it was a rat or a mouse. He watched her walk with the cage in hand from the table to the altar. She was too far for him to discern exactly what was happening, but he knew by the speed and confidence of her body movements that she was not a "bonded-one;" she'd clearly done this before. She bent down, assumedly to remove the animal from the cage. She then turned and reached for one of the ceremonial knives. Lifting her right arm above her head with her left still down on the table, likely holding the animal in place, with one fast movement she brought the knife down. She lifted both of her hands up to the idol, and Shad knew she had completed her offering to the bull god.

One tall, handsome man in a dark suit approached the table and handed over a wad of cash, bowing to the Molochian in front of him. Even through the shadowy robe, Shad could tell the priest was shocked at the size of the donation. "I'd like to procure one of the *special* offerings for the liberator."

"Of course, fellow liberated-one, we have the animals over here. I think we may have a racoon—"

"I don't want a rodent, you pathetic moron. I want the *Obsidian* Offerings," the man interrupted.

"Isn't that the banking guy? The one who does investments?" Shad whispered to Deckard.

"Who? Wait . . ." Deckard said, squinting and focusing on the man at the table. "Wow, yeah it is. Jerry Dink, I recognize him from the TV spots he does talking about the market and what not. I always thought he was a slimy creep, but this is next-level rich guy evil stuff."

"Aren't you a rich guy?"

"Bro, I'm below the poverty line compared to Jerry Dink." Another member of the Molochian clergy rushed forward, pushing the bewildered priest out of the way. This priest stood out, not only because the others were deferent to him, but because he wore a striking gold crown over his black hood, signifying some kind of authority.

"My most sincere apologies, Master Dink," the priest said in a heavily accented voice. "Please, if you'll come with me, I will escort you to the Obsidian Offerings myself."

"Lord Malochus, you didn't have to come personally," Jerry Dink responded, his attitude cowed by Malochus's presence. "If you'll just point me in the right direction, I'm sure I can find my own way. I hate to inconvenience you."

"Nonsense, Master Dink. The liberator is grateful for your continued generosity and support. It pleases me to escort you. Now, if you will?" Malochus extended his arm away from the table.

"Of course, thank you. I'm honored." The pair walked away from the table, but not toward the imposing black idol only about fifty yards behind them. They instead walked toward the same path that Deckard and Shad had used earlier.

"That's weird. Where the hell are they going?" Shad whispered to Deckard.

"Good question. The idol is right in front of us, but they just went out the way we came. Did you see where that sick guy went?"

"No, I didn't follow after they left the table."

"The priest took him in that same direction," Deckard said.

"My cultie-sense is tingling."

"Something is definitely up. Some kind of VIP area maybe? Let's check out the other cults and see if we can find out more," said Deckard as he led them away from their perch and moved toward the crowd of gyrating Asherians. One of their priestesses made her way toward Deckard, hoping to "worship" with him. They had an uncomfortable exchange after her very aggressive advance where Deckard declined her gropey proposition by using Shad as an excuse. Shad tried to play along with a fumbled story about Moloch and a rat sacrifice, but thankfully she interpreted his awkwardness as nervousness due to her sexual magnetism.

"I am a *terrible* actor," Shad said as they walked away.

"Yeah, that was pretty bad. At least she thought it was because of her, and not because we're total fakes."

"True. You being good with the ladies almost got us into trouble. You catch what she said about the goat lord? What was that all about?"

"I heard that, but I have no idea what it means. Moloch has the head of a bull. Baal is a man. He's got a weird, elongated head and he's made of gold, but still not a goat. And Asherah is, of course, a sexy lady, so also not a goat."

"Let's go to the Baalist area and see what we can find out over there. I don't think there's much else to find out from the Asherians," Shad said, starting to move in the direction of the Baalist worship area. They both continued to half-dance their way through the crowd, Deckard doing his best not to make eye contact with any prostitutes who seemed unable to resist trying to seduce him. The Baalist area was much more subdued than the orgiastic bedlam of the Asherians. It was quieter, save for the sound of drums from the other two cults. Worshippers stood or knelt at the base of the golden statue of their god, wielding blades and making their offerings. There were various places to sit or lie down placed all over the lawn area where worshippers were bandaging themselves or being bandaged. Some were receiving juice from the crimson-dressed, bald-headed Baalist clergy, having overdone it a little with their offerings. One was even receiving an IV therapy.

Shad spotted another lounge-like area that appeared to also be a sort of café for Baalists. "Let's check that out, looks like they're selling food."

"I am kind of hungry. Is it bad to eat cult food?"

"Well, it's not like we're eating food that was offered to the idols right? I think it's all right. I'm pretty famished, and it would help us blend in," Shad said, making his way in the direction of the café. They were seated by a young Baalist priestess clad in traditional red robes. Her head was shaved clean and any visible skin was ivory white with makeup. Cheekbones and her other endowments gave away that she was a priestess. She led them to a low couch with a coffee table that sat facing the idol and the worship area, providing them with an excellent perspective of the crowd.

"Thank you very much," Shad said as she laid down a menu and walked away. He turned to Deckard. "You have cash? I don't want my credit card ringing up here."

"Yeah, my tacti-pack is loaded," he said as he perused the menu. The options might have seemed out of place in another context, but made sense for Baalists: lots of red meat, beans, and fruits; the kinds of things you would want to eat if you had recently lost a lot of blood. Deckard flagged down a Baalist acolyte that was acting as a waiter and ordered some meatballs, black beans, and two large glasses of orange juice. Then the two friends sat back and tried to act natural as they continued to observe the cult activities surrounding them.

Everything Shad saw reminded him of his experience with the Baalist temple when he was in college. Lots of the same thing on repeat—people cutting themselves, wincing as discreetly as possible, bleeding into a trough or dish, and bandaging their wounds. As they sat in the comfortable lounge chairs, he watched that happen at least two dozen times with people of all kinds. While the majority were younger people, every race, age, and class were represented. The only group not present were children, likely due to the late hour.

A priestess arrived with their order, setting it down with a respectful bow. They both bowed in return from their seats, and reluctantly began to eat. "Gotta be honest, man. I feel weird about eating cultie food," Shad said to Deckard. "Even if it is absolutely hitting the spot right now."

"Yeah, I know what you mean. I feel dirty, like I'm committing adultery. But I have to admit it's delicious." Deckard wiped his mouth with a paper napkin with an outline of Baal on it. "Just when I start to cope with it, they piss me off again. Come on, look at this crap," he said, holding up the half-soiled napkin to Shad. "They can't even leave their religion off the napkins."

"It's their whole identity, man. Vegans on cocaine, right?" Shad said.

Deckard laughed. "You been watching the crowd? See anything that stands out?"

"Lots of cutting and bleeding, not much else. Let's finish up and head back to the Molochian area." Shad picked up the last meatball and washed it down with the rest of his orange juice. Standing up, he looked down at his watch. "Just about one in the morning and look at how many people are still here. Hasn't slowed down at all." They exited the café, thanking the Baalist clergy as they left, and stood outside, observing the area but looking like they were stretching and chatting after their meal. Still, the flow of Baalist offerings was as consistent as it had been during their break in the café.

Shad had just turned to Deckard to say they should move on when a young man caught his eye. He was in his late teens, still young but nearing adulthood. He had light brown hair that was unwashed and disheveled, stood about average height, and was skinny. Dressed in an oversized T-shirt and jeans that looked as though they'd never seen the inside of a washing machine, he had the air of an outcast. But it wasn't his appearance that made him notable; what made him stand out to Shad was the manner in which he moved. He walked briskly with a determined, deliberate stride. He was laser-focused on the idol to Baal, even blindly bumping into a few other devotees, one of which screamed loudly as the collision caused them to slip with their sacrificial knife and offer a little more than they had intended. As the young man walked, Shad noticed he was carrying a small axe in his hand when the light of the fires glinted off of the sharpened blade. Shad nudged Deckard. "You seeing this kid?"

"Huh?" Deckard asked, looking around. Shad gestured with his chin.

"The skinny one with the hatchet. He's heading to the idol."

"Got him. Wow, he's moving with a purpose. Why's he got an axe?" As they watched, the young man reached his destination. He held the axe in his right hand and raised his left up to the golden visage of Baal, saying something as he looked up. It was too far for Deckard and Shad to hear, but whatever he said got the attention of those around him, who immediately turned to him and watched. A few backed away, seemingly shocked. He then placed his left arm on the trough and raised his right arm with the axe high up in the air.

"No way . . ." Shad said as they both watched, transfixed by the gruesome scene taking place right before their eyes. They knew what they were about to see, they knew it wasn't something they'd normally prefer to observe, but they couldn't look away, like pedestrians witnessing a car accident on the street in front of them. Just as he began to bring the axe down, an attentive Baalist priest caught his arm mid-swing before he could complete his offering. The priest began to pull the young man away from the idol as another priest or priestess—they couldn't tell at this distance—arrived to assist. The young man resisted and struggled at first, but after the priests talked with him closely, he seemed to calm down, lowering the axe and ceasing his resistance. He nodded to the priests, and the second one to arrive placed his hand on the young man's shoulder and escorted him away.

"Look what direction they're walking," Deckard said. The priest and the axe-wielding youth were walking toward the same path that the Molochians had taken earlier that night.

Shad followed them with his gaze. "I guess we know where we're exploring next."

Chapter 7

THEY WALKED THROUGH THE crowd, passing the Molochian merchants who were still peddling offerings to eager festivalgoers. Deckard walked first, trying to appear as though he was guiding Shad, in case they needed to deploy their ruse about Shad seeking liberation. The Baalist priest and the axe-happy teen walked out of the large central festival grounds on the same path that Deckard and Shad had used to enter the area a couple hours earlier. Their shoes crunched onto the gravel as they continued down the path behind the two Baalists, weaving through groups of people as quickly as they could without running. "They're in a hurry, aren't they?" Deckard said.

"Getting winded?"

"Haven't smoked cigarettes in a while, douchebag. It's not really conducive with trying to power walk like a suburban mom." They followed the pair down the path, past the brightly burning braziers and against the flow of worshippers who were heading to the festival grounds. As they neared the park entrance where the path began, the priest led the young man off to the left, into another area of the park that was hidden under the blanket of darkness. Deckard and Shad followed close behind, trying their best to remain incognito. After walking a few minutes through dilapidated portions of the park that looked like they hadn't seen traffic in decades, the priest and the young man reached an old, single-story red brick building. Relieved that their pursuit seemed to be over, Deckard and Shad crouched behind a broken concrete bench for cover to continue to watch.

A basic, rectangular structure, it looked like some kind of storage or utility building for the park employees. The building sat off the path about twenty-five yards to the right, mostly blanketed in darkness except for one old light on the wall at the entrance. The yellow light illuminated a small alcove about three feet deep that housed weathered metal double doors. There was a sign over the alcove, but they were too far away to read it. The priest got to the doors first, reaching into his robes for something. Stopping for a moment, he raised his hand to the boy and turned away from him and toward where Shad and Deckard were hiding. Their hearts stopped. They held their breath and their bodies completely motionless, terrified. *What are we going to do? Turn around and run? Try to fake an excuse for being here?* Shad's mind was racing while the rest of him was as still as the concrete bench providing their minimal concealment. With the same suddenness that he had turned, the priest sneezed loudly and theatrically, a dozen sneezes in quick staccato succession.

"The hell? This guy a competitive sneezer?" Deckard whispered to Shad, still not moving. Shad had to cover his mouth to stifle a laugh. The priest shook his head after the sneeze attack, and turned back to face the doors of the building. He seemed to struggle with something on the door for a moment, and then reached back into his robes before opening the door and ushering the young man inside, the door closing behind them.

"Man, I almost lost it and blew our cover because of that absurd machine-gun sneeze that guy ripped out," Shad said.

"Some kind of mutant. What was that—like, twelve sneezes? Gotta be a cult thing, side effect of the moon's blood or whatever." The two friends knelt behind the bench, peeking their heads over the back rest at the old building.

Shad looked around. Seeing no one near them, he stood up. "Let's go," he said, resuming his crouch run. Instead of taking the lit path, he moved to the right of it, hoping to maintain a modicum of stealth in the black of night.

"Would be a lot more fun if I hadn't chain-smoked half of that pack of cigs you brought," Deckard said, struggling harder than Shad.

"Sucks getting old, huh?"

"You can't see it, but I'm flipping you off." The two reached the old building without incident, stopping in the darkness about a dozen yards away. They remained in the shadows of the tree line, observing the area. The building was big, but not imposing. A single-story, flat-roofed building that looked to be at least a century old, it was about fifty feet long and a hundred feet wide. The sign above the simple rectangular structure read "Cold Storage 4."

"Cold storage? What is this?" Shad asked Deckard, who was catching his breath as quietly as he could manage.

"This whole park used to be a massive stockyard, dude. You didn't know that?"

"Yeah, I think I had heard that, but why would a stockyard have cold storage?"

"Why do you think people would buy animals? To eat them. They'd auction off the livestock here, but not all of it was for ranchers to take to their land. A lot of the animals were slaughtered here so the buyers didn't have to bother with that part. This was one of the places where they stored the slabs of meat after the bloody part was done. I don't hear anything coming from inside. Want to see if we can get in and check it out?"

"We didn't come all this way to leave empty-handed." Shad began to move to the right, staying within the tree line to maintain the cover of darkness.

"No need to sprint this time, right?" Deckard asked. The tree line was uneven, with old oak trees getting as close as a few feet from the building, and then moving back as far as ten yards from the old redbrick walls. Luckily for them, there were no yellowing lights shining around that area, so they were able to move along next to the wall and remain concealed. The wall itself was broken up by large, equally ancient single-pane windows with glass so hazy from years of weathering and neglect that it might as well be painted over. They attempted to peek into the interior at each window they passed, but between the opaque glass and the darkness inside they were unable to discern anything. When they reached the final window before the wall became a corner, they both looked inside and stopped. It was faint, but both could distinguish a single light inside the building.

"Some kind of utility light? The kind of thing that's just always on?" Shad asked.

"Yeah, maybe. I think the park staff use these old buildings for storing their maintenance equipment now. Let's keep going, none of these windows look like they open."

"I didn't even think to check for that."

"Goody Two-shoes."

"Done a lot of breaking and entering?"

"No comment," Deckard said.

"That's a story I need to hear."

"Let's figure out this weird cult stuff first and then we can tell more stories. Tonight's little adventure will be a story I tell, that's for sure."

"Yeah. I don't know what they're all up to, but something strange is going on. I mean, more than the usual strange cult stuff. You sure you're up for pushing forward here? I don't know how risky this is. I've got a lot invested in this, but it isn't your problem," Shad said as he gazed through the cloudy window at the faint light inside. Deckard turned to face him.

"It's everybody's problem now, whether people realize it or not. These culties or alts or whatever you want to call them, they're only going to keep pushing until everyone bends the knee. I don't want to live like that. And yeah, you have a lot more to lose than I do. That's exactly why I'm here to back you up. Bros before hoes, or whatever. Not that Alina is, you know . . . she's a lovely lady—"

"I get it, you're good. Thanks, dude," Shad said. Deckard held his fist out for a bump. Shad nodded and reciprocated. "Let's find a way in and see where everyone went," Shad said. They continued around the corner to the back of the building. They found more ancient dark windows and some roller doors that were almost as tall as the building itself, but no points of entry. Following the wall, they went around another corner so that they were now on the opposite side from where they'd started and found a rusty ladder that went up to the roof of the building.

"Maybe there's a way in from above," Deckard said, pointing up to the sky with his thumb. "Want to check it out?"

"Wouldn't it be easier to just use the same door they did? We might be able to pick the lock or something."

"Picking locks isn't as easy as they make it look in the movies. Without the proper tools, it's a pain and takes forever. And did you see how much the priest struggled? He had to fight with it and he had the actual key. Not to mention that whole area is pretty brightly lit. If someone else comes along and catches us it'll be tough to talk our way out of that"

"Crap. Fine, you're right," Shad said, looking up at the ladder. "I hate heights."

"Meowwwwwwww."

"Yeah, yeah, yeah. I'll go first." Shad put his shoe on the bottom rung of the ladder and tested it with his weight. It didn't move or even make a noise. "This thing feels as solid as the wall. Good craftsmanship. They don't build things like this anymore . . . I guess I should head up."

"Quit stalling, chicken."

Shad glanced at his friend angrily and began climbing up. The ladder held strong the whole way, providing Shad with easy access to the top of the building. At the end of the ladder, he hoisted himself over the lip of the wall and on to the flat roof. It was pitch dark on the roof except for the yellow glow of the old lamps near the entrance of the building, on the opposite side from where they were. Deckard scaled the ladder more effortlessly than Shad, unburdened by a lifelong fear of heights.

"So what are we looking for? What's a roof entrance look like?"

"We'll know it when we see it, I guess. This could be a bust, dude. We might have to resort to the old-fashioned guest key—a brick through the window," said Deckard, stretching out his back and looking around. Shad did the same, and started making his way around the dark rooftop. His eyes began to adjust to the obscurity of the night, and he spotted a triangular skylight near the center of the roof. He made his way over to it. As he approached, it became clear it was made of the same cloudy glass as the windows downstairs. Luckily, much of the grime seemed to be on the outside. Shad cleaned a few panes with his bare hand, wiping it off on his pants.

"Wiping your hands on your pants? What are you, a kindergartener?" Deckard said.

"Sorry bro, I left my Windex and paper towels at home."

"Real men carry a handkerchief," Deckard replied, producing a white cotton hankie from his back pocket. He took it and wiped off a few more panes and replaced it in his pants pocket. "You can see the light we spotted earlier," he said, pointing down. "Looks like it's outside of some more doors. I can't see any signs or anything, so who knows where they lead."

"Look at the floor. Is that foot prints?"

"Seems like it. Must be super dusty in there. If it's so old and unused that the floor is caked with a layer of dust, why are all of the culties bringing people here? What could be in there that they'd want?"

"Let's find a way in." As Shad walked in the direction of the front of the building, he tripped over something solid on the surface of the roof. He fell hard, barely breaking his fall with his arms. Deckard, like a true friend, reacted with stifled laughter.

"Even through the darkness I saw that happen," he said through muffled laughs. "Walking is tough dude, but you'll get it eventually. I believe in you."

"Screw you, I tripped on something," Shad said, sitting up and brushing himself off. "I hope no one was in the building below, there's no way they wouldn't hear me land. That hurt."

"Break your hip?"

"You're older than me, idiot."

"What did you trip on?" Deckard asked, walking up to his friend and extending a hand.

"Not sure, something over there. Felt like a curb," Shad replied, grateful to have Deckard's aid to stand up. He brushed himself off and began squinting at the ground, attempting to spot the obstruction that took him down. "Ah, right there. I think that's it," he said, walking a few feet from where he landed. "Get out your phone flashlight."

Just as Deckard was pulling out his phone, he froze in place.

"You hear that?" he whispered, alerted.

Shad pointed to the place in the ledge where the yellowed lamp light couldn't reach and hurried over to it. Squatting down below the ledge, he waited for Deckard, who tracked just behind. Peeking over the edge, they saw a small group coming down the path. As they neared the building, he counted a total of four approaching. Three were dressed as cult clergy; two Asherians and one Molochian. The fourth was small in stature, dressed shabbily, and walking oddly. The person appeared to be shuffling, or stumbling along, being led by the Asherians.

"What's this? Two Asherians and one bull god guy, right?"

"Yeah, and one other person. Doesn't it look like they're walking, like, wrong? Something about the way that other one is moving just seems off. I can't tell what it is."

"Looks like a drunk walk. Maybe one of the worshippers showed up to the festival wasted? These culties are taking them to sober up?"

Shad started to respond, but as the yellow light of the lamp hit the group and he could see more clearly, he stopped. The fourth person was a young woman, maybe college-aged. As she got closer, he recognized the logo of the local community college on her tattered hoodie. She looked disheveled and dirty. Shad tightened his grip on the wall.

"That doesn't look right," Deckard said.

"I don't know what we're looking at here, but this isn't normal." They both watched as she stumbled, her left arm supported by an Asherian priest and her right supported by a priestess. The Molochian followed a few paces behind them. Shad and Deckard could see them all clearly when they reached the door to the building. The coed was swaying woozily and had to be steadied frequently by the Asherians as the Molochian approached and opened the door. They went inside, the old door closing loudly behind them. Without even consulting each other, both Shad and Deckard quickly and quietly shuffled back to the skylight and resumed their observation from directly above. The group below reached the solitary light in the building and the door it illuminated. The Molochian opened this door as well, but it wasn't locked. After the Asherians led the student inside, the Molochian looked behind them and scanned the room, perhaps feeling he was being watched. Shad and Deckard both pulled back from the window as quickly and soundlessly as they could. They heard the door below them close, and they both looked back through the skylight to find the room empty again.

"She looked young, like a college kid. She was filthy, definitely drugged. She had a Mapleton Community College sweater on," Deckard said.

"Follow me," Shad said. He crawled back toward the object that had tripped him earlier. Deckard pulled out his phone and turned it on with a low setting, providing just enough light to reveal that the object that had taken Shad down was a trapdoor. Shad moved his hands around it and found the clasp that secured it to its frame. It was held in place by an old, rusted padlock. "Find a brick." Deckard shined his light around until he landed on a piece of heavy pipe, covered in rust and grime.

"Hope you've had a tetanus shot," he said, holding the pipe up so Shad could see it.

"That'll work." He walked over to the roof access door, raised the pipe, and slammed it down on the oxidized lock. It gave way, breaking into multiple pieces across the roof. They struggled to get a good grip through the decades of filth that had accumulated around the edges of the port, but eventually they were able to break it free. It opened with a loud protest from the hinges, which were just as rusty as the lock had been. They both stopped moving the door and looked at each other, waiting and listening to see if anyone had heard the trapdoor's scream. After a few silent beats, they continued lifting the cover slowly. It still produced an awful squeak, but it was much quieter when they opened it gradually. After what felt like an hour, the door was completely open.

"So, what's the plan?" Deckard asked.

"We go down there, find them, surprise them, grab her, and run. There weren't that many with her. With the Baalists and the Molochians, there's maybe one or two dozen here, right?"

"Yeah, probably. Can't imagine it'd be more than that."

"Probably too many for us to overpower them head on, but if we keep the element of surprise, maybe we can get her out and get to the cops."

"All right, that works for me. We have to try something." Deckard nodded.

They both looked down into complete darkness below them. Deckard pulled out his phone again and shined the tiny LED downward, revealing the top of a metal ladder. About halfway down, Shad pulled his own phone out and activated the flashlight function. Through the dim light he could see the floor and some dusty shelves lining the walls of a small room, stacked with hardware and machine parts that hadn't been disturbed since the last millennium. He continued scaling the ladder downward and Deckard followed soon after, a few rungs above.

"Could really use some night vision goggles right now," Shad said as he reached the bottom. After stepping off of the ladder, he looked around the dusty room and spotted a door on the opposite wall, about twenty feet away.

"Some kind of storage closet?" Deckard said as he completed his descent.

"Looks like it. Bunch of tools that haven't been touched since before we were born. The door is over there," said Shad, pointing across the room. Deckard nodded and inspected the shelves before quietly making his way to the door. Leaning toward it, he stood quietly and listened for any signs of life on the other side. "Anything?"

"Nope. Want to do the honors?" Deckard asked, gesturing to the door.

Gingerly, Shad twisted the handle to see if it would budge. At first it didn't move and Shad feared it was locked, but with a little more pressure it slowly opened and the door moved inward with a scraping sound. It wasn't very loud, but it wasn't completely silent either. He gritted his teeth with every noise it made, opening it just enough for him and Deckard to get through. Looking around, Shad saw that they were near the locked front door that the cultists had used to enter the building. It was secured by an antique push-bar lock that was halfway covered in rust.

"The light we saw is over there," Deckard motioned across the building toward the solitary light mounted next to another set of double doors. He pointed at the shoe prints in the ground. "If anyone looks, they'll be able to see someone came from the storage closet. We can brush it off but it'll still be obvious," he said.

"Worth a try, maybe we can just obscure the whole area?" Shad said, dragging his foot back and forth around the area to disguise their dusty prints coming from the closet in addition to all of the others in the area. He kept sweeping up to the entry door, and then back to where the path of footprints moved toward the solitary light illuminating the doors deeper in the building. "At least that doesn't make it as clear, right?"

"Good enough for government work."

"So, bad?"

"It's not great, but I think you're right. It'll make it hard to tell that someone came from the closet. Should cover us."

"Hopefully that's all we need." Shad said.

They both walked carefully toward the light, doing their best to step within the existing foot prints on the way to the door. They both reached it at about the same time. Shad looked up at the skylight above, where they had both looked down on the group with the college girl about a half hour before. Remembering how powerless and dazed she looked, he shuddered and shook his head, his determination steeled. Deckard reached for the door handle and looked back at Shad. "Are you ready?"

"I haven't been ready for any of this, but we can't go back now."

Deckard looked down solemnly for a beat. He knew who had entered that door before them and he dreaded what they would discover when they finally found where they had gone. Taking a deep breath, he nodded, and opened the mysterious door.

Chapter 8

SUNDAY, 1:59 A.M.

THEY BOTH HELD THEIR breath as Deckard opened the door, expecting a banshee-like screech from the old hardware. Unlike seemingly every other hinge in the building, these were in good enough shape to open up silently. Exhaling in relief, Shad entered as Deckard held the door. He followed, and secured the door quietly behind them. He tried it just in case, making sure it hadn't locked behind them. In front of them was a short landing and a stairwell downward into darkness beyond. A dusty, worn copper sign on the wall read "The Under Yards Employees Only," with an arrow pointing toward the stairs.

"The Under Yards?" asked Shad.

"No way! Let me see that," Deckard said, inspecting the sign. "Dude, I thought this was an urban legend!"

"What is it?"

"I heard that the stockyards had an underground facility where animals could be shown, auctioned, butchered, everything they normally do, even in the harshest seasons. It was built in an old quarry that was out of commission. Instead of leaving a big hole in the ground there to fill up with water, the city decided to use it to make a facility they could use all year. It was pretty cutting edge at the time. In the winter it was warm and in the summer it was cool. This was back in the day before air conditioning was everywhere, you know? Animals would get shipped to Mapleton from all over because even in the dead of winter, the stockyard could keep operating."

"An underground stockyard? I guess that's a pretty smart way to make a huge hole in the ground useful. Did they use it for anything else?"

"Yeah, I think they'd do events there, sports and stuff. It's just a big arena, but underground and protected from the elements. It was also the fallout shelter for the whole city during the Cold War, they'd do drills and basically all of Mapleton would drive down here. It was big enough and the town was small enough back then that they could literally just drive their cars down and park them in the arena and wait for the drill to end. Anyway, the official story is that the place collapsed decades ago, even before the park above was built. But the urban legend is that the collapse was a lie created by local government to keep people out because the Under Yards are haunted," Deckard said.

"Haunted? By angry cow ghosts?"

Deckard snorted. "Never heard the full story, just that the place is massive, it's pitch dark, and it's scary as all hell."

"Awesome. That lines up with how the rest of this night has gone," Shad said.

"We should have just kept drinking and eating steaks."

"Yeah, but we're idiots," Shad said with a laugh. "We both had a feeling something was off with the cults. Now we *know* something is very off. We've got to find out what Alina is getting into so I can warn her. If we can get proof, I know I can get through to her."

"Down we go," Deckard said, turning and taking the first step down and Shad followed closely behind. The stairwell was as wide as the double doors and turned to the left about fifteen steps down. After they rounded the corner, they could see the landing at the bottom, dimly lit with flickering light. They continued down quietly, knowing they were completely exposed in this tunnel with no place to hide. If someone started heading back up the stairs, they'd be caught and would need to rely on their improvisational skills to get them through. Shad counted the stairs as he went, distracting himself from the panic growing in his gut the deeper they went.

"Ninety-six," Shad whispered to Deckard when they finally reached the bottom.

"What?"

"Ninety-six stairs. That's a lot, right? We're pretty deep underground?"

"Makes sense, it felt like a lot. Yeah, we're deep. That's like five or six stories. It even feels cooler down here," Deckard said. Ahead of them the landing widened significantly to three sets of double doors. A sign above the doors read "Service Entry." The area was lit by yellowed, flickering bulbs hanging from the ceiling in dust-covered stainless-steel fixtures. To their left, there was a single door in the wall that opened into a booth with three windows facing the hall where they stood. The door had a faded sign on it that read "Employees Only." Each window had a circular hole in the middle and had the bottom six inches missing, presumably so that whoever used this service entrance could check in with the stock-yard officials at the Under Yards. The room was dark, and looked to have been abandoned for decades. Shad turned from the small booth and approached the concourse entry doors quietly, doing his best to listen for sound on the other side. He and Deckard placed their ears against the doors, waiting in silence. After about a minute, Deckard spoke first. "I don't hear anything, do you?"

"No, nothing. But who knows if we'd hear anything through these old metal doors."

"Only one way to know for sure," Deckard said.

Shad nodded. "I'll open this one, you look through." Deckard responded with a thumbs up. Standing a pace from the door, Shad grabbed the handle with both hands, expecting it to be difficult to open. To his surprise, the door opened easily, causing Shad to open it much more quickly than he had planned. Deckard jumped back, startled. He caught himself, and looked through the opening after Shad had closed it a little.

"Looks clear. My pants, however, are now filled with pee. Thanks for that," Deckard said.

"My bad, I thought it would be hard to open like all of the other ancient doors in this creepy place."

"After you," Deckard said, gesturing forward to Shad. Begrudgingly, Shad moved through the open door with Deckard following shortly after. The concourse was wide and open and dimly lit. It looked like many of the other sports arenas Shad had seen throughout his life, but with a 1940s aesthetic. To their left and right, the concourse curved on beyond their view. Throughout the walkway, dozens of huge wooden crates, metal fencing, and other livestock equipment were stacked haphazardly. The concourse was lit by the same kind of stainless-steel fixtures that they had seen at the entrance, but many of them were not operational, adding to the area's dilapidated ambiance. While they hadn't heard anything through the doors, the sound of rhythmic drumming was clearly discernable in the concourse. Upon recognizing the sound, Shad and Deckard instinctively hid behind one of the larger pieces of equipment to their right, a cast-iron device that appeared to be used on livestock for some purpose they couldn't deduce.

"Sounds like we're getting closer," Shad said.

"Yeah, also sounds bigger than we thought. That's a lot of drumming for a couple dozen people. We need to be even more careful now. We know they came down here, so we know we're not alone. Want to go right or left?"

"They're obviously in the arena. It's darker to the left, so let's move right and see if we can find a way to get in without getting seen," Shad said.

"Works for me. I'll go first, stay close," Deckard responded before quietly stooping down and running to a stack of wooden crates about ten yards from their position. Shad followed right behind him, doing his best to stay in the unlit areas.

"It looks like they dragged all of this stuff from the arena out here to the concourse," Shad said, pointing to drag marks along the floor.

"Had to make room for whatever cult party we're hearing," Deckard said. The drumming got louder and louder as they moved, and after advancing about thirty yards down the concourse they came to a set of double doors down a short hall on their left. Above the entry was a sign that read "Sections 300–399." Muted light shone through the cracks in the door, with the thumping beats of the drums emanating clearly from the other side. Another ten yards down the concourse, the sound of drums was much louder and light shone brightly through a similar short walkway.

"Open doors?" Shad said, pointing down the way.

"Worth a look," Deckard said, creeping closer. They passed doors to restrooms on their right, both looking dark and unused for ages. Perching behind a stack of rusty feeding troughs, they had a good view through the two open doors. The arena was filled with a large crowd of people. The light shining through the open doors was from fiery braziers like those they had seen outside in the park, lining the outside perimeter of the arena. Inside the arena they could see the shadow of idols, lit erratically by bonfires set around them. The drum beats were loud now, sounding as if they were coming from all over arena.

"That's enough!" shouted a voice from the direction from which they'd come. One of the bathroom doors they had passed on the way suddenly burst open and an Asherian priest exited walking backward, struggling with someone. "This is the highest of callings. Remember that you chose this, you came to us first," he said. Shad and Deckard snapped to each other, wide-eyed. They both looked around for another place to hide, the troughs they hid behind leaving them completely exposed to the oncoming Asherian and whomever he was forcing along.

"But I told you I changed my mind," the captive responded. It was the young woman they had seen earlier. "I just want to go back to the way it was before; I don't want to do this anymore."

"There is no going back for you. Once you offer yourself, you are sealed. You will not be cleansed if you are an unwilling sacrifice, but it makes no difference to us," he said, dragging and pulling at her as he held the door open with his thigh. Grabbing Deckard's arm, Shad pointed about ten feet further down the concourse. Behind some metal livestock pen fencing was a darkened concession stand. Rising as quickly and quietly as they could, both made a break for it. There was a narrow gap between two pieces of fencing that was big enough to climb through. Shad nearly jumped through it, scaling the countertop and landing heavily on his stomach on the dusty concession floor. Just behind him came Deckard, gracelessly landing on Shad's back, knocking the wind out of his lungs. Shocked by the fall and the sudden loss of his breath, Shad panicked and began loudly gasping for air. Having righted himself, Deckard quickly covered Shad's mouth, which only served to amplify Shad's rising terror. Grasping at Deckard's hands, he began to flail.

"Calm down, calm down, they'll hear us! Breathe through your nose!" Deckard whispered as intensely as he could. "Your breath will come back, you're fine, don't panic. My fat butt just knocked the air out of your lungs. Sorry, man. That's it, breathe through your nose." Deckard held his friend's face close to his, his hand still covering Shad's mouth. Shad slowly began to recover, taking his breath through his nose greedily. He nodded at Deckard, signaling that he'd regained his wits.

"Crap, that hasn't happened to me since I was in junior high," he whispered to Deckard, rubbing his own chest as if it would bring comfort to his lungs. Deckard responded by holding his finger to his mouth, signaling for Shad to be quiet as he pointed in the direction of the concourse. Shad snapped his mouth shut and listened.

"This is not only for the goddess, but also for the inverted one. You have no idea what an honor it is to give of yourself during the Blood Moon Equinox. You should be proud!" he said to the struggling coed.

"Then why don't you offer yourself instead?" she asked.

The concourse echoed with the sound of a slap as the priest responded to her question decisively. There was more struggling, and Shad risked a peek. He saw the priest holding her by the throat from behind, pulling a gag out of his tunic and tying it over her mouth. "This is what you were born to be, the sooner you accept that, the easier this will be. Release yourself from the bonds of the light of this world and the darkness will embrace you," the Asherian said over her muffled protests. It appeared that despite the clumsy chaos of their escape, the Asherian didn't hear them hide in the concession stand. Still, Shad ducked back down to ensure they would remain concealed. The muffled screaming continued, but got more and more distant. They both knew he was taking the sacrifice into the arena.

"That was her, wasn't it? The college girl from before, the one we saw them dragging into the building?" Deckard whispered.

"Yeah, that was her."

"We have to do something, Shad. We have to help her."

"We are going to do something, just not what we thought we'd be doing. Did you look into the arena? There are way more people than we expected. Hundreds, even thousands of culties. The best we can do now is get proof and then go get help. We're going to record this and bring it to the cops," Shad said. "We just need to figure out how to get a view of what they're doing without getting caught."

"I hate letting him drag her away like that. You heard her just like I did, she wants out. She doesn't want to be here. Who knows what they're about to force her to do? She's just a dumb college kid, probably got duped by some professor, she didn't know what she was doing when she got into this," Deckard said.

"I know man, I know. But our surprise and run plan is done. There's too many people. The hell are we going to do? We'll just get caught and then no one will know what's happening here."

Deckard sat quietly for a moment, thinking. "I know you're right, even if we grabbed her we wouldn't make it out of the park before the culties swarmed us. But doing nothing is killing me. I hope this is the right call."

"I hate it too. This is the only way we can help her," Shad said. "I think my breath is back to normal. We need to find somewhere high up so we can record as much as possible." Shad rose to a squat and peered over the top of the counter. The Asherian and his captive were no longer visible through the double doors, he only saw the same distant movement through the dancing firelight, punctuated by rhythmic drumming.

They climbed back over the counter and exited the concession stand, much more slowly and delicately than their messy entrance. They perched behind the troughs and checked to ensure no one else was coming, and then continued again in the same direction down the concourse in search of a way up. Moving from one obstruction to another, they made their way down the concourse and deeper into the facility. Just before they reached the arena entrance marked as "Sections 800–899," Shad spotted a nondescript door on their right, marked "Service" with letters about one inch tall. Some metal livestock pen fencing was propped in front of the door, obscuring it from view. Shad nudged Deckard and pointed at the door, approaching it slowly. Deckard tripped on something and stumbled forward a few paces.

"I guess I'm lucky that's the first time I tripped with all of this garbage out here." They continued to the door. The fencing was in front of the door but not against it, so Shad was able to get behind it to the door without trying to lift and move the heavy obstruction. The door opened with a little struggle, but didn't creak. Shad entered a completely dark and silent room. He pulled out his phone and activated the flashlight, revealing some kind of mechanical room; he was greeted with a mishmash of rusty piping, knobs, handles, gauges, and various other things that made up the guts of the arena. In the far back corner was a metal ladder, enclosed in a safety cage.

"Bingo," Shad whispered back to Deckard.

"Crap, where's my phone?" Deckard said, panic on his face as he patted his pockets. "I must have dropped it when I tripped back there. I'll go check," Shad waited in the service room with the door ajar, looking outside while Deckard turned back to find his phone.

"Well, hello, Molochian," said a familiar, seductive voice. Shad instinctively crouched, shoved his phone in his pocket, and pulled the door almost closed in one quick movement. He left the door open just enough to look out at what was taking place on the concourse. The Asherian priestess who had tried to engage in "worship" with Deckard earlier in the park above had just walked in from the arena entrance. "What are you doing out here?" she asked Deckard.

"Oh, hey there. I was leaving for the bathroom and accidently dropped my phone," Deckard said, looking down. He bent down and grabbed something and stood up, facing her. "Hah, found it!" he said, holding up his phone.

"Where's your friend?"

"I invited him to come here with me, but I guess I spooked him or something. He decided he wasn't ready, so he went home," Deckard said.

"Too bad, I could have helped you give him some guidance," she placed her index finger on Deckard's chest. "But now we can worship the goat lord together," she whispered, tracing her finger down Deckard's torso to his crotch. "I have to head to the potty," she grabbed him between the legs firmly and decisively. "But you'll find me later tonight, right?"

Deckard coughed. "Ab-so-lutely," he grunted, emphasizing each syllable of the word. The priestess smiled, kissed Deckard fully on the mouth, released his most prized possessions, and walked away, all in the span of about fifteen seconds. He stood still, mildly stunned by the interaction and the fact that he had evaded being caught in his subterfuge. After shaking his head and shuddering, he bolted over to the door where Shad was waiting.

"And the Oscar goes to . . ." Shad said, opening the door for him and closing it after he entered. "You played that perfectly."

"You think she bought it?"

"Looked like she did. She's going to be disappointed when you don't show up to 'worship' with her." Shad made air quotes.

"She's got the grip of a seasoned arm wrestler. What's the deal with this room?" Deckard asked, rubbing his family jewels tenderly as he looked around the dark room.

"Some kind of utility room? No idea what all of this stuff does. The good news is there's a ladder at the back. I think we should see where it leads."

Deckard shook his hips and grimaced. "All right, you go first. I'm still trying recover from that surprise physical little miss vice grip gave me."

"Shad walked over to the ladder in the corner of the room and shined his cell phone's flashlight upward. "Can't see anything, looks like it goes up pretty far. I think I see a light flickering up there," he said. He thought of the young girl, struggling as she was dragged into the arena by the Asherian priest. Gritting his teeth, he began to climb.

Behind them, the door to the mechanical room was just barely open, letting in a sliver of light. As Shad and Deckard climbed up the ladder, it was closed quietly with deliberate delicacy, darkness sweeping back into the subterranean room again like an avalanche.

Chapter 9

THE PAIR HAD ASCENDED sixty rungs up the ladder, digging through darkness most of the way, until a single, flickering bulb near the top began to light their way. Shad counted rungs to distract himself. He wasn't really claustrophobic, but he definitely wasn't enjoying being inside a cramped metal tunnel, perched multiple stories high on a rickety metal ladder that was old enough to collect Social Security. On top of the fear rising to the brim of his psyche, Shad's limbs were starting to ache with the effort, causing him to slip off of the old metal ladder rungs more than once. Near the top, he slipped off completely and hit his back on the ladder cage. Fortunately, the cage caught him and stopped his descent. Unfortunately, the cage also had a protruding rusty bolt that cut deeply into his back. Deckard had stayed far enough beneath him that he wasn't hit by Shad's flailing foot.

"Dude, that was close. How are you doing?" Deckard asked.

"How I'm doing is, uh, relative? I'm not falling and you're not falling, and I'm back on the ladder, so that's definitely on the plus side. Something on this cage cut the crap out of my back. I'm pretty sure I'm bleeding," Shad said. "Looks like we're pretty close to the top. I think I see a passage."

"Sounds like a great place to pass out. I'm done with this stupid ladder, let's get up there."

Shad nodded and took a breath to try to slow his racing heart down to a manageable pace and focused on the rungs. With violent protests from what felt like every joint, muscle, and tendon in his body, he slowly began to climb again. He reached the top where the flickering bulb was housed, lighting the way to a passage across from the ladder. A grimy sign on the right-hand wall read "Catwalk/Light Grid" with an arrow pointing down the tunnel. "Touchdown, Deckard. This leads to the catwalk above the arena."

Deckard breathed a sigh of relief. "Well, at least this was worth it. Can we get off of this horrible ladder now?"

"Gladly." There were vertical handles on either side of the tunnel entrance. With one hand on the ladder and one on the handle, Shad pulled himself over to the landing, standing on the firm walkway for a moment before he collapsed and sat down, facing the ladder.

Immediately after, Deckard followed suit. He extended his middle finger at the ladder as he crossed the threshold, and collapsed next to Shad. They both sat for a few moments and recuperated before Deckard unzipped his 'tactical' fanny pack.

"Let me see your back," he said, digging around in the bag.

"Got any painkillers?"

"No, but I have some bandages."

"Really? I thought you'd just have a flask and some condoms in there."

"I have that too," he said, holding up a small stainless-steel flask with the letter *D* engraved on it. Shad turned around and pulled up his shirt. "Can you hold your phone flashlight over your shoulder so I can see what I'm doing?" Shad complied, and Deckard responded by inhaling sharply through his teeth. "Bro, that tunnel absolutely messed you up. You're going to have a nasty scar. Too bad it's in a place where you can't really show it off. Also, this is going to hurt."

"It already hurts. How could it get wors—Ow!" Shad screamed as Deckard poured the flask over the wound and wiped it with some gauze. "Holy crap man, some warning, please?"

"Dude, I told you it was going to hurt. What else do you want?"

"A countdown or something?"

"OK—three, two, one," he said before packing the wound with some kind of powder.

Shad screamed with his mouth closed, clenching his teeth. "What are you putting on there?"

"I got this cool powder off of Bezozon.com that's supposed to be what paramedics use to pack wounds to stop bleeding. And apparently it works, because your bleeding just stopped. Now I'm going to put on some butterfly strips to pull the skin together." Deckard sat quietly for a bit, focused on his task. Shad gritted through the pain of having his split skin pushed back together between Deckard's fingers. He heard the sound of tape being pulled off of a roll and torn, and felt a bandage on his back.

"Done." Deckard said.

"I admit, I thought that fanny pack was stupid, but that came in clutch."

"I brought it as kind of a joke, to be honest. I was drunk shopping one night and thought it was funny to have a tactical fanny pack. Never thought I'd use it, so thanks for justifying the money I spent."

"Happy to contribute," Shad said. He stood up and stretched his legs, shaking his muscles out. "How are you feeling?"

"Pretty exhausted, but sitting here has helped a lot. I'm glad we ate that cultie food earlier, I'd have passed out by now if we hadn't refueled. How long is this walkway?" Deckard asked, straining his eyes down the tunnel.

"Can't be too far, right? I'm a little turned around after being in that nightmare climb, but that room where we came up was just off of the arena's concourse. The catwalk must be close."

Deckard stood up and stretched, cracking his neck. "Onward," he said. They came to a ninety-degree turn in the tunnel with another sign with an arrow, like the one where they had entered. The muffled sound of drumming echoed in the distance.

"Hear that?"

"Not very far after all," Deckard said. They both continued down the path, the rhythmic thumping increasing in volume as they went. They came to a metal door with a sign on it that read "Catwalk/Lighting Grid—Authorized Entry Only." Deckard turned to Shad. "I authorize you to enter, Shad."

"Thank you, sir." Shad reached for the knob. The door protested a little at being awakened from decades of hibernation, but it opened nonetheless. A wave of sound and light greeted them, and they were both stricken with a sense of vertigo at the sight of the arena far below. After reorienting themselves for a moment, they both moved forward onto the catwalk cautiously. They were above the arena, but not so high that they couldn't clearly discern what was taking place and feel the heat of the fires below. The catwalk was structured in a sort of wheel and spoke system, with a perimeter catwalk that went around the edge of the entire arena and straight paths that broke off of the perimeter toward a center hub where lights and speakers were mounted. As far as they could tell, none of the equipment mounted on the catwalk was being used by the cultists, so they were confident that they could move freely without being noticed. Shad went first, leading the way around the perimeter catwalk toward a platform about twenty yards from the door where they'd entered. It looked like it had been used for photographers when the Under Yards were at the height of use, with some metal stools set up at a counter-top that overlooked the entire arena. Despite being covered in dust and cobwebs, everything had been perfectly preserved over the decades of dereliction. The counter was about ten feet long and one foot deep, just high enough that Shad and Deckard could sit on the stools and rest their elbows while watching the action beneath them. The friends sat next to each other, pulled out their phones, and tapped their camera apps. Shad's elbow bumped into something on the counter that he hadn't seen. Picking it up, he raised an old pair of binoculars to Deckard.

"Well, how about that? I guess it makes sense these would be here." Deckard ran his hand along the counter and came up with an additional pair of binoculars as well as a pencil and a faded press badge.

"Do they work?" Deckard asked, putting the binoculars he found up to his eyes.

"Yeah, mine are good. Yours?"

"Left side is shot, but the right is clear. Better than nothing," he said, setting his phone down. "If you see something we should record, call it out. I'll focus on the right half of the arena, you cover the left," he said, motioning to the sides of the arena with his left hand as he held the broken binoculars with his right hand.

"How's your phone's zoom?" Shad said.

"Not great, but good enough. It's a little grainy but you can tell what you're looking at here." Deckard picked up his binoculars and began to scope out the arena. "So, I see the Baalists, Molochians, and Asherians," he said, pointing to the idols to each of the cult gods as they were placed in a semicircle along one side of the arena, on the opposite side of where they were currently perched. "But what's the big boy in the middle of the others? I've never seen that one." There was a massive idol towering behind and in the center of the others, standing at least twice as tall as the three other idols. It appeared to be a man with the head of a goat, with huge horns and wings on its back. It had a pentagram on its forehead, with both arms extended outward, one pointing up to the sky and the other pointed down diagonally toward the ground. And while it had the head of a goat, it had a human torso. The idol was constructed to look more lifelike than the others and appeared to be built out of sundry materials, with canvas for skin, fur made of rope and fabric, and other features fashioned out of wood and metal. Its goat head was tall enough that they could see it clearly without their lenses.

"No idea," Shad said. "But it's creeping me the hell out. Does it have boobs?"

"Uh, yeah. It does. And a huge hog too."

"You're joking," Shad said, turning his binoculars down toward the midsection of the idol. "No, you're not joking. This thing must have taken weeks to build. What the hell are we looking at?" The idol had large breasts on a human torso above the legs of a goat, but between the legs hung the distinct tools of a male human.

"Well, it looks like a she-male goat person with wings. Because, why wouldn't it be?"

"Whatever it is, it seems to be more important than the other idols . . ." Shad snapped his fingers. "Dude, remember that Asherian chick? The one you bumped into in the concourse?"

"Yeah, the grabby one with the grip of an Olympian weight lifter? I'm going to be honest with you, she's close to hot enough to convert me, even if she almost popped my balls like water balloons," Deckard said.

"You need higher standards. When we were talking to her, she said something about the goat lord. 'We're all one before the goat lord' or something like that. This has to be what she was talking about. Look at them. All of the culties are worshipping it. Seems like they make offerings to their idols, and then they go to the goat thing and make another one," he said, motioning to the movements of the worshippers below. They sat and watched what took place in the arena through their old lenses. What they began to see froze their hearts like liquid nitrogen.

"Left side, by the Baalists. At the base of the idol. It's the ax guy. See him?" Shad said.

"Yup, I see him. That priest is with him too." They could both see the young man from earlier in the night, the ax he carried was still in his right hand. The priest made a dramatic motion toward the young man, appearing to draw some sort of symbol in the air over him and then over his left arm. He then knelt down before the idol to Baal as the young man turned to face the golden man. Turning his head up toward Baal's face, he appeared to speak as other Baalists near him looked on. And with a quick, fluid motion he placed his left arm on the trough in front of Baal, raised his ax with his right arm, and brought it down with ferocious speed on his left elbow. Blood sprayed up from the wound, spattering those around him, including the Baalist priest, who reacted with elation.

"What the . . ." Shad watched the young man hack two, three, and four more times at his arm until it was severed completely at the elbow. Their viewing angle only allowed them to see his profile, but he had a maniacal grin on his face and looked as though he might even be laughing as blood sprayed from the stump where his arm was once attached into the trough in front of the idol. The young man began to stumble back, growing faint from blood loss. Two priests grabbed him and put a belt around his stump to stanch the torrent and conclude his offering.

"So that's why they brought him down here," Deckard said. "They don't want people cutting off their freaking limbs in public, but they're OK with it if it's done in secret." The priests helped the young man back to the trough where he picked up his severed left arm in his right hand. They then walked over toward the massive goat-thing where golden altars were set all around with huge fiery pits behind them. Engraved atop each altar was a pentagram with the star inverted and a goat's head in the center, clearly resembling the idol to which the altars were dedicated. The young man, still supported by both priests, raised his severed arm up toward the goat and placed it on the altar in the center of the pentagram. He and the two priests bowed and made some ritualistic motions toward the idol, and then the man stood up and threw his severed arm into the fire. The worshippers around him cried out together, rejoicing. He looked overjoyed, waving his remaining arm and his bloody stump in the air.

"I'm guessing you didn't record that, did you?" Shad asked.

"No, I . . . I wasn't really prepared for that," Deckard said. He hesitated, taking a breath. "I knew what he was going to do, you know? We knew it when we saw him in the park. It was clear, he had the ax, he tried it right there in front of everyone. We saw them take him here. I knew what to expect, man. But even still, seeing it happen . . . We're making a lot of bad memories tonight."

"I have a feeling we're going to make some more before we're done," Shad said, picking his binoculars back up. Deckard stared off into the distance blankly for a few moments, processing the violence he'd just witnessed in the service of a man-made god. He breathed a sigh through his nose and steeled himself, unlocking his phone's camera app and raising his broken binoculars to resume their observation of the events below. They both searched for ten or fifteen minutes, which felt like an eternity. Deckard recorded a half dozen more particularly violent offerings by

Baalists—more people cutting off parts of themselves as acts of worship—
but they didn't catch anything else that stood out from the other two cults.
Asherians were performing their regular sexual offerings and Molochians
were sacrificing animals, all things they would expect to see. They did cap-
ture a few dogs and larger livestock being sacrificed, but nothing quite as
salacious as what they'd seen from the worshippers of Baal.

Shad put his binoculars down and rubbed his eyes. "Is that all we're
going to get? What if we've missed our chance to expose what's going on
here?" he asked Deckard, who was still scoping out the crowd below.

"We have plenty to expose them with already, dude. Cutting off body
parts for Baal? They don't put that in their radio ads. Besides, there's still
time. We haven't been here that lo—" he stopped. "Pick up your binocs.
Look down by Moloch. Is that Dink?"

"The rich tool bag from the offering table? The one that got the VIP
treatment?" Shad asked, lifting his binoculars back to his eyes.

"Yeah, Jerry Dink. He's down there. I've got to get this. I think this
is what they meant by 'Obsidian' Offerings. Where is he, where is he?"
Deckard said to himself frantically as he grabbed his phone. "Got him."

They both sat quietly, Shad glued to his binoculars and Deckard focused on his screen. Jerry Dink was being led up the steps of a platform
in front of the huge, dark idol to Moloch by a hooded Molochian clergy.
Dink wore a black robe similar to the priests, with only a white vestment
laid over his shoulders. The symbol of Moloch was embroidered in black
on each end of the vestment. The priest carried one of the curved bronze
ceremonial blades unique to their cult. The two walked toward one of
many large stone altars placed before the idol to the bull god and stood
with the altar between them and the dark statue. The idol was surrounded by a large pit of burning coals that was continuously being stoked and
tended by priests and priestesses in their dark robes, creating a burning
moat between worshippers and the bull god. Laying there on his back on
the stone table, dressed only in a white linen cloak and looking up at the
idol's unmoving countenance adoringly, was the sick man they had seen
be escorted away from the Molochian offering merchant. Neither Shad
nor Deckard spoke. They both knew what they were about to see, but just
as before with the young man with the ax, even knowing how it would
end didn't prepare them to watch it happen.

Dink stood to the side of the Molochian who was perpendicular to
the altar, right around the old man's midsection, facing the bull god.
The Molochian appeared to speak and raised the knife up with some sort

of ceremonial motions, then handed the blade to Dink, who bowed and held the blade pointed up with both of his hands. The hooded clergy then performed some hand movements over the old sick man, who reacted with exultation. After another bow, Dink traded places with the hooded clergy, first raising the blade up and bowing to the idol. He then waved the blade over the old man's body, head to toe, occasionally gesturing back up to the idol. His movements looked practiced, rehearsed; he'd clearly done this before.

Shad clenched his jaw and ground his teeth, anticipating what was coming next, unable to avert his eyes or even blink. Deckard was motionless, completely focused on his phone's screen. When it happened, it was different than the young man with the ax. Dink's movements weren't sudden and quick, they were slow and deliberate. He stabbed—or more accurately, inserted the knife in the ailing man's lower abdomen. Savoring each moment, he gradually dragged the blade up toward the man's chest. The old man couldn't help but struggle involuntarily from the pain, but was held down by four Molochian clergy, two at his shoulders and two at his knees. He was clearly screaming, and even though it was unlikely, Shad thought he could hear him from their perch. Even if he couldn't actually hear the man's cries of agony, he certainly felt them. Spitting up blood, the man's struggles became weaker and weaker. Dink laid the knife down on the table gently, raised his hands up to Moloch, and then plunged them down into the gaping abdomen. He began pulling the man's insides out, one at a time, and throwing them into the fiery moat between the table and the idol, occasionally slicing pieces free from the sinews and tendons within the old man's now twitching body. To their disbelief, the old man's face was still alive with an absurd blend of agony and ecstasy as Dink eviscerated him. And then, like a candlelight being pinched between two damp fingers, he was gone; his vitality finally snuffed out in the name of this cast-iron god.

Shad dropped the binoculars on the counter, turned and collapsed to his knees on the floor, dry heaving. He closed his mouth and forced himself to swallow the vomit that came up next, fearing he might spray the contents of his stomach on the cultists far below and give away their position. Deckard held the screen with his right hand, his mouth covered by his left, his eyes agape at the ghastly spectacle on his screen. The offering's death didn't slow Dink's butchery down at all. He continued apace, cutting and hacking at the frail body and tossing pieces into the coals. Eventually the body was completely eviscerated and dismembered, leaving only vital fluids, tattered linen, and the old man's head on the sacrificial altar. Dink stood at the table, breathing heavily, bathed in the blood of his offering to Moloch. In his right hand he held the now idle heart of the sickly man. A Molochian priest walked up with a large bronze dish, about twenty-four inches in diameter. He placed the decapitated head on the platter and presented it to Dink, bowing. Dink returned the bow, placed the heart next to the head and took the platter in both hands. Standing up straight in a formal manner, he turned and began walking off of the platform. He was followed by a procession of Molochian clergy and other worshippers who had been witnesses to the savage spectacle.

Having recovered control over his digestive system, Shad sat back on the stool and raised the binoculars back to his eyes with a cold resolve. He hated what he had seen and would see, but he was determined to see it so that he could testify to anyone who would listen about what had taken place in the Under Yards that night. Deckard took a deep breath and shook his head slowly, still stunned. They both watched in silence as Dink and his posse of worshippers made their way over to the huge goat-thing idol, arriving at one of the golden altars exactly like the one where the young man had presented his severed arm. Dink placed the head and heart on the altar in the center of the pentagram and performed ritualistic movements similar to those that the armless man had performed earlier. He then tossed the head and the heart into the fire and cried out in celebration. Everyone near him erupted joyfully; even the normally somber Molochians were animated, as if they had been jolted out of their shadowy dispositions with electricity.

Shad was the first to break the silence. "Did you see the old man's face?"

"He was happy. Maybe even grateful," Deckard said.

"People need to know what these cults *really* do. They present them like they're just another lifestyle. 'Alternative religions' they say, like they're another Protestant denomination. They're on TV shows, they're in movies. They're presented as victims of discrimination, innocent people just trying to live their truth, worship as they feel they're meant to worship. If people really understood their core, if they really knew the real, sinister darkness we've seen, no one would accept it. It's not worship, it's murder," Shad said. "I'll never be the same, man. I don't even know how to begin to tell Alina about this. She won't believe me. No one will believe me. But she has to know. She has to know. *Everyone* has to know."

Deckard nodded. "I know people with Molochian tattoos, you know? There's this one girl at the office. She's so sweet, really nice, super shy and quiet. So young and innocent, probably twenty-five. Really good designer too. She has the symbol of Moloch tattooed on both wrists. She goes to the idol every single day in the morning and after work. I kept seeing her on that altar down there. That young, promising girl with her whole life ahead of her, butchered and flayed, a meaningless death on these altars of counterfeit self-fulfillment. And she'd probably smile like that old man did. She'd believe she was doing the most righteous thing. She'd probably think she was ascending to a new spiritual level. But there's nothing spiritual about it. She'd just be dead, wasted on this screwed up insanity, this soulless individualism," Deckard said, leaning back onto the counter as he vented.

Shad had resumed observing the arena through his binoculars. He took a deep breath and exhaled heavily. "Oh, no," he said, barely audibly.

"What now?"

"I see that college girl. The one that they dragged into the building, the one we saw struggling with that priest down in the concourse."

Deckard closed his eyes, grimacing. "It's going to get worse, isn't it?"

"We're going to need to move, we can't get a good angle here. The Asherians are on the opposite side of the goat idol," Shad said, rising from his stool and gathering his binoculars. He placed them back on his eyes and used them to look around on their level for another post. "Over there," he said, pointing. "Around the perimeter to our right there's another photographer's platform just like this one." Deckard nodded and stood up, grabbing his broken binoculars and his phone. The two moved swiftly and silently along the catwalk toward the other perch. This one was exactly the same, although it was cleaner than the other one had been.

"She's down about ten or twenty yards in front of the Asherian idol, surrounded by a half dozen priests and priestesses," Shad said, trying to stifle the churning cauldron of emotion in his chest. Deckard hesitated. Shad lowered the binoculars and turned to look at Deckard. "I know, bro. I know. But we have to record as much as we can," he said.

Deckard nodded. "If I wasn't an alcoholic before, I'm definitely going to be now," he said, unlocking his phone to begin recording. "I see her. Looks like they're moving her toward their altar." He zoomed the phone in on the college student. She was more alert now, but was no longer struggling against her captors. She appeared resigned to her fate; she'd accepted it, but was far from an enthusiastic participant like the old man had been. Wearing a linen robe, she looked as if she had bathed, or had been bathed. Her hair was slicked back and looked greasy, and her face had been decorated with heavy makeup. She was held by two Asherian priests, one gripping each of her arms. All around them more Asherians were dancing and gyrating erotically. The rhythmic drum beats continued, a metronome for all of the rituals that they had witnessed that night. The altars before the huge bronze idol to Asherah were ornately carved wooden structures decorated with ribbons of all colors and looked like they would fit perfectly in the Asherian temple Shad drove by on the way to work every day. In the middle stood a single wooden post, about ten feet high, also ornately carved and wrapped in ribbons. Standing next to the post in her golden silk gown was the Asherian high priestess, her voluptuous curves clearly discernable and proudly displayed for all to see.

Stoic and defeated, the young woman shuffled along with her jubilant captors. *If Alina only knew what really happened with these cults, she'd react like this. She'd want out as soon as she found out the truth. I have to tell her, I have to show her that she's been lied to*, Shad thought as he watched the college girl being walked to the altar. The Asherian high priestess stepped down and took her hand and led her up to the wooden post. The priestess's movements were a continuous primal dance of lithe pulsations, she flowed more than she walked, her presence that of an ethereal intoxicant. She began to stroke the coed's face, tracing her lips affectionately and passing her fingers along her neck and down her chest. As she continued her path around the captive, the high priestess leaned in and ran her hand slowly up her cheek and into her hair as the young woman stood still and unreactive before the undulating crowd, indifference the only remaining act of defiance she could manage.

The high priestess extended her hand and an Asherian priest quickly placed leather straps into her open palm. Continuing to meander erotically, she grabbed the college girl's hands and began to dance with them on the large post, as the crowd of Asherians looked on, enraptured. The student didn't resist, she just stood limply, allowing her body to be manipulated like a lifeless marionette. The high priestess lightly spun her around so that she faced the crowd, placed her back against the post, and used the leather straps to lash her to it. The priestess tied her hands behind her back and around the post, then fastened her ankles. After testing the bonds to make sure they were tight and secure, she rose to her feet and faced her captive, standing only a few inches away from the college student's face. The high priestess simultaneously raised both hands up toward the huge bronze goddess that towered over them. With that signal, all of the dozens of Asherian priests and priestesses gathered at the altar rushed up to join the high priestess around their captive. There were so many, it was hard to discern what was happening. Shad focused the binoculars. "What are they doing to her?"

"I can't tell, they're moving so much, they're all over the place," Deckard said, watching the scene on the phone's screen. Shad zoomed the binoculars out a little, providing a wider perspective and adding much-needed context. The Asherians had engulfed their prey with their bodies; each of them was dancing all around her, a wild debaucherous bedlam. He could see that the young woman was now screaming and crying, her rigid resolve disintegrated, pleadingly searching the crowd for any sliver of hope that she might be rescued. She found none.

The linen that she wore was tugged and torn by the ravaging Asherians as she wept, her face awash in tears and snot. The high priestess stood behind the pole, dancing alone amongst the torrent of human flesh. Leaning in, she joined the group, and appeared to be hugging her around the neck from behind. Shad blinked and squinted, concentrating his vision. Something dark flowed down the coed's chest, washing over her frail form. Then, like the crack of a whip, the reality of what he had seen snapped into focus in his brain. The high priestess hadn't been hugging her, she'd had a blade in her hand, and she'd used it to split the young woman's throat wide open. Her body was now covered with a shimmering, sanguine drapery, cascading down to her toes. Her mouth was still open, but the priestess had robbed her of her tools to scream. Her forlorn eyes continued their frantic search of the faces around her for salvation and, finding only fanatics, she sputtered her last few breaths—childlike, penitent, alone.

Shad and Deckard watched in frozen silence as her body offered one last feeble shudder before its final surrender. The leather bonds were released and the gaggle of Asherians, crazed by their ritual act of sensual violence, lifted her broken corpse up above their heads. Leading the way, the high priestess floated and wisped her way toward the goat lord. The young woman's body was lain on the golden surface of an altar, and all of the Asherians danced together in celebration of their sacrifice, first to their goddess and ultimately to this horned abomination. They gyrated almost in unison, presenting even more offerings as they kissed and copulated. As the group continued to entangle itself more and more in a slippery mixture of sweaty bodies, the high priestess approached the altar. She bent down and kissed the college girl's lifeless forehead one final time, running her hands affectionately through her hair. Rising and looking up, the priestess lifted her arms up in the air in some religious gesture to the idol. And with a quick bow, she motioned to two priests, who picked the dead body up and tossed her into the fire, the last remnants of her vitality sizzling away into ash before the endless staring eyes of the goat lord.

Shad stood up, running his fingers through his hair. "You, uh . . . you got all of that, right?"

Deckard sat almost completely still, holding his phone with his left hand. He raised his right hand to stop the recording, but his hand was trembling so hard he couldn't manage to hit the button without multiple tries. After he succeeded, he let the phone fall from his hand onto the counter in front of him, staring blankly into the distance.

"Did you get that, Deckard? Did you record it all?" Shad asked again.

"Yeah," Deckard said. "I recorded the whole thing."

"We've got to get that out there. Far and wide. To everyone, everywhere. How do we do that? Do we send it to a newspaper? Or like a news channel?" Shad was pacing back and forth on the platform, his eyes wide open with anxiety and shock. Deckard continued to sit as motionless as a statue, dumbfounded by the horrific finale they'd just witnessed. "Deckard, are you hearing me?" Shad said, touching his shoulder.

Deckard jumped at the unexpected physical contact, lurching off of his stool and toppling it over. It began to roll toward the edge of the platform. Shad watched it moving, as if in slow motion. He sprung forward, stretching his arm out and catching the stool at the last moment just before it cleared the lip of the platform where it would have tumbled multiple stories into the crowd beneath them. Standing up, he righted the stool and approached Deckard who was staring wide-eyed at the floor and breathing heavily.

Shad placed his hands on Deckard's shoulders. "Look at me. Deckard, brother, look at me," he commanded his friend. Deckard complied, directing his astonished stare at Shad. "We've got to pull ourselves together and get this out there. I know you're messed up. I am too. We've watched living nightmares, barbaric violence I've never even imagined. I want to say we're going to be OK, but we're not. We're not going to forget this, ever. And that's exactly why we have to take what we've seen and show the rest of the world, so we can stop this madness before it happens again. We have to stuff it down so we can get out of here safely and get this video to the public," Shad said.

Deckard nodded, his breathing steadying to a normal cadence. "No newspapers or news channels. They're all crap, both sides of the spectrum. They're all pushing this cultie stuff now. We put this on the Internet, social media. That's the only way it spreads."

"OK, cool. So we put it on Yeller, PostSpace, VidHole, what else? Spinstagram?"

"Everywhere. I'll handle it, I do this kind of thing for work all the time," Deckard said. "We've got to get out of here first."

"Yeah. We're going back down the ladder tunnel from hell?"

"I guess so—" Deckard was interrupted by the sound of doors opening loudly behind them. They both turned around to face a small crowd of cult clergy walking with calm purpose straight in their direction.

Chapter 10

A SET OF DOUBLE doors opened behind them, revealing a group of a dozen people. Each cult was represented with priests and priestesses, as well as some men in black suits that looked like private security. At the front of the group walked a man that neither of them had ever seen. He looked around their age, perhaps in his mid-thirties, and was wearing a finely tailored tuxedo that looked to have been perfectly cut for his lean build. His bearded face was meticulously groomed, with no single hair out of place, framing the most immaculate smile Shad had ever seen. Shad and Deckard experienced the oddest cascade of emotions they'd ever felt in a matter of moments, from shock to fear to a sort of disarmed admiration. The man walked with the impeccable blend of confidence and ease, relaxed and yet completely in control. From his slicked back hair to his mirror-polished shoes, he was flawless.

"Before you head out, I was hoping we could have a word," the man said, his buttery smooth voice flowing charmingly from his picture-perfect smile. Acting on their instincts, Shad and Deckard began to back away slowly, even though they had nowhere to go. "Don't worry, we're not here to detain you or hurt you. You'll be free to leave as you please once our conversation has concluded," the man said.

"If that's true, why did you bring along your mob of culties?" Shad asked.

"Culties? Come now, Shadrick, we've come in peace. There's no need for pejoratives. That term is very frowned upon these days. We prefer the alternative religious, or alts," he said, his smile never fading even slightly. When Shad stood quietly, he continued. "No? Well, that's OK. Even if you choose not to be civil, we 'culties' as you say so disparagingly, are not here for a conflict. Just a conversation."

"You didn't answer my question," Shad said.

"Oh, them?" said the man, gesturing to the group around him carelessly. "The nature of my position is such that I am never able to go anywhere alone, really. I can hardly use the toilet without an entourage! Heavy lies the crown, as they say. But we'll get to that later. I've come to speak with you and Mr. Culpepper about why *you* have come to our religious festival."

"How do you know my name?" Deckard asked.

"Deckard, *really*? You thought you had snuck in here like some kind of secret agents?" the man said, prompting laughter from his group of companions. "As usual, bonded-ones underestimate us. You were flagged as soon as you walked through the gates. You see, when you're a part of a group that is regularly persecuted by ignorant people, you become attuned to the presence of outsiders. You gain the ability to recognize threats, to sniff out wolves in sheep's clothing. After you entered our festival gates and impersonated a liberated, Deckard"—he gestured scoldingly with his index finger at him—"our people began to keep an eye on you. They followed you to the worship grounds, they stayed near you throughout your tour of each of the alternative religions, they even observed your meal. I have a copy of your receipt, if you've lost yours," he said, pulling a piece of paper out of his pocket, clearly demonstrating the breadth of his reach in the festival and his penchant for the theatrical. "I do hope it was to your liking, by the way. The Baalists take a lot of pride in their charcuterie, and I believe it shows. Anyway, when you both began to follow one of our clergy as he ushered a faithful worshipper to our private sanctuary here in the Under Yards, your escorts escalated the alert to their supervisors. There was quite a bit of debate about how to deal with you. You were very nearly arrested! We did lose sight of you at one point, I must confess. You disappeared into the darkness near our building up in the park. The next time we spotted you was when Deckard encountered Jasmin down in the concourse," he said, pointing to the Asherian priestess who had been so interested in Deckard earlier. She smiled at Deckard and waved, raising her eyebrows suggestively. "Naturally, she immediately notified our security team that you had gained entry to our private ceremony. When we saw you go up the ladder, we knew exactly where you were going. How did you know about this catwalk, by the way? No one has been here in ages. I come up here sometimes for some peace and quiet, the view of our beautiful rituals is spectacular, wouldn't you say?" he said, motioning to their surroundings. Shad and Deckard remained silent and still, refusing to engage with the man.

"Well, you can keep your secret. That was an exceedingly long answer to your short question, Deckard. While you made your way through our sacred celebration, our people began to dig into both of your lives and backgrounds. We know your names, your addresses, your employers. We know the names of your family members. We know where you went to school. We have all of your social media accounts mapped out. We know that Shadrick is clean as a whistle! No criminal record. Very good, Shadrick!" he said. "But you, Deckard. One arrest for drunk and disorderly? *Two* arrests for drunk driving? It sounds to me like you might have a drinking problem, my friend."

"Screw you," Deckard said.

"I meant no offense, Deckard. Just making an observation, we didn't come here for an intervention. Not about your drinking, at least," he said, his crowd of followers snickering at his jab. "And Shadrick, we didn't even need to research your family. We know them very well already, it's really quite serendipitous! Allow me to introduce High Priest Malochus," he said gesturing to one of the dark-robed Molochian clergy in his posse who stood out from the crowd due to his golden crown. "Lord Malochus told me all about your beautiful bride Alina and your absolutely precious princess Isla. They're just *darling.*"

"You keep the hell away from them," Shad said, rushing forward with his arm raised, ready to strike. Two of the suited guards immediately closed ranks in front of him, forming an impenetrable wall of muscle and copious amounts of odious cologne that stopped Shad in his tracks.

"Thank you, guards, thank you. That's OK, he won't try to hurt me, will you, Shadrick?" said the mysterious man, gently moving his guards aside. "You misunderstand, Shadrick. We are not recruiting your wife. *She came to us,*" he said, his smile taking on a sinister shadow.

"That's not true. You had that cult thing at Isla's school, that's all. Alina told me about it," Shad said.

"Did she, Shad? I'm sorry, can I call you Shad?" he asked without waiting for an answer. "She told you about the festival at the school, sure. But did she tell you everything about it?" Shad stood silently, his anger fuming more every moment. "She was there, Shad. The entire day. She volunteered to be a parental sponsor to help with the children's festival. She's been very interested in Moloch. Your daughter's teacher has been providing her with guidance about gaining freedom from her bonds. As a matter of fact, afterward she spoke with Lord Malochus about liberation, didn't she? Perhaps even at this very festival. Is that correct?" he asked, turning to the Molochian.

Malochus bowed his head affirmingly. "That is correct," he said.

"She was rather enthusiastic as I understand it. Awestruck, even. Isn't that what you told me, Lord Malochus?"

Malochus bowed again. "It is," he said.

"I apologize for Lord Malochus, he's not much of an orator. It seems as though your sweet wife has kept a few secrets from you, Shad. She is well on her way to becoming a liberated member of the cult of Moloch. And how apropos for her to be liberated this weekend, at the very same festival that you visited. Truly a family affair! But she's clearly wiser than you, since she's waiting until the apex of the festival tomorrow during the Blood Sabbath. The most important day of the year in our religion, a very special day to be freed from your bonds. Perhaps you should ask her about her personal interest in being liberated by Moloch, Shadrick? You must feel so left out."

"Who *are* you?" Shad asked. "What do you want? Stop playing with us!"

"Playing with you? I'm disappointed, Shadrick. You've missed my entire point. What I'm trying to tell you"—he said, his smile fading into solemnity in an instant—"is that I'm *not* playing. I'm very, very serious. You need to understand that about me, gentlemen. I don't like games. Games are for children, and we're all adults here, correct? Now as to your first question, I apologize for not introducing myself immediately. I'm afraid I got carried away in the excitement of the moment," he said, his smile returning. "I am Nezzar, prophet of the inverted one, Baphomet." He bowed as he spoke.

"Can't say I'm pleased to meet you," Shad said. "What's Baphomet? Is that the huge goat thing down there?"

"Goat thing? *Shad*," Nezzar said. "We really must educate you on how to speak about our religions with the respect they deserve. Yes, Baphomet is the inverted one you see represented below, the axis about which the lesser gods rotate. The prince of darkness, may his wings envelope us all," Nezzar said, bowing his head. The entire group surrounding him followed suit robotically.

"I've never heard of Baphomet. Is that a new cult?" Shad decided he might as well take advantage of the predicament and learn as much as he could.

Nezzar laughed, more genuinely than any other time in the conversation. "New cult? Ah, bonded-one, your ignorance is most amusing. No, Baphomet is not new. In fact, Baphomet is the first, the prime of the rebellious, the original darkness to counter the wretched light of the world. He has many names, but we the faithful refer to him as Baphomet, the goat lord, the inverted one."

"And you're his prophet? What about the priests and high priests?"

"Ah, now we're getting to some good questions, Shad. There are no priests or high priests. There is only the prophet of Baphomet, and I am he. The normal hierarchy to which you are referring helps keep the lessers organized." Nezzar waved his hand around at the group surrounding him. "But Baphomet has no need for that. Baphomet is above all. The head, if you will."

"If Baphomet is such a big deal, why haven't I heard of him? The other cults are everywhere, but I've never seen a Baphomet idol before."

"Sadly, our backwards culture isn't ready for Baphomet just yet. But they will be soon, we're making great progress."

"So no one worships Baphomet yet?"

Nezzar laughed, prompting his posse to follow suit. "I'm sorry, I shouldn't laugh. Your questions are like those of a child! It's almost charming. Moloch, Asherah, and Baal are all servants of Baphomet. Everyone who worships one of the lesser gods is worshipping Baphomet, whether they realize it or not," he said. "You had another question, didn't you? What was it . . ."

"What do you want with us? Why are you here?"

"That's two questions, Shadrick." Nezzar held up two of his fingers. "Lucky for you, they have the same answer! I am here to tell you that we know you are here, that we know why you came, and we know what you've done. And even still, we are going to allow you to leave."

"Allow us? Is that a threat?" Deckard asked.

"You've been up here, watching our ceremonies below, correct? You've observed quite a bit. What do you think? Do you think it's a threat? Do you think anyone will leave this place unless we explicitly allow them to leave? And for those who will never leave this place, do you think they will ever be found?"

Shad and Deckard stirred angrily, but remained silent.

"Having witnessed all that you have tonight, you should both know that we have no need for *threats*," Nezzar said. "I know you recorded our religious services on your phones, but you can keep those. I wouldn't want you to forget what you saw."

A chill ran down Shad's spine as Nezzar made eye contact with him. His heart began to race, fear washing over him with the revelation that they were completely exposed. Nezzar didn't just have the upper hand, he had all of the hands. He and Deckard were completely powerless before this charming, yet ruthless man. "So, that's it? We can just leave? Right now?" Shad asked.

"Yes, you're free to go." Nezzar's attractive smile was back in all of its intoxicating glory, as he gestured to the doors behind him. "I recommend you use this passage; the press entrance will be much more pleasant than the service ladder you used before."

"Why?" Deckard asked. "If you know we have these recordings, why are you letting us go? Why aren't you just making us disappear?"

"Because *I have other plans*," Nezzar responded, speaking slowly to emphasize his words.

"You must know we're going to expose you," Shad said. "We're going to put this on the Internet, we're going to go to the cops. We're going to tell anyone who will listen about this. You're killing people. You murdered that girl! That old man, he was gutted alive. You tell people you just want to 'be free to live the lives you were called to live,' to worship 'your own way,'" he continued, making mocking air quotes. "But you're hiding the truth. And the truth is that you're taking advantage of vulnerable people, people who are desperate for meaning, for hope. People who just want to feel like they're a part of something. And you're brainwashing them, mutilating them, *killing* them! All for your vile, evil religion. People need to know the truth, and *we're going to show it to them*!" Shad screamed the last words.

Nezzar took a few deliberate steps forward and looked Shad right in his eyes, never blinking a single time. "Go ahead."

"Wh–what?"

Nezzar laughed. "Go ahead. No one will believe you. They will call you hateful, ignorant, bigot. You'll be completely isolated and ostracized. And then we'll crush you, Shadrick," he said, his voice absent any anger or rage, which made it far more intimidating. "You know nothing about the world you've barged into, that you're attempting to disrupt. These powers, these principalities, they are *absolute darkness*. And they rule this world," Nezzar narrowed his eyes. "After you launch your little crusade and it fails completely, it will have been as futile as a mouse attacking a serpent. You won't just lose; you will be *consumed*. You and everything that you love. But, Shad, my friend"—he smiled again—"it doesn't have to be that way. You can join us. I don't even care to which of the gods you bend your knee, take your pick. All you need to do is submit. Abandon your self-righteous quest, bonded-one. Pledge your allegiance and be liberated. If you do, I can guarantee that you and your family will be protected."

"Go to hell," Shad said through clenched teeth.

"Are you sure? No do-overs, no second chances. It's now, or never." Shad stood silently, fuming. Nezzar pantomimed washing his hands, wiping them together. "OK, I gave you the choice, Shad. Remember that. So, go ahead and carry on with your grand plan. I want you to see what happens. I want you to know—and not just to know, I want you to *feel* the pointlessness of your *witch hunt*," Nezzar said, stepping back to his place next to his two imposing guards.

"We have video. Video of that man getting disemboweled. Video of that young woman being molested and having her throat slit," Shad said. "And you think that doesn't matter?"

"I *know* it doesn't matter, Shadrick," Nezzar said.

"You're wrong. You think you're invincible? People are going to see the truth and they're not going to tolerate this garbage anymore. They're going to see through your lies. They're going to see that these cults are nothing but a bunch of psychopaths preying on the weak! And we're going to put a stop to this barbaric madness. When this is over, every idol will be torn down and smashed. These cults will be extinct."

"Is that a threat?" said Lord Malochus, who was still standing next to Nezzar.

Shad turned to him. "That's not a threat, that's a promise. *Stay away from my family.*"

"Oh, we will, Shadrick," Nezzar, said his hands raised in a symbol of contrition. "I already told you; we won't lift a finger to pursue Alina. But we can't prevent her from coming to us. Or from bringing your sweet daughter Isla along with her."

"I'll kill you!" Shad screamed, lunging forward. Deckard grabbed him by the shoulders to hold him back as both guards again closed ranks in front of Nezzar, who was laughing loudly.

"Time to go, gentlemen. It has been an *absolute pleasure*," Nezzar said. "Until next time, I bid you both farewell." He turned around and walked away through the double doors without a moment's hesitation or a second look back. The group of cult clergy and guards all followed closely behind him, each of them completely disregarding Shad and Deckard as they stood flabbergasted, as if they had disappeared from the platform. Deckard let go of Shad, who relaxed from his fighting posture. The doors closed and the sounds of the group descending the staircase began to fade, leaving only the ambient sounds of the continuing festival taking place far below.

"I guess we should go," Deckard said.

"Did that just happen? What just happened?" Shad said.

"I can't believe this night started with us getting drunk, smoking cigarettes, and eating steaks on my back porch. I thought we'd come down here, make fun of some culties, maybe get into a fight and get thrown out. I never thought it was the dawn of a crucible," Deckard said.

"It was like an avalanche. It just kept going and going, getting bigger and bigger, and before we knew it, we got buried. And now we have to find a way to dig ourselves out."

"I don't know, Shad. He was pretty confident. I don't know what we've gotten ourselves into."

"I don't have a choice. I have to try to convince Alina, I have to try to keep her far away from this. You saw what I saw, man. What if it was her on that table? What if it was her on that post? Or Isla?" Shad said, his voice breaking when he spoke his daughter's name. "I have to do everything I can to stop this, I have to try and protect my family. You don't have to help me, Deckard. I won't hold it against you. I mean that. Just send me that video you recorded and I'll do the rest. You can just go home and forget about all of this."

"No amount of alcohol or hypnosis or mystical peyote journeys in the desert would be enough to erase this night from my memory. Don't get me wrong, you can bet good money I'm gonna try. But I know I'll fail. And I couldn't live with myself if I knew I let you do this alone. I'll help you however I can, old friend. I already queued up the video to send to you once I get signal and set it all to back up to the cloud."

"Thanks, brother. I owe you," Shad said. "Let's get out of this hellhole."

"You think he was telling the truth about Alina?" Deckard asked as delicately as he could manage.

"I don't want to believe it, but my gut says he was. It lines up, that's why it pissed me off so much. Some of the pictures she showed me make a lot more sense now that I know she probably took them herself," Shad said, shaking his head. "How could I have missed this? My own wife, right under my nose, exploring an entirely new *religion*." He entered the double doors and started down the well-lit stairwell. "I was just on cruise control. Went to work, came home, played with Isla, had some small talk over dinner, watched TV, scrolled through my phone, went to bed, woke up, went to work. Same thing every day. I got complacent, I got lazy. I forgot to connect with my wife, to actually talk with her. I had no idea this kind of thing was even on her radar, you know? I thought she was happy. I was happy, or at least I was content. Totally clueless, that's what I was. My own wife was struggling right in front of me and I missed it. And these culties swept in and gave her the support she needed."

"Don't drag yourself for it now, Shad. You can't go back. The important thing is what you do about it today. That's our priority, we've got to show her that this isn't just some harmless new religion, this is evil," Deckard said as they reached the bottom of the stairs, which opened back onto the concourse. In front of them was another set of doors leading into the arena, where the familiar thumping of drums greeted them like an old friend. This portion of the concourse was mostly clean and free of debris, with all of the overhead lights functioning, giving new life to the aging facility. While it was free of boxes and livestock equipment that filled the rest of the concourse they had explored, this area was filled with busily moving people and their corresponding sounds. Talking, walking, moving, laughing—it almost felt like a window back in time to when the Under Yards were heavily used by the local community, except instead of cowboys and businessmen, it was clergy and worshippers from each of the three cults making their way around the area. Along some of the walls were more tables where offerings and other religious items were being sold. There was also another concession stand like the one where Shad had fallen, except it was lit, staffed, and fully active, selling food and drinks to the festivalgoers who were in need sustenance after whatever rigorous ritual they'd recently performed.

"We're not too far from where we entered. I think it's down that way," Shad said, pointing to their right.

Deckard pointed to an area about thirty yards to their left. "I guess we know how they got all those huge idol pieces in here," he said, gesturing to huge roll-up garage doors.

"And all of these people too," Shad responded, pointing a little further down at a huge entrance, complete with turnstiles and a neon sign that read "The Under Yards." Just like the entrance to the park, people were coming in and being screened by priests and priestesses from each of the cults. "I guess we used the service entrance?"

"Where does that lead topside? I didn't see a big group of people except around the idols. How are people getting down here? And the garage doors, where are the entrances for trucks to bring down equipment?"

"There must be another building where they're all entering and coming down. Obviously, this is a VIP, high-ranking thing, they're not just letting any random cultie down here. They're hiding it somehow," Shad said.

"These can't all be locals, right?" Deckard asked. "We don't have *this many* culties in Mapleton, do we?"

"I think we're a hub for the cults in the region, so I'm sure a lot of these people came here from out of town just for the festival. Especially if they're VIPs like that Dink psycho, they're probably willing to travel for the special kinds of offerings they make here," Shad said. He began making his way down the concourse away from the crowd to find the entrance they had used earlier that night. They reached the end of this main concourse and lobby where the path had been cordoned off with metal cattle fencing. They scaled the barrier and continued, looking for the doors where they had covertly entered earlier. Encountering no more surprises, they found the doors and exited the concourse. Once they mounted the stairs, they both realized just how exhausted they were after their eventful, sometimes frenzied evening. They both pushed through their fatigue, reached the top of the stairs and cautiously entered the Cold Storage 4 building, leery of meeting another group of cult members escorting a new offering. The building was still and silent, so they took a moment to catch their breath and then continued to retrace the path they'd followed earlier back to the door with the rusty push-bar lock. Deckard and Shad stopped just outside the building, breathing in the early-morning air, happy to be back above ground. Sunrise was still a couple hours away, so the park was just as dark as when they had entered the building hours earlier.

"Is your phone still on? I think mine's dead," Shad said.

Deckard pulled his phone out of his pocket. "Yeah, it's on low battery mode, though, so I can't upload anything from here."

"All right, let's get back to your house so we can start throwing this all online as soon as possible. And then we can pass out on your fancy couches," Shad said, beginning a light jog toward the park entrance. The cool, fresh air felt great in their lungs, even though their tired muscles were complaining with each movement. They reached the entrance path where the braziers continued to burn brightly and they stopped to get their bearings. Deckard pulled out his phone.

"I'm going to see if I can get Lexi back here," he said, looking down at his phone. Shad stood next to him, his hands resting on the top of his head as he caught his breath from the jog back. He spotted a pair of police officers walking up the festival path in their direction and seemed to catch their eye. They began walking in his direction.

"Hey, there's a couple cops over there, I'm going to see how I can file a report," Shad said, setting off toward the police as Deckard continued messing with his phone.

"Oh no . . . Shad, stop! Shad!" Deckard said, just as Shad reached the officers. He looked back over his shoulder to Deckard and waved him off.

"Hello officers. Um, I'm not really sure how to say this, but how do I report a crime? Can I do that with you, or do I need to call, or go to the police station?" Shad said. Having never even received a speeding ticket in his life, he quickly realized he'd never really interacted with law enforcement directly and wasn't sure how to conduct himself.

"Oh, you have a crime to report, do you?" said the officer on Shad's left, a stocky woman. Her tone was much more aggressive than Shad expected and it threw him off even more.

"I'm sorry? Uh, yes, I do have a crime to report. Can you help me?"

"We can definitely help you, you bigot, put your hands behind your back!" said the officer on Shad's right, a middle-aged man, sporting the stereotypical beat-cop look, complete with a receding hairline, paunchy midsection, and a push-broom mustache.

"Wait, what? What's going on? I need your help, what are you doing?" Shad did his best to comply, but the officer who was cuffing him wasn't hiding his disapproval in his rough demeanor. "I witnessed two murders! I have video, my phone is dead but my friend can show you. He's just over . . ." Shad looked over to where Deckard had been earlier, desperate for an ally who could clear up what must be a misunderstanding. Deckard was gone.

Chapter 11

SHAD LOOKED AROUND THE area as best as he could while being man-handled by the officer, expecting to find Deckard looking at his phone, oblivious to Shad's predicament. He looked everywhere around him, but Deckard was nowhere to be found.

"Stop squirming. You witnessed some murders, huh? Sure, you did, you anti-alt prick. You're under arrest for making criminal threats and for aggravated malicious harassment." The officer then proceeded to read him his rights. "Where is that friend of yours? We'd like to have a talk with him too."

Having seen plenty of cop shows on TV, Shad decided to keep his mouth shut. After cuffing him, the mustached officer patted him down and emptied his pockets. Shad winced when he patted his back. "What's your deal?" the officer said.

"I'm hurt, I have a cut," Shad said.

"Oh, of course you do . . ." the officer said sarcastically before lifting up the back of Shad's shirt. "Ah crap, Booth, call it in. We're gonna have to run this idiot by the ER before we book him."

"What? That'll be like twice the paperwork," said the female officer, apparently named Booth.

"Yeah, I know. This cut looks pretty bad. Hope it hurts, douche," said the male officer, dropping Shad's shirt back down.

"I have a lawyer, please call my lawyer," Shad said.

"What was that?" Booth asked.

"My front left pocket, there's a business card. Tom Rodriguez. That's my lawyer, please call him."

"Hold it," she said to the other officer. "If this is some kind of play, you're gonna regret it," she said. Booth patted him down and then delicately reached into his pocket to retrieve the card. "He was telling the truth," she said to the other officer as she placed the card in her pocket. "Your lawyer will be notified of your arrest when we book you."

The male officer grunted and grabbed Shad's arm and led him toward the park entrance. Booth spoke into a radio, notifying the dispatcher that they had made an arrest but that the perp was injured, so they would be stopping at the hospital downtown before they brought Shad into the police station. Shad was grateful that it was as late—or as early—as it was, since there were much fewer people at the entrance to the park than there were when he and Deckard had entered. The small crowd that was there watched him be escorted out attentively, many looking at their phones and pointing at him, while others recorded his walk of shame with their cameras. Unlike so many other situations, the police didn't seem to mind being recorded this time and even gave off an air of pride as they pushed Shad along toward their patrol car. Booth opened the rear driver's side door and the other officer pushed Shad into the back seat. With a grunt of pain, he landed roughly in the uncomfortable, well-worn bench on his right shoulder and back, aggravating his cut.

"Come on Christiansen, get your act together!" Booth scolded.

"Get over yourself, Booth. He's fine," Christiansen said. He got into the driver's seat and Booth walked around to the passenger door. As they drove away from the park, Shad tried to avoid looking outside where onlookers continued to record him through the smudged and hazy police car windows. *What is going on? What was he even talking about? And why the hell is everyone looking at me like I'm a celebrity getting arrested?* Shad thought, his mind and heart racing. He was pumped full of adrenaline again; he couldn't even count how many times that had happened that night. Closing his eyes, he focused on breathing and tried to calm himself down.

"Don't get too comfortable back there, chump. The hospital is just a few blocks away and Booth already let them know we're coming. After they patch you up you can cozy up in a cell at the station," Christiansen said. Shad ignored him and continued to take deep breaths to slow his heart rate and calm the torrential flow of thoughts in his head. Try as he might, he couldn't figure out why he was under arrest. He'd heard the charges, of course, but to what did they refer?

Christiansen wasn't lying; within a few minutes they arrived at the doors of the emergency room at Mapleton Mercy Medical Center. Since Shad wasn't an emergency, they parked in a normal parking spot and

Christiansen extricated him from the back of the cruiser. The ogling continued in the lobby of the emergency room, again with people looking at their phones, looking at Shad, and either talking or recording him. He continued to walk compliantly with Christiansen as they were checked in at the reception desk.

Three doctors refused to treat Shad. The first said she "wouldn't be party to aiding a hateful bigot" with a nasty scowl on her face. The second said "if he hates people like me so much, he can stitch himself up" before he walked away haughtily. The third was the least confrontational and actually apologized, saying "I'm sorry, but my nurses are alts and they would never forgive me," before she left. Finally, the fourth doctor came out. A grizzled older man, he walked out with a chart in his hand and didn't even look up from it when he called Shad's name. As they stood up from the chairs, he turned around and made his way to an exam room without greeting them. The officers led Shad down the hall and into the room, where he sat on the exam table.

"Go ahead and uncuff him so I can take a look at what I have to work with," said the doctor. He looked to be in his late fifties or early sixties, and based on his apathetic attitude, he'd been working in the emergency room for a long time.

"No can do, doc," said Christiansen, relishing his moment of power. "He's under arrest for making threats. That's considered dangerous, he's gotta stay restrained."

"Fine, then uncuff him so he can get his shirt off and then cuff him to the table. Then wait outside. I'm not a lawyer but I know he's got a right to some privacy here in this hospital." The officer scowled a little and hesitated. "I've been through this before, officer. I know how it works. You don't need to be in the room, especially if he's restrained. So please wait outside." Christiansen didn't budge. "You want me to stitch him up or not?" Booth stepped forward and uncuffed Shad so that he could remove his shirt. She then cuffed his left hand to a handle on the exam table.

"Let's go, Christiansen," she said. "He's not going anywhere. And even if he tried, we're in a hospital. This guy isn't an escape artist."

"We'll be just outside, tool bag. Don't get any ideas," Christiansen said, before reluctantly following Booth out of the exam room.

When the door closed with the officers outside, the doctor breathed a heavy sigh. "Now then, let's get you taken care of young man," he said as he began looking at the wound on Shad's back. "Somebody gave you some decent first aid. How did you get this cut? It's pretty jagged and ugly, clearly not a blade."

"I fell down an old ladder, caught myself on a bolt," Shad said, wincing as the doctor probed the wound with gloved fingers.

"So between a rusty bolt in the back and falling off of a ladder, you chose the bolt?" he asked. Shad nodded affirmatively. "Must have been a tall ladder."

"Yes sir, it was."

Shad scowled and groaned as the doctor began to clean the wound. "I'm going to put some local anesthetic here. I've cleaned the surface, but I need to dig in and make sure there's no debris inside the wound before I stitch you up. You're going to have a hell of a scar. Do you know if you've had a tetanus shot recently?" Shad shook his head that he didn't. "Then we'll get you one before you leave."

"Um, doctor, can I ask you something? Something not, uh, medical?"

"You can ask whatever you want, but I'm not going to promise I'll answer," he said.

"Do you know why everyone seems to hate me? I know what they said when I was arrested, but I really don't know what they're talking about. People keep looking at their phones and recording me. The cops took my phone and it was out of battery anyway, so I have no idea what's going on."

The doctor laughed. "So they nabbed you before you even saw it, huh? The nurses showed me when they handed me your chart and told me no one wanted to treat you. Guess I was the last resort. Apparently, I'm the only doctor who remembers the Hippocratic oath." After placing his medical instruments on a steel tray and removing his blue gloves, the doctor pulled out his cell phone. He grumbled to himself as he tapped the screen. "Ah, there it is," he said, turning the phone to Shad so that he could see it. "Looks like it's up on all of the social media websites, or apps, or whatever they're called."

Shad's jaw dropped. He was staring at a video of himself, there on the veteran doctor's scratched-up cell phone screen. The video was shot from the side, somewhere to Shad's right. The doctor hit the play button, and Shad's recorded voice filled the exam room: "You think you're invincible? People are going to see the truth and they're not going to tolerate this garbage anymore. They're going to see through your lies. They're going to see that these cults are nothing but a bunch of psychopaths preying on the weak! And we're going to put a stop to this barbaric madness.

When this is over, every idol will be torn down and smashed. These cults will be extinct."

Shad winced, knowing exactly how it looked. The camera turned to Lord Malochus, who stood such that Nezzar was blocked from view by his hooded figure: "Is that a threat?" said Lord Malochus.

The camera returned to Shad: "That's not a threat, that's a promise. I'll kill you!" The video stopped playing just after Shad lunged in the direction of Lord Malochus, and the doctor locked the screen and replaced it in his white coat pocket.

"Oh no . . ." Shad buried his face in his hands. Nezzar had baited him. They'd been recording him the whole time, hoping he'd lose control and say something terrible. And that's exactly what he did. They'd edited the video at exactly the right times. It was perfect.

"That you?" asked the doctor, putting on a new set of blue medical gloves.

"Yeah, but that's not the whole story. I mean, it's not everything I said. That's totally out of context."

"It usually is on the Internet. Little pinch here," he said before poking a needle in Shad's back. He grimaced but remained still as the doctor worked.

"Look kid, I wouldn't say I'm exactly on the same page as you. You seemed pretty pissed off there and I'm definitely not on board with making any people extinct," the doctor said. "However, I will say that I can empathize. Somewhat."

"If you only knew," Shad said.

"Maybe, but before you go on, you should remember that the cops can subpoena me. Doctor-patient confidentiality does exist, but they'll push. Also, I guarantee that walrus of a cop out there has his ear to the door right now, so I'd recommend you focus on listening more than talking. Sound good?" Shad nodded in response.

"Good. Now, where was I? Oh yes, I can empathize. Do you know how many of those stupid Baalists I treat every day? I can't even count how many come in here, trying to get their fingers sewed back on because they decided they didn't want to offer them to Baal after all. Pretty much every night now I get at least two of them passed out from blood loss because they cut themselves too deep." He stepped around to face Shad with his gloved right hand held up. "Hand to God, they brought one in two days ago who had already bled out. They dragged this little guy in here, maybe twenty years old, couldn't have weighed more than 110 pounds. He was as white as the paper you're sitting on. Two gouges in his wrists, must've squirted out like a fire hydrant. Poor idiot probably had a pint of blood left in his entire sorry corpse. I had to waste my time confirming the obvious to those clowns who call themselves priests. Such a waste of life," the doctor continued as he worked on Shad's wound. "I've been working emergencies and trauma for thirty years. Longer than you've been alive. I've stitched up thousands of wounds like yours. I've saved countless lives. I'm not bragging, it's just a fact, bullet points on my résumé. When you've seen what I've seen and done what I've done, you learn to appreciate the value of life. The real emergencies I deal with, these are people who didn't choose to come in here. They had a car accident, or they fell off of a bike, or their house caught on fire while they were sleeping. Those people are desperate to live and I'm desperate to keep them alive. I fight like hell for every person who comes in here with even a thread of life left in them. And sometimes we can save them, but a lot of times we can't." His voice cracked a little, and he took a deep breath before he continued. "And when these moronic cutters come in here, squandering their perfectly good lives, cutting up their perfectly good bodies for some statue," he sighed, "it just ticks me off, the waste of it all. For nothing."

He stepped back around, his hands pointed upward with some of Shad's blood on the fingers. "You know one of those idiots actually scheduled an appointment and came in to ask me to teach him how to cut himself 'safely'? I asked him, 'Do you know what 'do no harm' means, kid?' He was so shocked that I'd say no. I told him there is no safe way to cut yourself, there's always a risk, and I sent him packing. I'm not going to teach you how to mutilate yourself, you fool boy. You'll probably be done with this religion in a month, you'll move on to the next hip thing. And you want to do permanent damage to yourself for this passing trend? Because all of your friends are doing it? Because of some girl you like? The gall, the absolute disrespect! To squander this gift, it's reprehensible!" The doctor growled in anger, then returned to his work.

After giving him a moment, Shad spoke. "It's so much worse than you know. That's all I'll tell you, but I promise you'd be even angrier if you saw what I saw."

"Well, once you get this sorted out," the doctor said, tapping the handcuffs, "you come back here so I can check on this cut and you can tell me about it." Shad heard him drumming on his skin. "Feel that at all?"

"Nope."

"Good. I'm going to stitch you up, put a bandage on you, and then you're back with Officer Sunshine."

"Thank you, Doctor . . . I'm sorry, I never asked your name."

"Doctor Gaines. Funny, most patients in here never ask for my name. Never get a chance, you know with the bleeding and all that." Gaines chuckled at his own joke. Shad heard the sound of tape unrolling and felt pressure on his back. "Done. Fifteen stitches. Not the most I've ever done by a long shot, but that's a decent wound. Keep it clean and come back here in two weeks. Ask for me."

"Thank you, Doctor Gaines. Thank you for even being willing to treat me, I really do appreciate it."

"Keep your head up, kid. You seem like a good egg, you'll get this cleared up," Doctor Gaines said as he took off his gloves and threw them into the medical waste bin. He went to the door and knocked on it twice. It opened immediately and Officer Christiansen entered the room, clearly eager to get Shad back in his sight. "He's all yours, Officer." Christiansen walked over to Shad and unlocked the cuff from the table and placed it back on his other wrist, locking his hands behind his back.

"You mean Officer Walrus?" Christiansen said to Doctor Gaines with a scowl. The doctor erupted in laughter. Shad stifled his laugh, fearing retribution.

"Told you to shave that ugly thing," Booth said with a smirk.

"Shove it, Booth."

Christiansen led Shad out of the room, through the hallway and lobby, and back to the car. Fifteen minutes later, they were in the parking lot of the police station and Christiansen was again removing Shad from the back seat that felt like it was made of concrete. Shad went through the standard booking process, mug shot and all, and was placed in a group cell with a half dozen other men. One was vomiting enthusiastically into the shared toilet. Another was passed out on the bench against the wall. Two others were talking quietly in a corner. One older man sat against the wall, silent but alert. The final man was very big and looked very angry, pacing back and forth in the cell with a terrible scowl on his face.

Shad sat in an empty spot on the bench near the sleeper and tried his best to keep to himself. He hoped that none of these men were members of one of the cults, or that they were locked up before the video of his tirade went viral. *It's still really early. Maybe Alina hasn't seen it yet. If I can get my call, I can talk to her before she sees it and explain myself.* As Shad sat lost in his thoughts, a tired-looking, middle-aged woman walked up to the bars of the cell.

"Cool your heels, big guy. I'm opening this up, and if I get even the slightest impression you're heading my way, I'll put you down without a second thought," she said to the angry pacing man. He snarled at her, but he stopped moving on the opposite side of the cell. "Bengoade, Shadrick. Get up, you're coming with me." Startled at the sound of his name, Shad got up and walked to the cell door. "All right Danny, open it up," the woman said to someone down the hall. The cell door began to open. "Turn around, Bengoade." She pulled cuffs out of her back pocket. Shad complied, and she cuffed his hands behind his back.

"What's this about? Who are you?"

"I'm Detective Caceres. I caught your case, so I get the distinct privilege of asking you some questions," she said, leading Shad down the hall. They passed a few closed doors and finally came to one that was open. Inside was a metal table with two chairs on either side, lit with the familiarly brutal white light unique to buzzing fluorescent tubes. There were no windows—no windows to the outdoors, at least. There was one mirrored window, and Shad had seen enough television and movies to know that was an observation room which likely also housed a video camera and more police. He also spotted a camera up in the far corner of the room, its light winking at him every few seconds, indicating it was live. "You going to give me trouble, Bengoade? The report says you didn't resist and you're not violent, so I don't mind uncuffing you as long as you're not going to make me regret it."

"No trouble. And you can call me Shad, that's what everyone calls me."

"Good answer, Shad," she said, uncuffing him before leading him to the chair that faced the one-way mirror. "What kind of name is Shadrick Bengoade anyway? Never heard that one before. Some kind of Eastern European?" she said as she sat down with her back to the mirror and placed a manila folder and a black plastic bag on the table in front of her.

"Honestly, I'm not sure. My parents just always told us we were Americans. I think my great-grandparents were from somewhere in the Middle East, but that's all I ever learned."

"Fair enough. Let's get started, Shad. Do you know why you're in here?"

"I think so. There's a video on the Internet of me."

"Yup, it's on the Internet. Getting a lot of play, you're a little famous this morning. But specifically, Lord Malochus called the police after you were thrown out of the Blood Moon Equinox festival by his private security. He also sent us the video."

"I wasn't thrown out, I left on my own."

"Toe-may-toe, toe-mah-toe," she said.

"Does anyone actually call them toe-mah-toes?" Shad said, partly out of impatience, but also because he was feeling introspective and was thinking too much about everything.

"Is now really the best time to have a bad attitude, Shad?"

"Sorry, it's been a long night."

"I get it, long night of threatening alts and then getting arrested for it."

"Do you have my phone?"

"You'll get your call soon enough. My questions come first," Detective Caceres said.

"Not for a call. I have video on my phone that will exonerate me."

"Is that a fact? How convenient!"

"Get my phone or call my lawyer." Shad crossed his arms in front of his chest.

"That's how you're going to play it, Shad? We're just having a conversation here." Detective Caceres adjusted to a conciliatory tone. "I just want to know why you were there and what you meant by what you said on the video. Maybe this was just a misunderstanding. I'm sure we can talk with Lord Malochus about dropping charges if you apologize and explain that you just lost your temper. Too much to drink. You and that friend of yours were pretty lit, right? Who was that friend, by the way?"

"What friend?"

"Shad, don't be like that. Make this easy for both of us. It's too early for games. Or late, right? Have you gotten any sleep? Let's get this over with and I'll get you a cell all by yourself away from all of those weirdos so you can get some rest. What do you say?"

"Get my phone or call my lawyer." The detective lifted up the manila folder and pulled out the plastic bag that had been beneath it. She opened the bag and pulled out Shad's phone.

"This phone?"

"It's dead, you'll need to charge it," Shad said. She responded by pulling a phone-sized battery out of her pocket.

"Do I look like a rookie, Shad?" she said, plugging his phone into the backup battery. The screen popped on with the charging indicator. "Now we'll just give this a couple minutes to charge. Want some coffee? I'm going to get some coffee." Shad nodded in the affirmative. "Black?"

"Two creams, two sugars."

"Black it is." She walked out of the room and left Shad by himself. He wondered for a moment if this was some kind of test. If he went for the phone, would she burst in and cuff him again? *It's not illegal to use my own phone. I know they're recording me, so it's not like I can hide. If she asks, I'll tell her the truth.* He thought to himself. Taking one last look at the door, he took his phone and turned it on. Seconds dragged into hours in his mind as the phone's logo sat on the screen during its boot-up process. Shad felt himself begin to sweat, and once again his heart was racing from adrenaline. His eyes kept snapping back and forth from the phone screen to the door; he was sure he was going to get caught in the act. Finally, his home screen came to life. He immediately swiped to his photo app. Selecting everything from that night, he sent it all to the cloud folder that Deckard had set up. He also set everything to back up to his personal cloud folders, which were encrypted and passworded. Now he knew that even if the police took his phone, Deckard could still send it out. Shad then deleted all of the texts between himself and Deckard from earlier that weekend so that the most recent text with his friend was Deckard's standard birthday message: *Happy Birthday, dude.*

Caceres still hadn't come back and Shad had already accomplished his goal, so he felt kind of stupid for panicking the way that he had. Feeling aimless, he decided to comfort himself by looking at photos of Isla and Alina. Even after Nezzar had revealed Alina's secrets, even after their fight, her leaving, her hostility, even after she threw away the flowers he'd brought her—all of that baggage couldn't suffocate his love for her. Knowing that she'd been searching so sincerely for meaning, she'd felt such a deep need, and knowing that he'd been completely oblivious to it made Shad feel a desperate, contrite devotion for her. He wanted more than anything to redeem himself to her, to show her that she wasn't alone, that he could help, and they could find that meaning she was seeking together. She didn't need Moloch or any idol; their love had been enough for them both before. It could be enough again.

Before he even realized what was happening, a tear slipped down his cheek, followed by another. And then he was quietly crying, staring at a photo of their family vacation from six months before. Even though they hadn't gone out of town or done anything particularly special, it had been such a perfect time. During the days they had gone to the zoo, the local arboretum, the aquarium, and so many parks, taking advantage of all of Mapleton's sites and attractions that they had always been too busy to enjoy. The weather had been flawless, and each day was idyllic; beautiful memories of Isla running and laughing while Alina and Shad held hands and basked in their daughter's joy and wonder. The nights after Isla had been put to bed were peaceful and content, with Shad and Alina sharing drinks, telling stories, catching up on shows, and sincerely enjoying each other in the way that married couples should. The photos from that week filled Shad with such a warm delight that he lost himself in the moment, so much so that he didn't even realize Caceres was standing in front of him, holding two steaming cups of coffee. She cleared her throat, and he nearly jumped out of his chair, fumbling with the phone and clumsily wiping tears from his cheeks.

"Oh, I, uh, I'm sorry, I just—I wanted to—I'm sorry." He handed her the phone. "I wanted to see my family."

"That's OK, Shad. To be honest, I wanted you to do that. It's important for you to remember what you have to lose," she said, taking the phone from him.

You have no idea, lady, Shad thought. "Yeah, thanks."

"I did what you asked. I brought out your phone. It's charging, it's turned on. What's on here that's so important?" asked the detective, tapping on the locked phone screen. Shad held his hand out for the phone. She handed it to him, and he unlocked it again. He swiped back into his photos, found the video of the teenage girl and the Asherians, and tapped to play it. He raised the volume and turned the phone on its side so that the detective could see it more clearly. The phone's microphone hadn't captured much beyond the sound of drums beating and the ambient noise of cult worshippers, but the camera had captured more than enough detail to prove his point. Shad watched her face as the ritual progressed.

"I watched this happen. I recorded it. This took place before the conversation in the video that Malochus sent." Caceres didn't respond, she just kept watching the screen. She grimaced, visibly sickened by what she saw. Shad could tell she was keeping a tight rein on her emotions, trying to stifle her reactions so that she could continue to keep her cards close to the chest. The blood drained from her face, and Shad knew she'd just watched the girl's throat get slit open. "Are you starting to understand my side of the story now?" Caceres looked up from the screen and made eye contact with him.

"No, I'm not, Shad." She took the phone out of his hand, stopped the video, and turned the phone completely off. "All I saw were the alternative religious celebrating their freedom to live and worship as they please," said the detective, placing his phone back in the plastic bag. "And this may disappoint someone like you, but everything I saw was perfectly legal." She pushed her chair back and stood up. "Furthermore, as people continue to educate themselves, everything I saw will become increasingly accepted by our society. Eventually the ignorant like you will come around. What's not legal, Shadrick, is to make threats against people for their religious beliefs. You need to do better, *be better*." She stood in front of him, looking down with her arms crossed as she lectured him. "We've already spoken to the district attorney, and they're ready to pursue hate-crime charges against you. We have you dead to rights on trespassing and harassment, Shad. The hate-crime charges might not stick, but the headlines definitely will. This video is going viral even as we speak. Now, of course, I'm a proponent of a fair and unbiased justice system! But we can't control what members of a jury see on the Internet and how those things influence their opinions." Shad was flabbergasted. He was absolutely sure the video would be his get-out-of-jail-free card, but the detective was unmoved. *She's one of them. She has to be, there's no other way.* He thought to himself. He'd played his trump card, and it was a dud.

"I'm not a psychic, but I'm pretty sure I can predict how this video is going to impact a jury of your peers, buddy, and it isn't good for you. Before you respond, I'm going to take you back to a cell so you can get some rest and think this over. You need to get ahead of this, Shad. We're giving you a chance to clear this up. You should take it."

She walked over to him and motioned for him to stand up. Once he did, she replaced the cuffs on his hands and grabbed his arm to lead him out of the room. They passed the group cell where the scenery was just as they left it, the pacing angry guy eyeing them both maliciously as they walked. Rounding the corner, they entered a corridor of individual cells. Caceres stopped at an empty one and looked back over her shoulder to a camera. "Open seven." A buzzer responded, and the cell lock clicked, signaling it was now disengaged.

The detective turned back to Shad, leaning in at a somewhat odd angle, her head down near his shoulder. "Don't react to what I'm about to say. Stand here as if I'm not saying anything at all. If you react, I'll have to tase you and act like you were attempting to overpower me. If you understand, clear your throat." Shad's eyes were wide open with surprise, but he complied. "I'm sure you saw that mirrored glass and you know that's not just there so you can look at your own pretty face. My chief was behind that glass and he's got a hard-on for you and your case. Why? Because he's a Molochian. Malochus sent that video of you directly to him," she said, fumbling with his cuffs. "Stop wiggling, Bengoade, if you keep struggling, I'm going to tase you," she said loudly.

"I'm sorry, detective, I'm just tired and these cuffs are tight," he said, playing along.

Caceres continued whispering as she unlocked and removed the cuffs. "There are a lot of us on the force that know there's something going on with these cults and your recording confirms it. You need to understand that this is a lot bigger than Malochus and our local temples. There are some very powerful people way beyond Mapleton who are on their side, pulling strings, protecting them, pushing their agenda at every level. I meant what I said. You can't beat this, not head-on. And especially not locked up in here," she whispered. She put her cuffs in her pocket and pushed Shad into the cell. "Think about what I told you, Shad. I'll be back in a half hour so you can make your call." They made eye contact before she left, and Shad nodded to her subtly.

After she turned and left, he lay down on the thin cot. His mind was racing, but he was completely spent. The night had made his adrenal glands work overtime, producing more than they probably had in his whole life. He had so much to think about, so much to figure out, so much to plan for his call to Alina, but he just had nothing left. Closing his eyes, he fell immediately into a dreamless sleep.

Chapter 12

"RISE AND SHINE" DETECTIVE Caceres tapped on the cell door with the toe of her shoe. When that didn't rouse him, she clapped a few times. "Time to make your phone call, Bengoade."

Shad shot up from the cot, completely confused by his surroundings. He sat for a moment, blearily looking around as he cleared away the fog of sleep and his mind caught up to reality. "How long was I asleep?"

"I let you grab an hour or two. You were out cold; I've been standing here a while making noise. I guess you need some rest, but I thought you'd want to try and make your call sooner than later."

"Yes, thank you. I've got to try and reach my wife."

"Stand up and put your hands through the slot," she said, pointing at a rectangular opening in the cell door. Shad stood up unsteadily, took a deep breath, shook his head to remove the last vestiges of slumber, and did as the detective asked. She replaced the cuffs on his wrists and turned to the camera in the ceiling. "Open seven." The buzzer sounded again, and the lock disengaged. After opening the door, she grabbed Shad's arm again and escorted him out of the cell. They walked down a couple more corridors until they arrived at a bay of pay phones.

"These belong in a museum," Shad said, looking at the anachronistic technology.

"It's either these or carrier pigeons. Your choice," said the detective as she handed him the appropriate change to use the phone.

"Thanks. How long do I have?"

"It's slow now and I have some emails to catch up on, so I'll give you a warning when it's time to go, all right?" She walked over and sat down on a bench along the opposite wall, pulled out her cell, and began thumbing the screen furiously. Shad stood still for a moment and stared at the scuffed-up phone in front of him. He was more terrified of this call than any of the horrors that he'd encountered the night before. He didn't know what to say. How could he even start? Where would he begin? Would she answer and give him a chance to speak? Palms moist with anxious sweat, he picked up the sticky receiver and placed it to his ear as he slid the coins into the slot with his other hand. Audible clicks registered his payment, clearing the way for him to dial her number. His index finger hovered over the first digit. He stood, frozen in place.

"Pull the Band-Aid off, Bengoade. You don't have much time, don't waste it being a coward," Detective Caceres said from the bench behind him. Bracing, Shad dialed Alina's number. It began to ring once, twice, three times. His heart began to sink. *She's not going to answer. It's a weird phone number she's never seen, she'll probably ignore it, thinking it's someone trying to sell an extended car warranty. Or what if her phone shows it's from the jail?* he thought in the time it took for the phone to ring a fourth time. Suddenly, the ringing stopped with a click.

"Hello?" Alina said on the other end of the line.

"Alina, I'm so glad you answered. Please don't hang up," Shad said more quickly than he had intended.

"Shad, is that you?"

"Yes, please just listen to me. I went to the Blood Moon Equinox festival in the park yesterday. I got arrested, I'm in jail. But that's not important right now. What's important is what I saw, Alina. The cults, they're not what you think they are. They're evil. They're violent. They're killing people, for real. Gutting them, cutting their arms off. I saw it, you have to stay away." He blurted it all without taking a breath.

"Shad. Stop. What you're saying is *insane*. I saw the video already. I had so many people send it to me before I was even awake. All of my social media accounts are absolutely swamped. I'm getting DMs from reporters. People even sent it to my mom!" Alina said. "What you said in that video was disgusting, Shad. I'm glad they arrested you! I'm so embarrassed, I don't even know what to say. I hope this is a reality check. Look where your hate got you! You're in jail, Shad! What am I supposed to tell Isla?"

"No, Alina, that video isn't real. I mean, it's real, but it's not everything."

"It's not real? Are you saying it's like a deepfake or something?"

"No, it's not a deepfake, that's not what I meant. I meant it *is* real, but they edited it, it didn't happen like that. Alina, did you hear what I said? They're killing people, I saw it! You have to stay away!"

"Killing people? Get real, Shadrick. You'll say anything to cover your hate, won't you? Just leave us alone. I don't even know you anymore."

"Alina, please! You have to listen to me! *I'm telling you the truth!*" The line was dead. She'd hung up on him. Shad stood still, speechless. The phone's receiver fell from his loose grip and dangled on its metal cord, eventually beeping in protest at being off of its cradle. Detective Caceres said nothing, she just sat behind Shad and waited. "What do I have to do to get out of here?" Shad said without turning around.

"Just record an apology. Say you were wrong, disavow your statements and anything else that might come out. We have a list of things for you to cover."

"Then I get released? I can leave?"

"I can't guarantee the timing, but it's your best chance. Legally, anyway. We can't do anything about the Internet."

"I'm ready, let's do that."

"That's the right choice, Shad. For you, and for your family. You're not the David for this Goliath. Let's go, we'll use the same interview room." She walked over and grabbed Shad's arm to lead him again. He walked with her in a daze. He'd known that Alina wouldn't just change her mind after a short jail-house phone call. He knew she wouldn't believe him. Not immediately, at least. But even if you see a fist about to hit you and you know it's coming, it doesn't change that it feels like getting punched.

They arrived at the room where they had first spoken earlier and returned to their prior positions, with Shad facing the one-way mirror. "I need to get the paper with all of the points you need to make and the camera I'll use to record your statement. I'll just be a couple minutes. Don't go anywhere!" Caceres chuckled at her own joke as she left the room. "Can't help myself."

A few minutes passed, and then a few more. Fifteen minutes after the detective had left, Shad put his head on the table to try to get some more uncomfortable sleep. As soon as he rested his head on his arm, the door opened again. Shad raised his head, irritated at the timing of the detective's return, only to see her leaning into the room with her hand still on the door handle. "Change of plans, Shad."

"What? I told you that I'm ready to say what I need to say. What changed?"

"What changed is that your lawyer is here."

"Don't say another word, Mr. Bengoade," said Tom Rodriguez, the drunk man that Shad had rescued from calamity at Bullseye almost twenty-four hours ago. "They never should have interviewed you without your representation present," he said, turning to the detective. "And anything he *did* say, I will get thrown out in court as inadmissible. You know better, detective."

"I know you can screw off, counselor," Caceres turned to leave.

"Charming!" Tom said. "Shad, get up, we need to make it to your bail hearing. It's in ten minutes in the courtroom downstairs." Shad responded by lifting his hands to show he was still cuffed to the table. "Give me a break. Detective! Detective!" he called down the hall. "Would you mind uncuffing my client? Why is he cuffed in the first place? He's not violent. That's unnecessary and excessive."

"My most sincere apologies," Caceres said. She walked back into the room and uncuffed Shad, bowing down in mock-penitence.

"Uh, thanks?" Shad said.

"Come on, come on," gestured Tom from the door. "We already have an uphill battle; I don't want to add being late to our hearing to the mix." Shad picked up his pace, matching Tom's rapid walking speed.

"Thanks for coming, I don't know if I can pay you . . ."

"Don't worry about that. I came as soon as the desk sergeant called me. I also saw the video of you this morning and the videos of you being arrested. You bailed me out of a bad situation, consider this a favor returned," said Tom as they hurried down the hall. They reached a staircase and an elevator bank. They waited a few seconds for an elevator, but Tom looked down at his watch anxiously and then urged Shad toward the stairs. "Come on, we can't wait." They got down two floors in what felt like record time, with Tom maintaining the same speed as they looked for their courtroom. They entered it and made their way to their table at the front just as the judge was entering.

"All rise," said the bailiff. "The honorable Judge Brown presiding." Everyone stood as the judge made her way to the bench.

"This is not good for us," Tom whispered quietly to Shad. "I'm going to do my best here, but she's probably one of the worst judges for our case. She's a devout Asherian."

As she sat, the judge nodded to the courtroom, indicating that everyone else could sit down. The bailiff continued, reading the case information. "The case before the court is the state vs. Shadrick Bengoade, case number 22231837. The defendant, Shadrick Bengoade, is charged with aggravated malicious harassment and making criminal threats," said the portly bailiff, an aging man who appeared to be on mental autopilot.

"Your honor," interrupted the prosecutor from the table to Shad's left, a young woman who looked fresh out of law school, perhaps in her late twenties. "I apologize for the late notice, but after evaluating the evidence, the state is enhancing these charges as hate crimes."

"Clerk, please make a note," Judge Brown said. She then turned to Shad and Tom, looking down from the bench over her glasses. "How does the defendant plead?"

"Not guilty," said Tom, standing up. "Your honor, given Mr. Bengoade's strong ties to the community and his lack of a criminal record, the defense requests he be released without bail pending trial. He maintains a job at a local business, and has a wife and a daughter who attends school here. He has other family in the Mapleton community. As such, he does not present a flight risk," said Tom.

"And the state's position on bail?" asked the judge.

"Your honor, given the hateful nature of the crimes of which the defendant is accused, including specific violent threats,the state is requesting that bail be set appropriately to deter additional harassment or worse. We request bail be set at $100,000," said the young lawyer. Shad lost his breath in the moment, and he nearly spoke up himself but was waved off tactfully by Tom.

"Your honor, if I may," Tom said.

"You may not." Tom abruptly closed his mouth compliantly. "I've seen the video in question, and I tend to agree with the prosecutor. Without adequate disincentives, it seems likely the defendant may feel emboldened to continue to harass the victim or even act upon the vicious threats he made. And I want to be clear here, Mr. Bengoade, while there may be mitigating factors presented to the court that may provide context for the horrible things you said, the evidence of your crimes is irrefutable. You said what you said, and hateful discrimination like that has no place in our community. So, while I agree with the prosecution's request, I disagree with the amount requested," Judge Brown said. Shad began to feel hope return for a moment. "Bail is set at $200,000," said the judge, obliterating Shad's splinter of hope with the bang of her gavel. The courtroom spun around Shad as people began to stand. He steadied himself on the table, attempting to comprehend what all had taken place as the bailiff approached to take him into custody.

You won't just lose; you will be consumed—Nezzar's words from just a few hours ago echoed in Shad's mind. Shad hadn't even been out of the Under Yards for a half hour before Nezzar's declarations had manifested into this terrible reality. How could he know? How could he be this powerful, this pervasive?

"Don't worry," Tom said, interrupting Shad's stupor. "They'll process the paperwork and take you back to a holding room. I'll meet you back there." He placed a reassuring hand on Shad's shoulder. The bailiff grabbed his arm and escorted Shad out of the courtroom as the judge watched contemptuously from her perch above him. He was led back into the jail facility, where he went through the rest of the intake process, including changing into an orange jumpsuit. The entire process took about a half hour, but Shad hardly noticed as he muddled through the motions in a sort of trance. Once all of the paperwork and procedures were completed, he was taken to a meeting room where Tom was waiting with his briefcase resting on the table in front of him.

"What just happened?" asked Shad, sitting down at the table. "I was ready to record whatever they wanted so I could get out of here. I was about to do it. They weren't coercing me, I was willing. *I have to get to my family, Tom.* I have to talk to my wife. I can't be stuck in here while she's out there. I have to get to her. Now my bail is set at $200,000? I'm screwed, I'm going to lose her. I'm going to lose Isla."

"Shad, Shad. Relax. It's going to be OK. It's all good, your bail has already been posted. They're processing it now, you'll be out of here," he looked at his watch. "I'd say in a half hour, so by about 11:15 a.m."

"*What?* My bail was posted? How? I don't have that kind of money, and even if I did, Alina isn't coming to help me," Shad said. He was getting used to getting blindsided.

"Not sure, it was posted anonymously. Got any rich friends that might know you're in here and be inclined to help?"

Shad immediately thought of Deckard and chuckled. "Yeah, I do. No idea how to repay that, but I'll probably never live it down. Speaking of payment, how do I pay you? I've seen your house; I don't think I can afford your hourly rate."

"Oh, you absolutely couldn't afford it," Tom said. "Like I said before, don't worry about that. I'm taking your case pro bono. You saved me at Bullseye, and you didn't have to do that. You could have left me there to get myself thrown in jail. I wasn't there to stop you from ending up in cuffs, but I can get you out of them. That judge was vindictive and we have an uphill battle, but luckily, I'm good at this whole lawyer thing and I've made a lot of cheddar over the years, so it's not a problem to do this one for free."

"Wow. I'm not even sure what to say. Thank you. I'd be screwed without your help."

"Now we're even. Or we will be, when I get you a not-guilty verdict. Like I said, you were my guardian angel yesterday. I would have ruined my own life and you had my back even though you didn't know me from Adam. So let's stick together and get you out of this bind. Sound good?"

Shad laughed, unable to believe the day's wild mixture of terrible misfortune and extraordinary luck. "That sounds good. Man, I needed some good luck. I've got to get to my family." There was a knock on the door. Tom stood up and opened the door for an officer who stood in the hallway.

"Bail is posted, we're ready to process Mr. Bengoade out," said the officer, a stocky young man with a shaved head and a goatee who looked like he spent way too much time in the gym.

"That was quicker than I thought. Ready to go?"

Chapter 13

SHAD AND TOM WALKED out of the municipal justice building into the late morning air. As soon as they exited the building, Shad pulled out his phone and powered it up. No messages from anyone. He started to text Alina, but stopped himself and instead texted Deckard.

You OK? What happened to you?

After a few moments, Deckard responded.

Safe at my house. Already posted the vids. Sorry I bailed on you, man. I wasn't sure what to do. Are you texting me from jail? Did you store this phone in your butt?

Shad snorted.

Idiot. No, I'm out. Long story. You did the right thing, no use in us both being locked up. Can you send me the links? I'm with my lawyer. I'll call you later.

Dots showed Deckard responding.

Yeah, I'll send them right now. I'm going to try to sleep. Just come by whenever.

Shad locked his phone and put it back in his pocket as they walked toward the parking lot. Sunlight shone brightly through a cloudless sky, slowly burning away the crisp morning chill. Tom's car—a German coupe that likely cost more than Shad's house—was shimmering decadently in the sunshine. Knowing Deckard was safe and unmolested by the police or the cults gave Shad some peace of mind. The videos they'd recorded being out in the wilds of the Internet gave him some comfort as well, but also made him anxious. He wondered if it might impact his case.

"So, you're my lawyer, right?" Shad asked as he opened the passenger door.

"Certainly seems that way. I don't have a contract, so you need to pay me to make it official." Shad hesitated, looking surprised. "Relax, it's just a dollar so that I can call you a client without all of the paperwork. We'll get the official stuff signed later. I wasn't kidding about taking your case for free."

"OK, cool. I might actually have a dollar in my wallet." Shad retrieved his wallet and fished out a folded dollar from one of its crevices. The bill had clearly been wedged there for a long time. He handed it to Tom, who held it between his index finger and thumb. "It's not dirty or anything, it's just been in there for a while. I never use cash."

"This will work," Tom said, jamming the dollar in his pocket.

"OK, so I can tell you anything, right?"

"Yup, I'm your lawyer now, so everything we talk about is privileged. Got something to share?" Tom asked as he turned on the car.

"Well, I figure I should tell you what happened last night. Because a lot of it just got uploaded on the Internet."

"Yeah, that sounds like something I should know. I'm hungry, want to tell me over an early lunch?"

"Yes!" Shad said enthusiastically, desperate for the comfort of a delicious meal. They drove to the nearest LottaBurger and got into the drive-through lane. The voice of what was most likely some teenager in a headset came blasting out of the speaker.

"Hail the Blood Moon and welcome to LottaBurger. Would you like to try the Triple Meat Moloch Monster Burger with Baal sauce and an Asherah's Ecstasy Shake?" said the recently postpubescent voice through the tinny speaker. Tom shook his head and turned to Shad.

"They've even gotten to LottaBurger," he whispered. Tom ordered their food and they both sat quietly as they ate in the car. Shad basked in the meal, finding solace in the familiar tastes.

"Now, what's the story you wanted to tell?"

"Get comfortable, it's a long one. And there's video to go with it, although if you have a weak stomach, we might wait on that part." Shad recounted all of the events of the night before, starting with the drunken ride to the park. Tom was attentive throughout the story, muttering curses under his breath, the details clearly striking close to home.

"You saw Jerry Dink do that? You're sure it was him, the same guy you saw in the park?"

"No doubt in my mind. And it doesn't matter what I say, we have video that shows Dink gutting that guy," Shad said.

"That complicates things, but we'll figure out our actual legal strategy later. Keep going."

Shad continued relating everything he'd seen, sparing no details of the horrific events they had witnessed during the Asherian ritual. Given Tom's familial association, Shad was cognizant of the weight he was placing on his newfound friend's shoulders.

"We can stop it, Tom. We can prevent this from happening again. We'll find a way, we have to, we can't let them get away with this."

Tom started to nod, as if to dislodge the shock from his mind. "What happened after . . . the college girl? Did you just sneak out?"

"We tried to, but we got ambushed. It was . . . bad, but in a different way," Shad said. He told Tom about Nezzar and his posse showing up and confronting them, and how that led to the video that was secretly recorded of Shad threatening Nezzar.

"You don't have any video of that interaction, something that could clear your name?"

"No, we only recorded those sacrifices. We were about to leave when they all showed up. We didn't think to pull out our phones, we were deer in the headlights the whole time he was there. He knew he had the upper hand. I should have known better than to let him get under my skin, I fell for it."

"And he positioned himself so that you never see him, it looks like your confrontation is with Lord Malochus, who is well-known in our community, you know, not just with Molochians but with all of the alts. He also has some goodwill built up because of their homeless initiative. That makes your situation that much more complicated, because public opinion is going to be against you. Going to be tough getting a fair trial," Tom said.

"Nezzar said that too. Now we know what the homeless initiative is *really* about. I just wish I had controlled myself."

"Don't beat yourself up too much, Shad. I probably would have done the same thing."

"I feel so stupid now. He's been two steps ahead of me since we walked into that cursed park."

"What happened after the confrontation?"

"After that, we did exactly what Nezzar said. We left. We went back up to the ground level the way we came and were on the way out of the park when I spotted the cops. I went to them to ask about filing a report, thinking they'd be eager to help when I told them what I saw. Then they arrested me immediately, so I didn't even get a chance to tell them."

"You did all this with your friend Deckard, but he didn't get arrested?"

"Yeah, that's right. When they arrested me, they asked me about my friend, so they knew I wasn't alone, but they didn't know who had come with me. Deckard's face isn't in the video they recorded, it's just me. I didn't tell them anything when I realized that they would probably arrest him too. When he saw them arrest me, he took off and went home so he could upload all of the videos."

"Probably the smart move," Tom said. "That's a hell of a night, Shad. I have to be honest, I did not know what I was getting into when I came to the jail to help you out. This is a lot more serious than I realized. Dink is just one ultrarich alt, but there are so many more like him. If they're all involved in stuff like this, they're going to fight hard to crush you. I don't know if I have the resources to get you through this, but I'll take it as far as I can."

"You've already done more than enough, Tom. You got me out of that jail. No matter what happens next, you gave me the chance I need to get to Alina, to convince her that she's wrong about the alts. Speaking of her, now that we're done going through everything that happened, would you mind taking me to my mother-in-law's house? She's staying there with our daughter. I think if I talk to her in person, I can get her to listen. Once she sees my face, she'll be able to tell I'm sincere."

"Are you sure? Didn't you just talk to her? You think she'll be ready to hear from you?"

"I don't know, man. But I have to try. I can't stand by while she goes to that horrible festival. Especially if she's planning on bringing Isla, I'll do anything I can to stop that."

"Maybe she'll listen if we both talk to her?"

"That's a great idea, that will show her I'm not on some vendetta," Shad said.

"When do you want to go?"

"Can we go now? It's almost noon, they should be about to have lunch." Shad told Tom how to get to the neighborhood where his mother-in-law lived, and Tom put the car in gear and began to drive. It wasn't far and Tom apparently liked to drive his fancy car fast. "Up there on the right, a few houses down."

There was an inconspicuous blue sedan parked on the street in front of the house next door to his mother-in-law's house. Leaning against the driver's side door was Detective Caceres. "What the hell is she doing here?" Shad said.

"That's a really good question. Let me do the talking, all right?" Tom pulled the car up behind hers and they got out as Caceres walked toward them.

"I knew you'd come here, Shad," Caceres said.

"You can talk to me, Detective," Tom said. "Shad's bail has been posted, he's free to go where he wants. If you keep harassing him, I'll go straight to the judge and get you tossed off of this case."

"Relax, counselor." Caceres patted at the air with her right hand as she spoke. "I'm here as a courtesy."

"I fail to see how stalking my client is a courtesy."

"You lawyers are always so dramatic," Caceres rolled her eyes. "Shad's wife filed a temporary protective order against him."

"She did *what*? A protective order?" Shad asked.

"Yeah, she must have called it in right after she hung up with you this morning. The black-and-whites who caught it came to me to give me a heads-up since it's my case," Caceres said. "I told them I'd take the first shift because I knew Shad would come here as soon as he could. I didn't want him getting jammed up by freaking out on the officers."

"I need to talk to Alina. I have to see my daughter," Shad said, starting to walk toward the house.

"I'm sorry, Shad, you can't." Detective Caceres blocked his way. "I'm not going to arrest you, but if you go to that house and she calls the cops, I can't stop whoever shows up from arresting you. You have to leave."

"So you're here out of the goodness of your heart, Detective? Do you have a copy of this order? Forgive my skepticism, but I like to see things before I believe them," Tom said.

Detective Caceres turned to Shad. "You didn't tell him?" She pulled a paper out of her back pocket and handed it to Tom, who began to examine it immediately.

"No, I just went through what we saw at the festival, then we came right over here," Shad said. "Didn't really seem important, to be honest."

"Someone want to fill me in, here?" asked Tom.

"She's being honest. She's just trying to watch my back. So what do I do now? How can I legally see my wife and daughter?" Shad said.

"For the next forty-eight hours, you can't."

"But I can," Tom said, folding up the paper. "The protective order is against Shadrick himself, but it doesn't prevent someone acting on his behalf. I can go and speak with her, Shad."

"Do it, please. You've got to tell her that I'm not a bigot, I'm not even angry. I just want to keep her and Isla safe. She has to see the videos, she has to see what I saw."

"I'll reason with her, don't worry," Tom said. "I do this for a living." He patted Shad reassuringly on his shoulder and began walking toward Alina's mother's house. Shad stayed behind with Detective Caceres and watched from a distance, standing next to Tom's gaudy car. They watched him make his way up the sidewalk to the front door, where he punched the doorbell and waited, standing with his hands behind his back. The door opened, and Shad could see his mother-in-law Eliana was still playing gatekeeper.

"Mother-in-law?" Caceres asked.

Shad sighed. "Yup."

"Battle-axe?"

"When it comes to Alina, yeah, definitely. She's never really liked me. Never thought I was good enough for her daughter."

"What about her dad?"

"Her parents divorced when she was in high school. He died of cancer when we were dating."

"That's rough," Caceres said.

"They never had a good relationship; his death was a hard time. So she's super close with her mom, which made it even harder for me to win her over. And honestly, her mom isn't too off base. Alina has always been way out of my league, but somehow, I convinced her to love me," Shad said. "I'm still trying to figure out how I screwed it up this badly."

"Well, I don't know your business, but in my experience, it takes two to blow up a marriage. Also takes two to fix one, so keep that in mind as you go after her. You can only do so much, Shad. And I'm speaking from experience." Caceres exposed just a splinter of vulnerability.

"I'm not going to give up. I can't, I don't know how. She needed me, and I missed it. I have to at least apologize to her, to tell her that I should have been there for her instead of getting stuck in a rut."

"Maybe, but you're human. And she could have talked to you about it instead of running to the culties. Sorry, I mean 'alts,'" Caceres said, making air quotes. "But she didn't, she went to them instead of talking to her husband. Look where that got you both. I'm not saying it's all her fault, but I *am* saying it's not all your fault either."

"That doesn't look good." Shad gestured at the house. Eliana looked back inside, then said something to Tom and closed the door. A few minutes passed and Tom looked like he was about to give up, when the door opened again. Shad's heart skipped a beat as he saw Alina lean out of the doorway and begin talking to Tom. When Shad began to move, Caceres grabbed his arm and shook her head.

"I know, Shad. I know. But you can't, not yet."

"Yeah, OK," Shad said, barely restraining his instinct to sprint across the grass. He stood back in his place and continued to watch with Caceres. Alina seemed to be nodding in agreement. "Whatever he's saying, she's not slamming the door in his face, so that's good, right?"

"It's not bad," Caceres said. Tom bowed slightly toward Alina and raised his hand, an ostensible valediction, and turned to leave as Alina returned the gesture and closed the door.

"OK, OK." Shad nodded. "That seemed to go pretty well, right? Maybe she'll drop the order."

"Hold your horses, cowboy," Caceres said. "Let's not count our chickens before they hatch."

"Did you learn to talk from a western?" Shad smiled. "I'm trying to be optimistic, all right? I'm due for a win." He turned to Tom as he approached. "That looked like it went pretty well. What did she say?"

"I didn't push her very hard," Tom said. "Her mom is . . . protective."

"Very diplomatic way of putting it," Shad said. "You might also say she's a psychotic helicopter mom, or that she thinks she's Alina's personal Secret Service detail, or that she's just a crotchety old bi—"

"Yeah, we get it." Caceres turned to Tom. "Get to the good stuff so you can get back to chasing ambulances."

Tom threw a derisive glance at the detective before continuing. "I told her about the videos, I told her you were telling the truth. I told her I had seen the videos, that it was real."

"Did you show them to her?" Shad asked.

"No, I gave her my card and I told her I would send her the videos, she just needed to email or text me. She was open to what I was saying, but I didn't want to push my luck by asking her to watch them with me. This way, she's reaching out and making the choice. She was still guarded and defensive, but I think I got through to her. I don't think she expected you to respect the order, so sending a lawyer on your behalf was a surprise."

"Did you see Isla? Did she mention her?" Shad asked.

"No, but I could hear a TV in the background. I think she was watching cartoons."

"Eliana never respects our screen-time rules," Shad said. "I'm worried she'll go to the festival tonight. I don't know what they'll do to her, but she was already on their radar and now Nezzar has it out for me. She doesn't have to believe everything I say, I just don't want her to go to the festival."

"As soon as I hear from her, I'll send the videos," Tom said.

Shad turned to the detective. "Thanks. You could have let me get arrested again, but you went out of your way to protect me, and I won't forget that. I owe you." Shad reached out to shake her hand.

"Get the word out, Shad. But watch your back, you've already made some serious enemies, and they aren't going to stop," Detective Caceres said, shaking his hand. "Here's my card. I can't promise anything, but if I can help you, I will." She handed Shad a card and started walking to her car.

"Holly? Your name is *Holly*?" Shad asked after reading her full name on her business card.

"Screw off, *Shadrick*, at least my parents named me after a classic beauty."

"That's fair. Thanks, Holly!" he said, holding the card up. She responded with a middle finger as she opened her car door. "See you later, briefcase bandit," she said to Tom, who only glared at her.

"Want a ride home?" Tom asked as Caceres drove away.

"Can you drop me off at Deckard's house? My car is parked there. It's not too far from here."

"Sure. You should get some rest, probably the longest night of your life." Tom unlocked the car and got in the driver's seat. He pulled out his phone when he sat down, tapped the screen, locked it and put it back into his pocket as Shad got into the passenger seat. "Caceres is a pain."

"She can be annoying but I think she's on the level." He sat for a beat as Tom drove. "Lots of people are against me, Tom. How the hell am I going to get out of this?"

"One thing at a time, Shad. Let's focus on Alina, get you rested up, and then we'll hammer out our legal strategy. This exit, right?" Tom nodded toward the approaching sign.

"Yeah, that's the one. Got here pretty quick. How many speeding tickets do you get in this thing?"

"There's a reason I know every cop in this town, and it's not because of my job. Deckard has fancy taste," he said as they drove into Deckard's posh neighborhood.

"Arty people can't bear to live in a normal house like the rest of us."

As Tom pulled the car up, his phone dinged in his pocket. He pulled it out and looked at the notification without unlocking it. "I told you Alina would text me."

"It's her? Oh, thank God," Shad said, the warmth of relief evaporating the weight of anxiety from his chest.

"Yup, just give it a little time."

"You'll let me know what she says?"

"Absolutely. We got this, Shad."

"Tom, I can't thank you enough. I don't know how I'll ever repay you for all that you've done for me and my family." Shad got out of the car and leaned back in as they spoke.

"Oh, don't worry about that, we'll figure something out," Tom said. Shad smiled and nodded before closing the door and turning to walk to Deckard's front door. Inside the car, Tom pulled out his phone and opened his text messages.

Did you do what we asked? read the message on his screen.

Tom sighed. *Yes, I spoke to her. She believed me.*

Excellent. She won't hesitate any longer.

What do you want me to do now? My son is safe, right? Tom typed.

Ready yourself for this evening. You have an important part to play.

Chapter 14

ALINA AWOKE TO THE sound of her phone buzzing. Once, then twice, then over and over until she silenced it without looking at the screen, groggily assuming it was her alarm. She got out of bed and shuffled blearily into the bathroom. She emerged ten minutes later after completing her morning routines and went to the kitchen of her childhood home to check on her daughter, Isla. Her sweet little girl was sitting at the table, cheerily eating cereal with her grandmother's tablet propped up in front of her playing some cartoons, based on the sound Alina could hear. Alina sighed in frustration at her mother never respecting their screen-time rules.

"Already watching Granny's tablet, Isla? What's the rule about screens at the table?" she said as she walked in and sat next to her at the circular table.

Isla groaned. "Come on, Mom, we're on vacation! Granny said it was OK!"

"Oh, did she?" Alina turned toward her mother who was conspicuously silent as she fiddled in the kitchen. "Is that right, Granny?"

"It's just one cartoon, Alina, lighten up, you used to watch cartoons."

"You know that's not the same thing, Mom. Kids have screens in front of them all the time now. People treat it like a babysitter, which is what you're doing! Come sit down and talk to your granddaughter."

"Don't scold me, young lady. I changed your diapers," Eliana said, putting down a dish towel and walking over to the table. She sat across from Isla and placed her phone down on the glass tabletop. "I also let you sleep in this morning, so you should be thanking me."

"Thanks, Mom. It's hardly sleeping in, but I'll take what I can get." Her mother's phone dinged loudly. And then again, and again. "Dang, Mom, you're popular. Can you turn down your ringer? It's way too early for that."

"I don't know what this is about," Eliana said, picking up her phone and fumbling with the screen. "I never get messages, especially in the morning." She tapped the screen a few more times and then froze, staring at her phone. "Alina, get your phone."

"Mom, I don't need my phone with me all the time, unlike *some people*."

Eliana looked up and locked eyes with Alina. "Get your phone, *now*."

"Um, OK, fine." Alina stood up and walked back to her room, wondering what could possibly have made her mother react that way. She picked up her phone and saw she had fifteen missed calls and eighty-three unread text messages. Her heart began to race as she unlocked the screen. The first text was from Bella, Isla's teacher.

I'm so sorry, Alina.

After that, it included a link to a video on Yeller. Alina tapped it and her knees gave way beneath her, forcing her to the bed. Shad's face was on the screen, filled with an anger she'd never seen on it before. She sat on the bed and watched the video over and over again, not believing what she was seeing. It was all over every social media platform she checked, and each of her accounts was blowing up with mentions as people tagged her in the video.

Her thoughts raced so fast she could hardly keep up with them. *How could this happen? I know he was mad, but what is this? He looks so different. He's never been this angry. Is this my fault? Did I make him do this? Maybe I shouldn't have left with Isla. He looked so broken when I left. I should have at least talked to him when he came to see me. I can't believe I threw away his flowers, what was I thinking? That was a low blow. I pushed him. I did this.*

She scrolled through the thread and saw another video posted under that one. It showed Shad again, but this time he was in the park getting arrested by two police officers. She got another text from Bella just as she watched Shad being pushed into the back of a squad car.

Are you OK?

Alina stared at the screen, not sure how to respond. *No,* she finally typed.

What can I do to help?
I don't know.
Are you safe?
Safe?
Safe from him, Alina. You saw that video, he's out of control.

He's not violent. He's just upset because we left. It's my fault.

The phone began to buzz with a call from Bella. Alina tapped to answer it and put it on speaker.

"Alina, this is *not* your fault. You are not responsible for his choices. He's clearly a very angry, hateful person. That's not on you, that's on him."

"I've never seen him like that before." Alina's voice cracked as she began to cry. "He's so angry—that's not Shad. He's always been so laid-back, so passive. I pushed him too far, I caused this." She broke into a sob.

"What do you mean you pushed him? You can't blame yourself for this," Bella said.

"We fought on Friday night. I showed him the pictures of the festival at school. He got so mad about Isla being exposed to all of the alternative religions, I didn't even tell him that I was there or that I helped organize it. He was furious. He was so protective of Isla. I got really defensive; he made me feel like I put her in danger. I just kept thinking about how I organized the festival—I *did* put Isla in that situation, and I knew if I told him he'd flip out even more. I felt so guilty for hiding it from him, but I was also really mad." She rambled on through her tears. "I shouldn't have to feel guilty for learning about my truth, for following my heart to my calling. It's not wrong to want your child to experience the same things as you. But he was so mad, like he really felt like it was terrible for Isla. I didn't know what to do or how to feel so I just packed up some stuff, grabbed Isla, and left to my mom's house. I could tell it was hurting him that I would leave like that. I saw it break in his eyes; the anger just drained away. He begged me to stay, he begged me not to take Isla. He was desperate. But I was mad and I was sad and I didn't listen and I wanted to hurt him and now he's in jail, oh God, what did I do?"

"I'm so sorry Alina, that sounds *so hard*," Bella said. "I'm sorry that you had to defend yourself in that terrible fight and that you felt so unsafe in your own home that you had to leave, but you have to understand that you didn't cause this. Like you said, there's nothing wrong with being an alt. Nothing at all. If he has a problem with that, there's something wrong with *him*. You're taking the most important journey of your life and not only is he choosing to abandon you, he's doing everything he can to *stop* you. He's trying to keep you from true freedom, and that's evil."

"But he doesn't even *know* about me exploring Moloch—he was mad about Isla being in that festival. He was mad that she was exposed to all of the rituals, he was mad that he didn't even know it was happening. On top of all of that, he got in trouble at work because he didn't participate in a party they had for some alts there, so he was already worked up when he got home," Alina said, her sobs dying down.

"Obviously he doesn't know about your spiritual journey, Alina! How could you possibly feel comfortable sharing that with him when he's so biased against alts? And now you're telling me he got in trouble for discrimination against alts at work too? Sweetheart, how can you be so blind to this? He's a bigot, Alina. It's that simple. He hates alts just because of who they are, just because of what they believe. I know you love him, but people change, and sometimes it's not for the better. I bet he calls us evil murderers too. They all say that kind of stuff, they're all the same."

"What am I going to do, Bella? He's my husband, he's Isla's father. She adores him. *I love him.* How can I possibly fix this?"

"Take it one day at a time. He's in jail, you can't do anything about that. And more importantly, he can't stop you. Focus on you and your journey with Isla. Like Lord Malochus said, Isla is the key to your liberation. Tonight is the night you shed the chains of the light of the world and embrace the freedom of Moloch's shadow. You can't let Shad's hate keep you from attaining your purpose." Bella projected the kind of assurance that Alina needed to allay her near-crippling insecurity. As she was about to reply, Alina's phone beeped to indicate another call was coming in. She looked at her screen. It read "County Jail." Her heart skipped a beat.

"Oh no, Bella, he's calling me!"

"Right now? From jail?"

"Yes, right now! What do I do, should I ignore it? No, I can't ignore it. What am I going to say?"

"You answer it and you stand your ground. Tell him how wrong he is! You can do this. I'm here for you."

"OK, I'll call you later."

Alina tapped to answer Shad's call. It went terribly, but not in the way that she had feared. Shad wasn't angry with her at all, he was frantic, babbling as soon as she answered the phone. Bella was right, like she had been so many times; he immediately accused alts of being murderers. He didn't even ask about Isla, he didn't ask her how she was doing, he just starting rambling about cults and how they were evil and violent. Alina channeled all of the tumultuous emotions she'd been feeling that morning into her response, shutting him down in the middle of his wild speech. She put him in his place and hung up on him.

Then she called Bella to tell her about it, still so amped up on anger and adrenaline that she instantly began rattling off the details of the conversation without so much as an introduction. As soon as she was done giving her the play-by-play and stopped to take a breath, Bella was finally able to speak.

"You are *so* strong. I can't imagine having that kind of courage. Speaking directly with truth and not being afraid at all . . . just, wow, Alina. I'm so proud of you," Bella said.

"So you think it was good? I handled it the right way?" Alina's rage-induced confidence was waning.

"Absolutely. It was more than good, it was awesome. Seriously."

"You don't think I should have let him talk? I don't know, maybe I should have let him explain himself . . ." Alina's insecurity crept in, as it so often did.

"No, I think he said more than enough. In fact, I think you should get a temporary restraining order in case he gets out of jail soon. I have a contact at the police department that can help you get it set up really quickly."

"A restraining order? Isn't that a little extreme?"

"Alina, he's in jail for threatening alts. He got in trouble at work for discriminating against alts. You're about to become an alt. How do you think he's going to react when he finds out?"

"I don't know, honestly. I'm not sure."

"Are you serious? Come on, Alina! Listen to yourself. You know exactly how he's going to react; he's going to be furious! He's going to be out of control. You saw that video, he was on the verge of hitting Lord Malochus, and for what? Just for worshipping his god. When he finds out that you're walking the path toward liberation, he's going to lose his mind."

"I know what you're saying, Bella, and it makes sense. But you didn't hear him on the phone, he didn't sound angry. He sounded scared, not for himself, but scared for me. All he cared about was saying what he needed to say, like it was the most important thing in the world to him."

"Stop overthinking this and trust me. Get the temporary restraining order. It will protect you and it will protect Isla. It's temporary, they last only a couple days. When that's over, you can talk to him again. That will give him time to cool off and realize just how far he's fallen. By then, you'll be liberated and you can tell him all about it. You might even be able to change his mind with your experience."

Alina sat silently for a moment, considering Bella's advice. "OK, you're right. It's better to be safe than sorry. And if he's really concerned for me, he'll respect that I need some space right now. He'll understand."

Bella continued encouraging her for a few minutes, and then conference-called her contact at the police department. She stayed on the line while Alina provided all of her information to the officer, who filled out the necessary paperwork to establish a temporary restraining order. It took about half an hour, but before they ended the call, the order had been filed and was officially in place. Shad was not allowed within a hundred yards of Alina or Isla for the next seventy-two hours.

"Don't doubt yourself, this is the right thing to do," Bella said at the end of the conversation.

"I hope you're right."

"*Trust me*. I'll be by to pick you and Isla up around seven o'clock, OK?"

"Thanks again, Bella. Thanks for walking through this with me, I don't know what I'd do without you."

"Don't mention it. It'll all be worth it tonight, I promise!"

They said their goodbyes, and Alina went into the bathroom to clean herself up before she went back out to the kitchen. She didn't want Isla to be able to tell that she'd been crying. Her eyes were so red that she had to dig through her bags to find some eye drops. A little bit of concealer, mascara, and eyeliner, and she looked like she was ready for another day. Checking her watch, she realized she had been in her room for over two hours. Even though she had only just gotten out of bed, she felt completely drained. Isla and her mother had moved from the kitchen into the living room and were unsurprisingly watching more cartoons.

"Isn't there something to do in this house besides watching a screen?" Alina demanded. Eliana sat next to a rapt Isla.

"Yes, but Granny is tired and needed to rest her eyes," said Eliana, blinking the nap out of her eyes.

"Mom, it's not even lunchtime yet and you're already sleepy?"

"I'm old, Alina. I wake up at four-thirty in the morning every day. Without an alarm. This is like midday for me."

"You don't look a day over sixty, dearest Mother."

"How sweet of you. Stop avoiding it and tell me what happened."

Alina looked at Isla. "I handled it. I'll tell you the details later."

"Tell me the details now. Don't worry about her, she's so focused we could plan out her birthday gifts and she wouldn't hear us." Alina raised her eyebrows, unconvinced, and Eliana continued. "Don't believe me? I hid the dollhouse we got for Isla under your bed. It's not even wrapped, she could go grab it right now if she wanted." Eliana looked at Isla. As she predicted, the little girl continued to watch the screen and didn't react at all to what her Granny had just declared. Alina shrugged and told her mother everything.

"I didn't know he had been arrested. How terrible. I'm sorry sweetheart. He didn't seem angry at all when he came here yesterday. If anything, he seemed, I don't know, apologetic? Like he really wanted to make things right with you. Don't get defensive, I know that look. I'm just telling you the truth. I understand why you didn't want to talk to him, and I guess you were right. He must have had a lot of anger in his heart."

"I didn't expect it either, Mom. I really didn't."

"Did you really need the . . ." Eliana looked at Isla. "The T-R-O? He would never do anything to you or Isla, Ally," she said, using a childhood nickname. "You know that I've never been his biggest fan, but it was always because he's too passive. He never seemed to have any ambition, always content with what he had, never pushing for more. I wanted someone more driven for you." Eliana was always ready to share her feelings about Shad. "Anyway, my point is he doesn't have that kind of violence in him, Ally. And aside from that, he adores you and Isla. That's why you liked him, because he's always had you on such a pedestal."

Alina rolled her eyes. "Mom, I love him because I do, I have just always loved him. I still love him. The T-R-O is temporary, that's the point. Just to give him some time to cool down. Plus, he doesn't know that I've been talking to Bella about Moloch. I honestly don't know how he's going to react when he finds out."

"Ally, why are you getting into that stuff? It's so weird. We didn't raise you to be religious, we never did that kind of thing. Why are you trying it now?"

"I've always been religious, or tried to be. We go to church on the holidays, which is way more than you and Dad ever did. I like being a part of a community, a group of people pursuing a greater purpose. Especially when our beliefs are so marginalized, it feels good to be on the right side of history. You might like it, Mom."

"No, thank you. I'm too old to learn new tricks. And all of the blood and rituals . . ." Eliana's face had an expression like she'd tasted something gross. "It's just too much for me. I wish it was too much for you, Ally. If you want to be religious, that's fine. You said you and Shad go to a church already. Why not just get more involved there?"

"I don't know, every time we go, it's like we're lost in a sea of people. We don't know anyone, no one talks to us. It doesn't feel real or genuine, like everyone's wearing a mask. The music was always good, but it was almost like a concert. Shad has talked about trying to go more often, but I never really connected there, I guess. We're going through the motions. When Sunday comes around, we're just not motivated to get up and go. But when I'm with the Molochians, it's totally different. It feels real. It feels alive," Alina said. "Everyone is so interested in me. They listen to me, they talk to me, they seek me out. The high priest knows my name. He even knows Isla's name! I don't think I've ever even met the pastor of the church we've gone to for years."

"OK, it sounds like you've made up your mind. I trust your judgment, Ally. After all, I did raise you." There was a knock on the door and Eliana looked puzzled. "What could that be on a Sunday? I don't think I've ordered anything from Bezozon. She got up and walked over to the door. Alina could hear her talking to someone, but couldn't discern what they were saying. A few minutes went by, and Alina's curiosity got the better of her. She got up and walked over to the front door, leaving Isla mesmerized by the television screen. Her mother was still at the door, holding it slightly open and talking to someone Alina couldn't see.

"Who is it, Mom?"

Eliana turned around, startled. "Go back to the living room, sweetheart. I'll take care of it."

"Who's there, Mom? Is it about Shad? What's going on?" Eliana sighed in frustration.

"Excuse me a moment," Eliana said to the person outside. She closed the door and turned to Alina. "You've already dealt with enough this morning, Ally. Let me deal with this, go enjoy the rest of the day with Isla."

"Mom, tell me what is going on *right now*."

Eliana looked down and took a deep breath. "It's Shad's lawyer. He says he wants to talk to you. He's very pushy, but I had almost convinced him to leave until he heard your voice. Please, just let me get rid of him. You don't need to worry about this, you have plenty on your mind already."

"Go to the living room, I'll deal with it." Alina fortified herself for another confrontation.

"Are you sure, baby? I don't want you to be upset."

"Yes, Mom. Thank you for watching out for me, but I can handle this. I have to handle it, Shad is my husband." Eliana nodded and walked past Alina toward the living room. Alina opened the door and leaned outside just enough to be visible. Tom had his back to the door, appearing to be about to leave. He turned back, saw Alina, and smiled.

"Mrs. Bengoade, I'm Tom Rodriguez, your husband's lawyer. We know that you were granted a temporary restraining order against Shad this morning, which is why I'm here speaking to you instead of your husband. Shad wanted me to relay some messages to you on his behalf. Would it be OK with you if I did that?"

"Yes, I guess so."

"Thank you, I know he'll be grateful for that. He wanted me to tell you that he's sorry for everything he's said. He said that you were right, and he's glad you were brave enough to tell him the truth. He said he's sorry for putting you in this position, and he's sorry for scaring you. The hate you've seen from him is gone, he just wants things to go back to normal." Tom lied effortlessly. "It's my professional opinion, Mrs. Bengoade, that Shad is suffering from a nervous breakdown. I think the T-R-O was probably the best thing you could do for you, your daughter, and for Shad. It's been a reality check for him, and it's forcing him to really take a hard look in the mirror. Thankfully, I have a good relationship with the judge and the prosecutor who have Shad's case. I think I can plead him down to something like a misdemeanor if he apologizes, which I'm confident he will do. He's ashamed of how he's acted. From what he told me, it sounds like some recent stress at work has built up and he snapped and channeled all of that anger and anxiety toward alts, and by association, to you."

A wave of relief washed over Alina, clearing the dread from her heart and filling it with gratitude. "Oh, thank God," she said. "Or I guess I should thank Moloch!" she laughed. "You have no idea how glad I am to hear that. This morning has been such a terrible roller-coaster. I'm so happy to hear that he's coming around!"

"I'm happy to say it, we've had some really productive conversations," Tom said. "I won't take any more of your time. Thank you for speaking with me, Mrs. Bengoade. We'll be in touch after the T-R-O expires. I hope the rest of your day will be much more enjoyable than the morning has been." Tom nodded to her professionally.

"Thank you so much, Mr. Rodriguez. Please tell Shad that I'm so proud of him, and I love him, and I have so much to tell him!"

"I will absolutely tell him that," Tom lied, again. "Goodbye, Mrs. Bengoade."

Chapter 15

SHAD WALKED UP TO Deckard's front door as Tom drove off behind him. Raising his hand to the door to knock, he hesitated, remembering that Deckard was asleep and likely wouldn't hear him to answer the door. Thankfully, Shad knew the door's code in case of emergencies—the date that Deckard won his first advertising award after dropping out of college his freshman year. The electronic lock buzzed and opened smoothly after Shad entered the six-digit code. The house looked less alive during the daytime; its ambiance having been cultivated to bloom in the evenings. Shad headed to the kitchen where he could hear some light jazz playing softly. He was surprised to find Deckard awake, sitting at his breakfast table with a cup of coffee and a recently emptied plate in front of him. Deckard looked up at him, unsurprised.

"Make yourself at home, why don't you?" he said, getting up.

"I thought you were going to be asleep!"

"I tried. I really did. I might have slept an hour or two, but I just couldn't stay asleep. I was either anxious about everything, or I kept seeing . . . you know, everything we saw. So I finally gave up and made myself some food. Have you slept at all?"

"Same as you, a couple hours in the jail. You think I could grab a shower and borrow some clothes? This shirt is torn up and covered in blood. And I probably smell like a dumpster."

"Sure. There should be some clothes in the guest room closet. That bathroom is stocked too. Do what you need to do."

Shad walked down the hallway to the guestroom, grateful for Deckard's hospitality. He peeled his well-worn shirt off of his back, wincing as it stuck to his bandaged wound. He twisted his arm around behind him and uncovered the cut, examining the damage in the mirror for the first time since the doctor had stitched him up in the hospital. It looked about as bad as it had felt. The shower was as luxurious as the rest of the house, and although Shad wanted to remain in its lavish comfort for the rest of the day, he was eager to talk with Deckard about everything that had happened. He allowed himself ten minutes, and then got out and dried off with towels that were so soft he thought he had accidently picked up a blanket. Deckard had the medicine cabinet fully stocked, so Shad had no problems dressing his wound again before he grabbed some new clothes from the guest closet. He returned to the kitchen feeling reborn.

"That was the first thing I did when I got home, too," Deckard said. "Can't wash off what we saw, but it still felt like shedding skin."

"That shower is a little slice of heaven. Thanks for letting me use your stuff."

"No problem, glad someone is using it. Can't remember the last time I went into that guest room, to be honest. Anyway, I'm surprised you're here. I thought you'd be at your mother-in-law's house, talking to Alina."

"I wish I was, honestly. She got a temporary restraining order against me. She didn't believe anything I told her."

"What? You're joking, right?" Deckard said, motioning to a chair at the table. Sitting down, Shad told him about arriving at his mother-in-law's house, only to find Detective Caceres standing guard.

"She was there to watch your back? What's that all about?" Deckard asked. "You want some food? Coffee?"

"I'll take coffee. The detective is another story, I'll get to that. Tom, my lawyer, drove me there, so he went to talk to Alina, to convince her that I'm not crazy. He told her that the videos are real. She's supposed to be watching them right now, he sent them to her just before I came here," Shad said. "At least there's some hope that she'll see the truth once she actually watches the videos. There's no way she can ignore that. I understand why she was mad at me, hell, I even understand the restraining order. I was so mad on Friday, and then that video they shot was just so perfectly cut to make me look like the aggressor and not the victim. It was expert work, man. They nailed me. But if she sees our videos, I know that will change her mind."

"Glad Tom was able to talk to Alina." Deckard was grappling with his byzantine coffee machine; it began to bubble and hiss, filling a cup with a delicious-smelling brew. He placed it on the table in front of Shad and sat back down.

"It's so strange, dude. None of this feels real, none of it feels like it actually happened," Shad said. "But then I open my phone, and I see all of the notifications and texts, and it's definitely real. And we can't go back. It's happening exactly like Nezzar said it would. No one has believed us. My life is falling apart. They're crushing me."

"I'm sorry, brother. I really am. I feel terrible that you're taking all of the heat for this," said Deckard. "At least your lawyer has helped you out a lot. Speaking of, how did you land a lawyer so fast?"

"Tom is the drunk guy that I helped out at Bullseye. Remember that? Seems like ages ago, but it was what, forty-eight hours? I had his card in my pocket and gave it to the cops. If he hadn't showed up, I'd still be in jail right now."

"How was jail? You looked like you were walking normally. That's a good sign."

"Bro, I was in the local jail, not federal prison. I was in an orange jumpsuit for all of an hour!" Shad went on to explain everything that happened to him after he was arrested at the park, providing extra detail about the conversations he had with Doctor Gaines and Detective Caceres.

"At least there are a few people out there who aren't against us, even if they aren't exactly with us," Deckard said.

"The doctor would be with us if he saw our videos. Caceres is with us, I just don't know what her angle is, or what she could even do to help us. With the chief of police being a Molochian, her hands are tied. Showing up at Alina's mom's house to keep me from getting rearrested was above and beyond."

"Is she hot?" Deckard grinned.

"She's pretty, in a severe, law enforcement kind of way." Shad thought for a moment. "Not a bad match, if I'm honest. Anyway—did you upload everything?"

Deckard nodded, frowning. "The evil douchebags, they took them all down already. I'm either banned or suspended from Yeller, PostSpace, and Spinstagram. And VidHole gave me two strikes, one for each video I posted. If I get one more, they'll ban me there too. The videos were going viral before they got pulled. I was watching those views tick up before I went to lie down, we're talking hundreds each second," he said, punctuating each of the last few words with a stab of his index finger at the air. "They each had over fifty thousand the last time I saw them, so I have no idea how much they got before the censors found them. I can't even access the analytics data for the videos, they're just in some kind of video prison."

"If they're all against us, how are we supposed to get the word out?" Shad asked.

"I'm honestly not sure. I think I'm going to set up a stand-alone website that only shows the videos, but hosting is going to get expensive really quickly. There are a few alternative platforms that are attempting to compete with the tech cartels, so I'll try those too. I'm just going to try and post them everywhere I possibly can and see what sticks. I'm in some big group chats with some like-minded people. I'll share them there, maybe someone will have ideas. Going to have to do some guerilla marketing."

"Right up your alley," Shad said. "Can I help with anything?"

"Nah, man, like you said, this is my wheelhouse. I'll take care of it. And now I'm pissed, so I'm not going to give up. The idiots should have just limited the reach of the videos on their platforms so they would be live and available, but not getting any views. It would have taken me longer to realize what they were doing. Thankfully, they're stupid and couldn't help themselves, so they went for the most extreme option."

"So the bans are good?"

"The bans are definitely bad, but it's good that they played all of their cards. Now it's my turn," Deckard stood up from the table and picked up the empty coffee mugs and dishes. "You want to crash in the guest room while I figure this out?"

"Thanks, but I don't think I could sleep, either. I, uh . . ." Shad hesitated. "I think I'm going to go to church. Is that weird? Feels kind of weird. It's not Christmas or Easter."

"Well, it is Sunday. And after everything that's happened to us, that's probably the most normal thing to do. We need all the help we can get." Deckard placed the empty dishes in his dishwasher.

Shad checked the time on his phone screen. "I think there's an afternoon service that starts in ten minutes. I'm going to head over there. Text me if anything comes up. And watch your back. They haven't come after you yet, but they probably will, especially when you keep posting those videos. I never mentioned your name, but Nezzar knows you were there. So be careful."

"Don't worry about me, bro. I have this place wired up with cameras and a security system. And that fanny pack isn't the only piece of tactical equipment I own; I'll defend my castle. Besides, I'm a bachelor. All I have to lose is money, and I can make more of that."

"Sounds good, I'll see you in a couple of hours."

Deckard waved goodbye and walked away toward his office as Shad turned to walk out of the house. His trusty little SUV sat parked on the street, right where he'd left it the day before. Shad clicked the key fob, and the vehicle beeped to signal that the doors were now unlocked, the sound he'd heard a thousand times providing an odd comfort as a symbol of a normalcy that was now so foreign to him. The seat welcomed him back, custom formed to his backside after years of commuting and still just as comfortable as it was when he and Alina had purchased it new. They had been so excited, their future so full of hope and potential and dreams and plans. Now they stood apart, staring at each other across a bottomless chasm that threatened to consume everything they'd built with their years of love and toil. Shad sat in the quiet car, staring into an empty distance, grasping in his heart at the ethereal tendrils of his joyful memories, desperate for just one to materialize and replace reality. Drained, dumbfounded, forlorn, he sat in silence as he tried to comprehend the twisted wreckage of his once charmed life. He whispered a quiet prayer to God, known by name but otherwise obscure, and set about his quest to bring an appeal before him in person.

Chapter 16

Shad parked in a guest spot in front of the towering façade of Life Pointe Community Church, which he felt was actually quite appropriate given his perfunctory relationship with the institution. Looking down at his clothes, he felt underdressed as he got out of his car, but was quickly disabused from that impression by the other congregants walking by him in the parking lot. If anything, his borrowed pants put him ahead of a large portion of his cargo-shorts-clad fellow churchgoers. Music played to a perfectly choreographed fountain in the entryway of the massive church. Shad recognized the tune as a classic hymn and began to hum along as he approached the multistory, all-glass entrance. Looking up at the shiny glass, he remembered how wonderous the lobby looked in the holidays. Isla always loved coming to the Christmas Eve service because of all of the lights and trees the church would have decorating the entire campus. Even outside of the holidays, the massive building was still a sight to behold on a regular Sunday. The building was five or six stories tall, with the lobby wide open and cavernous. The stone floors echoed with the sounds of people making their way to the massive auditorium where services were held.

He'd never really taken the time to look around when he'd attended any of the holiday services, as he was always distracted with managing Isla. Now that he was here alone for the first time, he took in the sights and was impressed with the scale of the facility. To his left was a massive stone wall where other areas of the church building were housed. One sign read *Build Your Temple Fitness Center* above a set of glass doors. Inside he could see a receptionist and a massive, fully-equipped gym. On his right, outside in a beautifully manicured courtyard, there was a huge koi pond with tables and chairs set all around where people were sitting, talking, and reading. Set in the wall between that courtyard and the interior lobby where Shad was walking was a café called Tentbuilders, which served coffee and light food. Further into the lobby there was Scrolls, a large bookstore whose entrance was set into the stone wall, similar to that of the fitness center. Above both entrances on the large stone wall was the biggest television screen Shad had ever seen. It must have been three stories tall and just as wide, and was playing a video of a bird flying through the forest, through the mountains, and over the sea on a loop. A huge bank of at least a dozen escalators rose ahead of him, half of them lifting congregants to the entrance of the church's ten thousand–seat auditorium, the other half delivering them back to the lobby after the services concluded. Just to the right of the escalators was another receptionist behind a desk for the Spirit of Peace MedSpa.

Shad took the escalator up to the foyer, where smiling greeters were shaking hands and giving out programs for the service. He returned the toothy grin of a middle-aged man whose overly enthusiastic handshake gave Shad doubts about his sincerity. Walking past the wall of obligatory smiles, he happened to glance to his left and nearly jumped when he spotted his boss, Eddie, shaking hands and greeting people. Shad looked up and sent a grateful prayer that he had chosen a different escalator, avoiding what would have been an absolutely excruciating interaction.

He entered the gigantic auditorium, where the lights were already dimmed in preparation for the service beginning. Even though this was the fourth service of the day, Shad had to go to the upper level in order to find available seats. Spotlights slowly illuminated the stage, where nine people were standing, ready to lead the congregation in song. To the right and left of the stage were large screens like you might see at football stadium, displaying the lyrics to the songs and providing a more close-up view of the stage for churchgoers like Shad who'd arrived too late to get seats in the lower levels. The background of the stage was another enormous screen upon which a colorful display was projected, with a solitary wooden cross about eight feet high standing in the center.

"Hello, Life Pointe!" said the worship leader, a young twenty-something man with an unkempt beard and a man-bun. "Come on, y'all, you can do better than that. I said Hello Life Pointe!" he repeated, this time to a louder reply from the congregation. "That's more like it! We're so glad you could join us here on this Sunday afternoon. All are welcome, no matter your background. Maybe you're coming here from your house in a nice neighborhood, in your nice car, dressed in your Sunday best.

Awesome. Or maybe you came here from your college dorm room with some friends in a hoodie and basketball shorts. *Fantastic.* Or you know what, maybe you came here after a long night at the bars, just drinking, drinking your pains away. You know what? That's great too. We're not here to condemn you, we're here to welcome you," he said, strumming a pleasant chord on his guitar.

"I just want to share a little story that's on my heart right now, y'all. Listen here. Earlier today, I was hanging out at home with my dog Pookie. And we were having a good day, you know, just hanging out. And then, *out of nowhere*, Pookie pooped on the carpet. Just right there, right in front of me!" he exclaimed, prompting some of the crowd to laugh. "I was like, 'Come on Pookie! Don't poop on my carpet!' And I gotta be honest, y'all, I got mad. I wanted to punish Pookie. But then I was like, would God do that?" He strummed a minor chord, taking the tone of his story in a more serious direction. "And I realized, no, God wouldn't. We're always out there, pooping on God's carpet, right?" He smiled. "But does God punish us when we poop on the carpet? No, y'all. God forgives us, and that's how we have to live too." He paused for effect, strumming a major, triumphant chord. "Like God told us in His good, good book, love is the golden rule. It conquers all. Love doesn't rub our nose in our sin. It just picks them up, and flushes them away. We really believe that here at Life Pointe Community Church. Pray with me." He closed his eyes and bowed his head performatively.

"Oh, deepest of mercies," he said with a passionate, raspy tone. "Lead us to Your feet. Open us up and break our hearts. Let us dwell in Your beauty and wallow in Your mystery." His eyes were closed as he spoke. "May we fall in love with You today, just like the first time. Release us from our bonds, and liberate us. Amen. This song is called 'Over the Oceans'—sing it with me, church." He turned to the rest of the band, counting off to start the song.

The music began all at once, and was as good as anything Shad had heard on the radio; every musician was clearly professional and naturally talented. He found himself enveloped in the song, mesmerized by the thrumming guitars and the melodious voices; the punctuation of each drum beat resonating in his chest even in the upper levels of the auditorium. Without realizing it, he began to sing along to the words that were up on the screens as people around raised their hands in the air.

Over the oceans
Under the sea
Your love flies
Like a bird to me

Kiss my heart
With your redeeming love
I just wanna dance
With you above

Ohhhh
Hold my hand
Ohhhh
Don't let go
Ohhhh
Carry me
Ohhhh
Through the snow

Ohhhh
You'll never leave
Ohhhh
You'll never go
Ohhhh
I hope you see
Ohhhh
I love you so

The band continued to play for about twenty minutes. Shad had never seen the church's regular worship service and was floored by the production value. The lights, sound, and overall coordination of each element rivaled some concerts he had paid to see in his college days. After "Over the Oceans," the band played "I Give My Heart," "Dance of Love," "Fix Me," and closed with "We're All Together," a song that included some crowd participation in the form of hand-holding. After the music, a trendy-looking young woman with a nose ring, one of the many pastors of the church, walked onto the stage.

"Now we worship through our offerings. Life Pointe Community Church, this beautiful building where we come together to fellowship, this is only possible because of *your* support. Don't hold back! The Lord tells us that the more you give, the more you'll be blessed! You can scan the QR code on the back of the Bible in your pew to be taken to our donation website. We accept donations in the form of cash, check, all major credit cards, mobile wallets, cryptocurrency, stock, jewelry, vehicles, and real estate. If you're not sure about a donation, just ask! Chances are, we'll take it. Guests, please don't feel obligated to donate, but keep in mind that God's blessings are available to everyone—even if you're not a member of our church. As we pass around the donation baskets, we're going to play a few videos of members of the church who have given *big* and received *even bigger blessings* in return!" she said. Shad sat back and watched the videos, impressed again by the professional production value. These looked like documentaries he could have watched on any major streaming service or channel. They featured stories of people who had "stretched" to make significant donations to the church. Each of them then had remarkable things happen to them in the weeks and months after their donations; huge job promotions, large inheritances, and one man even won five million dollars after he "felt led by the spirit to buy an Ultra Millions lottery ticket" while he was filling his truck up with diesel. He'd picked the numbers that corresponded with his favorite Bible verses and, according to his testimony, God had returned his blessing. Shad had no money on him, so he passed the basket along to the next person who hesitated to take it, smiling and glancing down at it. He returned the smile, ignoring the clear judgment.

The donation period continued for about ten minutes, and then the lights came back up on the stage. Lead Pastor Bryan Delaney walked onto the stage along with another pastor that Shad didn't recognize. Delaney's face was on all of the billboards and ads for the church that were around the city, so he was hard to miss.

"Good afternoon, Life Pointe!" Delaney said. "It's so good to be here with you. As many of you know, I started Life Pointe Community Church in my living room with a few friends and family members. That was twenty years ago, and look at how we've been blessed since then! I never would have expected that our little house church would grow into this wonderful place, but God had bigger plans than I did. Unfortunately, those plans have changed."

He took a deep breath and looked down, standing silently for a few moments before looking up to the congregation. "I'm here to announce that I'm stepping down as your lead pastor. This will be my last service with you," he said to a cacophony of gasps and whispers from the congregation. "I know, I know. To tell you the truth, it's a surprise to me as well. The elders and the board voted earlier this week to fire me and to hire someone new, to take this church in a different direction." He began to pace across the stage, and as he spoke, the other pastor that came up on the stage with him started to follow him. "This was *not* my choice, and I don't think you should support it. Spread the word! They're taking everything we've built and destr—" His mic went silent, and Shad could barely hear his voice from the stage.

"Thank you so much, Pastor Delaney," said the other pastor on the stage. Two ushers walked purposefully onto the stage and escorted Delaney away. He resisted a little at first, but then relented. "It's a very emotional day, as we can all understand. Let's have a hand for Pastor Delaney!" he said, pausing for the crowd to clap for the ousted leader. "His faith led him to plant the seed that grew into this church, and his faith has now led him to step aside and let this church blossom with the next generation. I'm John Garza, Life Pointe's Pastor of Administration, which means I'm the guy that helps to keep things running behind the scenes! I was mentored by Pastor Delaney when I was just starting out as a youth minister. In many ways, he's responsible for the pastor that I've become. I'll always be indebted to him for all that he taught me. Let's all keep him in our prayers as he goes through this tough transition into God's next call on his life," Garza bowed his head in ostentatious admiration.

Having been removed from the auditorium, Delaney's protests could no longer be heard, making the whole scene a little less uncomfortable to behold. "You all must be anxious to discover who our new leader will be, right?" Pastor Garza leaned toward the crowd as if to listen closely. The crowd remained silent, tension from Delaney's graceless exit still filling the air. "I'm thrilled and honored to introduce our new Lead Pastor—Gloria Julian," he exclaimed, clapping and turning to his left as a middle-aged woman walked onto the stage.

Physically, she was totally average; she was neither short nor tall, neither fat nor fit, neither beautiful nor ugly. She wore unremarkable clothes and had a common hairstyle; she looked like someone you could pass in the aisle of the grocery store and immediately forget. Still, something kept Shad's eyes locked on her as she walked to take her place next to Pastor Garza. She exuded a magnetic energy, a strength and confidence that made Shad want to listen to what she had to say. The congregation clapped for her as she smiled and waved. When she got to Pastor Garza, they exchanged a cordial hug, he nodded to her as he continued clapping, and left the stage.

"Good afternoon, Life Pointe! There aren't words to describe how excited I am to be here with you today. Let's have another hand for Pastor Delaney!" she said, smiling and nodding as she clapped. "Such a rich spiritual legacy, he really leaves some big shoes to fill. He really does. I'm grateful to Life Pointe's elders and board for the opportunity to try to walk in those shoes, and to lead our church down a new path toward true forgiveness, freedom, and fulfillment for *everyone*."

Someone in the congregation said "Amen" loudly. Pastor Julian laughed. "That's right! Amen. We're about to journey together to a new place, a new level of spiritual awakening. Are you excited? Because let me tell you, brothers and sisters, you absolutely should be!" she said, eliciting cheers from a large portion of the congregation, while some maintained a silent skepticism.

Shad wasn't sure what to think; he felt disoriented by the unexpected turn of events. He had wanted to come to a church service to clear his mind and ground himself after such a turbulent weekend. Instead, he walked into what felt like the introduction of a stepparent after a sudden and unexpected divorce. Regardless, she appeared to be winning people over. The tension that had filled the air just a few minutes earlier had now mostly dissipated. "I hear you, I'm so glad you're with me. Like Pastor Garza said, we're beginning a new era here at Life Point Community Church. Are you ready?" she said, pausing for response.

Most of the congregation stood up from their chairs and gave her what she wanted with a loud "Yeah!" Many were clapping happily.

"One more time, just so everyone in the building can hear you!" She goaded the anticipatory crowd. "All right, brothers and sisters, I believe you. I won't make you wait any longer. Welcome"—she paused, stepping to the side and gesturing toward the cross that stood behind her at the center of the stage's backdrop—"to the new era of Life Pointe!" Above the cross, three huge black tapestries dropped from the ceiling.

Shad's knees buckled, and he sat down involuntarily. Aghast, he sat gripping the armrests tight enough to turn his knuckles white. He couldn't believe what he was witnessing. He looked frantically around him, hoping to find others who were equally shocked, but he found only disappointment, as everyone he could see was standing and cheering.

Each of the black banners was elaborately embroidered with a symbol representing one of the three cults. Asherah was on the left from the crowd's perspective, Baal was on the right, and Moloch was in the center. Julian was clapping and looking back and forth from the banners to the congregation, which continued cheering, as if hypnotized. "Brothers and sisters, Life Pointe Community Church has always been a place for everyone to come and find forgiveness and freedom. That's not going to change! In fact, we're doubling down on forgiveness! We're going all in on freedom! Today our doors are open to anyone in our community. Today, we accept *everyone* as they come. The elders and the board brought me here to usher in a new vision of *unbiased* church. Forgiveness and freedom for *everyone*." She waved her arm across the whole congregation for effect. "God's truth is everywhere in this world, and we're going to join with our community as we embark upon the journey to learn more about liberation. Meet our new staff members!" Julian said, turning to her right as she clapped. Walking up the stairs to the stage were a Molochian priest, an Asherian priestess, and a Baalist priest, each in their traditional garb. The Asherian waved at the crowd and smiled as she walked, while the Baalist nodded in affirmation to the crowd. The Molochian held his hands crossed in front of his chest and moved forward as if the congregation didn't even exist.

Shad was floored. He sat in his chair, paralyzed with disbelief at what was taking place on the church's stage right in front of him. "Now, please join me in a prayer of united holiness," Julian said. Shad could no longer bear it. He got up from his seat and began to leave, apologizing politely to the other congregants as he made his way down the row toward the aisle. When he reached it, he realized he was alone; some congregants were still seated, but no one else was leaving as Julian introduced Life Pointe Community Church's new Alternative Religion Pastors. Shad walked down the aisle toward the exit and locked eyes with a young man about his own age who was sitting down, his young wife and children seated in the row next to him. They held each other's gaze for a beat, and then the man looked away, ashamed, although he then stood up and directed his family to stand as Shad continued down the aisle toward the door.

Shad popped the door open eagerly, anxious to get as far away from the cult leaders as possible. He couldn't escape the lingering whispers of Nezzar's voice that his fight was hopeless; he'd already lost, he just hadn't realized it yet. Ahead of him were the escalators that led to the expansive lobby, but Shad wanted to get out as quickly as possible. A set of double doors to his left had an illuminated *EXIT* sign above them, so he began walking in that direction. Punching the push-lock with enthusiasm, he entered a long corridor with some offices and conference rooms.

He followed more illuminated signs until he finally reached a door that went outside. The afternoon sun greeted Shad with a blast of warmth, and he felt uncaged, as if he'd escaped something terrible. Looking around, he realized he had exited on a side of the building he didn't recognize. He started to walk out of what was apparently the building's service entrance in the vague direction of his parked car. Heading around a corner, he found a sidewalk lined with some parking spots that seemed to belong to employees of the church, each with a sign on the wall specifying the owner. The closest spot's sign had been removed, but it was still occupied with an unassuming gold sedan that looked well-maintained for being over a decade old. Its trunk was open and Shad could hear the sounds of someone shifting things around. He decided that whoever it was, they'd probably know the quickest way to get to his car.

"Hello? I think I left out of the wrong door. Could you tell me how to get to the visitor's parking lot?" Shad asked. The vehicle's owner raised his head above the trunk, and Shad stopped in his tracks. The face greeting him was none other than Pastor Delaney himself, looking a little frazzled and disheveled, but still bearing a warm smile.

"Sure thing. In fact, if you could give me a hand with these boxes, I'll do you one better and drive you around front so you don't have to walk the whole way. I know it's a bit of a trek to get around the whole church," he said, more cheerily than Shad would have expected from someone who had just been unceremoniously fired and thrown out of the building that was essentially his life's work.

"Oh, wow. Um, hi, Pastor Delaney."

"Well, as I'm sure you heard, I'm not a pastor here anymore. Just call me Bryan," he said, extending his hand. Shad shook it, feeling a little starstruck.

"I'm Shad, it's great to meet you."

"Pleased to meet you too, Shad." Delaney returned to his task of packing bankers boxes filled with books and personal effects in the back of his car's rapidly filling trunk. "How long have you been coming to Life Pointe?"

Shad reached down and picked up a box to hand to him, then took a deep breath, trying to recollect the first time they'd attended. "My wife and I have been coming for seven or eight years, I guess."

"Wow, that's a long time. I'm sorry to just be meeting you now. Especially under these circumstances!"

"Well, we really only came on holidays. Christmas Eve and Easter, usually. This was actually the first regular Sunday I had ever come."

Delaney set a box down and began laughing heartily. "Of all of the Sundays for you to come, it had to be this one?" He took a breath. "Some luck you have, huh, Shad?"

"Yeah, it's kind of been that way for me this weekend."

Delaney returned to packing the trunk as he spoke. "Sounds like we're both having a tough time. Want to talk about it?"

"Oh, I wouldn't want to bother you with it. You have plenty of problems of your own," Shad said. "Wait, I didn't mean that—sorry. That came off worse than I meant. I just meant that I don't want to burden you."

Delaney looked up at Shad from the trunk with a kind smile. "Honestly, Shad, you'd be doing me a favor. There's nothing I'd love more than to make the last thing I do on this property be genuine pastoring. So if you'd feel comfortable, unburden yourself!"

Shad's desperation for help and advice overcame his taciturn nature, and so he did exactly as Delaney asked. They finished packing Delaney's trunk and then got into the car as Shad recounted everything that had taken place that weekend. Delaney drove Shad around to the front of the building and parked in the guest spot next to Shad's car, where they sat and talked until Shad was finished.

"I'm really sorry that you're going through all of this, Shad. Your predicament sounds much more precarious than mine."

"Really? You were just forced out of the church you built for decades. They threw you out in front of your whole congregation. How's my situation worse?"

"Please, don't pull your punches, Shad! I hear you, but you have to understand, I am in this position because of my own failures, so I don't think our situations are exactly apples to apples. So much of what has happened to you this weekend has been outside of your control. Now, granted, you're right that you could have attended more to your bride. It's good that you see that now. This situation presents you with a real chance to show Alina that you're still the man she married. The question is how you can get to her before she does something she may regret, and that's a subject I'm afraid I'm not equipped to address. That's your own trial to overcome." He paused to think. "All I can tell you is I believe you're right to fight for your family. Protecting your daughter and your wife is your primary responsibility as a father and as a husband. And I would put it in that order, because your daughter is innocent of all of this. Your wife has made her own choices and she's responsible for those, but you still have to do everything you can to lay yourself down for her. She's definitely making it tough for you, but I don't think you're too late."

Shad sat for a moment, letting everything the pastor had said soak in. "Thank you for that advice, Pastor. I'm not sure what I'm going to do, to be honest. I feel totally powerless. I'm not sure how to get to her, but like you said, I have to try everything. I have to do anything I can."

"The right opportunity will come. Keep knocking, eventually a door will open," Delaney said.

Shad turned to Delaney. "What about you? What are you going to do now? You're clearly still good at this pastor thing."

"I appreciate that, Shad. Pastoring is all I've ever done. I can't imagine myself not doing it, really. But as you and everyone else saw today, I failed this congregation. I let down all of these people who were my responsibility, and I'm still sorting out my own challenges along those lines. I have to come to terms with the destruction that I've wrought."

"What do you mean? I thought they fired you? It's not like you handed Life Pointe over to the cults."

"Not that directly, no. But over the years, yes, that's exactly what I did. Inch by inch, Shad, I gave way to the darkness of this world until there were no inches left to give. It was never as stark as what you saw today; that would have been easy for me to resist. It was little things, little compromises made in the spirit of acceptance, or tolerance, or growth. What I didn't realize was that you can't compromise just a little of the truth. You can't give away just a little bit of your integrity. Once I had given away an inch, I had given it all away." Delaney looked through the windshield at the church building. "We always wanted more people to come to Life Pointe. We always wanted to reach more of our community, to get bigger. I told myself that growth wasn't the goal, that we were really trying to share the gospel with as many people as possible, but I see now that I was lying to myself. I was lying to the church, to God. I put the growth of the church ahead of the truth of the message. We watered things down to make them easier to sell. Of course, we never called it sales, but that's what it really was. We were marketing the gospel—and telling people they need to repent of their sins and change their lives or they will burn in hell isn't really the kind of thing that sounds good in a commercial!" Delaney laughed. "So we focused on the things that we could put on a billboard and we left the rest out. I don't think I ever really changed Life Pointe's actual doctrine; I just ignored a lot of it. I'm sure somewhere on a pamphlet or an obscure page of our website there's a statement of doctrine that says all of the right things, all of those things that we used to preach. I bet most of the people in there right now have never seen that, though."

Delaney chuckled again. "I just realized I don't even know what Bible translation we have in the chairs. I used to be such a stickler for that!" He shook his head.

"What about everyone else at Life Pointe? The other pastors, the other leaders; why are they allowing this to happen? Pastor Garza said that you mentored him."

"I really don't know, Shad. I'm sure they mean well. I'm sure they have good intentions. John was always so bright and energetic. I'd like to think I taught him to be open and inviting, so maybe he's just taking that a little too far. I always told John that it's better to find common ground and focus on that. No one likes to be the person who tells someone that they're wrong," he said, staring off into his memories. "I didn't expect this from John, but I'm also not surprised. This didn't start here, believe it or not. Life Pointe is a part of a national church organization called the National Evangelical Convention. They've played a central role in leading us down this path. They began passing small, subtle changes to their statement of faith . . . I think it started over ten years ago. They gave an inch to the culture here, another inch there, and fast-forward a decade and now they have priests of each of the alternative religions on their pastoral counsel. I'm not trying to pass the buck; I absolutely own my role in this catastrophe. I saw the compromises they were making and I didn't resist them. I embraced them. Shoot, I even spoke in favor of them at the conferences where they were approved! But the point is, this is a lot bigger than our church here in Mapleton. This is happening in churches everywhere."

Delaney shook his head. "Everyone is going to have to face this, one way or another. I know there are good people still in that building right now as we speak, feeling terribly conflicted, unsure of what to do. They've been going to Life Pointe for years and they trust the leadership, but they know what's happening isn't right. They're afraid to act, they're afraid to speak up and get involved. There are a lot of people like that, Shad. People who are sitting on the sidelines, watching terrible things happen and doing nothing because it isn't directly impacting their lives. It's not happening at their church or school or job, so they think they can just ignore it and it will go away. But they're going to end up the way we did here at

Life Pointe—it was minor, it was easy to excuse, and then all of a sudden, everything was different, and now you have to pick sides, and the side you'd like to pick just got kicked out the door. Everyone is going to have to face the fact that they can't serve two masters. You can't be both the darkness and the light. One side is going to win. I'm sure that they'll keep saying that Life Pointe is a *church*, they'll keep calling what they do *Bible studies*, they'll even keep some of the same songs and hymns, but none of that will be true anymore. This is a temple of the cults now." He pointed at the building, deep sadness in his voice. "I cracked the door open and let a little of the darkness in, years ago, and now it's snuffed out all the light."

"So what now? How can we possibly beat this?" Shad asked.

"Learn from Life Pointe. Learn from me and my failure. Don't compromise your principles, your beliefs. Not even a little bit, not for anything. It might be the path of least resistance. It might feel safer. They'll make it sound that way; it's just one sacrifice, it's just one offering. I'm sure Gloria made it sound noble, didn't she? Probably said something about acceptance, or condemning bigotry. But what they really mean is submission, and there's no such thing as a partial surrender," Delaney said. "You keep doing what you're doing and *you don't quit*. Fight with your whole heart for your family. That's your calling, that comes first. If you give up even a little bit, you've lost everything."

"I will. I can't give up on them. I just hope it's enough."

"Give your all, because that's all you've got," Delaney said, as if he was reciting something he'd said many times before. "And that's all I've got. Thanks for letting me preach one last sermon."

Shad laughed. "I hope that's not the last one you ever give. You could always start another church in your house. And if you do, I promise I'll go more than just on the holidays."

"I'll hold you to that, Shad. I'll be praying for you and your family. You're not alone in this fight," said Delaney as they shook hands. After they exchanged contact information, Shad got out of Delaney's car and walked over to his SUV, which sat in the shadow of the large church. The building that had looked like a welcoming refuge from his travails when he walked in earlier that afternoon now loomed over him, dark and foreboding—a mocking reminder that his struggles were far from over.

Chapter 17

As Shad drove back to Deckard's house, he was zoning out as he reflected on everything he and Pastor Delaney had spoken about. While it hadn't exactly been encouraging, Shad still felt reassured after the conversation. Much of what Delaney had said resonated deeply within him, and it was heartening to find another ally in the war that had come to his doorstep. The trill of his phone ringing through the car's speakers shattered his reverie. His car's screen showed Tom was calling.

"Tom? Have you heard from her? Did she watch the videos? What did she say?"

"Easy, easy. I sent her the videos, but she hasn't responded since then. I'm going to follow up with her soon, but she might be ghosting me. I'm sorry, Shad."

Shad cursed under his breath. "Don't give up, Tom. You're the only connection I have to her."

"I'm not, I'm not. But I don't think you have to give up, either. I know you're worried about Alina going to the festival and you're doing everything you can to stop her. If she doesn't watch these videos and she still goes to the festival, I have an idea about how you can get in. That's the other thing I wanted to tell you. I called my son to try to find out if he was going to the festival today, and he told me some really interesting details you're going to want to hear. I'm pretty sure you can get back into the festival. If Alina is going, you can at least be there to try to talk to her as one last-ditch effort," said Tom.

"Won't that violate the restraining order?"

"Only if you get within fifty feet of her. And only if you get caught. If they do catch you, I think you can plausibly say that you went to the festival to try to make things right with Lord Malochus and you had no idea that Alina would be there, since you haven't spoken with her. That part has the added benefit of being true, you really *don't* know if she'll be there. That won't get you off of the hook entirely, but I think that's plausible enough that I can use it to mitigate any significant issues."

"Why did your son tell you anything? Doesn't he know that you're against him doing the Asherian thing?"

"After what you showed me, I have to be honest, I panicked. I just wanted to make sure my son wasn't going to end up like that girl did. So I just asked him directly what he'd be doing. I asked him to tell me about it. I didn't know what else to do. He was very hesitant at first, understandably skeptical. Eventually he told me that he'd be ascending, but not down in the Under Yards. My ex-wife is going down there for something called the Obsidian Mass Ascension and he's going to attend as a spectator, but he's not participating. He said he's too new to be allowed into that ritual. Blessing in disguise, I guess," Tom said. "I'm not happy about him ascending. He's just a kid, he doesn't know what he's getting into. I'm not going to give up on him, but I'm just glad he's going to live through the night."

Shad shuddered as he thought about the college girl and what he'd watched the Asherians do to her. "I get it, Tom. There's no good option, you have to pick the least bad thing." He was quiet for a moment as he drove, considering his own options. "So what do I need to do?" Tom went on to explain the plan to Shad as he sat in his car, parked in front of Deckard's house. It sounded simple enough; in order to gain entry to the festival, Shad would have to dress as a Molochian priest. Their priests very rarely speak, if ever, so there wouldn't be much risk of being exposed by a conversation. He would enter at the special Obsidian gate, reserved for VIPs, high-level clergy, and their assistants. This entry was heavily guarded, with sentries posted at each doorway on the way down to the Under Yards. If any of them asked Shad who he was, he'd just respond that he was a steward to Malochus. According to Tom, getting questioned was unlikely but he should still be prepared. At each entrance, he would have to provide a specific passphrase to signal to the guards that he was a member of the exclusive group who could use the Obsidian entry. Apparently, Tom's ex-wife and her new husband were Obsidian-level members of the cult of Asherah, so Tom's son had the special phrase and had told his dad. When greeted by the guards with the traditional phrase *Hail the Blood Moon*, Shad only needed to respond with *Hail the Blood Moon and kneel before the goat lord*. Once he said that phrase, the guards would know that he was an insider, and they'd let him through, according to Tom.

"OK, sounds simple enough," Shad said. "But where am I going to get traditional Molochian robes?"

"That's the big question, but I have a pretty promising lead for you there too. My ex-wife gets her Asherian stuff dry-cleaned at Five Star Cleaners. Apparently, they specialize in getting out the kind of stains that the cults end up with after their . . . activities," Tom said. "I don't know for sure, but if the Asherians use this dry cleaner I'd say there's a good chance the Molochians do too."

"So I'm supposed to head over there and steal some robes from the dry cleaner?"

"Things get lost at dry cleaners all the time. As long as you don't get caught, it won't be a big deal. I doubt they have a robust security system. It's not like the cops are going to show up because two sets of robes are missing."

"Two sets of robes?"

"Isn't Deckard going with you?"

"I don't know, we haven't really discussed our next steps. He's still working on getting the videos up, but I haven't talked to him since I went to church."

"You went to church?"

"Yeah, I guess it seemed like the best place to be right now."

"How was it?"

"Terrible at first, but ended up pretty good. Long story."

"Did you find God?"

Shad thought for a moment. "I don't think He was the one that needed to be found." They concluded their conversation with Shad committing to keep Tom apprised of their plans and progress in case they got into a bind and had a need for a lawyer again. Punching the button to turn off the car, Shad got out, locked it, and went back into Deckard's house. He found Deckard stationed in front of his desktop computer, clicking and tapping at the keyboard.

"How's the uh . . . Internet stuff going?"

"Internet stuff?"

"I don't know what you do, bro. There's a reason you're rich and I have a minivan," Shad said.

Deckard nodded. "I'm making progress. The video is still banned on all of the big platforms, but I'm getting traction in other places. Message boards, messaging apps, and some of the mid-tier video sites. There's this crypto thing where you can post a video to the blockchain and it's basically there forever. It's a big-time niche spot, but at least they can't delete it. I'm trying to meme it into popularity using my anon accounts on Yeller and PostSpace. I'm friends with some influencers on Spinstagram and they're talking *about* the videos, just not posting or linking to them. So far, that hasn't caused them any trouble. That's the strategy on every other platform, trying to get people to talk about the videos to build up interest without linking directly to them. I've been able to get #SheDiedAlone trending, at least until the thought police realize what it means. The moronic thing about censors is that when they try to take something away, it just makes people want it more. It's like they've never heard of the forbidden fruit. The Drysand effect, right?"

"What the hell does this have to do with Deborah Drysand?" Shad said.

"Dude, you don't know about this? You grew up in the Internet age. Back in the early 2000s, someone got a hold of some pictures of her house. She tried to sue and stop those photos from being published online. Well, it backfired on her. The increased attention she created by trying to ban the photos just made people more interested in them, and they went viral. So thanks to her stupidity, we now call it the Drysand effect. I use it as a strategy at work all the time to make products go viral. We fake a ban on social media, do something to make it difficult to get directly to the product, like making it seem like the site has been taken down or our account has been suspended, and then we sit back and watch people just go completely rabid trying to find what we're selling. Works every time, even when the product is stupid. I literally got a million dollars in sales in two days by convincing people that thongs made from recycled plastic bags were being suppressed by the 'big undies' industry. It was a total lie and those thongs were terrible. Actual garbage made of garbage. But people still bought them because I convinced them that *someone was trying to keep them from buying them.*" Deckard laughed as he continued to focus on the screen. "The same thing is working in our favor this time; except this time, we're not faking it. There really are major forces trying to keep people from seeing our videos," he said, finally turning from the screen to look at Shad. "These guys are serious, Shad. I'm making progress, but their speed, their reach—it's pretty scary, man. I've only been doing this a few hours, and they've already banned four different accounts on three different platforms. Those platforms are owned by entirely separate parent companies, like with different stock symbols, bro. And yet, some-how, they are all coordinating and sniping me across the Internet at the exact same time."

"How? How can that even work?"

"Just wait, that's not even the scariest thing. Thankfully I'm not just a pretty boy who likes to do art, I've got my geek side too. I have my whole house set up with a hardware and software firewall, and I'm using a high-end VPN that's invite-only. I'm also routing all of my traffic through the dark net and posting to these platforms that way."

"I can barely work a spreadsheet. What did you just say?"

"Take my word for it, tracking me would take some serious juice. Like, government level. And someone has gotten as close as my firewall *twice* already. That has *never* happened. I'm not bragging, bro, I have liter-ally *hacked the actual government* and they've never been able to track me down. But today, with our videos of the cult insanity, they've already found me not one time, but two times."

"That sounds bad," Shad said, looking to the front door involuntarily.

"My firewall is rock solid and I have enough of a smokescreen up that even though they got close, they still can't tell where I am in terms of actual geography. But yeah, man, I'm spooked. I think it's just a matter of time before they give up on the videos and just come after me. Like I said, these people aren't lightweights. We're swimming in the deep end now. This isn't even David versus Goliath, this is like David versus Godzilla."

"So a slingshot and some rocks aren't going to take them down? What can we do, short of divine intervention?"

"We can't stop what they're doing. But the good news is, they can't stop what we're doing either. They may have people in every one of these companies, but I still have the real videos and I'm still posting them. We're at war with the cults. This is just the beginning."

"You don't seem as discouraged as I am."

"I'm not. I'm determined. We're in the right here, dude. We have the truth on our side. I'm not discouraged by what they're doing. It's the opposite, I'm energized. They're only slowing us down. Anyway, I'm at a good stopping place—I just basically vaporized my trail and reset everything so whoever is trying to find me is about to get really pissed off because I just sent them to square one. Enough about the tech stuff. How'd it go at church?"

Deckard stood up from his desk and motioned for Shad to follow him onto the back porch. They lit up cigarettes from the pack they had broken open the day before, sat back in Deckard's unusually comfortable patio furniture, and spent the next twenty minutes talking through everything Shad had experienced at Life Pointe.

"I guess at this point we should have expected it," Deckard said. "They're around every corner, under every rock, behind every curtain. We can't get away from the cults, they're in everything, taking over everything in society. I'm sure people who see the videos online think we're on some kind of crusade, that this whole thing is a vendetta against alts. But the truth is that we just want to be left alone, and the culties can't seem to allow that. They keep pushing and pushing, injecting their religion into everything until it can't be avoided. I mean, you can't even go shopping at Bullseye without a full frontal cultie assault. So people like us—normal people who were neutral, people who didn't care, people who really are tolerant and just want to live their lives and let other people live theirs—they're forced to engage in this battle to protect their own. We're only fighting them because they didn't give us a choice."

Deckard walked to the minifridge in his outdoor kitchen. He pulled out two sparkling waters, sat back down, and handed one of the bottles to Shad.

"I was definitely frustrated after what happened at work, but it was those photos that Alina showed me of Isla doing those pretend rituals at school that really set me off," Shad said, taking a sip of the fizzy water. "Like you said, before that I was neutral. But there's no going back to that now, not with what we've seen. Not with everything that's happened. We can't just walk away after the festival, the rituals, Nezzar, jail . . . Speaking of jail, I still haven't thanked you for bailing me out. That was a lot of money dude, and I'm absolutely grateful, but don't make me do anything too humiliating as payment, all right? I have a kid, I need to maintain at least a little dignity."

"What are you talking about?"

Shad's smile faded. "My bail. It was two hundred thousand dollars. Tom said that it was posted anonymously. I just figured it was you, since you're the only rich friend I have and you were the only one who knew I was in there besides Alina."

"I'm flattered you think I have that much cash lying around. Don't get me wrong, if I did, I definitely would have bailed you out, but it wasn't me."

"If it wasn't you, then who the hell paid my bail?"

"Your guess is as good as mine. Maybe some rich guy who saw your video also watched the ones I posted and realized you were being set up.

Wanted to help and paid your bail anonymously? For some people, that much money is nothing. Like Jerry Dink but not evil," Deckard said.

"Could be. Whoever it was, I'll take it. If I was still in there, we wouldn't be able to sneak into the Blood Moon Equinox festival again tonight to make sure that Alina is safe."

"Say again?"

"Don't worry, I have a plan."

"Oh, OK, no problem then. What the hell are you talking about? We can't go back there! Going the first time has basically ruined your life."

"Relax, Tom hooked me up with some key insider information that will get us into the festival through the VIP entrance. I don't know if Alina is even going to be there, but if she is, then I have to be there, too, so I can try and stop her. It's my battle to fight, but I could really use your help if you're willing."

Deckard thought for a moment. "What's the plan?"

"It's actually pretty simple. We steal a couple sets of robes from the Moloch guys and we walk right in like we're one of them. Tom got the passphrase from his son, he's an Asherian."

"His son is a cultie? And we're trusting him?"

"He's just going to be there as a spectator. That's why Tom called him. They're estranged because Tom's ex got his son into the cult of Asherah. It's a long story. Tom's ex and her new husband are both Obsidian-level Asherians. That's how his son knows the special password to use the VIP entrance."

Deckard considered the plan for a moment and then nodded, satisfied. "So we have the secret handshake now, but where do we get the robes?"

"Tom told me where his wife gets her Asherian stuff dry-cleaned. We don't know for sure if the Molochians use the same place, but there's a good chance they do."

Deckard pulled out his phone. "What's it called?"

"Five Star Cleaners." Deckard began tapping away on his phone screen.

"Oh yeah, this place definitely has robes," he said, turning the phone toward Shad. The website for the dry cleaners had symbols for each of the three cults as the hero image with a large pentagram as the icon in their logo. "Up until now, we haven't actually done anything illegal, are you sure you want to cross that line?"

"Bro, I was literally in jail this morning. That ship has sailed, don't you think?"

"That's not what I meant. The charges against you are bogus, trumped up by the culties to make you look bad and discredit the video evidence we're posting. But if we do this, we'll be doing something actually illegal. We'll be stealing. You're OK with that?"

Shad sat back and took another drink of his sparkling water as he contemplated Deckard's question. "I've never had so much as a parking ticket, but my wife is in danger. If I have to get hit with a charge for petty theft, it's worth it as long as she doesn't end up tied to a post like that poor young woman."

Deckard nodded. "The teleological suspension of the ethical."

"Yeah? Yeah, that thing you just said is what I was also thinking," Shad said.

"Philosophy was one of the only classes I took before I dropped out, some of it stuck with me. Anyway, the point is that your obligation to your wife outweighs your obligation to the law. I agree, and so would the sad Danish guy who came up with that complicated phrase."

"I'll take your word for it. I skipped a lot of that class and barely passed. Not my bag," Shad said, taking one last draw from his cigarette before putting it out in Deckard's art-deco ash tray. "Ready to do some crime stuff?"

"Easy, kingpin." Deckard looked back at his phone. "Looks like they close in about forty-five minutes. It's ten minutes away. Let's head over there, maybe we can catch a lazy employee, ready for the shift to end." Shad stood up in agreement and followed Deckard to his garage.

They made their way to the dry cleaners and, after Deckard worked his masculine magic on the attention-starved cashier and insisted he had lost his dry-cleaning tickets, they left with two sets of Molochian robes.

"One sec, I told Tom I'd keep him updated on our progress." Shad tapped away on his phone for a few moments as they walked back into Deckard's kitchen from the garage. "What are we supposed to wear under this? Does it come with special underwear?"

Deckard thought for a moment. "I don't think so, magic undies are for the Mormons. I was going to say we should go commando, because why not? But if we need to get out of these robes quickly and get lost in the crowd as normies, we should probably have clothes on underneath. Just grab something else out of the closet in that guest room you used earlier," he said before he walked down the hall to the master suite. Shad nodded and headed toward the guest room. Before he dug through Deckard's stash of old clothes and got dressed, Shad went to the restroom. After depositing the processed sparkling water in Deckard's toilet, he washed his hands and splashed his face with cold water before staring at himself in the mirror, contemplating his immediate future.

There was a chance that he and Deckard could successfully infiltrate the festival entirely unnoticed. There was a chance that they'd go down to the Under Yards and not find Alina there. She might change her mind and stay home, in which case Deckard and Shad might just turn around and leave. No confrontations, no violence, no sick feelings, no bottomless pits in their stomachs, just walking in and walking right back out. Compared to their last night in the Under Yards, there was a chance that this night could be uneventful, even boring. Shad told himself that was possible. But he knew it was a lie.

Chapter 18

CREDITS ROLLED ON ANOTHER episode of Isla's favorite cartoon before her completely predictable request to watch *just one more*. After Shad's lawyer Tom had left earlier that day, Alina was completely exhausted and decided that the stress of the morning justified an exception to the no-screens rule. Three generations of their family sat on the plush couch and took in episode after episode of cartoon inanity for the better part of the afternoon. They'd eaten a late lunch of frozen pizza in front of the screen, with Isla wondering how it could be possible for life to get any better. Eliana nodded off periodically into short naps, while Alina snuggled her little daughter and found comfort in her childish joy.

Even though Isla was basking in the bliss of seemingly unlimited screen time, she still wanted one more thing: her daddy. Isla had looked up at Alina more than once and sweetly asked if her daddy could come to watch the next episode with them "if he promised to be nice." Choking against the lump forming in her throat, Alina had just brushed her hair with her hands and said he'd come as soon as he could. Just before she was about to end their animated marathon, her phone buzzed with a text from Bella. "Fine, fine, but this is the last one!" Alina said to Isla as she unlocked her phone and sat up.

How are you feeling? read the text from her friend.

I guess I'm OK. Shad's lawyer came by. He said . . . a lot. Shad knows he's got work to do, so that's encouraging.

That sounds promising! Definitely seems like he's hit rock bottom, so hopefully he'll make the right choices now.

Alina thought for a moment before tapping out her response. *I don't know, I just feel overwhelmed. I've been snuggling Isla all afternoon.*

It's been a really tough day, but you're getting through it like a CHAMP. You are an absolute WARRIOR!

lol thanks. I don't know about that . . .

Trust me! You are SO strong.

Doesn't feel that way. Alina had a lot of feelings about herself, but wouldn't have picked any of the words Bella used.

Well it looks that way to me! Tonight is going to be great for you. Are you ready? You're going to be liberated!!!

Alina hesitated. Her heart jumped at the reminder of her liberation ritual before Moloch and his followers, her future community. She'd been fantasizing about it for so long, the idea of it being so close gave her goose bumps. But after the emotional roller-coaster she'd been on that day, part of her wanted to delay it and just stay home with Isla until things settled down with Shad.

I'm excited. I'm really looking forward to being liberated.

There was a pause before Bella responded. Alina started to type more, but deleted it.

Feels like there's a "but" coming?

Haha yeah, you know me too well! Is today the right day? With every-thing that's happened, I feel like it might be better to wait until life settles down.

Bella didn't text back quickly like she had been, like she always did. Alina watched the clock on her phone, waiting for Bella to respond. One, two, and then three minutes went by with her text showing it was received and read, but with no response in return. Insecurity began to creep in and settle into her stomach as an acidic void, making her squirm uneasily on the couch next to her oblivious child. Was Bella mad at her? She was just trying to be honest; she didn't mean to make her angry. If Bella would just respond, Alina could explain everything. Nine minutes elapsed; still, nothing. She locked her phone screen and set it face down on the cushion next to her and focused on the cartoon mania on the large flatscreen television. The mobile phone remained immobile, screaming to be turned over and checked because *what if she'd missed it?*

Bella must be very angry; she was really holding her ground. What if she just checked? Would that really be a big thing? Maybe she was being crazy. Who would care if she just checked to see if she had a notification? *No one would know,* hissed the serpent in the garden of her mind.

She decided to just do it. It wouldn't be a big deal if Bella hadn't responded. What was she, a teenager? This was stupid. She could handle it if there was no text. She turned the screen over and unlocked it.

Are you there? She typed, unsure of what else to say that wouldn't reveal her near-crippling insecurity.

Mercifully, Bella sent a response.

Yes.

Alina's thumbs hovered over her screen keyboard as she considered how to respond. She knew that Bella was upset, but she still wanted to avoid any conflict.

Did I say something wrong?

That did it. Bella began to type. And type. And type even more.

I vouched for you, Alina. I put my reputation on the line with the whole community. Lord Malochus is trusting me to provide you with guidance. He's relying on me. For you to change your mind on a whim because you had a bad day makes me think this isn't really that important to you. Is this just a distraction from your boring life? A little hobby you're exploring for fun? Well, it's not for me, Alina. This is my life. And it really hurts to be used and then thrown away like a cheap toy. On top of everything, it's the Blood Moon Equinox! It's our most important religious holiday. To be invited to be liberated by the High Priest himself is an honor that people LITERALLY dream of. Especially during the festival. People who have been coming to the temple for months don't get that. BUT YOU DID ALINA. If you don't show up, it would be such a huge insult. I don't think we could be friends. I don't even know if I could keep teaching Isla. I hope you change your mind.

Alina's jaw hung open. Her mind was blank, unable to construct a response to the textual deluge Bella had finally released. She'd been so hyped up waiting for her friend's message that she hadn't even taken a moment to imagine what Bella might say. Now that the wait was over, she was totally unprepared for the unvarnished honesty that she had received. She knew that Bella was mad, but she'd unleashed such a haymaker that Alina was dazed.

I'm sorry. Was the response she finally settled on. Bella didn't respond immediately, so she sent another message quickly after that one. *I wasn't thinking. I'm just feeling overwhelmed and I panicked. Please forgive me.*

Bella waited a few moments to respond. Alina's thumbs hovered over her keyboard, ready to continue groveling if Bella started another volley of silence. Thankfully, it wasn't necessary. *It's OK. I'm sorry too. I should have been more understanding. I know you have a lot on your mind. I just really want this for you. We've been chatting about it for such a long time and it's such a great opportunity. I'm so excited that Lord Malochus chose you to be liberated today.*

Am I the only one being liberated tonight? I thought it was a lot of people.

At the general festival there are probably more, but Malochus was impressed by you. He selected you for the Obsidian festival.

What's that?

It's where truly loyal followers of Moloch make their offerings. It's very, very special. I'm a little jelly, tbh! I'm just glad I get to be there with you.

The levity was a welcome respite, allowing Alina to relax for the first time since the standoff had begun twenty minutes earlier.

I'll be there. I want to do this, and I don't want you to be disappointed with me.

That's so great Alina! You and Isla will never forget this night.

Alina sighed. *So what's the plan? When do we go? What do we wear?*

I'll pick you up at 7 tonight. You should eat first, there won't be any food there. Do you have white dresses for you and Isla?

White? I thought we'd be wearing black because of Moloch . . .?

Now Bella's response was rapid. *You aren't liberated yet. The white represents that you're still bonded by the light of this world. Once you're liberated, you can wear black in the presence of the bull god.*

OK that makes sense. I don't know if I have anything white here for us both. I might have to go back to our house. Alina paused to think.

Don't worry about it, I have some dresses for you both. They have basic dresses for the bonded at the temple, I grabbed some just in case.

You really thought of everything! Thank you!

No problem girl! I just want to make sure everything is perfect tonight. Moloch will be pleased by your offering!

I HOPE SO! lol is it weird that I'm nervous? Because Alina was. Very.

Not at all, I was nervous too. You're going to be great. So is Isla. This is going to be so special.

I'm getting excited!

Good! No more cold feet!

lol definitely. I'm sorry again, I didn't mean to upset you.

Don't mention it. I'll see you at 7!

Alina responded by tapping a heart icon on Bella's message. She locked the phone screen again, this time with contentment instead of a knot of anxiety. Putting her arm around Isla and ignoring the fidgety protests, she settled in to enjoy the rest of their time together before Bella came to take them to the Blood Moon Equinox festival.

Time passed quickly; Alina surprisingly held her ground and didn't allow Isla to watch another episode of her cartoon. Peeling her daughter off of the couch, she forced her to into the kitchen where a slightly groggy Eliana began to prepare dinner. Alina and Isla helped, which basically consisted of following any orders that Eliana gave them. She ran her kitchen with an iron fist; Alina had learned early in her life not to ask questions and to do exactly as she was told, absorbing any knowledge she could by watching her mother's meticulous preparations. Enchiladas were her specialty and required multiple steps to get them just right, from rolling the enchiladas themselves, to making the sauce from scratch. Alina loved seeing Isla's fascination with Eliana's work, her daughter asking as many questions as she could get away with. Disarmed by her granddaughter's sincere interest, Eliana was way more patient and permissive than she'd ever been when Alina was that age, which Alina was very quick to point out to her mother.

"Old age has made me soft," Eliana said, waving off Alina's criticisms. They sat together as the enchiladas baked in the oven, laughing as they listened to Isla excitedly recount the storylines of the cartoons they had all watched together that day.

"Can we watch more tonight mama?"

"No sweetheart, we're going to the festival with Ms. Meyerson-Smith! Remember? You're going to stay up past bedtime tonight," Alina said, raising her eyebrows to Isla to emphasize what a big deal it was.

"Are you sure that's a good idea?" Eliana asked, getting up from the table to refill her glass.

Exasperated, Alina rolled her eyes. "Yes, Mom, it'll be fine. It's just one night and she's off school tomorrow so she can sleep in late and take a nap if she needs it."

"I just don't understand why she needs to come with you," said Eliana. "This is your decision, right? Or are you going to raise her to have the same beliefs?"

"Don't tell me you're going to start too. You know I have enough of *this* right now, Mom." Alina emphasized the word with her hands, being vague to avoid talking about Shad in front of Isla.

"That's not fair. I'm just asking questions, Alina. That shouldn't be a problem."

Alina sighed, frustrated at having to explain herself. "I don't know, Mom, the high priest said that I needed to bring Isla with me. I'm not sure how all of this works; I'm just doing what they said I need to do to get liberated."

"Liberated? What is that? Like an initiation?"

"Mom, come on," Alina said with a groan, regressing more to her fifteen-year-old self.

"What? I don't know about these alties, I read some things but I don't understand it. Why can't you explain it to me?"

"Yes, it's sort of like an initiation. It's the way that I officially join the temple of Moloch. I make my first offering. That liberates me from my position as a bonded-one."

"OK, I think I understand. What does Isla do?"

"I don't know, I guess she's just there with me."

Eliana looked at Isla who was wiggling in her chair. "Issy, do you need to go potty?"

The little girl thought for a moment. "Yeah, I do."

"OK, sweetheart, please go to the potty and don't forget to wash your hands."

"I will, Nana!" Isla slid off of her chair and headed to the bathroom. Once Isla was out of earshot, Eliana turned to her daughter.

"Shad is still her father, Alina. He's still your husband. You know he wouldn't want her to go to this ceremony."

"Mom, it's not your business. It's my family, and I'll do what I think is best. Shad's bigotry is his problem."

"Bigotry or not, there's no reason for you to intentionally make it worse." Eliana looked past Alina, recalling her own decisions. "I was stubborn with your dad. He wasn't perfect, but I was no angel. I didn't see it then; I could have let my guard down. I think he would have met me halfway. But I dug my heels in, and we divorced, and he was never the same after that."

"That wasn't your fault. He had a temper, just like Shad does."

Eliana laughed. "Darling, do you know me? Do you know yourself? We are stubborn. More than that, we're vindictive, and we know exactly how to cut the deepest. Your father loved me. I have no doubt of that. I never did, to be honest. I always knew he loved me. But he was human, he made mistakes. And when he messed up and hurt my feelings, I would never let it go. I would punish him relentlessly," she said, frowning involuntarily. "Sweetheart, I am old now. I see things much more clearly than

I did when I was your age. I let him die without ever telling him these things. I'm embarrassed to admit that it took losing him—really losing him, permanently—for me to realize that he wasn't a villain. I wasn't either. We were both just regular people, trying to make a life together. We could have succeeded. I know we could have, and I have to live the rest of my days with my regret, with my memories of him, and knowing that I failed. Please, don't make the same mistakes that I made. Shad isn't perfect, but he's your man. He gave you Isla. Don't do things that you can't take back." Tears slid quietly down her cheeks.

Alina sat quietly as her mother wiped her face with a paper napkin, blowing her nose lightly. "I'm sorry, Mom. I don't want you to feel like this."

"Alina, please don't miss the point. My sadness is not important. Your choices are."

"I've thought a lot about this. This ritual is significant to me and my life. They asked me to bring Isla, and I want her to share it with me. Maybe Shad will get mad, but I can't stop that. I think this might actually help him see that the alts are a healthy, positive community and that it's OK for Isla to explore it as she gets older. I'm not forcing her into it, I just want her to learn about it. What better way for her to learn than to experience a liberation firsthand, with her mother. The more I think about it, the more excited I am," Alina said. She heard the pitter-patter of Isla's sock-covered feet coming across the room and she turned to face her.

"Did you wash your hands?" she asked.

"Yes, Mom."

"Did you dry them?" Alina asked, raising her eyebrows. Isla began rubbing her hands on her shorts.

"Yes," she said. Alina laughed and turned back to her mother.

"I appreciate your concern, but I know what I'm doing. We're going to be OK. I know you're worried, but I'm not you, my marriage isn't like yours. I'm not making the same mistakes." The timer went off, indicating that the enchiladas were ready. Alina started to get up to take them out. Eliana placed her hand on top of Alina's.

"Just think about it, my love. Please."

Alina hesitated for a moment and then pulled her hand away without responding.

They sat together at the round, glass-topped table and enjoyed the enchiladas while Isla continued to retell and reenact cartoon episodes.

"Isla, are you ready to go on a special adventure with Ms. Meyerson-Smith?" Alina asked.

"We're going to school?"

"No, silly. We're not going to school. We're going to the Blood Moon Equinox Festival at the park downtown with Ms. Meyerson-Smith. Remember all those special activities we did at school on Friday?"

"The scary ones with the statues?"

"Scary? Baby, you had a lot of fun. Remember the dancing?" Alina said.

"That was weird. Then we did the ones with the blood and I didn't like that at all." Isla had disgust on her innocent face.

"Oh, we're not going to do that tonight, sweetheart. That was the Baalists. And the Asherians are the ones who do the dancing, we aren't doing that either."

"What are we going to do?"

"Do you remember the last one we did? With the black statue?"

Isla's eyes widened. "The ones where they cut open the puppies?" Eliana, sitting between Alina and Isla at the circular table, never took her eyes off of Alina, who could feel her mother's penetrating stare.

"Yes sweetie, those were offerings you made to the bull god Moloch. That's called being liberated. Mommy is going to be liberated tonight and you get to come!" Alina tried to hype up the ritual to her apprehensive six-year-old daughter.

Isla's face began to melt with sadness. "You're going to cut a puppy?"

"No, sweetheart, I won't be cutting any puppies. It will be a piece of meat that's already been cut up, like a steak. Remember the steaks that daddy made last weekend on the grill?"

Isla sniffled a little bit. "Yes."

"It will be like that, baby. No puppies, I promise," Alina wondered if she'd just lied to her daughter, since she actually had no idea what her offering would be. "You get to wear a new white dress."

Isla's mouth slowly improved from a frown to flat line. "Will it be a pretty dress?"

"Will it be pretty? Isla, would Mommy ever put you in a dress that wasn't *the prettiest?*" That did the trick, and Isla slowly began to smile.

"Where is it? Can I see it?"

"Ms. Meyerson-Smith is going to bring it when she picks us up! Won't it be fun to hang out with your teacher outside of class?"

Isla thought for a moment. "Yeah, I guess so. Will my friends from my class be there too?"

"No, I don't think so. I think it's just you, me, and Ms. Meyerson-Smith."

"How come no one else from class is coming. Am I in trouble?"

Alina placed her hand on Isla's. "No, baby, you're not in trouble! It's the opposite. You get to go because you're so special! In fact, you're so special that tonight you don't have to call her Ms. Meyerson-Smith, you can call her by her first name."

"Really? Are you sure?"

"Yup, I'm sure. Tonight, you get to call her Bella." This was truly a revelation for little Isla, who could hardly conceptualize that Ms. Meyerson-Smith existed outside of the classroom, much less that she had a regular first name.

"When is Ms. Meyerson . . ." Isla paused. "When is Bella coming to get us?"

Alina looked at her phone. "She's coming at seven, so in just about an hour. Before she gets here, we have to do our bath time, so go get started and I'll catch up with you." Isla bounced out of the chair and took off toward the bathroom in an eager jog. After she had rounded the corner, Alina spoke without even turning to her mother. "I don't want to hear it, Mom."

"Good, because I don't think I need to say it." Eliana stood up and began to clear the table, then helped Isla with her bath-time routine while Alina took a shower and straightened her hair. Bella texted at 6:54 p.m. that she was outside, and Alina greeted her at the front door.

"You look great! I hope these fit, I think you're about my size," Bella said as she walked in carrying two dresses. Alina's dress was a little tighter than she'd like, which she'd never admit out loud to anyone except maybe Shad. Thinking of him as she looked at herself in the mirror sent a current of anxious electricity through her chest, which she immediately worked to suppress. The child's dress fit Isla perfectly and she loved it. She twirled around, giggling as the skirt flowed around her.

"You two are absolutely perfect," Bella said. "Tonight is going to be unforgettable."

"Thanks Bella!" Isla eagerly took advantage of her special privileges at every opportunity. The three began to walk to the front door, where Eliana was waiting to see them off.

"I'll be asleep when you get home, so I wanted to make sure to say goodnight to my beautiful girls. Those dresses look great on both of you! So pure and angelic." She took a step back, taking them in. "OK, come give me hugs. Yes, you, too, Alina." Alina begrudgingly complied after Isla nearly sprinted into Eliana's legs.

"Nana! We're going to the park! I'm staying up past my bedtime! And I get to call my teacher Bella!"

Eliana laughed involuntarily, the only normal reaction to a child's unbridled joy. "That sounds so fun, princess. You stay close to your momma and make sure to do what she says, OK?" Isla nodded enthusiastically. Eliana looked up to Alina. "I love you, daughter of mine. Be safe. I will see you in the morning." She hugged Alina again, more tightly than usual.

"I love you, too, Mom. Don't worry, we'll be fine. Bella is going to take care of us," she said, smiling at her friend and her daughter's teacher, who nodded and smiled before looking down at her shoes. "All right, we've got to go. Don't want to be late!" Eliana waited in the open door as they left, leaning on the doorframe as she watched them walk to Bella's car. She watched every moment until they drove off, just like she always had when Alina left, ever since she was old enough for sleepovers.

"Everything OK with your mom?" Bella asked.

"Yeah, she's just worried. She doesn't know anything about alternative religions besides what she's seen on TV and heard from her friends, so she's just filling in the blanks with her fears. Typical. She'll be fine."

"What about you? No more cold feet?"

"Oh, come on, you're never going to let that go, are you?"

"Of course not!" Bella said, laughing. "You really gave me a scare. You'll never live it down."

They continued to chat and joke about everything and nothing, passing the time as Bella drove to the park. Traffic intensified as they neared the festival, the roads filling up with faithful cult-members hoping to attend the apex rituals of the Blood Moon Equinox. When they finally reached the park, Bella drove past the regular parking lots to a gated entrance with two guards clad in black suits. She rolled down her window and leaned out as the guard approached. "Bella on behalf of Lord Malochus." The guard lifted up a clipboard and activated a small but blindingly bright flashlight, flipping through pages. He nodded to her and waved her through as the other guard activated the gate's opening mechanism. It rolled to the side and Bella drove in to a small lot filled with more expensive cars than Alina had ever seen in one place.

"Wow, this looks like an exotic car dealership. These cars are worth more than all of the money I've ever made in my life!"

"Obsidian members. Like I told you, you're very special. I wasn't kidding." Bella parked next to an ostentatious European sedan.

"I didn't think you were kidding, but I guess I thought you were being, you know, nice. Like exaggerating to make me feel better," Alina said. "But yeah, this looks really exclusive, I feel kind of out of place already." Her eyes were wide as she looked around.

"Momma these cars are pretty. Can we get that one?" Isla pointed to a pearly white SUV that likely cost more than their house.

"Not a chance, sweetie, but you can go take a closer look if you want to," Alina said. Isla gleefully complied, running across the quiet parking lot. Compared to the masses of people at the main area of the festival they had passed driving in, the Obsidian entry was very quiet. The parking lot was mostly full, but there were no people around. Bella began walking toward a single-story brick building at the other end of the parking lot and Alina followed, calling back to Isla to come with them. She came running, ogling all the fancy cars and pointing them out to her mother as she ran. As they approached, Alina could tell the building was large, even if it wasn't tall. The wall they approached had a bank of garage doors, six in all. Apparently at some point in time this area served as a loading dock. Above the garage doors Alina could just make out letters in faded paint that said "The Under Yards" in a decades-old retro script. Bella was walking toward a set of double doors over to the left of the garage doors.

"What's the Under Yards?" Alina asked.

"It's an old underground arena built into a quarry, basically abandoned for years. Used to be for cattle and stuff, that's why they had these loading docks."

"So we're going underground?"

"Yeah, it's the only place we could use. We needed something big, just wait until you see the idol to the dark one we have down there!"

"Don't they have a big idol to Moloch in the park already?"

"This one is bigger. And the park is more for regular worship. We're using the Under Yards for followers who are at a higher level, more serious about their dedication. You'll see what I mean." They reached the double doors and Bella stopped, banged on the metal surface, and stood back. After a few moments the door opened and another guard in a black suit who looked like he could be a clone of the one at the gate came out, scrutinizing Bella suspiciously.

"Hail the Blood Moon," Bella said. "Bella for Lord Malochus. We're on the list." She gestured to the clipboard in his hand. Nodding, he opened the doors and waved them inside the building. Turning to Alina, Bella motioned toward the entrance. "These doors lead down to the Under Yards. This is the back, private entrance."

"I feel like such a big shot. I guess this is what rich people and celebrities feel like. Why is Lord Malochus doing all of this just for me?"

"I keep telling you that you're special, Alina." They began to descend the brightly lit stairwell.

"But how? What makes me *this* special?"

"I don't know, honestly. That's between you and him. I just know he recognized something in you. He'll explain everything during your liberation ritual," Bella said. Satisfied, Alina turned to Isla as they reached the bottom of the stairs and started down a corridor toward another set of doors and still more suit-wearing guards.

"What do you think, honey? Pretty cool, huh? We're VIPs!"

"What's a vip?" Isla said, pronouncing it as a word instead of an acronym.

"Very important person, silly. We're special, so we got to go in the same entrance as the other special people. Isn't that fun?"

"Where are we going? It's cold." Isla was unimpressed with the pomp of their entrance.

"Oh, don't worry, it'll be warmer in the Obsidian lounge," Bella said. They reached the next set of doors, which were again opened for them by the black-suited guards. After they entered, a hall about fifty yards long opened into the arena ahead of them. It was far enough that they couldn't see much other than light, but they could hear the beating of drums and the muffled cacophony of masses of people. Alina's heart began to flutter with excitement. She stopped and turned to Bella.

"Is that the arena down there? Where I'll be liberated?"

"It sure is." Bella grinned.

"It sounds like there are so many people there. They're all going to be there for my liberation?"

"Yeah. It's awesome, right?"

Alina responded by hugging her tightly. "Thank you so much for guiding me here! This is going to be unbelievable." She picked up Isla, spinning her around in a hug. Isla giggled giddily.

"Honestly, Alina, it's a special gift for me to be able to guide you. Yours will be a liberation for me, too, in a way. I can't wait to see it happen," Bella said, smiling wider than Alina had ever seen. They continued down the corridor until they reached a door on their right that had no handle on the outside. Bella knocked on it, and again it was opened by a guard. Because of the direction the door opened, Alina couldn't see the guard, she could only see his hand on the outside edge of the door. "We're here for Lord Malochus," Bella said to the unseen guard.

"Name?"

"Bella."

"Where's the offerings? The lady and the kid?"

Bella's brow furrowed and her lips pressed tightly together in a flash of anger. "The offerings should be stored *inside with you*. The *bonded one* is here with me." She motioned to Alina and Isla.

"Apologies, my mistake," the guard said as he peered around the door to see Alina and Isla waiting patiently. "Please, come in to the lounge and relax." He pushed the door flat to the wall so that it was totally open.

"Thank you," Bella said. She nodded to Alina and walked into the open door, who followed behind with Isla in tow. They entered a moderately sized room that was splendidly decorated. Leather couches were positioned in different places around the room, some lining walls, others opposing each other with a coffee table in between. There was a buffet of refreshments along one wall staffed by two smiling, beautiful young people. The room was dimly lit, but not dark, providing the same relaxing aura as a posh downtown bar. A small Bluetooth speaker played soothing music, evoking memories of the kind of miscellaneous tunes that were played during the therapeutic massages that Shad had gotten her as a "push present" after she had given birth to Isla.

Bella led them over to an L-shaped leather sectional in the corner with an ornately carved square coffee table in front of it. They sat down, both Alina and Isla taking in their surroundings. There was no one else in the room except for the guards and the waitstaff. Bella walked across the room and knocked on another door. Alina couldn't hear what she said, but when Bella turned around she was followed by a Molochian priest. She recognized him as Lord Malochus by his modest golden crown, and stood up to greet him as he approached. Anxious to make a good impression, she turned to Isla, who was distracted by all of the new sights and sounds and hadn't noticed her mother standing, and waved her hand frantically to get her attention. Isla complied, and stood excitedly next to Alina just as Bella and Lord Malochus arrived.

"Hail the Blood Moon, bonded-one," Malochus said in his thickly accented voice, bowing his head in greeting. "This must be your precious daughter, Isla."

"Hail the Blood Moon, Lord Malochus." Alina bowed in return. "Thank you for giving us the opportunity to be here tonight. I'm very excited to be liberated and I'm so grateful to be able to share this with my daughter."

"Oh, I assure you Alina, the joy of your liberation will be shared by all of the worshippers tonight. Such a wonderful offering to be made to the bull god. And to the goat lord, as well. Please, sit," he said, gesturing to the couches.

"I'm sorry, did you say goat lord? I thought I was being liberated by Moloch, what's the goat lord?" Alina asked as she sat down again. Malochus sat down on the couch opposite of hers, while Bella remained standing by his side. The two waiters walked over silently, bearing silver trays with snacks and drinks. They placed a glass of dark liquid in front of Alina and Isla, along with a plate of various snacks—including candy. Isla immediately squealed in delight and attacked it eagerly.

"Yes, yes," Malochus said smoothly, nodding as he spoke. "This is the Blood Sabbath, the most sacred part of the Blood Moon Equinox. Tonight is the apex, when we partake in the blood communion. Part of that ritual is making offerings to the prime of our gods, Baphomet. Even Moloch serves Baphomet. So, yes, you will be liberated by Moloch, but your offering will be presented to Baphomet after it is presented to Moloch."

"Oh, OK, that makes sense," said Alina, embarrassed at her own ignorance and feigning more understanding than she actually had.

"Please, enjoy the hors d'oeuvres and the drinks. That's a very fine cabernet for you—one of my favorites from my own collection—and of course a grape juice for your beautiful little one."

Alina smiled and picked up the glass, grateful that she could sip on wine instead of trying to think of something else to say. Isla had already had half of her glass of grape juice. Lord Malochus hadn't exaggerated; the wine was absolutely exquisite.

"Sweetheart, slow down on the candy. You're going to make yourself sick," Alina said to Isla as she was reaching for another piece of chocolate. Isla grunted in response, reluctantly acquiescing to her mother's command. Alina turned back to Malochus. "I'm sorry, I thought I had studied the Molochian liberation ritual but I didn't know about the Blood Sabbath." She took another drink of her wine.

"That's no problem at all, bonded-one. The true rituals of the Blood Sabbath are not widely known. In fact, they are a closely held secret. It is not surprising that you were unaware. That is by design."

"Why are they so secret?"

"Well, I'm afraid the nature of the rituals is such that they would be difficult for many to accept. Up in the public festival"—Malochus pointed up, indicating the festival in the park—"they have what I would call a sanitized version of the Blood Sabbath. Something more palatable for the majority of our society. Thankfully, we are making great progress, there are liberated in very powerful positions everywhere now, always making changes. A little here, a little there; we're slowly transforming this culture into our likeness. Alas, that is still a distant goal. There are many who remain very resistant to the freedom offered by the alternative religions. People like your husband Shadrick."

"I'm so sorry about what he did," Alina said. She was starting to feel tired and drowsy. "He knows he made a mistake; his lawyer told me. He'll come around. My liberation will change his mind. I'm feeling kind of sleepy," she said, her words starting to slur a little. She turned to look at Isla, only to find her sound asleep, slumped over on the couch in an odd position. "What happened to Isla?"

"We gave her something to calm her nerves. We gave it to you too," Malochus said. Bella remained still by Lord Malochus's side, her smile looking less and less friendly to Alina.

"You did what? In our drinks? Why? I came here willingly, I want to be liberated," she said, stumbling through her words.

"Yes, you have said so. And I do believe you are sincere in your desire for liberation." He paused for a moment. "You will be liberated, bonded-one. You will be. But yours will be a very special liberation. Very few throughout history have ever been liberated in the way that you will. A Blood Sabbath liberation is such an incomparable honor, your names will be remembered for many years to come."

Alina was fighting to stay awake; her eyes were heavier than any weight she'd ever lifted. It felt like she had to relearn how to speak in order to get any words out. "I wanna go home. I changed mind. I wanna go home. Shad gonna be mad. Need take Isla home for bed." Lord Malochus and Bella both laughed disdainfully as she struggled to plead.

"Bonded-one, you will never go home. You still don't understand. Our guard almost gave it away when you arrived. Thankfully my initiate Bella is very quick, very clever, indeed." Malochus reached over and stroked Bella's cheek tenderly. "She covered for his mistake and maintained the ruse *just* long enough."

At that moment, the guard who had opened the door was dragged into the room by two other guards. His face was bloodied, hardly even recognizable. Bella stepped back and stood behind Lord Malochus, who slipped a long, pointed ceremonial knife out of his robe as he continued speaking. "You are so *very important*, bonded-one. This man's error almost ruined our Blood Sabbath ritual," he said, gesturing at the man with his knife. "There is no forgiveness for such a severe failure."

With the last word, Malochus's hand flicked with lightning speed, splitting the man's throat wide open, blood spraying spectacularly outward as if to exclaim its surprise at being released into the open air. There was a sickening wet sucking sound as air was pulled inward through the wound before the man began to choke on his own blood as he bled out.

Malochus made a dismissive motion with his hand and the guard's now-dead body was dragged off. "You said that your husband's mind will be changed by your liberation. You are more correct than you even realize, bonded-one. He will come here tonight, because of you. And we *will* change him."

Alina's last vestiges of consciousness were spent in abject horror, just barely aware, but cognizant enough to know she'd just watched a man be murdered nonchalantly, like a toy being disregarded by a child after it had lost its luster. With all of her remaining strength and control, she reached for Isla, desperate to protect her young child in the face of such capricious violence. Gripping Isla with hands and arms that felt ghostly and numb, she turned to Malochus and Bella and managed to utter one final word. "*Why?*"

Lord Malochus approached her slowly, wiping the blood off of his blade with a napkin that one of the waiters had handed to him. Tossing it aside carelessly and sheathing his blade underneath his robe, he knelt down in front of Alina and placed one hand on her knee. "Because, bonded-one, there will be no offering, no sacrifice for your liberation. There will be no paltry steaks to slice. No ribeye or filet mignon," he said, prompting a giggle from Bella who was looking on, perpetually in his shadow. "We won't be slitting the throat of some pathetic rodent or spilling the guts of some farm animal. No, no, not on Baphomet's Blood Sabbath. Tonight, our Blood Communion will be decanted from your families' veins directly into our chalices. Tonight, we will consume your blood, your breath, your heart, your *life*. Tonight, bonded-one, *you* are the offering. And on the altar, you will be *made free*."

Chapter 19

WALKING OUT OF DECKARD'S guest room clad in black from his neck to his toes, Shad felt divided. He carried the hood into the kitchen and took a seat at Deckard's table, rubbing the soft fabric between his fingers as he sat and thought about their plan. Shad had no idea what he would do if he did see Alina at the festival. Maybe he would call out to her, or try to sneak up next to her in his disguise and whisper to her, or throw her over his shoulder like an ancient barbarian and make a run for it. She was petite, he felt confident he could carry her and maintain a decent sprint with the power of adrenaline aiding his efforts. Deckard walked in and interrupted his visions.

"Looking pretty contemplative there, my friend. Pregame ritual?"

"Trying to avoid rituals." Shad laughed. "I'm wondering what I'll do if we do end up spotting Alina. We'll be completely surrounded by culties. We can try to run for it, but I don't see how we make it out of the Under Yards. I really don't know what I'll do. She probably won't listen to me, she won't want me there." The gravity of the task before him lay on his shoulders like an albatross. "I don't know how to save her."

Deckard thought for a moment, his usual jocularity fading into pensiveness. "To tell you the truth, I don't either. I've thought a lot about it too. Our plan kind of ends with sneaking in, right? No one's going to mistake us for master spies," he said with a remorseful chuckle. "But I don't think we need to be. Let's get down there. Let's get to Alina. We'll find the right path at that point. We've made it this far, we'll know the right choice when we get there."

"Are you saying we should have faith? I thought you were an atheist," Shad said.

193

"Hey, I've never called myself an atheist. I'm agnostic, all right? And with all of the things we've seen . . ." He shook his head. "If evil like that is real—and I know it is because I've seen it with my own eyes—if that's real, then the opposite has to exist, too, right? Goodness *has* to be real. Because if it isn't, if there's nothing out there to counter that darkness we witnessed, then we should just give up. There's no hope."

"This is your pep talk?" Shad blinked.

"Let me finish, let me finish. My point is, even though I wouldn't quite say I have faith at this point, or even that I know what I would have faith *in*, for that matter, I will say that I do believe that goodness exists. There's light that's countering this darkness. I see it in you. I feel it in me. It's in some of the people you've met this weekend. That doctor, that detective, your lawyer Tom. We all know that what we're seeing is wrong; deep down in our guts we all know this stuff is evil. And we know it independently. We came to that conclusion, each of us, without being told, without being pushed. Even though we're all totally different people with different stories and experiences, we're all bound by this unavoidable sense that what these cults are doing is wrong. I can't explain that. I can't explain how we all just *know* that, all on our own, except that there's some source of goodness out there that's telling us the difference between good and evil, tying us together. Something deep in our souls is telling us that this is wrong, this isn't how we're meant to live. I don't know what that thing is. I don't know if I ever will. But I know more than any other time in my life that it's real, and I'm going to pursue it."

"But is that goodness enough? The cults are everywhere, they're in everything. The cops, the government, the media. Honestly, we probably don't even know the half of it."

Deckard looked Shad directly in the eyes with a more serious expression than he'd ever remembered seeing on his friend's face. "It has to be."

The two sat for a few minutes in silence, a spirit of sober determination settling over them both. Shad stood up from the table, slipping the hood of his disguise into his pocket. "Time to go."

Deckard nodded and rapped his knuckles on the table for a moment as he thought. Resolute, he stood and walked toward the garage quietly. They drove to the park in silence. Shad texted Tom again to let him know they were on the way to the park.

Heading to the festival. Wish us luck.

Godspeed. Keep your phone on in case I need to reach you. Set it to Do Not Disturb, but set me as one of the contacts with override. I won't text you unless it's important.

OK, done.

Tom responded to the final text with a thumbs up and Shad put his phone away. When they were close to the entrance to the Obsidian parking lot, Shad put his hood on. They weren't as concerned about anyone knowing who Deckard was. Neither of them knew whether or not Molochians wore their hoods while they drove, so they just made a guess that they didn't and hoped it was accurate. The guards at the gate accepted the passphrase without hesitation and waved them in. Deckard parked his blacked-out SUV next to a little sedan that stood out among the luxury vehicles in the lot. Putting on his hood, he turned to Shad before they got out of the car.

"How do I look?"

"No idea."

"I guess that's the point," Deckard said, opening his door. Before they started off, Deckard stopped Shad. "If anyone says anything, I'm going to do the talking. We can't risk that they recognize your voice from the video."

"Got it. Thanks for doing this, Deckard."

"Bros before hoes."

"What?"

Deckard shrugged, letting his attempt at defusing their mutual fear hang in the air for effect, and then began walking toward the large brick building. Now that they were both in their full disguises, they tried to walk the way that they had seen Molochian priests walk before, holding their arms over their abdomens, one arm on top of the other, their heads slightly bowed as they moved silently. They reached the doors to the building and once again Deckard provided the passphrase response to the guards. Just like at the gate, they were granted entry without hesitation or hassle. Nodding a slight bow to the guards as they opened the doors, they walked into a beautifully adorned reception area. So far, Tom's information had been flawless. There was a black carpet that led from the entry door over to their right, where another set of double doors was attended by two black-suited guards. There were a handful of Obsidian VIPs relaxing in the lounge.

He and Deckard maintained a steady pace along the black carpet, providing no indication that they were observing the people in the room as they walked. There was a woman reclined on one of the couches, sipping on a glass of white wine. Shad recognized her as a congresswoman from her reelection campaign signs that had popped up all over town. He had to stop himself from doing a double take when he realized that the man she was talking with was none other than their local weatherman, Donny Breezeman. Seated in a plush leather couch at the far end of the room and picking at finger foods provided by a stunningly attractive waitress were a man and a woman Shad immediately recognized.

After gritting their teeth to resist talking to each other about the people they were seeing, they went through the next set of doors and began to descend again to the heart of the Blood Moon Equinox festival—the massive Under Yards arena. Once the doors closed behind them and he was confident they couldn't be heard, Deckard spoke first.

"I always knew that Breezeman guy was a creep. Totally makes sense he's a cultie."

"You see the two in the corner? The guy was the police chief!"

"Sitting with that chick?"

"Yup, he's the reason I got arrested so fast. Malochus has him on speed dial. And the chick he was with? That's my prosecutor," Shad said as they continued down.

"He told us they had people everywhere. Nezzar is an evil monster, but he didn't lie to us," Deckard said.

When they reached the bottom of the steps, instead of walking into the concourse around the arena like they had the first time, they were in some sort of tunnel that went directly from the stairs and onto the grounds. As they walked down the corridor toward the rhythmic pounding of the ritual drums, a door ahead of them on the right opened and a Molochian priest walked out, accompanied by a guard. Shad and Deckard were far enough back that they weren't noticed, but they still slowed their pace to keep their distance and minimize the amount of noise they made as they followed. Because of the tiled walls, they were also able to eavesdrop on their conversation.

"See to it that the offerings are closely guarded. They mustn't be harmed in any way. Even the slightest scratch will diminish their value before the bull god and the goat lord," the priest said. They both immediately recognized the voice as Lord Malochus as he continued. "I want you to keep an eye on the initiate as well. She did well to bring us these offerings, but she's still not to be trusted with their care. They're too important.

Without them, there is no Blood Communion. And if there's no Blood Communion on the Blood Sabbath, Nezzar will have my head."

Malochus and the guard reached the end of the walkway and began walking on the grounds. They stopped as Malochus turned to face the guard and continued speaking. Deckard and Shad kept following, knowing that if they stopped walking to avoid Malochus, they would look even more suspicious. "And if he has *my* head, I will guarantee he takes the heads of everyone who failed me. Do you understand me?"

"Yes, Lord Malochus," the guard said.

"Good. Make sure the rest of your people do too. When the offerings wake up, make sure they are kept comfortable and as calm as possible. The mother will be angry, of course. You won't be able to help with that, just try to keep her contained. The initiate may be able to help, but her credibility with the mother is gone, now that she knows the truth. If the presence of the initiate aggravates her further, expel the initiate from the lounge. She can wait outside," Malochus said.

Shad and Deckard were close enough now to enter the guard's periphery, and he turned to face them.

"Who are you? What are you doing here?" said the guard. They stopped in their tracks, bowing their heads even more.

Deckard spoke, doing his best to adopt a submissive tone. "Hail the Blood Moon, Lord Malochus. We are here to serve."

Malochus turned to them. Even through his hood, they could feel the scorn emanating from his face. "More stewards? Fine. Get to the altars and clean. They must be *pristine*. Dozens of Obsidian offerings are still being made as we build up to the Blood Communion and we cannot have them slowed by lack of available altar space."

When Shad and Deckard didn't move, he turned to face them. "What are you pathetic idiots waiting for? Clean those altars and do not embarrass me! Now get out of my presence!" They both bowed to Malochus obediently and walked off more quickly than they had before.

Having entered on the perimeter of the arena on the side opposite of the idols, they were surrounded by the observation and recovery areas. The arena was teeming with activity; crowds of cult members all around them, walking, running, standing, talking, dancing, kissing, simply being. It had been busy the night before, but the Blood Sabbath was notably more crowded. Lounge structures were built all along the walls of the arena for cult members to rest and recuperate after completing their ritual offerings. Tending to these lounges were more cult clergy, bringing members food, drink, and whatever else they may require. There were also some medical tents for those whose offerings were more physically demanding than others. Shad noticed a half-dozen or so unmarked black tents around the area and wondered what they housed. Cult members who wanted to observe could sit up in the old arena seating. Now seven or eight decades old, it must not have been comfortable or even totally intact, because the stands were sparsely populated. Most people who were observing stood around in small groups or enjoyed the scenery from the comfort of one of the lounges.

Now that Deckard and Shad were actually down on the ground in the arena of the Under Yards, the festival took on a new level of reality. As they walked away from Malochus and the tunnel exit, they were greeted by elements they had seen from a distance, but not really experienced firsthand. They could feel the heat of the fires, they felt the pounding of the drums as it shook their clothes, and the smells—the smells were overpowering. The coppery stink of blood, the stale saltiness of sweat, and a disgusting cocktail of sundry body fluids was so strong in the air that they could taste it. Layered on top of everything else was the smell of burning meat. They had to remind themselves that it wasn't delicious barbeque they were smelling, but the stink of cooking human flesh. What they'd experienced the night before had an element of disconnection that made it intangible or fantastic. Like the difference between seeing a car accident happen and being the driver when a car crashes, it felt like something they had *seen* but not something they had *lived*. Now they were down in it, immersed; it was on them, around them. It was real.

They were no longer looking at people through screens or binoculars, they were at arm's length now. They could feel the breeze of air swish through their robes as people walked by, they could hear their conversations. Shad could see the oceanic blue-green eyes of the young Asherian woman looking sheepish as she walked with a much older man whose loathsome cologne was loud enough to scream above the deafening smells for a moment. He could see the thin smile lines in the cheeks of an old Baalist man, looking woozy as he was escorted away from the altars, a bloody rag wrapped where his left hand used to be. And as they walked, he saw the light shimmering off of a blade as a Molochian VIP walked away from the altar, his ritual knife still dripping with fresh human blood.

"Where are we supposed to go?" Deckard said to Shad as they walked through the crowd.

"Let's make our way to the idol to Moloch."

They continued weaving through cult members in the general direction of the huge black bull god. When they neared the altar area, Shad spotted a Molochian priest who seemed to be in charge. One hooded figure stood alone on the altar platform, appearing to direct others as offerings were made by Obsidian cult members. The priest noticed them as they got closer, turning to face them.

"State your business, stewards," a female voice hissed angrily behind the dark hood, surprising both Deckard and Shad. The Molochian robes made it almost impossible to discern the sex of the person under them. Both bowed to her in deference, doing their best to stay in character.

"Lord Malochus sent us to aid in the cleaning of the altars," Deckard said.

"He is wise. Both of you go to the fourth altar. There's an offering being made there now that should be almost complete. The stewards from the third altar have been cleaning them both and they can't keep up," she said. They nodded and shuffled off toward the altar.

Luckily, she had pointed at the one she was talking about, because the altars weren't labeled and they had no idea how to tell the difference. Looking toward the other altars, they saw Molochian stewards tending to their posts and tried to emulate them. Each altar before the bull god consisted of an ornately carved stone table on top of a semicircular platform raised a few feet off of the ground. The front of the platform faced the rest of the festival and other worshippers who were there to observe the Obsidian offerings. On the rear, concave side of the platform was a small walkway where the stewards waited to assist in the ceremony and clean after each offering. The platform was high enough that the stewards remained concealed when they were in the walkway, but they were still able to see over the platform to the crowd and beyond. Past that walkway was a pit of burning coals surrounding the pitch-black idol, the same pit into which they'd seen the sick old man's body tossed the night before. Shad looked up at the idol towering menacingly over them; the light of the fire at its base flickered and reflected off of its perfectly polished surface. He began to sweat from the sweltering heat of the burning pit as he approached the fourth altar. The other two Molochian stewards had already stationed themselves in the walkway below, waiting to assist. They stood next to a small wheeled cart with cleaning supplies and a huge fifty-gallon trash can filled with clean, white rags.

"Is that—" Shad said, looking up at the active offering taking place at the altar they would soon be cleaning.

"Donny freaking Breezeman," Deckard said as they approached. They slowed their pace when they were about ten yards away. It seemed appropriate not to crowd the platform during the ritual, and they also wanted to keep their distance while Breezeman did his work. Thankfully, the bossy priestess had been correct, the ritual was almost complete. They saw Breezeman hacking away at the body on the altar, just as Jerry Dink had done at the end of his offering. Another steward who had presumably been on the other side of the platform out of view walked up a set of stairs, carrying a round bronze dish. Shad and Deckard steeled themselves, struggling to maintain their composure as Breezeman threw limb after limb from the dismembered corpse into the fiery pit. He failed to throw one of the arms hard enough, and it bounced off of the edge of the pit and fell into the walkway below, landing with a wet thud next to one of the stewards. Without hesitation, the steward picked up the arm and threw it over the edge into the fiery pit. He then retrieved one of the white rags from the trash can, bent down and wiped the blood off of the floor, and then threw the bloody rag into the fire.

"I guess they don't waste anything," Shad said to Deckard.

"Not even the blood."

The rest of the ritual went exactly as it had with Dink the night before, with the steward on the platform placing the decapitated head into the bronze dish, bowing to Breezeman, who then returned the bow and placed the offering's heart into the dish next to the head. The face of a young man hung slack and lifeless as it sat unnaturally in the dish, his terrified final expression now frozen forever. Breezeman and the steward then left the platform in a procession toward the idol to Baphomet. One of the stewards in the walkway grabbed a handful of white rags and turned, heading to the stairs that led from the walkway up to the platform. Noticing Shad and Deckard standing there, he stopped. Realizing they'd been seen, they walked toward him.

"We were sent by Lord Malochus to take over cleaning and preparing the fourth altar," Deckard said.

"We have been blessed to serve our lord of darkness at two altars," said a nasal male voice.

"Oh, OK. We can wait while you continue to enjoy Moloch's blessed work."

"No, we would never disregard the guidance of Lord Malochus, may he be bathed in darkness," the priest said. Deckard bowed in return. The priest turned around and walked back to his partner. After whispering quietly, the two went to the third altar.

"What was that all about?" Shad asked after the other two priests were gone.

"Sounded like he didn't want to come off as eager to leave as he actually was. Probably afraid we would rat him out to Malochus. I guess the Molochian priests don't have a healthy internal culture. Not very collaborative. Not a lot of synergy. They need to do some team-building," Deckard spoke quietly. "So we wipe up whatever is left up there and toss everything in the fire? Sounds pretty simple." He looked at the altar above them.

"I guess so. Hopefully Breezeman already disposed of most of his offering. At least the platform will give us a great vantage point to look out for Alina."

"This wouldn't be too bad of a cover job if it weren't for the fact that we're standing in front of the mouth of a volcano." Deckard pointed to the pit next to them. "And, you know, all of the human blood and guts we're about to be mopping up."

They walked toward the cleaning cart and examined the tools the Molochians had provided. A bucket of basic bleach-based cleaning solution with multiple spray bottles, black nitrile gloves, coarse sponges, and a very large bottle of hand sanitizer. Shad squirted some sanitizer on his hands and turned to Deckard. "I'm just glad they keep their human sacrifices sanitary. I'd hate for someone to get hepatitis."

"Very responsible," Deckard said, reaching for the sanitizer. "Don't want to get AIDS either. Or monkeypox."

"I don't think that's how you get monkeypox."

"Know from experience?"

Shad responded with a middle finger.

Deckard wore his trademark smirk as he snapped on a pair of the nitrile gloves. Their cleaning equipment now prepared, the two reluctantly made their way up to the altar to assess their job. The stone surface of the altar was covered with a pool of blood from edge to edge. The upper portion of the young man's torso sat in the center of the small blood pond, with the liquid's smooth surface littered with gnarled pieces of flesh, bone, and viscera. Out of the corner of his eye, Shad could see the other two priests watching them from the walkway behind the third altar. Attempting to look like he'd done this before and didn't find it deeply repulsive, he began to gather pieces of the young man's body and toss them into the pit. "Just right down to business?" Deckard asked.

"The other two are watching us. Trying to act like I know what I'm doing," Shad said, gritting his teeth in disgust. Snapping into action, Deckard followed suit and began gathering chunks to burn. "Help me with this," Shad said, approaching the torso.

"This is an actual nightmare. I thought what we saw last night was terrible. Being down in it? This is infinitely worse," Deckard said as they lifted the mutilated remains and heaved them over the edge into the coals. They could smell the flesh cooking in the coals as they mopped up the blood with rags. "Are we really doing this?"

"Just focus on the work. Pretend it's paint. It's not real. Try to look for Alina. We have to give it some time before we can be sure that she's not coming," Shad said quietly. Deckard nodded, his reluctance evident even through the Molochian robes. As they continued soaking up blood with more and more white rags, Shad began to observe the rituals taking place all around them. Everywhere he looked was unimaginably obscene bedlam, nightmares made flesh. Each of the three cults were engaging in the kind of rituals they had witnessed the night before, but on a much wider scale. It wasn't just one offering at a time, it was multiple offerings taking place simultaneously; all of the horrific rituals of the three cults Shad and Deckard had previously seen, now turned up to eleven. Sexual depravity, brutal mutilation, and death enveloped them like a fog, overwhelming their sensibilities and numbing them both into shell-shocked stupor.

The cult of Baal had several altars like the cult of Moloch did, each occupied with an active offering. Shad saw people cutting off their own limbs, cutting off the limbs of others whose willingness to participate looked questionable at best, including an elderly man whose limbs were being offered by what seemed to be his adult son. The old man was held down by two Baalist priests, with another standing in wait with medical equipment. The man must have been in his seventies, thrashing against the priests who were restraining him as much as his feeble frame would allow. His son, completely unmoved by his father's cries, was hacking away at his leg below the knee. Shad saw all of that in just a matter of seconds and looked away involuntarily, overwhelmed by the sight. Unfortunately, he turned his eyes to another Baalist altar where a man was sitting on the stone surface, naked from the waist down. Shad closed his eyes before he could see what would happen next.

Shad tried to focus on the blood he was wiping up, but the pandemonium in his periphery was impossible to totally ignore. Capitulating, he looked toward the cult of Asherah and found no respite from revulsion.

As he continued cleaning the blood of the young man hacked to death by their local weatherman, he saw every conceivable sex act performed in every combination possible. Individuals, couples, and groups, all kinds of people. Averting his eyes from the mass of undulating bodies, he realized he had been gripping the side of the stone altar so hard that he had folded the nail of his middle finger backward. He mashed it back down with his thumb, grimacing. All he could think about was how these wicked cults were being promoted to innocent children like his own daughter, Isla.

"Have you looked around?" Shad asked Deckard, throwing his last clump of bloody rags into the fire, the altar now cleaned.

"Man, I'm really trying not to, but I can't avoid it. Even out of the corner of my eye, everything I see is like we're inside some Renaissance painting of hell," Deckard said. "It's what we saw last night on steroids. And we're courtside now."

"We've been here like what, twenty minutes? Keep trying to tune it out. I know it's horrible. We have to make it through until we're sure she's not coming. Are we done with this?" Shad asked, motioning to the altar. He and Deckard inspected it closely, walking around its edges, hoping to maintain the legitimacy of their cover by being meticulous. The stone was free of any blood or viscera, all evidence of the life there extinguished now erased by their efforts.

"I think we just need to do a final spray with the cleaning solution and it should be done," Shad said. He went down to the walkway to gather the bleach spray before completing the job. Deckard performed a final wipe and polish of the surface before they both returned to the walkway to await the next offering. It didn't take long. Just a few minutes later, the next VIP arrived with their offering. They didn't recognize the Molochian this time, an older woman with gray hair. The sacrifice was a middle-aged woman who seemed woozy as she walked. Her skin was leathery and worn, as if it had seen too much sun far too many times, making her look older than she probably was. Shad surmised she was likely homeless, recalling billboards he'd seen earlier advertising the Temple of Moloch's homeless outreach program. Unlike the old man they had watched Dink butcher the night before, this woman was not willing. Once the ritual began, she had to be held down by guards and priests of Moloch. Her screams pierced the air; the Molochians apparently unperturbed by her protests. She was eventually silenced by her own blood filling her throat before she gurgled her last, desperate breath. Both Shad and Deckard stared forward, gritting their teeth as they listened to the horror taking place just above them.

After the poor woman was divided and the Molochians paraded away toward Baphomet again, Shad and Deckard went back to work cleaning the altar. They were quicker this time, having improved their ability to tune out the abominable ambiance.

Again, minutes after they completed their grisly task, a VIP arrived with an offering. And again, this one was worse than the last. A middle-aged woman walked toward the altar, holding hands with a little boy who looked just a little bigger than Isla, maybe nine years old. They looked similar enough that it was clear they were mother and son, sharing hair, eye color, and basic facial features. The boy looked terrified, gripping his mother's hand tightly and looking up to her over and over again as they walked, searching for reassurance. She would look down and say some-thing to calm him down, but he seemed to get more frantic as they neared the altar. He could clearly see what was taking place all around him and was beginning to realize something wasn't right. When they were just a few feet from the steps up to the altar, the boy's flight response took over and he slipped his hand away from his mother, making a sprint in the direction that they had come. Within a few feet, he was swept up in the arms of a tall, lanky Molochian priest who had been walking behind them. The thrashing child was carried up the stairs and held down on the altar by four different Molochian clergy. He wailed and wept, begging his mother to stop and take him home. Over and over, he screamed for his daddy. His cries went unanswered. As they listened to the vile ritual being performed, Shad choked back tears, thinking of his own daughter in the boy's place. He had to reach over and restrain Deckard from interven-ing, his tolerance for inaction having been exhausted. "We *can't*," Shad whispered.

Deckard resisted. "He's just a *child*!"

"Don't you think I know? We can't save him!" Shad felt a depth of remorse that he knew would haunt him for the rest of his life. Deckard hesitated, and then relented. They both knew that a successful interven-tion was a long shot, and it was a long shot they could only take once. Shad wouldn't waste it on a stranger, no matter how much it made him hate himself.

They cleaned up in total silence after the child had been given up to the bull god by his own mother, each of them nauseous from a cock-tail of anguish, frustration, and disgust. In a conflicted daze of shame, they shuffled back down to resume their positions in the walkway as yet another VIP approached. Shad spoke, dazed. "I think I'm numb. I can't process anything else."

"Yeah," was all that Deckard could manage as a response.

Two more offerings came and went, but they couldn't say much about who made them or who was offered, having reached the point where robotic disconnection was necessary for their sanity. They sopped up blood, disposed of entrails, and sanitized the surface each time, now an established routine that they could complete like clockwork. They no longer noticed the mayhem taking place at the other idols, their minds having retreated as much as they could before reaching actual unconsciousness. Shad continued looking for Alina, his eyes trained to skip over all of the horrors they beheld, like searching for a specific piece in a puzzle of nightmares. They stood, motionless automatons in the walkway beneath the table of death above them, staring forward into nothingness.

Bumped. Bumped. Bumped again—Shad was jarred out of his stupor by a pain in his arm. Looking down, he realized Deckard had been elbowing him, trying to make him snap out of the torpor. "Listen!"

Shaking himself back to cognizance, Shad quickly realized what had pierced the fog to get Deckard's attention: total silence. No more drumming. No talking; not even a whisper. No voices crying out in agony or ecstasy. No dull slapping of moist skin-on-skin collisions. None of the sickening ripping and tearing of blade meeting flesh. None of the ambient ritual noises to which they'd grown accustomed. No footsteps; no movement at all. Nothing, just stillness and the crackling of fires still burning, oblivious to the sudden change.

Looking around at the cultists in the arena, they were all motionless, their eyes fixated in one direction. Shad followed their gazes to the central idol of Baphomet. Behind the golden altars and at the foot of the goat lord statue was an empty stage, now lit with a single, piercing spotlight. The crowd waited silently in anticipation until, without warning or introduction, a man walked out into the light. Immediately, the mass of cultists erupted in deafening cries of adulation. The man stood, his back to the crowd, his arms raised toward the idol of the goat lord, as if to channel the cheering directly toward it. He then turned to face the crowd and motioned for them to quiet. Shad knew him immediately; a face he would never be able to forget. It was Nezzar.

"Welcome, welcome, fellow worshippers!" he said to more cheering and applause. "Thank you, yes, thank you. Hail the Blood Moon!"

Nezzar shouted, the crowd then repeating the phrase back to him joyously. "Tonight is the Blood Sabbath, the most sacred night of our festival when we bring our final, most precious offerings before the goat lord, Baphomet. And accordingly, as the priest of Baphomet, I will perform a sacred rite on your behalf. An offering to cleanse us all until the next Blood Moon Equinox—the Blood Communion. The goat lord, the leader of our liberation from the tyranny of the light, the prince of darkness; our *freedom*. Tonight, we will offer him our communion, our worship, our allegiance, and if it pleases him, he will accept it, and he will bless us!" Nezzar exclaimed to more raucous cries, his cadence reminiscent of a televangelist. "He will bless us, and his power will shatter the chains of the light, delivering each of his faithful servants into the unrestrained, unrestricted, limitless life *we each deserve*! Soon we will make our offering and I must emphasize to you, faithful servants of the lesser gods, the offering I will make on your behalf is a very, very special one. The requirements for correctly presenting the Blood Communion to Baphomet are extremely strict. It is very difficult to find the right offering to satisfy the prime recreant, the first among rebels. But I am happy to tell you all that our own Lord Malochus has provided the perfect specimen to please Baphomet." Nezzar stood still, waiting for the cheering to die down to a hush. "I could not be more pleased to reveal our offerings to you. Their lives given on this stage to sate his hunger and earn us all his precious blessings. Behold, our Blood Communion!"

Shad's heart stopped; his breath caught in his chest as the world around him entered slow motion, his vision tunneling to only the stage. He stood watching, paralyzed as two figures clad in all white were led out by priests of each of the lesser cults. The crowd went absolutely wild as the two offerings were slowly walked to a set of posts on either side of Nezzar where they were tied. Shad couldn't move, he couldn't think, he couldn't comprehend what his eyes were telling his brain. There on the stage, bound and gagged in front of a crowd of crazed cultists, were the only things in the world that Shadrick Bengoade loved unconditionally, irrationally, uncontrollably—his wife and daughter.

Chapter 20

NEZZAR LOOKED OUT AT the screaming crowd, grinning with pride and anticipation. "Aren't they magnificent?" he said, waving his arms toward Alina and Isla like a salesman in a showroom. Ropes were wrapped around Alina's legs and chest just above her breasts, pinning her to the post with her hands bound behind her back. Little Isla was bound the same way next to her mother, struggling feebly against ropes that were almost as thick as her arms. "A young mother and her sweet daughter, perfect offerings for our Blood Communion. I must commend Lord Malochus again, *they really are exquisite*. Many of you may not know this, but there have been years in the past when we completely forego the Blood Communion due to a lack of an acceptable offering." The crowd gasped and groaned in disapproval. "I know, I know. It is terrible when we must make that choice, but there can be no compromise when we take the Blood Communion before Baphomet. Rather than displease him by offering something substandard, we simply skip the offering altogether, depriving us all of his blessings until the next opportunity arrives," Nezzar said.

Stunned, Shad remained still, unable to do anything but watch and listen. He felt himself lifted up by Deckard, and only then did he realize he had fallen to his knees.

"We'll get them, brother. We'll get them," Deckard said. "Now we know where they are. Get your breath, shake this off, and let's find a way to get closer to that stage." Deckard patted Shad on the shoulder encouragingly. Shad took a few deep breaths and felt the numbness begin to wear off, the strength returning to his limbs. He stood on his own again and turned to Deckard.

"I think I'm good, thanks. Isla is up there, Deckard. I *have* to get to her." Desperation was beginning to take root, like a weed that feeds on rationality.

"We will. But we need to be smart about this, we can't just sprint at the stage. We need to stay under the radar until we're as close as possible. Let's start making our way toward them. Once we're near the stage, we'll find a way to get up and free them." Shad nodded and swallowed the dryness in his mouth.

"I'm so glad that you're as excited as I am about our offerings," Nezzar said from the stage, feeding off of the accolades from the eager crowd. "However, my fellow servants of darkness, I must confess that I misled you a little bit. These two beauties are not our only offerings for the Blood Communion. There is one more." Screams of glee filled the arena again. "Yes, yes, there is one more. You see, to maximize the blessings of the goat lord, the sacred rites of Baphomet's Blood Communion require three specific offerings. We have not had a Blood Communion with *all three offerings present* in at least a century. First, the innocent child." Nezzar motioned to Isla, her eyes red from sobbing, her gag covered with snot leaking slowly from her tiny little nose.

Doing their best to appear nonchalant and blend in with the other cultists, Shad and Deckard were in the crowd now, two or three dozen yards away from the stage. From their position, they could clearly see Nezzar, Alina, and Isla. Like a boa collapsing upon its prey, Shad's insides constricted with overwhelming anxiety at the sight—the spectacle—of his family on display as Nezzar gloated in front of thousands of cultists.

"Second, Baphomet asks us to bring a desperate mother. I can confirm for you from my conversations with Lord Malochus that this woman fulfills that requirement exactly," he said as he pointed at Alina. She struggled against her bindings as she attempted to turn her head so she could look at Isla, her face contorted with indescribable sorrow as her effort was in vain. "Some years we have one, or at best two of the required offerings. But tonight, tonight we have all three."

The crowd again responded to Nezzar's sermonizing with applause, providing Deckard and Shad with an opportunity to advance closer to their goal. They deftly weaved through more and more of the crowd, continuing slowly as Nezzar spoke. "And that brings me to the final offering that Baphomet requires on this hallowed night. It truly is a blessing of the goat lord's will that this offering presented itself to us. I am proud to say that I personally participated in the cultivation of this sacrifice when the opportunity became clear. You might say the third sacrifice walked right in to my door." Nezzar paced along the stage as he spoke. "You see, friends, along with the innocent child and the desperate mother," he said, pointing, "the final portion of what we must offer to Baphomet is the grieving father."

Shad and Deckard froze in place, as if through their inaction they would blend more convincingly into the cultists around them. Sweat beaded on Shad's forehead as the familiar rush of adrenaline spilled into his veins, sending his heart into high gear. Trying to remain natural and loose, Deckard took on a defensive posture as he eyed the people in their near vicinity.

Nezzar looked out to the mass of people in front of him, as if he was searching for a specific face. "And that grieving father is here, right now, among you," he said, eliciting gasps and murmurs from the crowd. "Don't worry, no need to look around. I know exactly how to find him."

Nezzar raised his hand up and snapped his fingers. Shad's phone suddenly rang loudly with the sound of a cascade of text messages, one after the other in quick succession. Everyone around him instantly turned to look at him as he scrambled to pull his phone out of his pants pocket underneath the Molochian robes. Finally retrieving it, he pulled it out and saw on the screen that he had received dozens of messages from his lawyer, Tom. They all said the same thing.

I'm sorry.

"There he is!" Nezzar snapped his fingers again, stopping the texts instantly. "Shadrick, why don't you come up here and join your family. And bring your friend Deckard, too, will you?"

They both hesitated for a moment, considering their options. Could they run? They could try, but they probably wouldn't get far now that all eyes were on them. Even if they could get away, Shad couldn't leave without Alina and Isla. The iron weight of defeat settled into his gut, crushing any remaining vestiges of hope he had left. He looked to Deckard, who remained still next to him, and nodded before removing his hood as he began to walk toward the stage. Deckard held on to his determination for a few seconds longer before he accepted reality and followed his friend through the crowd of gawking cultists.

When they arrived at the stage, two guards greeted them at the base of the stairs. Shad winced as his hands were pulled roughly behind his back where they were bound together with the familiar buzz of zip ties being fastened. The guards escorted them up to the stage where Lord Malochus was waiting.

"Isn't this a violation of your restraining order, Shadrick? I don't think this is going to help your court case. Would you like to call your lawyer?" The guards continued to push them along toward Nezzar. When they were within a few feet of him, the guards kicked the backs of their knees, forcing them to collapse to a kneel.

"Oh, I'm sorry, you've already heard from Tom, haven't you? Would you like to say hello? He's just over there." Nezzar pointed to the side of the stage. The guards twisted them around so they could follow Nezzar's direction and they saw Tom standing there, looking down at the ground, unable to make eye contact. "Tom chose to be here, Shadrick. When you gave the police his card after you'd been arrested, we called and offered him a deal. He didn't even hesitate before he sold you out. Didn't you think it was crazy that your bail was posted so quickly? I was a little worried that you wouldn't believe it! That wasn't cheap, Shadrick. You'd better not leave town!" Nezzar said, prompting chortles of laughter from the enraptured crowd. "But you never suspected a thing. He chose to betray you, even though you helped him when he needed it most. He chose his family."

"And Deckard, why don't you wave to Bridget? You do recognize her, don't you?" Deckard looked up and saw the clerk from Five Star Cleaners standing next to Tom just backstage. "You really thought you had charmed your way into snagging those robes, didn't you?" Nezzar laughed again triumphantly. "So terribly sorry to burst your bubble, Deckard. I tried to warn you, gentlemen. But you didn't listen. I told you that we were everywhere. I told you that no one would believe you. I did lie, a little bit. The truth is, most people probably *do* believe you."

Nezzar continued to pace and gesticulate as he spoke, feeding off of the energy of the crowd. "Honestly, most people probably *agree* with you too. But that's where our power enters the equation, the power that I warned you about. Even though most people agree with you, they're all too afraid to say it. They're too afraid to speak up and do anything about it. They don't want their faces on the next viral clip labeled 'hateful bigot' like yours was. People all over the country have seen your face, Shad! And you didn't make a good first impression," he said with a mocking shake of his head. "People don't want to be you. So they just stand by and do nothing, hoping they can keep their head down and stay out of it. Some others went a little further and feigned outrage, bloviating about 'hate' and 'alt phobia' to their alternative religious friends and family." Nezzar paced on the stage like a professor giving a lecture. "Many of those same people posted on social media about how upset they were about what you said, changing their profile picture to the alt flag, or to one of the cult symbols to show 'solidarity.' They all think that getting likes on their words of righteous indignation will act as some sort of social armor, protecting them from any criticism. As if painting their doors with virtue signals will make the alts just pass them by." This elicited laughter from the adoring crowd.

"Whatever happened to 'live and let live'?" Deckard shouted, interrupting Nezzar's diatribe. One of the guards immediately backhanded him, drawing blood from his lower lip. Shad tried to get up from his kneeling position in response and was also struck by a guard in the face, knocking him backward. The guard then picked him up off of his back and placed him back on his knees.

"Enough, enough of that," Nezzar said, waving off the guards. "No need for violence. Don't you see that the pain these men are feeling is far more intense than anything we could inflict? These men are *failures*. They have *failed entirely*. You are looking at the faces of utter defeat. Even their little Internet crusade is going nowhere. We don't need to abuse them. They're destitute."

"What if I hadn't come?" Shad asked. "Since you need me for your sacrifice, what if I hadn't shown up?"

"We knew you'd either come with Alina, or come for her. And, if for some reason you opted out entirely, we have friends whose cars have flashing lights on top that would have escorted you here whether you wanted to come or not," Nezzar said.

"Now, back to your question, Deckard. *Of course* we believe in letting every person live freely however they may choose, that's the core of our faith! We don't want to restrict anyone's personal liberty to live their truth. Our members are called 'liberated' for a reason!" Nezzar drew cheers of agreement from the onlooking crowd. "We just want to stamp out hatred, Deckard. If your beliefs restrict someone else's freedom, that's hate. That's what we've been fighting against. Hateful bigots who want to keep the alternative religious from worshipping their gods however they see fit. It shouldn't be controversial to oppose hate, should it? No one thinks 'Oh, Hitler was a bad guy, but live and let live,' right?" The crowd chortled on cue.

"You're killing people. You have a woman and child tied to a post behind you. That's the exact opposite of letting people live freely," Deckard said, spitting blood onto the stage.

"What an antiquated, one-dimensional view of freedom, Deckard! Just last night you recorded the man who gave himself up to Moloch. Deacon Dink didn't kill him, he set him free from the bonds of his agonizing life. The people who participate in our offerings are all being liberated, regardless of whether they're standing in front of the altar or lying upon it."

"I've seen the people butchered on your altars tonight. I've heard their screams, watched them fight for their lives, heard their last breaths. They weren't all willing participants. They were murdered," Deckard responded.

"Whether they realize it or not, everyone who takes part in one of our rituals is in need of liberation. It's true that some are more"—Nezzar hesitated, thinking of the right word—"more eager than others. Regardless of their levels of enthusiasm, they still receive true liberation, the most precious gift we could ever give them. They may not thank us in this life, but they will in the next one."

"I saw a dad cut his own son's arm off for Baal. Did that kid need to be liberated from his arm?"

"What an honorable offering for him to make. It will bless him the rest of his life," Nezzar said without hesitation.

"What about the people I saw get molested by the Asherians? Will they be blessed by those terrible memories? By that trauma?"

"They've been liberated, Deckard! My answer is yes, they'll absolutely be blessed. Don't you understand? They're free now. They will never be the same," Nezzar said.

"We agree there," Deckard said. "And the boy I saw get killed by his own mother? How is he free?"

"He's the freest of them all," Nezzar said. "He's been liberated eternally, the most precious gift his mother could give him."

"My family doesn't want to be here, Nezzar. You're not freeing my wife or daughter, you psychopath! They're tied to posts! You kidnapped them, let them go!" Shad screamed, struggling against the grip of the guards.

"Oh, Shadrick, where do you get these crazy ideas? We didn't kidnap anyone. Your wife came to us on her own. She was excited to be liberated! She wanted her old life back. The career, the excitement. She wanted fulfillment; she was desperate to break free from the banal routines of life as a stay-at-home mom, the boring life *you gave her*. She even brought your precious daughter Isla along to share in this momentous experience. Now, I will admit, she's feeling some apprehension now that she knows exactly what liberation will mean for her. But she chose this, Shadrick. *She chose Moloch over you*. And if you had done what I asked of you, she could have had a more 'mainstream' liberation ritual up in the public festival," he said, pointing at the ceiling. "All you had to do was *submit*. If you had just pledged your allegiance last night when I asked, this could have all been avoided. I told you what would happen, didn't I? You didn't listen. Tom listened." Nezzar pointed over at the lawyer, who was still looking down at the ground in shame.

"He bent his knee before Asherah. He also had to help us with a few things, of course, like making sure you were here tonight and instead of sitting in a jail cell. But he fulfilled his obligations, and now his son is up in the park, joyously ascending, instead of being liberated as an offering like your sweet little Isla will be tonight." Nezzar stroked Isla's hair as he looked Shad in the eyes. Shad let out a deep growl and struggled to his feet again, the death-rattle of his defiant spirit, but was quickly knocked back to his knees by a punch to the stomach from the guard. "I warned you, but you thought you could beat us. You thought you could *expose us* to the world. I told you that we would consume you. That we would destroy you and everything you loved. You didn't believe me. But I bet you do now, don't you?" He looked at Shad with the blackest malevolence in his eyes.

"So now you're going to watch your wife and daughter become the Blood Communion offering to Baphomet, the goat lord. I am going to split their wrists and fill my chalice with their blood. Then I will drink it as we both watch them slowly die. And then I'll cut out their hearts and take their lifeless bodies and burn them on the altar of the goat lord as all of these people celebrate. And after you've watched them die and seen their bodies burned to ash, I'll take your blood last. Are you ready to watch your family bleed, Shadrick? Are you ready to see what your pride and your hateful crusade have gotten you?" Nezzar spit at him vindictively, unsheathing a curved ceremonial knife and running it along Alina's face.

Shad felt breathless, as if he'd had the wind knocked out of his lungs. He looked at Isla, his beautiful daughter, her eyes sparkling brightly with terrified tears as she stared at him, ripping a hole through his core like a bulldozer through a brick wall. He struggled against his bonds, and was again struck by the guard back down to his knees. Broken, he looked away, his own eyes filling with tears to match his daughter's. He took a deep breath, gathered his strength, and looked up at his bride, Alina. In that moment of anguish, they were at peace with each other. The anger and frustration that had burned so fiercely between them the past two days had gone, and all that was left when they locked eyes was a placid sea of regret. There were so many alternate paths they could have taken before now that would have led their young family far from this terrible place and they both knew it, and were now left with the hollow longing for missed opportunities. There was no blame, no bitterness, only the deepest mutual remorse. Still gagged and sobbing, Alina couldn't speak, but Shad could tell what she was trying to say.

"I'm so sorry, I'm so sorry," he heard through the muffling of the cloth in her mouth.

Her eyes were swollen from crying, her face a mask of guilt and repentance that can only be formed by a bankruptcy of hope. Forsaking any attempt at dignified restraint, Shad wept with abandon. He couldn't muster any sounds, but could only mouth words to her in response.

"I know, it's OK, I'm sorry. I love you. I love you. I love you."

Back and forth for what felt like an eternity, he went from his wife's eyes, filled with contrition, to those of his daughter, petrified and despairing. Shad looked around. Deckard knelt next to him, bleeding and crying but still managing a small amount of self-control that Shad couldn't achieve. He saw Nezzar looking down at him, grinning, relishing his absolute power and the suffering he had wrought. Looking out into the crowd, the hopelessness of the situation seemed to crystalize into certainty. Shad was on a stage deep underground, restrained and heavily guarded, his family bound to posts, surrounded by hundreds or even thousands of fanatics who would savor the opportunity to watch and cheer as their throats were slit before them. He considered making one last ditch effort at freeing himself. If he somehow got away from the guards who already proved they were familiar with violence, he'd have to figure out how to free his family, and then manage to evade every other person in the arena in order to escape to the surface above, where even more uncertainty was waiting. There was no chance at success. All was lost. He was beaten, and he knew there was nothing he could do about it. And then Nezzar spoke, his venomous voice breaking Shad's mournful reverie.

"But perhaps it doesn't have to be that way. It *is* the Blood Sabbath, after all. I'll give you *one more* chance to do the right thing. You are at a fork in the road, Shadrick. You are choosing the path, not me. Not even Alina is making this choice. If you bend the knee *right now*, in front of all of these faithful liberated, and pledge your fealty to Baphomet, I will release your wife and daughter. I will take your blood for their freedom. That's the last choice I will give you." Nezzar paced slowly between Isla and Alina menacingly. "*Are you ready to kneel now*?"

Shad didn't hesitate for even a second. "Yes, take me," he said, meeting Nezzar's gloating gaze. Even though he was conceding defeat to an enemy he hated with his whole being, whose power had proved to be overwhelming and unconquerable, even though he was relinquishing his principles and his life, Nezzar was offering him a pyrrhic victory he couldn't have afforded to even hope for just moments ago. Shad breathed a deep sigh of relief. Now that it was offered, he'd gladly pay for it with his own blood so that he could see his family freed.

"I'm sorry, what was that?" Nezzar asked, perpetually performing.

"Yes, I'll kneel."

Nezzar sneered. "You will bow before Baphomet," he said, lifting his arms up toward the massive goat lord behind him. Nezzar directed the guards, who then dragged Shad and placed him on the stage in front of Alina and Isla. He knelt before his family, his back to the mass of cultists, enthusiastic spectators of his disgrace. "Do you pledge your life to Baphomet, the goat lord, the prince of darkness, to be now and forever bound to his service, and henceforth liberated from the tyranny of the light of this world?"

Shad looked up at Alina and Isla again, their eyes glistening as they watched him be humiliated for their sakes, trading his convictions, his entirety, his life, for them.

"I do."

"Bow," Nezzar said, looking down at him. Steeling his nerves, Shad complied. "Further." Again, Shad complied. Nezzar placed his expensive Italian boot between Shad's shoulder blades and pushed him to the ground until his face was pressed against the cold metal of the stage.

"Thank you, Shadrick," Nezzar said, his foot still on his back. "As the priest of Baphomet, I accept your pledge. You are now liberated into the service of the goat lord," he said, lifting his foot. "You may kneel." The guards lifted him up and placed him back on his knees in front of

Nezzar, all while his wife and daughter watched. "I am a man of my word, Shadrick. I will now free your family."

Nezzar walked over to Alina first, unsheathing his curved blade and slicing the ropes that held her arms. She brought them forward gingerly, clearly sore from having been in the same position for so long. With a lightning-fast snap, Nezzar grabbed Alina's left arm and dug the tip of his blade into her wrist, dragging it down toward her elbow, splitting it open into an eight-inch furrow that erupted with bright red blood. Alina screamed through her gag and grabbed for the wound with her other hand, only for that arm to be snatched by Nezzar, who promptly carved an identical wound. Grabbing a chalice from a stand near the posts, he began to fill it with the crimson fruit of his labor. The crowd of spectating cultists erupted with cheers like wild fans at a championship game.

"No!" came the guttural cry from Shad's chest, disbelief transforming to sorrow and then fury in an instant. His muscles exploded with the strength of ten men, bursting forth from the ground and sending the two guards flailing backward. "No! No! I knelt, I knelt!" he screamed as he ran toward Alina, who was quickly spilling her vitality all over the stage.

Nezzar just barely dodged out of the way as Shad reached his wife. Slipping in her blood, Shad stumbled clumsily. Laying his head against her, his arms still bound behind his back, he whimpered in despair. "No, no, no, no, Alina, no baby, don't go, please don't go. I'm so sorry, please don't go." He kissed her cheeks and her forehead, resting his face against hers, and felt her weakening arms embrace him, soaking his back with her blood. "Please, please stay, please stay. I can't do this. Isla needs you, I need you, no, no, no," he pleaded with her over and over again, his forehead against hers, their eyes inches apart. With his teeth he pulled the gag out of her mouth.

"Everything is going to be OK, my love. I'm sorry, Shadrick. I'm so sorry. Please don't hate me. Mom was right. I didn't listen but she was right, she was always right. I love you, I'm so sorry. Take care of our baby," she said, her heartbeat slowing with every passing moment as it ran out of precious life to pump. Alina looked over toward little Isla and summoned all her strength to speak loud enough for her to hear over the din of the crowd. "I love you, little Pickle. Always know Mama loves you, OK? Be good for Daddy, he's gonna take care of you. I love you, I'll always love you." Isla, still gagged, just cried quietly as she watched her world shatter.

"Please hold on, please don't go, I love you so much," Shad said as he felt her slipping away.

"Oh God, oh God, please forgive me. I'm so sorry. I love you, Shadrick," she said, her vision fading, her body drained and withering quickly. As he wept and begged in futility, Alina looked into her husband's eyes, powerless to grant his appeals, forlorn as she faced her impending demise; she clung to her final repentant hope—and silently screamed that she loved him still, that she had loved him always. And then, with a flutter, her eyes slowly closed, and she was gone.

For only a moment, Shad stood and stared at the face of his only love, taking her in, unwilling to say goodbye. But then he remembered Nezzar, who was standing just a few feet away observing Shad's world crumbling like a sandcastle beneath an unstoppable tide, and he lunged toward the villain with all of the hate and hurt in his heart igniting in his veins like nitroglycerin. Although Nezzar saw Shad advance on him, he remained still, smiling. Growling like a wounded animal, Shad closed the distance in a second and was just inches from Nezzar's face when he felt himself abruptly change directions and then land roughly beneath someone's weight. The collision broke the zip ties that had restrained him, and with fresh adrenaline still pumping, he used his newly freed hands to pummel the person—no, persons—who had tackled him. Two of the black-suited guards were on top of him, struggling to restrain him.

In just a few seconds Shad had regained his footing and faced off with the guards. Without hesitation, he landed a clean right cross on the first guard, dislocating his jaw and knocking him unconscious. Shad defended against another tackle wildly, rabid with desperation, and landed one elbow heavily into the back of the guard's head with a sickening crunch. The man went limp and dropped to the ground, opening the pathway between Shad and Nezzar. Growling again, he attacked. Three more guards emerged from different locations on the stage. One took Shad's legs from behind, bringing him to the ground and preventing him from reaching his quarry. Once he was down, the other two thugs set about battering his face and torso with kicks and punches.

"OK, OK, you've got him. Stop hitting him. Keep him still, but I don't want him injured. I definitely don't want him unconscious." Nezzar smoothed his shirt and straightened his gleaming black tie as he regained his composure. "Whoa, that was close!" Nezzar said to the crowd for a laugh that was immediately provided to him. The guards dragged Shad back to his position next to Deckard, with one guard holding each arm and the third keeping him in a headlock.

"Why are you so upset, Shadrick? I promised that if you knelt before Baphomet, I would free your wife and daughter. I kept my word. Alina has been set free in the most profound way possible. As the Blood Communion, she will forever be freed from the tyranny of the light of this world. She's now been ushered into eternal darkness, liberated forever. You should be *thanking* me."

"Go to hell," Shad said, spitting blood spitefully onto the stage.

"I plan to," said Nezzar with a wicked smirk. "But I'm not done here, yet. We need three sacrifices to for a complete Blood Communion. The first is the desperate mother, which we've just added to our chalice," he said, raising his ceremonial goblet toward the crowd of cultists who responded with cheers. "We also need an innocent child, and a grieving father," he said, pointing his knife at Isla and then at Shad. "I know you're grieving now, Shadrick, but I've done a lot of research on this stuff. It's kind of my job. What I've discovered is that the ritual's requirement isn't just a person that is grieving that happens to be a father. It must be a person who is grieving *as a father.* Do you see what I mean? It's a crucial difference. You're clearly grieving now, but only *as a husband,* and that's not good enough for Baphomet. He wants your grief to be the kind only a father knows. So that's what I'm going to give him." Nezzar turned abruptly and began walking toward Isla.

"No!" Shad screamed again, his voice now hoarse from the night's terrors. Fruitless as it was, he continued thrashing as he watched Nezzar walk toward his daughter, his ceremonial blade hanging casually in his hand.

Suddenly, Nezzar's head snapped back. His body went rigid and began to shake, the knife slipped from his hand and clattered to the ground. Equally shocked, Shad and Deckard looked on in confusion as Nezzar collapsed backward to the ground, stiff and convulsing. The guards holding Shad were on high alert, searching around them for an explanation for why Nezzar had dropped to the floor. The one that had held Shad's neck in a chokehold released him and began running forward to assist his boss.

Shad noticed a multicolored streak moving across the stage. He turned and saw a woman dressed in Asherian robes running in their direction. She had something yellow in her hand that had thin wires attached to it. Behind her ran four or five more people dressed in cultist garb.

"Get your daughter!" the woman screamed. Shad didn't react, still stunned and unable to process what was happening. "Shad, get up and get your daughter *now*!" As she approached, Shad finally recognized her and all at once the pieces of the puzzle in front of him snapped together. It was Detective Caceres, and she was holding a taser in her hand as she ran. The cables that were extending from it were connected to electrodes which were now embedded into Nezzar's back. The other members of the cult clergy that were running with her were other officers. "Police! Police! On the ground! Get on the ground now!" Caceres yelled. The other officers pulled badges out of their disguises and allowed them to hang around their necks on ball chains.

Deckard reacted before Shad did, rocketing up from his kneeling position and smashing into the guard holding Shad's right arm, who was sent careening face-first into the stage. Taking advantage of the opportunity, Shad grabbed the guard holding his left arm and pulled him off-balance toward his colleague's splayed body, then kicked the man in the face as hard as he could as he broke into a sprint toward Isla. Nezzar was in between Shad and Isla, beginning to recover and get off of the ground, slowly pushing himself up. Recognizing another opportune moment and electrified with adrenaline, Shad used his momentum to kick Nezzar's extended left arm right at the elbow, snapping it backward in the wrong direction with a loud cracking noise. Nezzar cried out in pain and fell back to the floor, but Shad didn't slow down in the slightest. Less than a minute after Caceres had yelled at him, Shad was untying Isla's arms and picking her up. He took a few blissful seconds to squeeze her close, as if he could transfer his immense love to her through induction.

"I've got you, Pickle. We're going home," he said. Shad turned to survey the situation behind him and was pleasantly surprised at what he found. Nezzar remained face down on the stage, his hands cuffed behind his back. Deckard's hands had been freed, and he and Caceres were back-to-back, engaged in a riotous melee with the guards.

When they were in college, Deckard had always said that there was no such thing as a gentleman in a street fight. When they had gone to bars or parties and things got out of hand, Deckard wouldn't hesitate to clap someone's ears, pull their hair, or gouge their eyes in order to take the upper hand in a brawl. "Better to win dirty than lose honorably," Shad remembered him saying. He was happy to see Deckard hadn't changed his philosophy on violence, as he watched him wind up and land the full force of a kick squarely between the legs of one of the guards, producing a yelp that sounded like a cat that had been stepped on.

Caceres had a furious focus that came with years of professional experience, dispatching guards with precisely aimed headshots with a slapjack. The other officers grappled with more guards, the element of surprise having worked in their favor. For the moment they were winning the fight, but there were dozens of guards and clergy in the arena, not to mention the thousands of worshippers who were watching everything taking place in front of them on a brightly lit stage. The crowd was restrained by shock for the moment, but as the commotion on stage continued, that dam would likely burst and they'd be swamped. Shad ran toward the fight, gripping Isla tightly. "Let's go!"

"Booth! That crowd is looking like it's going to rush. You got this?" Caceres yelled toward one of the cops who was dressed as a Molochian and had just crumbled a guard with a knee to the stomach.

"Yeah, probably a good time to make ourselves known," she responded. It was Officer Booth, one of the officers who had arrested Shad in the park.

"Officer Booth? You're . . . you're on our side?" Shad asked.

"Surprise!" she responded. "Sorry about that prick Christiansen. Now go!" she yelled, pulling a gun out from under her robes. She pointed it to the sky and fired off a quick series of shots. The crowd, which had been accustomed to crying out in elation that night, now erupted with screams of fear as people scattered like rats and ran for the exits. The three of them followed suit, Caceres leading the way with her gun drawn ahead of Shad, who held Isla closely as he ran, while Deckard took up the rear.

"Back up! Police! Get out of the way!" she yelled at the clergy and guards who stood at the top of the stairs that led down to the arena floor. One guard remained static, squaring up for a confrontation. Deckard shot forward at full speed, executing a textbook body check on the black-suited sentinel. Even though the man was prepared, Deckard's momentum was too much for him to resist, and he went careening backward down the stairs. Caceres, Deckard, and Shad flew down the stairs three or four at a time, landing on the arena floor in a full sprint. "How do we get out of here?" Caceres asked, looking back at Shad as they ran.

"Head to the concourse. We can figure it out from there." Shad ran harder than he ever had in his life or ever would again. The rest of their escape was a blur that none of them could clearly recall afterward. Caceres had kept her gun out and at the ready, keeping most of the cultists at bay. Any resistance they met had been dealt with swiftly by more iceless hockey hits from Deckard or pistol-whips from Caceres. They had rocketed through the familiar cluttered concourse and quickly found the stairs they had taken the night before. They scaled the stairs effortlessly and kept up their Olympic pace, sprinting outside and breathing the cool air of early Monday morning without even mentally registering the old brick building they had passed through. The next thing Shad could remember, they were in Deckard's SUV racing back to his house, with Deckard driving, Caceres in the front seat maintaining a vigilant watch for threats, and Shad in the back seat, still clinging to little Isla as she hid in his arms. He stayed awake and held her as she slept, the consistent rhythm of her heartbeat the only thing keeping his own from shattering into oblivion.

Epilogue

THE CHAOS THAT ENSUED that night took weeks to unravel. Dozens of guards and lower-level cult clergy were arrested by Booth and the other officers who stayed behind after Caceres helped Shad, Isla, and Deckard escape. Soon after they had requested backup, the police chief had arrived with conspicuous speed and immediately took command in order to "secure" the crime scene. He insisted there was no evidence of any foul play recovered in the entire arena except for Alina's murder, which had been captured by the officers' body cameras and was, therefore, undeniable.

Unfortunately, in the pandemonium after Booth had fired her gun, Nezzar had somehow gotten away. He was now wanted for Alina's murder, but no records could be found anywhere of anyone with his name. No birth certificates, no driver's licenses, nothing in public databases, nothing on social media—Nezzar simply didn't exist. The most common working theory was that cultists high up in the government and tech companies had erased all evidence of his life order to brush the entire incident under the rug.

That theory was bolstered when the same judge who Shad had stood before in court ruled that the body camera footage showing Nezzar murdering Alina could not be made public and must remain sealed indefinitely. Multiple families came forward about people who attended the Blood Sabbath ritual and hadn't been seen since that night. Shad and Deckard were vocal about the dozens of other murders and crimes they had witnessed, and they even met with some of the families of missing people and gave statements to the police. The police claimed they were investigating their allegations, but Caceres told them they were just for show and that the detectives assigned to those cases were being stonewalled by the brass. Some of the guards and cult clergy were charged as accessories to Alina's murder, but they were out on bond within days of their arrests thanks to crowdfunding campaigns driven by social media trends that claimed they were victims of religious discrimination.

Alina's body was recovered from the Under Yards and a funeral was held four weeks later, delayed by a legally required autopsy. While Shad fired Tom as his lawyer soon after that night, Tom continued to make sincere efforts at penance. It turned out that after he had received Shad's text message that they were heading down to the Under Yards, Tom had called Caceres and told her everything he knew, which led to Caceres's heroic sting. He emphasized that he had no idea what Nezzar and Malochus had planned and was only told that Shad would be humiliated when he took Nezzar's deal. He was wracked with guilt over Alina's death. When her body was finally released by the police department, Tom insisted on paying for all of her funeral expenses and even set up a generous college fund for Isla.

Even with the overwhelming efforts from social media companies and mysterious cyberattackers, the Drysand effect remained undefeated and Shad and Deckard's videos of the rituals from the Under Yards went viral. Jerry Dink managed to avoid significant consequences by claiming the video was a deepfake. Forensic analysts challenged his claim, but it just became another hot topic on social media since there was no other evidence to prove he was actually there.

Shad and Deckard became minor celebrities, frequenting podcasts and news shows to talk about their experiences. They weren't shy about sharing exactly what they had seen, but for some reason Jerry Dink never sued them. They both developed large social media followings on Post-Space and VidHole, although their accounts were frequently censored and demonetized for violating the terms regarding "hateful" content. Deckard even went on the daytime talk show *The Shrew* to share his story, but spent most of the time defending himself from the hosts of the show who accused him of being a lying, hateful, anti-alt bigot. The resulting attention turned Alina's funeral into a massive public event, with thousands of strangers showing up to the memorial service to pay their respects. The graveside portion was kept secret and private for friends and family only. Shad asked Pastor Delaney to perform the service, and he graciously obliged. It was the second saddest day of Shad's life, but he was grateful that they could say goodbye and give her a proper burial, unlike so many other souls who had perished on the Blood Sabbath.

Nezzar's association with Baphomet made it easy for the leaders of the other cults to use him as a scapegoat to save face, publicly disavowing him and the worship of Baphomet as "fringe" and "extremism." Of course, they had no good explanation for why Nezzar or the huge idol to Baphomet were even at the festival in the first place, but journalists never pushed them with those tough questions. A movement of people who were skeptical of the alternative religions began to grow and gain momentum, especially online. They labeled themselves as "alt-skeptics," eschewing the popular "anti-alt" pejorative.

Wary of further scrutiny and hoping to fade into obscurity, Lord Malochus rescinded his complaint against Shad, resulting in the charges against him being dropped. While Shad, Deckard, and Caceres knew that Malochus and Bella had drugged Alina and Isla, they had no evidence to prove it. They were both captured in photos and videos of the Blood Communion ceremony so they couldn't deny that they were there, but each insisted in separate public statements that they had no idea that a murder was going to take place and they had no part in it, maintaining the new narrative that the worship of Baphomet was "extremism." Lord Malochus remained in his position at the Temple to Moloch, but made much fewer public appearances. There was a significant outcry from concerned elementary school parents about Bella remaining on staff, but the school board stood their ground and refused to fire her, even going as far as to have some protesting parents arrested at a school board meeting.

Shad and Isla lived with Deckard at first, unwilling to move back to their house, filled as it was with memories of Alina. Initially, Eliana and Shad both blamed each other for Alina's death, with Shad insisting she should have stopped her daughter from going to the festival and Eliana blaming Shad for pushing Alina into the arms of the Molochians in the first place. After a few weeks, Eliana showed up at Deckard's house unannounced and asked to speak with Shad. They had yelled at each other, spitting vitriol and venom as they condemned each other for the loss of the one they had loved so completely and uniquely, and then, almost simultaneously, they both began to crack and fall apart. Hugging and crying for an hour, they mourned together and buried their animosity. After that, Shad sold their house, and he and Isla moved in with Eliana.

Most of Deckard's clients fired him because they were afraid of bad press, so he eventually had to rebrand his advertising and consulting business, leaning into his newfound notoriety and offering services catering to others who had been ostracized for being "alt-skeptics." As the movement began to grow, so did his client list. The executives at E-Tech Data Systems met with Shad and basically begged him to quit, afraid of the negative attention he might draw to the company. After some negotiations, Shad was given two years' paid severance with health benefits in order to resign quietly. He went to work for Deckard, managing the operations of his growing business. With Deckard's help, Shad was eventually able to maneuver his continued activism into a podcast and book deal with a prominent alt-skeptical website.

Shad refused to send Isla back to her school, since Bella remained on staff there. Eliana wholeheartedly agreed with his decision and volunteered to homeschool Isla until they identified a school that didn't include any cult-indoctrination in their curriculum. One afternoon when Shad was sitting out on the back porch reading, Isla ran up and handed him a paper. Irritated at first by the interruption, as parents often are, his attitude completely changed when he looked at what she had given him. He immediately stood up and called out to Eliana, handing her the paper. She lit up with joy; Isla had drawn a beautiful sketch of Shad, Alina, and Isla at the park, that warm memory still alive and well in the little girl's heart. It filled them both with pride to see that Alina lived on in her daughter's natural artistic talent.

Just as Shad had predicted, Caceres and Deckard turned out to be a great match. They hit it off and became an exclusive item within a couple months of meeting. Her calm intensity was a perfect grounding force for Deckard's spontaneous, creative spirit. Caceres stayed on with the police department, but Deckard consistently tried to get her to go into the private sector. The police chief hated her for what she had done and had relegated her to overnight desk duty. She held on to her pride, insisting that the chief wouldn't break her, but night shifts and Deckard's appeals were slowly wearing down her resolve.

Pastor Delaney and Shad continued to stay in touch after Alina's funeral, and when Delaney reached out about starting a new church, Shad enthusiastically accepted his invitation to attend. He, Eliana, and Isla became active members of True Life Church, and even managed to convince Deckard and Caceres to start coming too. Shad struggled with the pledge he had made to Baphomet, but Delaney insisted that with sincere repentance comes complete forgiveness. Taking that to heart, Shad repented anew every single day, terrified that he'd given himself to the very evil that had stolen his wife from him and had robbed his daughter of her mother. He dedicated the rest of his life to fighting that evil, hoping to save other families from the brokenness he could never repair.

While the alt-skeptic movement consistently grew and maintained strong momentum, it remained mostly a grassroots effort. The cults continued to gain footholds in every established structure in society, increasing in power and becoming more and more difficult to avoid. People all over the country and the world were willingly, enthusiastically pledging their souls to darkness in the name of individualistic freedom, rejecting the light, whose boundaries they dubbed an unbearable tyranny. Small, dedicated enclaves of resistance continued to sprout and even thrive, made up of people like Shad, whose families and friendships had been ruined, or nearly, and many others who embraced the light and worked together to thwart the growth of these new religions.

Seemingly omnipresent, the darkness fell on them day in and day out, an everlasting deluge raining down on a ship of refugees. And so, they heaved and heaved, bucket after bucket, determined to keep the water out, resolutely afloat amidst the relentless, ruthless waves. As the indominable tide of darkness continued to rise, swallowing up the culture piece by piece, remaking civilization into its own malignant, idolatrous image, these weary faithful continued to row against the current, eyes stubbornly focused on the horizon, patiently awaiting the victorious return of the light that would rise and reclaim the world.

THE END